LUKE

C.J. PETIT

C.J. PETIT

Printed in the United States of America

First Printing, 2017

ISBN: 9781691254200

TABLE OF CONTENTS

PROLOGUE

Southwest El Paso County, Colorado
December 13, 1871

They had ridden away the day before when the weather was practically balmy, but now the wind battered the outside of the barn and the temperature had dropped until it felt as if hell itself had frozen. The frigid temperatures were almost painful but suited her purpose. She could have built a small fire to keep warm but didn't because it no longer mattered.

She knew she was taking the biggest risk humanly possible; she was gambling her immortal soul. She had been told that suicide was a mortal sin and would send her to eternal damnation but rationalized that she really wasn't committing suicide. She just wasn't doing anything to stay alive. If God saw that as failed logic and condemned her to the fires of hell for eternity, then she'd discover her error soon. *How much worse could it be than what dared call itself life now?*

Laura wrapped herself in a horse blanket to avoid the irritating hay, climbed onto the large stack then pulled hay over her and lay still. She was in her cocoon now and soon would morph into something else. She would be a spirit and free from this life, whether in heaven or in hell didn't matter. She would be done with this life, a life that she no longer wanted.

CHAPTER 1

Northern Pasture of the Circle S Ranch
Twelve Miles Southwest of Colorado City, Colorado
December 14, 1871

Luke was furious as he looked at his herd as it huddled together against the strong northwest wind.

"Damn it, Hal! Who rustles cattle in December?"

"Rustlers, I would guess. They must be hard up or something."

"I counted twenty-eight missing critters. Is that what you get?"

"Yup. Want me to chase 'em down, Luke?"

"No, I'll do it. It looks like it's going to be a hard one if the weather gets any worse, and I figure it might do just that. Let's get that fence repaired and then I'll go get my stuff packed and get after them."

Luke Scott and Hal Rawlings stepped down and made short work of repairing the cut fence before remounting and heading back to the ranch house. They reached the house, tied off their horses then quickly went inside where Luke dropped his saddlebags on the floor before heading to the kitchen.

Luke hurriedly packed food that he could eat on horseback into the saddlebags then walked to his bedroom and added two pairs of extra thick wool socks and his heavy green plaid scarf as Hal watched.

"Hal, I don't know how much longer that snow is gonna hold off, so I've got to get moving fast. I don't want to lose those tracks."

"You takin' the Sharps?" Hal asked.

"No, I don't think so. I'll take the shotgun in the second scabbard. It'll scare them more up close and I think I'll need the spread, too."

"That's a good choice, I think."

Luke hurled an extra union suit into his open saddlebag and snapped, "Damnation, this riles me something fierce! Hal, why didn't they pick on one of those big ranchers? They could afford to lose that many cattle and not even blink. That leaves me with just a hundred and forty-six and just when things were looking good, too."

He tossed in an extra box of .44 cartridges for his Winchester Yellow Boy and his modified Remington New Army that used the same cartridge along with a box of shells for the shotgun.

Luke finished his selections when he went to a spare bedroom and grabbed an extra blanket and a canvas tarp before turning to Hal.

"I should be back in a day or two, Hal. If I'm not back in a week, I left my will in the desk. It'll be your ranch if I don't return."

Hal shook his head and said, "Luke, it's downright stupid for you to go. I'll go and get 'em."

"My critters, Hal," Luke replied.

Then he tossed the blanket and tarp over one shoulder and his saddlebags over the other before grabbing his shotgun and striding across the main room, opening the door, and returning to the frigid outdoors.

The wind was building as Luke rode back to the northern pasture where he picked up the trail left by his cattle and the damned December rustlers. The trail swung wide to the north for a while before bending to the northeast.

He was wearing a sweater, his heavy jacket, a red scarf, a heavy Union suit, and even two pairs of socks. He was still cold as he began to follow the hoofprints of the cattle but grateful for the heat from his mount.

He counted four sets of shod hoofprints among his cattle's much different prints and it didn't take long to guess their destination. Not surprisingly, they were headed toward Colorado City some twelve miles away, and should be there in a couple of hours at this pace. He wasn't going to push his horse as the gelding would need every bit of energy he had just to keep from freezing.

He'd made the ride to Colorado City dozens of times and knew the route as well as possible but that had been on the road. Now he was following his stolen cattle cross country a good three miles from the roadway. He guessed they'd chosen this path because they didn't want to be seen but even though it was going to add a few extra miles to the trip he wasn't concerned.

He had ridden for about an hour when the snow began. It wasn't the pretty, gently floating large flakes that an artist might paint but began as small, icy pellets being driven by a rising wind. Luke should have turned back but he was almost halfway to Colorado City and he was stubborn. Those four rustlers weren't going to get away with his animals and he wanted to find them even if they'd already sold them off. It was going to be very close. His twenty-eight animals had been stolen the night before and might already be in Colorado City's stock pens but even at his slow speed, he was still traveling more than twice as fast as those cattle would move.

As he kept riding, the trail began to disappear under the quickly building coating of ice. It must not have been as cold as he thought it was because if it had been, the ice covering wouldn't have stuck, but that wind sure made it seem a lot colder. Mother Nature was playing havoc with him now, and he was losing the game. He thought that he didn't need the trail now anyway as he just had to ride to Colorado City to find his cattle, so when he lost it, he wasn't concerned too much. But the weather itself was suddenly a new problem.

Less than twenty minutes later, after the ground had been sheeted with almost a quarter of an inch of ice, the temperature dipped rapidly, and the icy pellets gave way to snow. The wind had continued to climb from the northwest, and he fought it by pushing his horse hard into the wind. His vision was diminishing rapidly as the snow thickened and the howling wind picked up more from the ground.

He was already in trouble and he should have sought shelter but didn't. Deep in his bones, he knew he was getting close to Colorado City, but his bones were lying to him. Once he had to lean into the wind, he made the mistake of thinking the wind was continuing from the northwest, but it had been shifting and was now blowing almost straight from the west, making Luke's new path almost due north. It continued to shift as it came out of the mountains and Luke shifted with it until he was heading northwest. Colorado City was now almost seven miles east and the distance between him and the town was increasing with each careful step of his horse.

Luke's long-lost trail under the ice and snow and left-curving path didn't change his mistaken belief that he was still riding straight to Colorado City. He kept his horse plodding along, his Stetson wrapped around his ears by the green plaid scarf and his heavy jacket feeling like a light shirt.

He'd been riding for two hours after the storm had started when he finally admitted to himself that he had made a lot of mistakes. He was lost and the snowfall was still increasing. He had to keep the horse moving but very slowly because of the ice. With those steel horseshoes, he was losing his footing every so often and Luke found his eyes looking almost straight down in front of the horse's hooves to make sure he didn't fall.

He turned briefly to look at his backtrail in the slim hope he could turn around and follow it back, but it was obliterated just twenty feet behind him as if he had never existed. He was beginning to wonder if that was a portent of his future.

Twenty minutes later, the snow was already over a foot deep in some places as it began to drift. The wind was still slamming into him and his horse making Luke's path take him even further away from Colorado City, but it had shifted more westerly sending him north rather than northwest.

Luke and his horse kept moving because he knew what would happen if they stopped. He had an extra blanket and the tarp, so he thought he'd survive if he wrapped the blanket around him then slipped into his bedroll and covered himself with the tarp, but the horse might die and if that happened, it wouldn't be long before he followed.

He began looking for some form of shelter, so the horse could get some rest. The mountains were all around but still too far away to offer any immediate help. All they did was make the wind more violent. He needed at least a stand of trees, but they didn't seem to want to cooperate either, not that he could see more than fifty feet in front of him to search anyway.

The wind began to pick up even more and the snow increased its intensity in concert, which he didn't believe possible. Luke was by no means panicking, but he was getting ready to accept any form of shelter. He finally spotted some trees off to the northeast that might provide him with some degree of protection, so he shifted in that direction.

It was six and a half hours since he'd left the ranch, and he had no idea where he was as he approached the trees. There weren't many, but it was the best he would find. He entered the stand of pines and felt the wind being partially obstructed, improving his visibility and giving him some hope.

The closer he rode into the trees, the more conditions improved, albeit marginally, so he continued into the small forest to improve the windbreak when he suddenly popped out on the other side. He was about to turn back into the trees when he stopped his rotation and stared into the snow. It may be a trick of his mind, but it looked like there was a barn a few hundred yards away. He was going to disregard the mirage and head back into the trees but the need of being able to stay in an enclosed space was too great, so he continued toward the illusion, the horse slipping as it tried to maintain its footing on the downslope.

But it wasn't an illusion. When he drew closer to the structure, the mirage morphed into a barn with a house just to the west. The barn doors were facing directly into the wind, but the back of the house was in the lee of the storm. There was no smoke coming from the chimney, so maybe it had been abandoned. In this weather, if someone was inside, they should have a fire blazing like holy hell in that fireplace.

Both barn and house were log structures and in apparently good condition. He decided to head for the barn and after the horse was put away, he'd go to the house and ask the owners if he could stay in the barn overnight, although he didn't expect to find anyone inside.

With an enormous sense of relief, he set the horse slowly walking down the last of the gentle but icy slope, still fighting the vicious wind and driving snow. By the time the ground leveled, the snow was well over a foot deep already with much higher drifts around the house and barn. It was going to be a lot of work getting the barn door open, but he'd get it done.

When he was close, he dismounted, dropped his reins and trotted to the barn, and found a bar across the doors.

He lifted the bar, but it wouldn't budge, and he initially thought it was being held in place by the ice but on closer examination, he found the wooden beam to be lashed down with pigging strings to keep it in the holding brackets. He pulled his eight-inch knife and made short work of the tie-downs, then after sheathing his blade, he removed the crossbar, tossed it into a nearby snowdrift, then tried to open the door. He wasn't surprised that it didn't swing very far. Between the snow and the driving wind acting like a cold, giant hand holding it in place, he could barely move it an inch.

He jogged back to the horse, pulled his rope from his saddle and looped it around his saddle horn, then ran it through the barn door handle tied it off, then trotted back to his horse.

He leaned into the wind, walked to the front of the horse, and led him away from the barn. The rope grew taut and the barn door began to move until there was a gap large enough for the horse. He left the horse in place and quickly returned to the barn assisted by the howling wind that almost blew him straight into the edge of the barn door. He went inside to find something to prop the door open and discovered an old plank about three feet long leaning against the back wall. He grabbed the plank, returned to the open door, and dropped it to the ground near the arc of snow left by the opened barn door.

Luke then followed the rope with his head down into the wind, reached the horse's nose, and backed him as slowly as he could to keep from jarring the plank out of position. The barn door finally caught on the plank's end and Luke waited to see if it would hold. Once he was satisfied that it would keep the door open, he turned the horse back toward the barn and leaving the rope still attached led him inside. He knew it was still bitterly cold inside the barn but without that raging wind, it felt practically balmy. He then untied the rope from his saddle horn and tossed it outside in case the plank gave way.

As he had expected, there was little ambient light in the barn, so after removing his gloves, he reached into his pocket and struck a match, found a lamp near the door removed it from its peg, and sloshed it around. There was some kerosene in the tank, so he struck another match and lit the wick. After closing the chimney and hanging the lamp on a peg, he donned his gloves again and quickly examined the inside of the barn.

There were two horses inside, their breaths making large clouds as they both stared at him. They were handsome animals too, which surprised and confused him. So, the place wasn't abandoned after all, but why wasn't there any smoke from the house yet the horses were still here? He didn't have time to wonder about it now, so he quickly unsaddled his horse, watching the steam rise off his back, and soon had him in a stall. He needed to add some hay, so he headed to the back of the barn and grabbed an armful of hay, at least that was his intention.

When Luke jammed his gloved hands into the large stack of hay, they crunched into something, which made him jerk his hands out. He grabbed two handfuls of hay and tossed it into the stall for his horse before returning to the haystack and began to shovel the hay aside with his fingers, wondering what was under the hay, and found a blanket. His earlier curiosity about the lack of smoke was intensified. *What were the owners hiding in the hay and from whom?* He suspected some form of contraband, maybe firearms.

He brushed away the hay, lifted the blanket back and stared at what had been revealed, and stepped back. It was a girl. He couldn't guess her age in the low light but thought she must be dead. The owners were hiding a dead body. *But why in the barn? Why didn't they just bury her?*

He walked to her head, then leaned close, peered down at her face, and was startled when he saw small clouds of condensation appearing from her mouth. She was alive but wouldn't be for long if she stayed here. He had to go to the house and get her inside quickly. *Who would do such a thing?*

He leaned closer to her head and spoke loudly, "Miss? Can you hear me?"

Luke wasn't surprised by the lack of response. She wasn't blue yet, but he knew she didn't have long and wasn't sure if he could save her life, but he had to try.

He turned and trotted to the wedged open barn door and slipped out, walked quickly head down into the wind for a few seconds until he passed the end of the barn, then turned toward the house and had to lean hard to his left to walk the fifty yards. He reached the front of the house and walked up onto the porch, reached the door, and began pounding. After thirty seconds, his foregone conclusion that the house was empty was confirmed, but as Luke looked at the door for a handle, he couldn't find one. He could see where there had been one, but it was gone now and had been replaced with a wooden plug. *How could anyone get in?* It must be barred from the inside. There were no glass windows and all the windows were shuttered and probably barred as well.

There must be a rope somewhere to lift the internal bar. He looked up and saw what he expected to find under the eaves, a good two feet above the top of the door. He spotted a peg with a rope wrapped around the end. Luke was an inch over six feet and could reach the rope without having to stand on anything, so he gave it a yank and then lifted his right boot to kick the door open and crack the ice. It turned out to be unnecessary as the wind slammed the door open without any assistance from him.

He quickly went inside and had to push mightily against the door before he had it closed and quickly dropped the door bar to keep the snow out.

He needed to act quickly. First, he had to get that fire going in the ice-cold room. There was a can of coal oil, a stack of firewood, and kindling near the large fireplace, so he tossed some kindling and splashed on some kerosene. He struck a match, tossed it onto the kindling and flames popped to life. He then quickly added some thicker branches and then when they caught fire, added two large logs.

With the fire going, he found and lit two lamps before he trotted into the attached kitchen, started a fire in the cook stove, and pumped some water into a coffeepot. He noticed that there was a decent supply of food, which added to his confusion, but this wasn't time to ponder the mystery; he needed to get the girl into the house. There was a second barred door in the kitchen, but the wind was blowing from the west and the kitchen door was on the east side of the cabin. He pulled off the bar and set it aside, opened the door, and then left it open as he carefully maneuvered back to the barn. He had taken almost fifteen precious minutes to start heating the house and hoped it wasn't too long. That girl was very close to death and for her, every second counted.

He slipped back inside the barn, went to his gear, and pulled out his extra blanket. He carried it to the girl and covered her completely noticing that she had no shoes. Luke was now more enraged than curious as he wrapped her in the blanket and lifted her. She wasn't very heavy, less than a hundred pounds, so he carried the still-living girl out of the barn and stepped into the wind again. As he turned the corner toward the house, he had to be careful not to let the wind shove him and his human cargo to the frozen ground. It was difficult, but he angled for the back of the house and as soon as he reached the house the wind disappeared in its lee. He quickly stepped in his own footprints as he climbed the back steps and through the open back door into the kitchen where the warmth was already noticeable as he carried her into the main room near the fireplace.

He gently set her down then trotted to one of the two open bedrooms and pulled the mattress and blankets off the bed and slid it into the main room near the girl. He uncovered her face, and in the better light, he could see that she was in her mid-teens, maybe even younger.

He set the pillow on the mattress lifted her again and placed her on the mattress, then covered her with the new blanket, and then left her there while he left the house again to return to the barn to get his saddlebags, rifle, and shotgun. He didn't like this whole setup. There were so many odd things about the buildings and whoever called it home.

Ten minutes later, he was back in the house and had both doors barred again. The back door didn't have a rope lift, so the front door was the only entrance if both doors were barred.

The water was boiling, so he made some coffee and set it aside on the warm side of the cook stove then began removing his gear. It wasn't warm in the house yet, but he was warm enough, so he took off his jacket, hat, gloves, and scarf and hung them around various locations in the kitchen where they could dry.

Luke then walked back into the main room to check on his patient.

He pulled one of the four straight-backed chairs near her head and sat down. She seemed to be breathing normally, so Luke stood and began examining the rest of the cabin which was more like a house, which was unusual for a home built of logs. There was the main room with the kitchen area, a table, and four chairs. There were two bedrooms, but only one had a door. Both bedrooms had two beds and a single, crude dresser. He also noticed that there were no jackets or hats hanging anywhere. *The girl had no jacket? How did she go outside?*

He had no idea what was going on but would do some more in-depth investigation when he had the time. His first job was to see if he could get the girl to awaken. If she did, then she could give him the answers.

He walked back into the kitchen and poured himself a cup of coffee, then half-filled a second cup and walked back to the main room, and sat in the chair at her head.

Luke leaned close to her and asked loudly, "Miss? Would you like some coffee? It'll warm you up inside."

There was no response, but Luke didn't really expect one. He added some more wood to the flames and knew all he could do was wait.

He returned to the kitchen area and while he was there, he drank his coffee and thought it would be a good idea to get some hot food ready for when, or if the girl awakened. He could use some hot food himself anyway, so he put a pot on the cook stove and poured in about a quart of water. He found some potatoes, peeled them, and cut them into small pieces before dumping them into the water then added some onions, a whole tin of canned beef, canned tomatoes, some salt and pepper, and finally, two cans of beans. Then he simply walked away and let it heat.

Luke needed to know more about the occupants of the cabin. Until the girl was awake, he wouldn't know how she had gotten here and why they were treating her so poorly. He had his suspicions and none of them were good.

He began in the bedroom with the door. There were two beds, and each room had a dresser of sorts. They had been crudely built but served their purpose. He began going through the dresser. The drawers contained nothing but men's clothing. He removed and held up the trousers inside and found that there were two different men living in the room. One was quite large, the second just about average-sized.

When he went through the drawers of the other bedroom area, he found that they held only men's clothing as well, again in two distinct sizes. So, there were four men living here and one girl. Judging by her treatment, she wasn't here voluntarily.

He returned to the first bedroom to take some of the socks to put on the young woman's feet and had one pair in his hand but when his hand closed over the second pair of rolled-up socks, he found them much too bulky and too hard for wool. He pulled out the socks and peeled them back to find a thick wad of currency. He stared wide-eyed at the money, then dropped the first pair of socks back into the drawer and began peeling off bills, laying them on the top of the dresser and counting. When he finished, he whistled softly. There were almost two thousand dollars in that sock, and he doubted if the money was obtained legally, so he just shoved it into his pocket. What he did with it was for him to determine later.

He continued his search through the large cabin, making other worthwhile finds such as a cache of six full boxes of .44 caliber rimfire ammunition for his Remington and Winchester, as well as a small keg of gunpowder, a box of lead balls, and another of percussion caps. It meant that these boys practiced a lot and probably used their guns often in whatever illegal jobs they had been doing. He took the cartridges out to the kitchen and set them near his Winchester and shotgun but left the powder, caps, and balls behind.

He returned to the main room, dropped to his heels to examine the girl to ensure that she was still breathing at least, then touched her forehead lightly, gratified to find that she didn't seem to be nearly as cold as she had been.

Luke then stood, returned to the kitchen, and then stirred the still-heating pot and took a good whiff of the steaming mixture. It was too early for a taste test.

The place was unnerving, and he believed that bad things had happened here. He knew it wasn't the cabin's fault, but he knew that the men who had done the evil would not be returning anytime soon with the storm outside.

But that being said, he found himself in a bit of a quandary. He was convinced that the men who lived here were probably outlaws and he should leave at the earliest opportunity, especially as he had their money in his pocket. But he also knew he couldn't leave the young woman here to be alone with them.

He sat at the table, rising every few minutes to stir the stew and look in on the girl. Her breathing was much better, but she was still asleep.

Forty-five minutes later, the stew was almost done and after a few tastes, added some more salt and pepper and a few tablespoons of sugar to take the bite out of the tomatoes. In another fifteen minutes, it would be ready.

He poured himself another cup of coffee and wandered back to the fire, then put two more logs onto the flames before sitting down in the chair near her head.

"Miss? Are you awake?" he asked loudly.

There was still no response, and now he was growing concerned. It had been over an hour since she'd been near the fire and he would have expected her to be moving at least.

He sipped his coffee and tilted his head to look at her. Her light brown hair was everywhere, but in her sleep, she looked so calm and peaceful that she appeared positively angelic. She was breathing normally, but she needed to get something warm into her stomach.

"Miss, would you like some hot coffee?" he asked loudly.

Laura could feel warmth all around her and heat on her face. It wasn't the fires of hell that she felt for what she had done, it was a soothing warmth. She realized that she had changed into a new life, that her soul was free from that other, horrible life and was now entering a warm, pain-free existence. She felt at peace as she had never felt before and kept her eyes closed, luxuriating in the freedom. She had gambled and won. She didn't go to hell for just letting herself die. God had forgiven her.

Then she heard a voice, a man's voice calling to her and her peace evaporated. S*he hadn't died at all! They were back and brought her into the house again! Why had they brought her into the house?* She knew they didn't care if she died.

The voice asked if she would like some coffee, causing more confusion. *Why would they be nice to her suddenly?* She opened her eyes just enough to see and saw a kind, handsome face. He wasn't one of them, maybe he was a new gang member, but if he wasn't, then maybe he could help her escape. She had to know.

Luke hadn't seen her eyes open into slits and thought she wasn't going to react, so he took another sip of coffee and was about to stand when he heard her speak ever so quietly that it didn't even qualify as a whisper.

"Who are you?" she asked.

Luke quickly dropped his eyes to the girl and saw a pair of dark blue eyes looking at him.

He quickly sat back in the chair and replied, "My name is Luke Scott, miss. I have a ranch south of here and got lost in the blizzard. How do you feel?"

Laura suddenly began to weep gently. *She was safe! Someone was here to save her!* But despite her incredible relief and joy, she became suddenly aware she was still so very cold.

Rather than answer his question, she quietly asked, "You have coffee?"

Luke leaned closer to her and replied in a low voice, "Yes, miss. I've made some coffee. Would you like some? You need the heat and the liquid."

"Yes, please."

"You stay bundled under those blankets, miss. I'll go and get you some coffee. I made some stew that will be ready in a few minutes," he replied as he stood to get her coffee.

Laura didn't waste any more energy in replying but simply nodded.

Luke smiled down at her and hurried to the kitchen, where he quickly filled another cup and then stopped to add some sugar from a tin near the cookstove. One of those bastards must have a sweet tooth he thought as he stirred her coffee and then carried it across the floor to where she lay near the fire.

After taking his seat, he asked, "Can you sit up by yourself, or do you need some help?"

"I'll try," she replied.

Laura struggled, and after almost a minute of trying, managed to sit up, but had to brace herself with her arms.

Luke held the cup to her lips, and she took a mouthful of the medium-hot coffee into her mouth and held it there. She closed her eyes and relished the coffee, unsure if she preferred the heat or the taste. It took her less than a minute to finish the cup.

When she'd swallowed the last drop, she asked, "Can you help me back down, Mister Scott? I may have a hard time."

"Certainly."

Luke stood behind her and put his hands on her back as she released her arms and he lowered her gently to the mattress.

"Thank you, Mister Scott," she said as she looked up at him.

“Call me Luke, miss. What’s your name?” he asked as he took a seat, her coffee cup still in his hands.

“Laura, Laura Harper.”

“Laura, I have a good idea of what’s happened to you, but can you tell me what is going on here?”

“These four men came to our ranch. They killed my father and hurt my mother then took all our cattle and they took me. One of them brought me here and the others came back a few days later.”

He looked into those deep blue eyes and asked softly, “Laura, you could have started a fire in the barn to keep you warm, but you didn’t. Why did you want to die?”

She closed her eyes and began to cry again as she whispered, “Because I think I’m going to have a baby. They kept using me.”

Luke suspected that she’d had a bad time of it but hearing her say it still made him sick, so he let her cry for a while before asking another question.

After almost a minute of Laura’s tears, he asked, “How long have you been here, Laura?”

“About three weeks, I think,” she answered and then sniffled.

“How old are you?”

“I’ll be sixteen on January 27th.”

“Well, Laura, I don’t want you to worry about anything anymore, alright? I’ll take care of you until we get out of here. Was your mother still alive when they left your home?”

"Yes. They hurt her and then threw her into her bedroom and told her that if she told anybody she'd never see me again. When they were riding away, I heard her shout my name from the porch."

"Laura, I'll get you all warmed up and then after the storm dies down, I'll take you back to your mother. Then I'm going to find these men and kill them all for what they did to you."

"Are you a sheriff?"

"No, I'm just a rancher, but men like this don't play by the rules, and neither will I."

Laura looked at him and thought he was the kind of man that would do exactly what he said he would.

"Mister Scott…" she began.

"Luke," he interrupted.

"Luke, um, I need to use the privy, but I can't walk," she said, obviously embarrassed.

"I'll get you something."

He stood, walked to the kitchen, and found a shallow pan, then opened his saddlebags and pulled out some privacy papers before returning to the fireplace.

"Alright, Laura, I'm going to slide the pan under the blankets. Do you think you can handle it from there?"

"I think so."

"I'll be in the kitchen. Call me when you're done, alright?"

"Okay."

Luke handed her the privacy papers and left for the kitchen. He had to check on his stew anyway.

Laura managed to clear her clothing out of the way and then somehow slide the pan under her. She understood the meaning of relieving herself when she felt the vast relief of answering nature's call. She carefully lifted her hips and slid the pan out from under her and almost collapsed from the exertion. She pulled it aside, beyond the blankets, and then readjusted her clothes.

"Luke, I'm finished!" she shouted, which was only slightly above a normal speaking volume.

Luke had been stirring his stew and sampled it again. It was just about ready, but the potatoes needed just a few more minutes.

When Laura called, he hurried into the main room, picked up the pan and carried it out to the kitchen, opened the door, and stepped outside. The storm was still in full force, but with the house breaking the wind, he was able to hurl the pan's contents to the left of the steps to avoid the creation of any yellow ice where they would be stepping later.

He returned to the kitchen area, closed the door behind him and pumped water to clean out the pan then set it aside for non-food use before he walked back to Laura.

"Laura, the stew is almost ready. Do you want to eat there, or would you prefer to sit in one of the chairs at the table?"

She glanced over at the chairs before saying, "Would you be able to help me to get over there?"

"Of course, I will. Are you ready to move?"

"I think so."

Luke helped her to sit up, then assisted her to her feet and slowly walked with her to the chair, and set her down. Once he was sure that she wasn't going to fall over, he trotted back to the mattress, pulled the two blankets, and returned to Laura, spread them across her lap, and wrapped them around her legs.

"That'll keep you warm on the outside and the stew will warm you on the inside, which is more important," he said as he smiled.

Laura tried to smile but didn't quite make it. Luke was surprised she did as well as she did, considering all that had happened to her. He quickly crossed the ten feet to the kitchen area, took out a bowl and ladled in two scoops of stew, made another cup of coffee for her, then took them both back to the table.

He set the bowl of stew and the coffee on the table, and asked, "Can you manage on your own, Laura, or do you need help?"

"I can eat all right."

Luke returned to the cookstove, filled a bowl of stew for himself, topped off his coffee then returned to the table to talk to Laura as they ate.

Laura still seemed very depressed, which didn't surprise Luke at all. To be her age and witness the death of her father and then be subjected to repeated violations by four violent men was excruciating. He sat down and began to eat, glancing up at Laura between bites. She seemed to be eating well enough, so he was sure that she'd make a speedy recovery now, at least physically. She was a very pretty young lady, yet her innocence had been stolen from her by those four men, and he felt his anger renewed at the thought.

"Laura, when I first talked to you, you said you were going to have a baby, but you've only been here three weeks. My wife didn't know she was going to have our baby for more than two months. How do you know?"

Tears began to slide down her smooth cheeks as she stared into her stew.

Her voice was shaking as she stammered, "Those…those men…they…they violated me."

Luke softly said, "I know, Laura. But I don't understand how you know that you're carrying a child already."

Her head snapped up and she said in a surprisingly strong voice, "Didn't you hear me? I said they took me! I'm going to have a baby now!"

Luke was surprised by her vehemence and her newfound volume but was confused by what she had said.

"Laura, my wife didn't get pregnant until we'd been married four months."

Now it was Laura's turn to be confused as she asked in a calmer voice, "Didn't you make love to her?"

Luke smiled at her and replied, "Dozens of times, if not hundreds. But it still took a while. I've known women who have been married for years who haven't had any children."

"But papa said that if I let a man do that to me, I'd have a baby."

Luke finally understood her worries and said, “Laura, your father told you that to try to keep you from dallying with a boy and having the risk of having a baby. But it doesn’t always happen.”

“It doesn’t? When he told me, I asked about Mrs. Charleston because she didn’t have a baby yet, and he said her husband never visited her.”

“No, it really doesn’t happen all the time. Now, there is a chance that you might be pregnant, so I won’t lie to you. But there’s also a chance that you aren’t.”

“How will I know?”

Luke never thought he’d have to explain such things to anyone, much less a teenage girl he’d known for less than a few hours, but it was necessary.

“My wife said she thought she was pregnant when she missed one monthly but had to wait until she missed two to be sure.”

Laura brightened up considerably and asked, “Then there’s a chance I’m not going to have a baby?”

“Yes, there’s a chance. How are you doing aside from that, Laura? Are you hurt?”

“Two of them hit me sometimes if I didn’t do what they told me to do, but not for a few days now.”

“Do you think you’d be able to ride tomorrow?”

“I don’t care if my behind was covered in bug bites, I’ll still ride to get away from here.”

Luke smiled and replied, "Good. Now, we need to figure out some things first. These four men, can you tell me anything about them?"

Laura took a big bite of stew and nodded, then Luke had to wait until she finished chewing for her answer.

She swallowed and said, "A man named Charlie Bassett is in charge. Philly Henderson is his best man and then there's Mack Johnson and Joe Pendleton. They're all vile, cruel men."

Luke hadn't heard the names before, so he asked, "How do they make their money, Laura? I found it hidden in a sock in one of the drawers."

"They steal cattle and take them to Colorado City. They were complaining about a man named Kingman trying to give them less money the last time."

"I know him. He's the purchasing agent at the railroad stockyards. They're probably the ones who stole my cattle."

She scraped the bottom of the bowl with her spoon, then looked at Luke and asked, "This is really good stew, Luke. Could I have some more?"

"Absolutely. When was the last time you ate, Laura?" he asked as he took her bowl and then returned to the cookstove.

"When they left two days ago. They lock me in the barn when they go out to steal the cattle. This last time was the third time since I've been here."

"If they're stealing cattle that often, I wonder why the law hasn't come down hard on them," Luke said as he handed her back the full bowl and sat down.

Laura accepted the bowl and solved the mystery by replying, "Charlie Bassett is the sheriff's cousin."

"That would explain it then, wouldn't it?" he said then asked, "Laura how soon after they leave, do they return?"

"Usually, it's three or four days."

"You've gone nine days without food in the past three weeks?"

She nodded as she dug into the stew.

He didn't add that at least it was nine days she wasn't being molested as he watched her eat. She wasn't taking small, lady-like bites either, but was devouring the thick stew. There was still plenty left, so he could reheat it later for dinner, and he'd already found some eggs and bacon available for breakfast.

"Laura when they returned, was it always from the same direction?"

She stopped eating and thought about it before replying, "I'm not sure. I was always in the barn when they got back, but I think they came from the south."

"Your ranch is to the east?"

She continued eating and nodded.

"We're going to have to fashion some cold-weather clothing for you, Laura. If the winds die down, it won't be so bad, but I think the snow will keep coming down. But even if it's still snowing, we'll have to leave in the morning. It was the wind that blew me off course, so we should only be on the trail for two or three hours before we get you home."

"They burned my coat when we got here."

"They put you in that cold barn for three days without anything to keep you warm?"

She kept her eyes focused on the stew as she said softly, "It wasn't too bad the first two times, but it was really cold this time. That's when I decided to let the cold just take me away to heaven. I wasn't sure if it was really killing me because I didn't do anything. I just didn't want to live anymore. I thought I was going to have a baby and those men would probably kill me anyway."

Luke was stunned by her conversational tone describing not only the terror of what they had put her through but the extraordinary moral dilemma she had to face.

"Laura, even if you are going to have a baby, there's never an excuse for giving away the most precious gift of all, your life."

She set her empty bowl down and pulled the blankets to her chin as she looked at Luke and said, "But I had no chance. They were hurting me."

Luke stared right back into those blue eyes and said, "Laura, never give up. Life is too important. You always have to find a way to fight for every second of life."

"But you don't understand! I had nothing. I was ashamed and thought that I was going to have a baby."

Luke could see the tortured pain behind her eyes, sighed, and said, "Laura, remember I told you that I was married? I was married to the most wonderful woman I've ever met. Her name was Ella. She was everything I ever asked for in a wife and friend. She was smart, kind, and just a joy to be around. We didn't have it easy at first because we were building up our ranch, but it didn't matter. We were so happy just to be together.

"She got pregnant four months after we were married and had our little boy, Mark, six years ago. He was a beautiful boy and Ella was so completely happy with her life and so was I. She didn't just go through the motions of living, either. My Ella lived.

"Then one thing after another went wrong. Mark died of croup when he was two and we were both devastated. But it was Ella who brought us both back from our despair. She insisted that we had to keep living and that maybe we'd be blessed with another baby. So, we returned to our happy lives hoping she would conceive again."

Luke took in and blew out a long breath and continued, saying, "Then…then a couple of months after we lost Mark, Ella noticed that there was a lump under her left arm. I took her to the doctor who said it was just a swollen lymph node and that it would go away, but it didn't go away. It kept getting bigger and I was afraid for Ella.

"Then when I took her back, he changed his diagnosis and said she had advanced breast cancer. He told her that because it was so far along, there was nothing he could do. Ella asked him how long she had, and he said less than two months. He offered her some laudanum to control the pain, but she declined. I wanted to shoot him for delivering the bad news, but Ella just took my arm, smiled, thanked the doctor and we left his office. I was crushed and wanted to let my anger out on someone but didn't have anyone to blame. I stewed in my boiling rage all the way back to our ranch, but do you know what Ella did when we got home?"

Laura could barely speak but replied in a soft whisper, "No."

"She knew how I felt, so she walked close to me, put her arm around me, and asked me to make love to her. I knew that she didn't ask to make herself feel better. She asked for my benefit to drive the demons from me. I was worried about hurting her, so I told her we shouldn't. She then insisted, saying she wanted to experience as much joy as she could in her remaining time. She knew that was the only reason she could give to me. How could I deny her?"

Luke was having a very hard time continuing and had to stop for a full minute to regain his composure before he continued.

"Over the next few weeks, she began to lose weight and I could see the pain on her face, but she never complained. She never asked for relief. We went through our life as normally as we could, and she still behaved as she always did. She would poke fun at me and expect me to do the same to her. Do you know how hard it is to make fun of someone you love when you know they'll be gone in just a few weeks? But I did because she asked me to.

"But as much pain as she was enduring, she never gave up her love of life. She was wasting away and in constant pain, but she still would manage a smile when she saw me. I knew she didn't have much time left and I spent her last four days with her and barely left the house. It was selfish in a way. I just wanted to keep her with me for as long as possible. She died on a Wednesday night right around midnight. I didn't weep or wail over her passing as I had long since accepted her death. I buried her on our ranch the next day by myself.

"Now maybe you'll understand why I believe you should never give up. I look at you and see a pretty, young woman who was probably abused terribly, but you're still healthy and can fight. My Ella had no chance at all but loved every second of her life. I know it doesn't seem fair to you, to compare what each of you went through and I don't diminish your suffering or pain. I really do understand, but I don't want you to throw away such a unique gift as your life."

"You lost your little boy and your wife in the same year?" she asked quietly.

Luke nodded, before she asked, "Didn't you want to be with her in heaven?"

"Not yet. Before she died, she extracted two promises from me. The first was that I would go on living as I had when we were first married. In other words, she wanted me to be happy. I promised I would and have tried to live up to that promise. The second was that she told me to remarry."

"Did you?"

"No. I've kind of cheated on that promise a bit."

"How can you cheat on a promise?"

"I don't socialize at all. I stay at the ranch most of the time and when I have to go to town, I take care of my business and return to the ranch right away. I've already talked to you more than I've talked to any other female in the past four years."

"That is cheating."

Luke smiled and said, "I know. I can almost hear Ella's voice chastising me for it. She's probably calling me all sorts of nasty little names."

"I had a boyfriend. His name was Jason Chandler."

"I'd be surprised if you didn't, Laura. You're a very pretty young lady."

She blushed and replied, “Thank you, Luke. But he won’t come near me now. I’ve been spoiled by those men.”

“Laura, that’s not true at all. You’ve been hurt, but any man who thinks less of you for what happened isn’t a real man and not worth marrying anyway.”

“Don’t all husbands expect their wives to be untouched when they get married?”

“Some do, which is kind of one-sided, don’t you think?”

“What do you mean?”

“Those are the men who like to think of themselves as experienced in the ways of women, meaning that they are far from being untouched themselves. Laura, if you find a man who truly loves you, what happened to you won’t matter a lick. In fact, it’ll be a good measuring stick. If you tell him and he balks, he’s not worth your time.”

“Was your wife untouched?”

“Yes, but it wouldn’t have mattered. Ella and I were close from the time we were in our fourth year in school. By the time we were your age, we knew we were going to get married. I went off to war and she waited three years, despite being a very popular young woman.”

“You were in the war? Aren’t you kind of young?”

Luke smiled and replied, “Hardly. I joined up when I was eighteen, and like a lot of other young men, I thought it would be a short war. I was gone for three years and returned when I was twenty-one. I married Ella and we lived on my father’s ranch. We had a small house built just for us. It was me and Ella, my father, and our foreman, Hal Rawlings. My father died the next year, so Ella and I moved into the ranch house and Hal moved into the small house. For the last four years, I've lived alone in the house. I asked Hal to move in, but he felt he should live in the small house or the bunkhouse because he wasn't family. Are you an only child, Laura?"

"No. I'm just the only one still at home. I have two brothers. John is the oldest and then there's Rob. My sister, Elizabeth, but we all called her Lizzy, is five years older than me. She got married and is living in Colorado City. My brothers left two years ago to go to the gold fields near Pike's Peak. They took Lizzy's husband with them, too."

"So, what happened to Lizzy?"

"She's still in Colorado City. I haven't seen her since Rob and John left. I think she's too ashamed."

"Why should she be ashamed if she was deserted?"

"I don't know, but my mother says it's because he took all their money. Rob and John took some cattle to Colorado City for money too, and my father was really mad at them."

"I still don't understand why your sister would stay in town if she had no money."

"She had some money left, but her husband, Richard, took most of it. It was her money, too. My father had given it to her in case her husband left because he didn't like Richard very much. I think he didn't want Lizzy to come back, either. That's another reason I haven't seen her in two years."

"Why did she marry him, then?"

"I think it was because she let him take advantage of her. My father was really mad at her and made Richard marry her. That's why he told me about getting babies, I think."

"But didn't you wonder why Lizzy didn't have a baby?"

"She did have a baby, but it died when it was born."

"Oh. What did your mother think of all this?"

"She was mostly sad because she misses Lizzy."

Luke paused then said, "So, promise me that you won't think about dying anymore, Laura. You're going to go back and see your mother tomorrow. It'll make her very happy to see you again, won't it?"

That brightened up Laura's face as she replied, "Yes, I think so."

"Now, tomorrow, the easiest way to keep you warm would be to wrap you in blankets and just let you sit on the horse. There are two horses in the barn, but I didn't see an extra saddle. If we wrap you up, I'd rather you sit in the saddle, so you can keep your feet in the stirrups and grab the saddle horn if you start to slip. We'll have you wearing two pairs of pants and at least two shirts and then I'll put my slicker over you to keep the heat in. You'll wear two pairs of socks and I'll cut up some of my tarp to make some makeshift boots to keep the moisture from your feet. You should stay nice and toasty for the trip."

"What about my dress?"

"You'll still wear your dress. You'll put the two pairs of pants on under the dress and the two shirts over your dress. Before you get on the horse, you need to roll up the dress to your waist, so you can sit on the saddle. Once you're in the saddle, I'll wrap the blankets around you and put on the slicker. I'll make sure to wrap the blanket over your head like a giant scarf, too."

"I'll look very odd."

"But you'll be warm and in a couple of hours, you'll be home, Laura. It's worth a little fashion embarrassment, don't you think?" he asked as he grinned.

She smiled back and replied, "I think so."

"Alright. Do you want to lie down again? I'll go and start getting your things together for the ride."

"I think that would be better."

Luke helped her stand and walked her slowly back to the mattress. He noticed that she was already moving much more smoothly as they approached the fire. Once they reached the temporary bed, he lowered her onto the mattress and covered her with the blankets.

"You rest now, Laura. No more worries. Alright?"

She smiled up at Luke, nodded then closed her eyes.

Luke smiled to himself as he picked up the empty bowls and cups before he walked to the kitchen. She was a sweet young lady and it made his desire to punish those who hurt her even stronger.

After cleaning the bowls and spoons, he began assembling the clothes to bundle Laura for tomorrow's cold ride. He chose one smaller shirt and one large, and then he found a pair of small woolen trousers that would be ideal for the inside pair and a larger, canvas set of pants for the outer covering then added two pairs of heavy socks to the pile.

He was going to head out to the barn to get his tarp to make some canvas moccasins but then went back to the drawers and found another pair of canvas pants which would work much better. He sliced off the legs and took them to the table where he had his sewing kit. He simply stitched the ends closed and set them aside. He'd just use pigging strings to hold the tops up over her legs. Satisfied he had everything he needed to keep Laura warm on the way back, he decided to check on the weather again.

He could hear the wind outside before he took off the bar, then opened the back door and looked around. It was early evening, so visibility was nil, but he could tell that the snow was still falling which meant that no one would be coming back soon.

After closing the door and dropping the bar in place, he poured himself another cup of coffee and took a seat at the table. Even though he didn't expect them to arrive in the storm, he knew that he had to prepare for that possibility. He walked to the front door and looked at the rope that lifted the bar, then hoisted the bar a few inches and slipped the rope off the end, effectively locking them inside. He thought it would be safe to sleep now as nobody could get inside.

Luke took a few minutes to clean and oil his Winchester and shotgun because they had been exposed to moisture for most of the day. He'd use some socks from the drawer to cover them for tomorrow's trip. Once he was satisfied with his weapons, he spent some time trying to think of the aftermath of their departure.

If he left the money where he found it, then they'd probably just stay in their cabin and leave him alone, but he didn't want them to leave him alone. He wanted them to follow him and try to get their money back. At the same time, he didn't want to put Laura or her mother in jeopardy, either. He'd figure out what to do after he got Laura home. Getting her back to where she belonged was the first big step.

He added a little more water to the stew and stirred it to blend it into the mix. It would probably taste better the second time. He added more wood to the cook stove and then quietly walked past the sleeping Laura and put two more logs on the fire.

Luke returned to the table thinking of things he might have missed but couldn't think of anything. He'd use another couple of pairs of pants as makeshift pack saddles for storing some of the food when they left. He wasn't absolutely sure that he'd be able to find Laura's home in two hours, but if he rode east, she should be able to recognize landmarks when they were close.

In a snow-trapped Colorado City, Charlie Bassett looked at Philly Henderson.

"We gotta get out of here, Philly. I'm already I' testy."

"We can't do nothin' about the weather, Charlie. All we can do is wait and enjoy ourselves. At least we got some female entertainment and other things to keep us goin'."

"That's one of the things that's got me testy. That girl is gonna be frozen stiff when we get back."

Philly laughed and said, "That's a good one, Charlie. She'll be a stiff that's frozen."

Charlie snickered at his own unintended pun then said, "At least we got the cattle sold, Philly. That damned Kingman tried to squeeze me when we dropped off the last bunch. He said he'd only pay us twelve bucks a head. I reminded him whose name was on those shipping sheets, so he gave us fifteen. We're gonna have to pay that fat bastard back one of these days."

"Let's get Mack and Joe and go downstairs to have a few hands of poker and maybe get some eats."

"Alright. Anything is better than just sittin' around. It'd better clear up soon. If it's only snowin' tomorrow, we head back. I don't wanna stick around here any longer than we need to."

"I hear ya, boss," Philly said as he grinned, then stood and followed Charlie out of the _____

Laura awakened an hour later and couldn't believe how warm she felt but wasn't surprised how hungry she still was, despite eating two full bowls of that tasty stew. She sat up easily and looked around for Luke, panicking for a moment to think he had already gone before spotted him sitting at the kitchen table, sipping coffee and thinking. Laura swung her legs out from under the warm blankets and slowly stood, feeling much better as she walked softly to the kitchen.

Luke was still thinking about tomorrow and didn't hear Laura's soft steps behind him.

"You seem lost in thought, Luke," she said, breaking his reverie.

Luke was startled but recovered quickly and was happy to see Laura walking on her own.

He turned to look at her and said, "Have a seat, Laura, and I'll get you some more stew."

"I was going to ask for some more. I'm still hungry."

"I'd be shocked if you weren't, Laura."

She was going to sit when Luke stood and pulled back a chair for her, making her smile. She'd never had anyone do that for her before and it made her feel like a lady. She sat, and Luke took the now-clean bowl and filled it with stew then set it down on the table, poured some of the freshly made coffee added sugar, and stirred it for Laura before putting it on the table.

"Aren't you going to have some more, Luke?" she asked as she began to eat.

"I haven't decided yet. You go ahead and eat."

After she had taken a few bites, she had to wipe some juice from her mouth, then giggled and said, "I'm not much of a lady, I guess."

"Laura, you're very much a lady. What do you think makes a woman a lady?"

"Oh, I don't know. Manners, nice clothes, and money, I think."

"You're completely wrong, Miss Harper. You just described a rich society matron. Nope, what makes a woman a lady, and a man a gentleman, for that matter, is consideration. A true lady or gentleman will treat everyone equally and courteously.

"I've met some well-to-do people who act like they're courteous to what they consider their social inferiors, but they're being condescending. You impress me as someone who no matter what your financial status, would always be truly courteous to everyone. That's why I think you're a true lady, Laura."

"I don't know about that, Luke, but I can tell that you're a real gentleman."

"Thank you, Laura. I work at it. Now, Hal, my foreman, has been with the family longer than I have. He doesn't speak

English well and can barely read and write, but he's as much a gentleman as anyone I have ever met."

"I'd like to meet him."

"Maybe you will, Laura. Let me ask you something. This really matters to me and it involves you and your mother, too."

"Okay," she replied and took one more bite before leaving the spoon in the bowl of stew.

"Tomorrow, when we leave, we'll go to your ranch to reunite you with your mother. Now, I have the outlaws' money in my pocket. I intend on keeping six hundred and fifty dollars for the cattle they stole and giving the other twelve hundred dollars to you."

"Why?" she asked quickly.

"Payback for what they did to you. They hurt you, and now we can hurt them. I know money isn't nearly enough, but to them it is. My concern is that they'll follow our trail back to your ranch and hurt you and your mother. If I leave the money here, they'll probably just ignore you. I don't care that much about the money. I'll probably be able to wring it out of Mister Kingman's hide when I get to go to Colorado City anyway, but I do worry about you and your mother. I intend on staying with you as long as it takes to ensure you're safe, or you can both come to my ranch where we'll have more firepower and Hal will be there as well. I'll do whichever you prefer, Laura."

Laura didn't think at all very long before replying, "Take the money, Luke. I don't care that much about it either, but my mother will probably need the help. I want to hurt them, Luke. If I could shoot a gun, I'd shoot them all."

Luke smiled and said, "That's the attitude to take, Laura. You did nothing wrong and have nothing to be ashamed of. It was all on them and you should be angry. Alright, we'll take the money. When we get to your ranch, we'll talk to your mother and find out what she wants to do. What's your mother's name, by the way?"

"Her name is Ann," she replied before she began to eat again.

She was feeling better all the time. Ever since they'd taken her, she had been planning to escape one way or another, but nothing had gotten very far in her mind as she could never envision what would happen if she got more than a few hundred yards from the house. Now she would make it all the way home and have protection on the way.

After she finished eating, Luke showed her the assortment of clothes she'd be donning in the morning, and she laughed as he explained how it would all work. Luke smiled when he heard her laughter, amazed at her resiliency. Laura was going to grow into a formidable woman. He could already see it in her eyes and the way she carried herself. To undergo that kind of nightmare and recover so quickly was nothing less than superhuman. He didn't even realize his own enormous part in helping her to cope with those nightmares, including her enormous worry about a possible pregnancy.

After everything was set for the morning, she asked about using the privy again. Luke advised against it but told her if she wanted to go outside for privacy, to use the north side of the porch. The wind was blocked by the house and there was no snow. She took his advice and after Luke removed the door's bar, she stepped outside quickly while Luke stood by the door and waited for her. She popped back into the house just a minute later and Luke quickly closed, then barred the door.

"Would you like some more stew, Laura?"

"No, thank you, Luke. I'm really full."

"Okay. I'll go ahead and finish it off and then, I'll just leave the pot on the stove to ruin the inside, so they can't use it."

"Why don't we just burn the place down when we leave?"

"I thought about doing just that but figured they'd just go and take some other family's house and kill them all. Let them stay here, but I'll make it hard on them to get inside. I had planned on cutting the rope pull for the front crossbar after we left so they would either have to sleep in the barn or figure out a way to break in. They'll be freezing their butts off by the time they do, too."

Laura laughed again and then he asked, "And do you know what else I'm planning on doing?"

"No," she answered as she grinned.

"After we get the horses out of the barn and get ready to go, I'm going to get a pail of water and toss it all over that bar they use to close off the barn. It'll just drive them nuts."

Laura loved all the small irritants that Luke was describing to her and asked, "Can I do some things to make them crazy, too?"

"Sure. What did you have in mind?"

"Can we close off the flue to the chimney?"

Luke grinned and replied, "That's a wonderful idea. It wouldn't be hard, either. One good whack with a sledge would do the trick. We're turning into mischievous elves, Laura."

“How about spreading pepper over the mattresses, too?” she asked, giggling.

“Anything you feel like trying, Laura, you go right ahead. Just hold off until the morning. You can go crazy while I’m saddling the horse and making a trail rope.”

“Okay.”

Laura was astounded by how the simple acts of vandalism lifted her spirits. Those four monsters would be sorry they ever heard of Laura Harper.

Just an hour later, Laura was snuggled into her mattress-bed by the fire after Luke had added three more logs to get through most of the night.

Luke stood over her and said, “Good night, Laura. I’ll get up early and check on the weather. I’d like to be out of here by early morning, but there’s no real rush because they’ll have to ride the fifteen to twenty miles from Colorado City in the deep snow.”

“Good night, Luke. Thank you for everything,” she said as she smiled up at him.

“You’re welcome, Laura,” he said as he smiled back.

Luke blew out the lamps in the main room but let the one in the doored bedroom burn minimally. He’d probably be up in six hours.

CHAPTER 2

Luke managed to awaken almost exactly six hours later. He had his boots off, so after he rolled out of the bed and stretched, he padded quietly across the floor into the kitchen, stopped, and restarted the cook stove fire before unbarring the back door and stepping out onto the porch. The wind was almost gone, but the snow was still coming down. It wasn't as thick as he had expected though, so they'd be able to leave.

After answering nature's call, he returned to the house and washed as well as he could. He felt his face and knew he should shave, so he took his shave kit from his saddlebags and lathered up. He didn't nick himself too badly, all things considered, but he felt cleaner. After putting away the shaving kit, he filled the coffeepot and set it on one of the cookstove's hot plates.

He snuck into the main room and saw Laura curled up like a ball under her blankets which made him smile. As quietly as he could manage, he restarted the main fire and began adding progressively larger logs. Once it was going strong, he stepped away and returned to the kitchen.

Laura slept for another two hours, obviously needing the rest to build up her energy. Luke had already gone through two cups of coffee and had selected two large pairs of pants, tied off the ends of the legs, and begun to fill them with food, the heaviest canned items were dropped in first, but he left the eggs and a half slab of bacon for breakfast. He packed a tin of sugar and all their coffee too and had almost finished when Laura walked up behind him, startling him again.

"Is the weather okay?" she asked.

"Better than I expected. There's only a little wind and the snow isn't too bad."

"Can I use the porch again?"

"Go ahead. I'll start our giant breakfast."

Laura smiled and trotted to the unbarred door, went outside, and was back in quickly before closing the door behind her. It was still nasty cold out there.

Luke had sliced the last half slab into a dozen thick slices and had the first six frying. While they were shrinking away to proper strips of cooked bacon, he broke the last of the eggs into a large bowl and whipped them up for scrambled eggs, and added some salt and pepper.

After all the bacon was cooked, he dumped the eggs into the large frypan and began to scrape and flip the eggs. Laura had already availed herself of a strip of bacon and was happily chewing as she waited at the table.

"Laura, while you're waiting, why don't you go and light all the lamps and get some more light in here. We'll just let them burn down until there's no more kerosene. It'll be another little gift from us to them."

Laura didn't need any more encouragement as she smiled then quickly hopped from lamp to lamp, setting their wicks aflame.

Luke had the eggs cooked and on the plates with the eleven strips of bacon on a separate plate in the middle of the table. He poured two cups of coffee and added sugar to Laura's before placing them on the tabletop.

Laura took her seat quickly and Luke joined her. It was a lot of eggs and bacon for them to eat, and they couldn't finish either the eggs or the bacon, but Luke found some butcher paper and laid the remaining four bacon strips on top and folded it into a large, greasy envelope, then set it into the food pants and turned to Laura.

"Well, Miss Harper, I think you need to get dressed while I go out and start getting the horses ready. The sun won't be up for another half an hour or so, not that we'll see it, but it'll be light enough to leave."

"Alright."

Laura trotted into the bedroom to don her bizarre wardrobe while Luke carried the two pants full of food with him out to the barn. Without the wind to worry about, his only concern was the ice that he knew was under the rising white fluff but soon stepped over the plank holding the barn door open, and entered the barn.

Luke gratefully set down the two heavy pantleg-bags and saddled his horse. He adjusted his stirrups to accommodate the shorter Laura and then grabbed another horse blanket and tossed it over a second horse. He lowered the two pants onto the horse's back and secured them at the bottom with pigging strings. He'd ride the last horse, so he fashioned a long trail rope that ended on the pack horse and then went through his saddle and ended in a large loop that he'd hang onto. Once they were underway, he could loop it over his shoulder. Satisfied that they were ready to ride, he made one last look around then left the barn and returned to the house.

Laura greeted him looking immensely cute in her oversized getup.

"I feel like a stuffed pig," she said as she grinned.

"You're the cutest stuffed pig I've ever seen," Luke said as he grinned back then said, "Alright, the horses are ready. We've eaten, so now, ma'am, we need to do our mischief."

Laura was smiling as she waddled over to the kitchen area, grabbed the tin of pepper, and carried it back to the bedroom. Luke could hear her giggling as she spread masses of pepper over the other two beds in the open bedroom.

"I couldn't find a sledge to jam the flue, but this big pot should work," Luke said loudly as he picked up a heavy cauldron.

Laura trotted out to watch as he lugged it to the fireplace and slammed it onto the flue handle, snapping it off in the closed position, then left the cast iron pot where it fell. He then turned to Laura and they both laughed at the damage.

"I have your homemade galoshes in my pocket with some pigging strings. Go ahead and sit down."

Laura flopped indelicately into a chair as there was no other way of doing it. She held out her right leg and Luke slid the canvas pant leg up over her thick pair of socks and tied off a pigging string loosely on the top then repeated it for the left.

He stood and examined his handiwork saying, "These won't keep out water, but it will keep the heat in. When you get to the kitchen door, just stay there. I'll bring around the horses and put you in the saddle, so your feet don't get wet."

"Okay."

"Once you're in the saddle, I'll wrap you in the blankets then I'll come back in here and bar the back door go out the front and cut the rope near the top. After I'm finished, I'll come around to the back and we'll head out of here."

Laura nodded, and Luke helped her stand and walk to the kitchen, having a hard time keeping from giggling himself at the sight. When she was at the doorway, he stopped and jogged across the porch and out to the barn. Three minutes later he was riding bareback out of the barn trailing the other two horses then stopped behind the house and tossed the loop of the trail rope over the bareback horse's neck that he'd be riding until he took care of his other jobs. He went inside and picked up his Winchester and shotgun, quickly slid them into their scabbards, and then slipped socks over both of their stocks before returning to retrieve Laura.

"Ready?" he asked as he looked into her eyes.

"Ready."

He scooped her into his arms and walked gingerly across the porch, slid her left foot into the stirrup, and told her to stand and try to swing into the saddle. She managed it with surprising ease, eliminating Luke's concern.

She held onto the saddle horn as he said, "I'll be right back with your blankets."

Laura nodded, then Luke turned, trotted back into the house, and picked up three blankets and then quickly sliced one halfway through the short side and tossed the split blanket and one of the others to the floor before taking the last one out to Laura. He tossed it over her shoulders, and she held onto it snugging it down into a giant shawl.

"Wrap that around you, Laura, and I'll be right back."

As Laura completed her wrapping, Luke returned to the house then reappeared with the other whole blanket, and just wrapped it loosely around her shoulders. The one he'd sliced was an idea he had at the spur of the moment.

He took the split blanket and walked to the front of the horse and tossed it over the horse's neck. Then he slipped it up onto Laura, so the split was on her front. He then wrapped each half of the blanket around her legs.

Laura felt like she was in a cocoon as all that was showing was her face, which was beaming at Luke. She was going home.

"I think I'm warm enough, Luke," she said.

"If you can still say that in two hours, I'll be happy. I'll be right back."

Luke returned to the house, barred the kitchen door, went through the already smoke-filled main room, reached the front door, and, after reattaching the rope, lifted the bar and exited the cabin. Once outside, he had to use the rope to pull the bar up again, so he could let it drop into its bracket. He pulled the door closed and let the bar drop. Once the door was secured, he reached up as high as he could with his knife cut the rope where it entered the house, and tossed the scrap into the snow. He verified that the pull rope was inaccessible then stepped down into the eighteen inches of snow and plowed through to the barn with only one more piece of mischief remaining.

He reached the barn and went inside cracked the ice in the trough then filled a pail of water and carried it back out through the still-propped-open door. Luke kicked the plank holding it open almost breaking a toe in the process, but then shut the door before putting the bar back into place. Then he secured it with pigging strings before he splashed water over the pigging strings and the bar knowing that the frozen iron of the bracket would freeze the water almost immediately. He tossed the bucket aside, then headed back to the horses and spied Laura grinning at him. He smiled and waved as he made it to the horses.

"We're going to go north for a little bit and then swing east. When you see any familiar landmarks, let me know."

"Okay."

Luke had planned on a grand leap onto the horse's back, but his heel found a thick patch of ice under the snow and his momentum carried his slide under the horse's belly and Luke found himself almost completely under a thick blanket of snow. He looked back and saw an upside-down Laura holding back her laughter.

Luke started to rise, pointed a finger at Laura, and shouted, "Not a word!", which had the opposite effect and caused Laura's laughter to become uncorked.

Luke was smiling as he boarded the horse more sedately and looped the rope around his shoulder before they set off to the north with Laura still laughing.

Charlie Basset sighed in exasperation as he looked at his oldest partner and said, "It's just snow, Philly. We can ride out to the cabin easy."

"Charlie, I don't trust this weather. That damned wind can come up really fast."

"The wind is gone. We gotta move fast now before the snow gets too deep."

"I suppose you're right. I'm gonna miss the female company, though."

“Just go get Mack and Joe and tell them we’re gonna go to the diner, get our breakfast, and head back. We should get there around noon.”

“Okay, boss.”

———

Luke had made the turn east after a mile or so and kept checking his backtrail to make sure Laura was all right and to see if the falling snow was covering their trail. With three horses, there would be a large canyon of snow that needed to be filled, and it wasn’t coming down that quickly any longer. The wind would take care of it in a couple of hours, but he’d rather not have any more wind. With any luck, the outlaws wouldn’t find where Luke and Laura had left the cabin, but it all depended on time and weather. If the snow kept coming down, it’s possible that in six or eight hours, they couldn’t be followed at all.

Then there was the darkness. It was almost the winter solstice, the shortest day of the year, so they could only track for nine hours a day. If they didn’t get back to the ranch until late in the afternoon, they might never see the trail. They could also be so distracted by all the mischief that they wouldn’t be able to get into the cabin for another hour or two and then, they might not miss the money for a while. That was a lot of ifs, but even if they followed the trail, they wouldn’t know about Luke. They’d think that Laura had managed to escape somehow and taken the horses, but they’d know where she’d be going, too.

He wished he had brought his Sharps, then he wouldn’t worry about them one bit. It would be too easy. With the snow restricting their movement, he could let them get within three hundred yards and pick them all off within minutes.

But those were all future concerns. Right now, he needed to get Laura home.

An hour and a half later, Laura called out, “Luke! I remember that stand of trees over there to the right. The one in the middle fell over. My house is about another five miles away but it’s more to the right.”

“Thanks, Laura. Still warm?” he yelled back to her.

“Yes, sir!” she shouted back.

Luke shifted their path more to the south and continued plowing through the snow.

Charlie Bassett, Philly Henderson, Mack Johnson, and Joe Pendleton were fighting their way through the snow riding west as Luke and Laura were pushing snow aside and heading east. At their closest, there were six miles between them. Laura and Luke were just three miles from her ranch, but the outlaws had another six miles to go before they reached their almost useless cabin.

Joe Pendleton was the least happy of the unhappy bunch. He had forgotten his scarf back at the hotel and hadn’t stopped whining about his discomfort since he discovered it missing. His constant complaining wasn’t sitting well with the others.

“I’m just so damned cold,” Joe moaned.

Charlie snapped, “Joe, it ain’t that cold. We’ve been out in a lot worse than this.”

“Charlie, the snow’s goin’ down the back of my neck. How much longer do we got to go?”

"About two hours. The snow's a little deeper than I thought. We'll get there sometime after noon. I don't wanna hear you no more. Just grow some, will ya?"

Joe simply sulked and wanted to blame somebody for his own forgetfulness.

"What are we gonna do about the frozen girl?" asked Philly.

"Take her out in back and leave her there. Let the critters take her away and save us some work."

"That's too bad. I was kinda lookin' forward to a little go-round with her when we got back."

"Jesus, Philly, don't you ever think of anything else?" Mack asked through his muffled mouth.

"Nope," he replied loudly as he grinned beneath his heavy scarf.

———

It was about an hour later that Laura told Luke that their ranch was less than a mile straight ahead.

Luke waved and headed in a beeline for the ranch and was beginning to feel the chill himself. They'd been on the trail for almost four hours, but they had almost reached their destination and Laura seemed excited. Luke was still impressed with Laura. Part of him wished she were a few years older as she was sure to make some lucky young man very happy.

Luke spotted the barn first and headed straight for it before the house appeared out of the snow a few seconds later. He doubted that the access road was on the western side of the ranch, but where were the fences? Laura had already told him what had happened to their small herd, but those rustlers surely didn't take down the fences.

"I'm home!" shouted Laura.

"You live in the middle of a field?" Luke shouted back.

He heard Laura laugh before she replied, "A field near my house is a lot better than that place."

"I'll grant you that, Miss Harper. Especially seeing that your field isn't covered in pepper."

Laura laughed again, and he could almost feel her joy from twenty feet away. He shifted toward the house and five minutes later pulled up in front. There was no point in hitching the animals as they weren't going anywhere. They were all tired and standing in deep snow.

Luke slid down and walked back to Laura.

"Hold on for a second, Laura. I've got to get you at least able to walk. I'm not going to carry you in. You can afford to get those things on the end of your feet wet now."

Luke began unwrapping Laura, tossing the blankets over the pack horse. When he unrolled the last blanket, he helped her down and she held onto his hand as they walked carefully up the snow-covered steps and porch. Once they reached the door, Laura didn't knock as Luke pulled the screen door open just enough to allow her to get inside. After the swinging outer door cleared most of the snow from the doorway, Laura opened the inner door and bounded inside.

"Mama! Mama! I'm home!" she shouted.

Luke walked in and closed the door, removing his Stetson as he stood in the doorway and waited for Laura to reunite with her mother.

In the kitchen, Ann Harper was having coffee when she heard the door open and was immediately terrified thinking that the men had returned but the terror was quickly supplanted with unrivaled joy when she heard Laura's shout.

She leapt from her chair, knocking it to the floor and spilling her coffee as she ran into the hallway to catch her daughter in her arms.

"Laura! Are you all right? How did you get here?" she asked between kisses, paying no attention to her daughter's outlandish garb.

She turned and smiled at Luke then answered quickly, "Luke saved me, Mama. He found me in the barn. I was almost dead from cold, Mama, but Luke saved me."

"Who is Luke?" she asked suddenly aware of the big man standing near the door with a smile on his face.

Before Laura could answer her eyes were ripped back to the hallway and she shouted again, "Lizzy! Why are you here?"

She left her mother and waddled quickly to her sister and embraced her before she had a chance to reply.

Luke took one look at the woman and was taken aback. She looked like an older, slightly taller, and shapelier Laura. When she looked up at Luke, he found himself lost in her Laura-like deep blue eyes. He would have recognized her as Laura's older sister without hearing Laura call her name.

Meanwhile, Laura danced back to Luke as well as she could while wearing all her mismatched clothing.

She took Luke's hand turned and said, "Mama, Lizzy, this is Luke Scott. He has a ranch south of here and he's the nicest man I've ever met."

Ann Harper approached Luke with tears in her eyes. She couldn't talk but smiled at Luke, but he didn't need any words to understand her gratitude.

Luke quietly said, "You're welcome, Mrs. Harper. I understand."

She nodded and wiped away her tears.

"Laura, I think you can get rid of all of those clothes now," Luke said as he turned to Laura with a smile.

Laura glanced down at herself and laughed before saying, "I think so. I'll be right back."

After she fast-waddled into her room, Ann Harper and Lizzy walked closer to Luke who was still in awe of Lizzy and tried to hide it.

Ann said, "Mister Scott, I can never thank you enough for saving my Laura. Was it bad?"

"You can ask Laura for the details, ma'am. But I've never seen anything like it. They had her in the barn without heat or a warm jacket. When I found her, she was almost frozen to death. She doesn't have a lot of fat to protect her, either."

Luke paused, deciding not to mention Laura's decision to end her own life, and then continued.

"In answer to your next question, she was repeatedly violated by the four men. It's a credit to her and to you, how well she's rebounded from that treatment. I'm very proud of Laura. She's only a day past being almost dead and she's acting like a normal young lady. I'm sure she'll still need all the support you and Mrs. Swanson can give her."

"Did they beat her?"

"She told me that two of them were rough with her, but she seemed all right. Laura has sand, Mrs. Harper."

"Both of my daughters were always very resourceful, Mister Scott. I'm proud of them both."

"Please, ma'am. I'd appreciate it if you and Mrs. Swanson would both call me Luke."

"We'll do that, but please call me Ann."

For the first time, Luke heard Lizzy speak and it did nothing to dispel her aura as her voice was melodious but still firm.

"Luke, please call me either Ellie or Beth. I've always hated being called Lizzy," she said as she smiled.

Luke had a hard time responding for two big reasons, the name Ellie and the smile.

"Um, I'll call you Beth, if that's alright."

"That's fine."

Laura bounced out of her room wearing just the dress and Ann gave her another hug. Luke had noted the source of the two daughters' fine features. Laura and Beth's mother was around forty-five and still a fine-looking woman.

Ann led Laura into the kitchen, and Luke prepared to follow when Beth stopped him, which was exceedingly easy for her to do.

"Luke, may I talk to you for a second?"

"Certainly."

Her deep blue eyes peered into him as she asked, "What did you hold back when you were talking to my mother? You had to think about saying something and didn't."

Luke was more than just a bit surprised. *Could she read everyone that easily or just him?*

"Um, I didn't think it was my place to tell her. I thought it had to come from Laura."

"Will you tell me? I won't tell my mother unless it becomes necessary."

Luke took a breath before answering quietly, "I'll tell you because you may understand it better and it'll help you if Laura has another bad experience."

"Alright."

"When I found her, as I told your mother, she was bundled up under some hay in the barn. After she finally awakened in the house a few hours later, she told me that she wanted to die. It was her plan to just go to sleep and never wake up."

Laura was startled and asked, "Was it that bad?"

"It was. But what had really pushed her to that decision was her belief that she was pregnant."

“She’s only been gone three weeks. How could she know that?”

“That’s what I had to tell her. I had to explain that she may or may not be pregnant, but she wouldn’t know for a while. It seems that your father told her that every time a man and woman join together, the woman becomes pregnant. She was horrified that it would happen then when added to the abuse, you can understand how bad it would be for her. But she promised me she’d never think of doing it again.”

“Even if she is pregnant?”

“Even then.”

She smiled at Luke again, and said, “You must be more of a preacher than a rancher.”

“That seems to be everyone else’s opinion, but not mine.”

“Thank you for telling me that, Luke. It helps me understand what Laura went through. Let’s go into the kitchen. I have a feeling you’d like a cup of coffee about now.”

“Yes, ma’am. It sounds pretty good, but I’ve got to get outside and take care of the horses and bring everything back inside.”

“I’ll make sure the coffee stays hot then.”

“I appreciate it, Beth.”

Luke headed back out the front door, grabbing his Stetson as he did, then opened the door and closed it behind him before he stepped across the porch and back into the snow.

“Let’s get you hard-working critters into the barn,” he said to the horses.

None answered as he led the three horses through the snow.

Inside the house, Ann was still talking to Laura about what had happened and, like Luke, was surprised by her seemingly normal demeanor.

"Mama, what happened to papa?" Laura asked.

"Well, sweetheart, I rode into town and told the sheriff what had happened. I didn't believe that evil man who took you when he warned me not to go to the law. Men like that never tell the truth. When I saw the sheriff, he told me he'd begin a search for you, but I don't think he ever did anything. The man has a murdering bunch of men ride in here kill my husband and take my daughter and he did nothing!"

"Mama, the gang's boss is his cousin."

Ann was startled by the revelation and exclaimed, "Well, that explains it! So, he thinks it's all right for his cousin's gang to murder and do other things, and he thinks that no one will notice? I wish I were a man. I'd make him pay for his negligence!"

"Mama, Luke will take care of the sheriff after he kills those four men," Laura announced matter-of-factly.

"What?"

"Luke was really mad with what they did to me and said he'd take the law into his own hands and kill them all."

"I'm sure he was just saying that, sweetheart. He really didn't mean it."

"Yes, he did, Mama. I'm sure of it."

Ann looked at Beth for support and received none.

"I think he's the kind of man that does what he says he'll do, Mama," said Beth.

"But there are four of them and they're all killers."

"Luke knows. Mama, when Luke comes in, ask him about the money, then you'll see."

"What money?" Ann asked as the revelations kept exploding.

"Just ask Luke," Laura said as she smiled then took a sip of coffee.

"It sounds like you're very impressed with Luke Scott, Laura."

"I wish I were older, Mama. He fed me, kept me warm, and made me feel alive and want to stay that way. He even made me laugh when I thought I'd never laugh again."

"Is he married, Laura?" asked Ann.

"No. He told me about how his wife and little boy died. It was a sad story, but he told it to me for a reason," Laura paused, realizing she had to tell her mother no matter how difficult it would be.

"Mama," she continued as she looked down, "I was so upset about having a baby and knowing that I'd never leave that I wanted to die. So, when they put me in the barn, I just let myself get cold, so I could die. When Luke gave me coffee and some stew that he had cooked, I felt better, but I was still sad until he told me about his wife, Ella, and his son, Mark. He said that even when she was dying and in a lot of pain, how she wanted to live. He told me that my life was too valuable to throw away and I should fight for it. So, I promised him that I'd never think of doing it ever again, and I won't either."

"His wife was named Ella?" asked Beth.

Laura nodded and Beth understood why he preferred Beth to Ellie.

There was a knock at the door and Laura jumped up to open the door for Luke.

When she did, Luke just put one foot in the door and swung the two pantleg-bags of food onto the floor.

"I'll be right back as soon as I get my guns," he said.

"When you come back, don't knock, Luke. Just come inside," shouted Ann.

"Yes, ma'am," he replied before closing the door.

"What's this?" Ann asked as she looked at the odd bags.

Laura smiled and replied, "When we left their cabin, we did a few things to make them mad. Luke took most of their food, locked their house so no one could get in locked their chimney flue closed, and froze their barn door closed. I spread pepper all over their beds."

"I don't know about the other things, but we could use the food. I was running a bit low."

"Mama, what will you do now that papa's gone?"

"I don't know, sweetie. I need to think about it. We don't have any cattle anymore. Our bank account is okay, but we can't hire any more hands, and with your brothers still gone, I'm almost at the end of my tether."

"I think Luke has something in mind, Mama."

"Is there anything that Luke can't do?" asked Ann with a smile.

"I don't think he can sew very well," she replied with a straight face.

Ann and Beth started laughing and Laura joined in.

Luke picked that moment to walk through the door with his Winchester and shotgun. After closing the door, he set them down in the corner took off his Stetson and scarf peeled off his gloves, and jammed them in his coat pocket, then noticed that all three women were looking at him.

"Can I leave my jacket over on that peg, Ann?"

"Go right ahead."

Luke hung the jacket, then walked to the cookstove found a cup then filled it with coffee, and took a seat between Laura and Beth.

"I noticed you have four horses in the barn as well as three saddles and a pack saddle. Do you have any panniers?" Luke asked.

"We have four in the storeroom. One of the horses is mine, the other three are my mother's," replied Beth, "I returned with my mother from town when she told me about what had happened with my father and Laura."

Luke nodded then looked at Laura's mother and asked, "Ann, can I guess that the sheriff took no action?"

"He did nothing. He let a murder and kidnapping go without doing anything. Laura just told me that the gang leader is his cousin."

"She told me that as well. Charlie Bassett is his name."

"She also said that you planned on killing all of them."

Luke paused, then replied, "Yes, ma'am. That's my intention. I just didn't want to involve any innocents like you three ladies, though."

"We're involved. Did you find anything interesting at their hideout?" Ann asked.

"I did. I found their cache of money. I was debating about leaving it there or taking it, so I asked Laura. I plan on keeping six hundred and fifty dollars to make up for my cattle that they stole. The remaining twelve hundred dollars is Laura's. Knowing Laura, I'm guessing she'll give it to you. Is that right, Laura?" he asked as he smiled at her.

Laura nodded with a grin.

"Did you want the cash now? It's kind of irritating having that much money in your pocket and I mean that literally, by the way."

As he was speaking, Luke pulled out the hefty stash of currency and set it on the table. He had already broken it into two bundles: one was his, the other Laura's.

"What would I do with it?" asked Ann.

"That's the bad side of the decision. Taking the money meant they'll almost certainly follow us to get it back. If I had left it there, they'd probably just leave you alone. Part of me wanted them to follow and part of me wanted to keep them away from you and Laura and now Beth. I do have a suggestion for you, though. Tomorrow morning, we ride into Colorado City. You can deposit the money in your account and then we'll head down the road to my place. You, Beth, and Laura can stay in my house. I'll move into the small house with my foreman, Hal."

"Why not go straight to your ranch? Isn't that shorter?"

"Yes, but those extra few miles will be well spent. When we reach the road into town there should be some traffic already, leaving paths we can follow. After we go through Colorado City, we'll follow similar paths on the southwest road out of town to my place. When we arrived, Laura and I rode cross country and left our own path. It'll be easy to follow. Tomorrow, we'll get lost in all the other traffic, so you'll be safe at my place."

"For how long?" asked Beth.

"Until they're gone."

"Do you mean gone somewhere else or gone forever?"

"Forever. After you're settled in, I plan on reversing my course and heading back to your place. I'll expect to find them here or someplace nearby, hunting for our trail. I'll engage them at long range with my Sharps to thin their ranks and probably have to shift to my Winchester after that."

"What's a Sharps?" asked Laura.

"You've never heard of it? It's a long-range rifle. It can easily put ten out of ten shots within a foot circle at six hundred yards, which is well out of the range of most rifles and five times the range of the Winchester or Henry repeaters that most outlaws seem to favor."

"Do you know how to shoot it?"

"I do. I wore the green in the War Between the States. Since then, I stay proficient with practice."

"Wore the green?" Ann asked.

"I was a sharpshooter. By the time we were disbanded, we were all wearing normal Union blue for a couple of reasons, but we were always proud to say we wore the green."

"Why did you go to war? Didn't you live in Colorado then?" asked Ann.

"I did, but I was young and full of foolish ideas. I thought war was like an adventure full of glory and honor. That perception was erased very early, then it became a job, a job of protecting my brothers. I had always been a shooter, grew up with a rifle in my hand, and used them a lot at the ranch on coyotes and the like. My father hated to waste ammunition, so I made sure I was always on target. I got so I could reach out with his old Kentucky long rifle a good three hundred yards.

"When I joined the army, they took notice and sent me to the sharpshooter brigade. I was issued a Sharps and wore a green outfit with no brass, so we could hide in the foliage better. Of course, when we weren't hiding, we were a big target for the Rebs. They hated sharpshooters. They had theirs too, of course, and we weren't too fond of them either. We were disbanded in '64 and I came home. When I returned, I bought my own Sharps that were better than the ones we were issued. It had been modified, so it was more of a sporting rifle. But I'm just as accurate with the Winchester and, to a slightly lesser degree, with my pistol."

"So, you intend to hunt them down," asked Beth.

"They hurt Laura and killed your father. They aren't men. They're feral beasts, preying on the innocent. Yes, Beth, I intend on hunting them down."

"Good. Can I help?" she asked.

Luke looked at her beautiful face and saw conviction in those deep blue eyes. She had the same grit that Laura had shown.

He could see the surprise in those blue eyes when he asked, "Can you shoot?"

Beth was surprised that he hadn't turned her down immediately as she'd expected but replied, "I've shot my father's rifle."

"What kind is it?"

"It's a Spencer."

He turned to her mother and asked, "Do you still have it, Ann?"

"Yes, it's on the fireplace mantle. It doesn't have any ammunition, though."

"I can get some ammunition when we stop in Colorado City."

He looked back at Beth and asked, "How often and how well did you shoot the Spencer, Beth?"

"I used it pretty often until I left two years ago. I was reasonably accurate."

Luke was torn about this. He would love to have a second long-range shooter with him but didn't want to endanger a woman, especially this woman.

"Let me think about it, Beth, but I need to examine the Spencer first."

"I'll get it!" exclaimed Laura as she hopped up from the table and trotted down the hallway before reappearing a minute later with the Spencer and handed it to Luke.

"It's not a rifle," Luke said as he examined the weapon, "it's the carbine version with a shortened barrel and stock. It shoots the same ammunition, though. It has a range of up to five hundred yards. It's not as accurate as my Sharps but it seems to be in good condition."

Luke opened the breech and peered inside. It needed a thorough cleaning and oiling as the action was getting stiff. He was grateful for the dry Colorado air as there wasn't any rust. He squinted as he examined the barrel. The rifling seemed solid and the barrel itself was clean. Overall, it was a good weapon.

"I'll clean the carbine and get it working more smoothly later."

Luke was already thinking along the lines of not taking Beth along and just adding the Spencer to his weaponry. He could reload the Sharps in three seconds, but the Spencer was quicker. He could fire seven shots in fifteen seconds as opposed to just three or four shots with the Sharps.

Then Beth asked another of her 'I know what you're thinking' questions.

"There is an advantage of taking me along rather than just taking the Spencer, you know."

"Yes, I know. Two shooters would cause them to have to split their shots. It is a lot more difficult to attack two shooters."

"I just thought I'd mention it," she said as she smiled.

"Beth, I can understand why you would want to get revenge for them killing your father, but this isn't going to be a picnic. It'll be cold, hard work."

"I know that. Let's just say that I want to go. I appreciate that you didn't say that this is no place for a woman."

"It's no place for most men, Beth. I still need to think about it though, alright?"

"Okay."

"Luke, will they do anything to my house?" asked Ann.

"It's possible. They're going to be very angry, but I don't think they'll do anything drastic like burn it down. That would bring attention to them."

"Well, it's just a house anyway. Luke, do you have any suggestions about what I should do with my ranch? I have no cattle. We only had a small herd anyway. The most we ever had was sixty-four, and my sons sold forty of them to finance their trip to the gold fields. Then those men took the last two dozen. With my sons gone and now my husband, I don't even have anyone to work the ranch anyway."

"You never put up fencing?"

"No, we didn't have the money. The cattle stayed near the water anyway."

"Do you have good water?"

"Oh, yes. We have a spring in the northern pasture."

"How big is the ranch?"

"Not very big. It's two sections."

"With the buildings and the water, you could probably sell it for three thousand dollars, but I'd wait until spring because nobody buys ranches in the winter. Until then, you and Laura can stay at my ranch. Beth, you can stay there as well, if you wish. Laura told me you live in town."

"Not any longer. I moved back here when my father was killed. Besides, I'll be coming along with you," she said as she smiled again.

Luke felt he had already lost the decision and looked at Ann wondering if she had the same iron backbone that her daughters seemed to possess.

"So, we'll leave in the morning for Colorado City. I'd suggest you take everything you value with you. With the packhorse, you should be able to take quite a bit including your clothing. Laura, do you have another coat you can wear?"

"Yes, but it's not very good."

"We'll stop in Colorado City and get you a new coat, some gloves, and anything else you need. Ann, I think you should buy all those things that you might need for a month or so. You know, soaps and things."

Ann asked, "That's a good idea. Do you have a bathroom in the small house?"

"No. It has a kitchen and two bedrooms, a small main room, and a small washroom. But it's well-built and it's easy to keep warm in the winter. It doesn't have a fireplace. We built it with two heat stoves instead. Like the main house, we added an inner and outer wall and used wool insulation between the boards and the windows have heavy shutters to protect the glass when we get storms like that blizzard. I have enough wood stored away to last the winter for both houses, so we're okay there. We'll have enough food to last at least three or four weeks."

"You say your foreman is the only other person on your ranch?"

Luke smiled and replied, "I call him the foreman, but we've never had another ranch hand."

He leaned back and continued saying, "My father started the ranch and hired Hal back in '45, the year before I was born. I've never known the place without Hal. He's more like an uncle than a foreman, and he's the best man I've ever known, including my father. He still lives in the small house, though. We have a bunkhouse, too. My father and Hal built it before they built the main house, so they could have someplace to live while they worked on it.

"After they built the bunkhouse, they built the main house before my parents got married and moved in. I was born later that year. My mother died in childbirth when I was four. Then it was my father, Hal, and me until my father died when I was sixteen. I had to stop going to school to devote all my time to the ranch and helping Hal. I was married to my Ella when I returned from the war in '65. We had Mark and then since '67, it's just been me and Hal."

Luke suddenly realized he'd rambled on a bit too much perhaps and said, "Sorry, I just kind of got carried away a bit."

"No, that's quite alright, Luke," said Beth.

Luke was still a bit embarrassed about how he had gone on and waited for someone else to say something.

Laura bailed him out by simply saying, "I'm hungry, Mama."

"Oh, I'm sorry, dear. Let's get lunch started."

If Luke thought he was uncomfortable before when he found himself alone at the table with Beth's big blue eyes on him, he felt downright fidgety, so he took the manly way out.

"I'll take the Spencer into the main room and give it a good cleaning and oiling," he said as he picked up the carbine and pulled his cleaning kit from his saddlebags.

He was breathing easier as he walked down the hallway until he realized his backtrail wasn't empty. Beth was walking behind him.

He reached the main room and took a seat near the table, set the Spencer down, and began to act as if he was working until he glanced up and saw those deep blue eyes boring into him. He stopped and faced her.

"Um, Beth, so you're not living in town anymore?" he asked.

"No. I was going to return here pretty soon anyway. I was almost out of money and thought I could live with my father's wrath rather than going without."

Luke recalled Laura's story about her sister 'Lizzy' and her forced marriage and departure from the family home.

"Laura mentioned that your husband had gone with your brothers to go to the gold fields."

Beth tilted her head as if to say, 'she told you that?', then smiled and said, "Ex-husband. I divorced him for desertion six weeks ago. It cost me twenty dollars that I'd rather have used to spend on something worthwhile, too. He almost emptied our bank account before he left, and he'd never contributed a dime to it, either. Or did Laura not mention that?"

Luke found himself growing more comfortable with Beth's intense gaze and returned her smile.

"She told me. It's not as if she was engaged in idle gossip. She was just angry at her brothers and your ex-husband for deserting you and Ann."

"I know. I just wanted to see if you knew."

Luke's momentary level of comfort vanished and was replaced by a growing feeling of being flummoxed.

"You know, I've never met any siblings that were more alike than you and Laura. She's a lot like you, but you've had more experience being you than she has being Laura."

Beth laughed, and Luke didn't find his level of flummox-ness decrease at all.

"We are a lot alike, but we do have our differences."

"I noticed. Aside from the obvious, that you're a bit taller and more, well, never mind."

Luke wasn't surprised a bit when Beth didn't let it go when she asked, "More what?"

"You know…more, well, more, um, more mature."

"Oh. You mean I'm older."

Luke found his ears getting warm and probably covered in an accompanying redness.

"Well, yes, of course, you're older. But not old, I mean. You're still much younger than I am."

"Did you mean to say that I'm more filled out than Laura?" she asked holding back her smile.

Luke had to admit what he meant and answered, "Yes, you're more filled out than Laura, as you should be."

"Why should I be?"

Luke knew he shouldn't have added that last phrase and almost smacked himself in the head.

Finally, he just rolled his eyes and asked, "Can I admit defeat and simply show my white flag? I'm digging myself deeper into a hole every time I open my mouth."

Beth did smile this time as she said, "Oh, I don't think so. Most women would take it as a compliment, as did I. It's been a while since I've heard a meaningful compliment."

"Really? I find that hard to believe, but it's more than that, Beth. I've only known Laura for a day and just met you but I can see it in both of you. You both have the inner strength of will, of character. For Laura to have given up, she must have been under incredible pressure. It was her ability to bounce back that showed me how strong she really is."

Beth looked at him quizzically and asked, "Does that mean you've decided that you're going to let me come along?"

"You couldn't wear a dress. You'd have to pick up some trousers and long johns at Salk's when we stop there tomorrow. Do you have some heavy gloves?"

"No. I need some gloves and a hat, too. I have a heavy scarf, but I'll probably want to get some boots and galoshes."

"Salk's has some rubber-covered boots that will work well. I have a pair at home. I should have brought them on the trip, but I didn't think I'd get hit by the blizzard."

"You'll have to tell me about the whole adventure sometime. Maybe when we're out hunting the bad guys."

"Beth, I know maybe you've probably shot some critters with that Spencer but shooting a man is an entirely different thing. It's hard to describe but it is much more difficult. I'll agree to take you along, but you have to think about what it will be like."

"I have, and I believe I'm prepared."

"So, I guess your mind is made up and I don't get a vote at all."

She shot him one of those big smiles and replied, "I guess not. Let's go and get some lunch. You can come back and hide from me after we eat."

Luke smiled before they both stood and returned to the kitchen. Beth was quite a woman. *How could that idiot husband of hers let her get away?* She was a lot more precious than that stupid yellow sand he and her brothers were hunting near Pike's Peak.

Charlie and the boys were within sight of their cabin after four and a half hours of plowing through the deep, wet snow. The temperature had been rising for the duration of the entire ride and was now approaching forty degrees, so even Joe stopped whining about being cold as the sun reflected off the blindingly white snow.

Unfortunately for the four men, the overhang from the barn had prevented the sun from reaching the frozen locking bar, so when they finally reached the barn and dismounted, it was Philly who first discovered the problem.

"Look at this mess. That damned blizzard froze the bar solid. I'm gonna have to cut the damned lashing."

He pulled out his knife and began to slice through the ice-coated leather strips, but just cutting it didn't help a lot as the bottom was still frozen to the ironworks, but once the pigging strings were cut away, it did allow them to try to free the bar from its brackets. It took them almost three minutes of banging to finally break it free.

"What do we do with that kid's body?" asked Joe as he threw the bar aside.

"Today, we leave it. We can drag it out behind the house later. I want some heat," replied Charlie.

They pulled the barn door open and walked their horses inside where they discovered the first anomaly.

"Where are the spare horses?" asked Mack.

"They sure as hell didn't get out on their own," snarled Charlie, "Go and check on that girl and make sure she's in there."

Joe trotted over and jammed his gloved hand into the hay, where they had found her hiding on the last two trips.

"She's gone!"

Charlie thought about it and said, "I don't care that she got out. She probably froze to death somewhere out there, but those horses will have to be replaced. Maybe they're around somewhere. Let's get the horses unsaddled and get into the house. I'm hungry, too."

Twenty minutes later, they all headed for the house carrying their Winchesters and saddlebags. It had been a good trip. They had sold Luke's stolen cattle for four hundred and twenty dollars, even though that bastard Kingman had tried to get them to take less. It took a whole minute of convincing before he understood that he shouldn't trifle with them, then relented and paid the previously agreed price of fifteen dollars a head. *Why should he try to be so cheap?* He was making over seven dollars a head just for falsifying a bit of paperwork. They did all the dangerous work.

Joe reached the house first reached for the pull cord and found it missing.

"Boss, the rope's gone!"

Charlie peered up at the top of the cabin door and asked, "How the hell did she manage that?"

"How are we gonna get in, boss?" asked Joe.

"Through a window," he growled as he pulled his knife.

He walked to the nearest window and slid the blade between the gap in the shutters. The gap had another board behind it to keep the wind from entering the house, so he'd have to carve a notch into the wood to allow the knife to lift the bar behind it.

He worked the tip of the knife back and forth for almost thirty minutes until the inside board finally had a long slot carved into it. He had to make the cut longer to allow the knife to lift the board higher. After fifteen more minutes, Charlie had the point of his knife into the crossbar and lifted it three inches.

"Try openin' the left shutter now."

Mack yanked open the left-hand shutter and it popped free allowing Charlie to yank his knife back from the window before he opened the right shutter.

"Joe, you're the skinniest, get in there and open the door."

"Alright, boss."

Joe Pendleton pulled off his gunbelt and handed it to Charlie before slipping through the open window.

"Damn! It sure is smoky in here!" he shouted as he hit the floor.

He found his way to the door, pulled off the bar, then swung the door wide as some of the residual smoke floated out of the door onto the porch.

The men entered the cabin and began noticing the immediate changes like the mattress on the floor near the fireplace, the broken flue lever, and the chair near the mattress.

"How'd she get in here?" asked Mack.

"She knew about the pull cord. Once she got outta the barn, she probably used a stick or somethin' to grab it," Charlie answered then said, "Alright, open the door again and get the smoke outta here. I'll get the flue knocked open. Joe, go back and open that back door, too."

It took Charlie almost ten minutes to get the flue open again, and the smoke was clearing rapidly now that the doors were both open. Once it was clear enough to close the doors, Charlie started a fire in the fireplace and Mack had already started one in the cookstove when he noticed that the larder was almost empty.

"Boss, most of the food's gone!" he shouted.

"That girl is gettin' me mighty riled!" Charlie snarled.

He had barely finished expressing his displeasure when the gang leader suddenly had a bigger concern and quickly trotted into the bedroom. He yanked open the drawer and looked for his cash-filled sock.

"Son of a bitch!" he screamed.

That brought the other three running into the bedroom.

Charlie was still staring at the empty drawer and shouted, "She took the money! *How the hell did she know we had the money in there?"*

"She was probably lookin' for somethin' to wear when she left. She didn't have a coat or nothin'," said Philly.

"That means our money is probably buried in the snow somewhere with her body," Charlie groused as his jaw muscles bulged.

"How are we gonna get it back?" asked Joe.

"We trail her. She left with two horses, so we pick up her trail and find the body."

"Can we eat first, boss? It's gonna be a long day."

"Yeah. We'd better get some chow. Mack, start cooking. I'm gonna see which direction she went."

"Okay, boss."

Charlie stomped out of the front door and stood on the porch for a few seconds to see if he could spot the directions she had taken. There wasn't a path from the front of the cabin, so he'd go and check from the back. As he pushed through the snow, he saw another problem as well. With the warming temperatures and the sun, the girl's trail would be disappearing, and they'd have to find it soon.

He walked quickly through the house and stepped out onto the back porch and soon spotted a slight depression heading north. Satisfied that he had a read on her initial direction, he returned to the cabin to have his lunch.

Luke had gone outside after lunch and was standing on the back porch. He saw the stream of water from the roof from melting snow and smiled.

Beth walked out behind him followed by Laura, then the sisters flanked him.

"This is good news. The warm air and sun will start to melt the snow. It'll flatten our path as the snow collapses. In a couple more hours, our trail will be almost impossible to follow. I imagine they're at their cabin now and not happy. I wonder if they've figured out if Laura had help or not. They may still be operating under the illusion that she escaped on her own, and that's a real advantage."

"Why would they believe that I escaped by myself?" asked Laura.

"Because it's the easiest thing to believe. All you had to do was find a way out of the barn. If they stepped back to look at it logically, they'd wonder why you tied the barn door bar closed again after you left. How did you reach that pull cord for the door? How did you pick up that heavy cauldron to break the flue lever? All those things indicated that you had help, but once your head is set in one direction, you fit the new evidence into what you already believe.

“They knew you were there and probably wanted to escape. Once they find you gone, they assumed you had escaped. It’s possible one of them will figure it out, but it’s not likely if the boss man is the one who is driving the assumptions. None of the others would challenge him on it.”

“How do you know all this?” asked Beth.

“During the war, I saw a lot of that. We would tell the sergeant or captain what we saw when we were out in the bush doing our job and they’d dismiss it more often than not because that’s not what they believed. I could tell the captain that I saw a full brigade of Confederates marching down the road and he’d say that it was impossible and that I probably just saw a scouting party. Then none of the lieutenants would question the captain because he was their boss. It happened more often than you’d think.”

“So, if we go to Colorado City tomorrow and then to your ranch, there’s a chance they won’t know we’re there?”

“A very good chance. I’d be surprised if they even think Laura’s still alive. Men like them have a very low opinion of women. They think of them as weak and unable to make decisions. Laura isn’t even sixteen yet, so they’d be shocked if she even made it a mile. I guess they don’t know Laura very well. There’s another advantage. If the snow melts enough, they’ll spend a lot of time looking for Laura’s body.”

Laura looked down at herself and exclaimed, “I found it!”, eliciting laughter from Luke and Beth.

Luke glanced at Laura and smiled. *What an amazing person she was!* He was a bit surprised that she hadn't asked to come along but didn't bring it up because he didn't want to inspire the idea.

Laura caught his glance and surprised him anyway when she winked. He had no idea why, but he returned her wink getting a giant grin in return. He hoped he hadn't just proposed marriage or something.

"It may be warming, but I think it's a good idea to go back inside," he said.

Laura and Beth then turned and headed inside as Luke took one more look around and followed them into the kitchen, closing the door behind him still wondering about Laura's wink. He'd have to ask her about it if he had the chance, which arrived sooner than he had expected.

Once inside, Beth announced she'd go to her room to prepare her clothing for tomorrow's ride and start packing. Ann said the same, but Laura didn't have that much and already had her shirts and pants, so she followed Luke into the main room.

After they had each taken a seat, Luke asked her about the wink.

Laura smiled and replied, "I just wanted to let you know that it was all right."

Luke was a bit confused and asked, "What's all right? Going to my ranch?"

"No, Mister Scott. It's all right about you and Lizzy. I mean Beth. I didn't know she didn't like that name."

Luke blushed again. It was becoming a habit since he'd arrived at their home.

"Excuse me, Laura. Did I miss something?"

Laura rolled her eyes and said, "You must have. I must admit, I was a bit jealous at first. I thought maybe I could convince you to wait a few more years, but then when I saw you look at Beth, I knew that it wasn't fair at all for me to expect any such thing. Beth needs you even more than you need her."

Luke was as stunned as he'd ever been as he asked, "Why? Beth seems just as strong a person as you are."

"Sometimes. But she's terribly lonely and she's still hurt by losing her baby and then having Richard leave her and taking all the money. My father's attitude didn't help, either. I told you that he made Richard marry her, but I didn't add that he made Beth marry him too. She didn't want to marry him, but our father insisted and told her he'd toss her out on her ear unless she did. Now she's alone and has nothing. At least she's back here now, but it's not enough. She needs you, Luke."

Luke sat back in the chair, shook his head, and said, "Laura, I've known you just twenty-four hours and you keep astonishing me. Are you sure you're only fifteen?"

"Yes, sir, but almost sixteen."

"We have to give it some time, Laura."

"Why? That's one of the dumbest things people say. I'll give you one week, Luke."

"Or what?" he asked as he smiled.

She grinned back and said, "You don't want to know."

Luke just stared at Laura in awe. She wasn't even sixteen and yet she seemed to understand people better than he did and behaved more like an adult than most of the adults he knew including himself.

The four men finished their limited lunch and followed Charlie onto the back porch.

He pointed at the shallow indentation in the snow and said, "See that trail? It heads north."

"I can see that, boss, but there's nothin' there. She's gotta go east or southeast. Her ranch was east of here about fifteen miles or so and Colorado City is southeast another nine. That's where she's gotta go."

"She's a girl, for God's sake, Philly! You think she has a clue which direction she needed to go? She just lit out and ran away as fast as she could. I wouldn't be a bit surprised if we followed that direction, we don't find her dead under the snow a mile away."

"We gonna go there now?"

"Yeah. Let's go."

They walked to the barn and saddled their horses again. Ten minutes later, they were fighting their way through the melting, heavy snow.

Just five minutes later, Joe shouted, "The trail is disappearing, boss."

"I can see that, Joe. Let's keep heading in the same direction. We'll ride for another hour or so."

They continued to ride their animals up mild inclines and then back down the other side. The horses were all breathing heavily, and after another forty minutes and no more trail to follow, Charlie stopped the parade.

"Damn! I don't see a lump anywhere. Let's go back. I figure tomorrow we'll head over to her ranch house and see if she made it there. It'll be easy enough to figure out if we find our horses."

They all swiveled on their mounts and Mack, who had been trailing, took the lead back. It wasn't as bad because the path was already there, but it wasn't great either. By the time they made it to the barn, the horses were exhausted.

After dinner, Luke began lining up the filled panniers. All four were stuffed and packed tightly at that. He'd still need the pant-bags for some things, and they'd be stopping at Salk's and probably adding another three or four bags. Luckily, they had a spare horse. He'd pick up another pack saddle at the livery and four more panniers which should be enough.

The three ladies were all watching and when he stood, he turned and said, "When we get to town, Ann, you can go to the bank and make your deposit, then you, Beth, and Laura, can head over to Salk's and start to pick up what you need. I'm going to take one of the spare horses down to the livery and get another pack saddle. I'll come back to Salk's and we'll load your purchases. We'll need the basics like flour, sugar, coffee, and eggs. Make sure you get what you need, and I'll get some more ammunition for the Spencer. Beth, you'll need a pair of those rubberized boots and some warm clothing."

"Do I get a pistol, too?"

"I have a spare at the house you can have. It has a gunbelt, too."

He turned to Laura, and said, "And, Laura, we'll finally get you a nice, warm coat."

She grinned and replied, "It's about time."

"Just like this morning, I'll probably be up very early to get the horses ready to go. Beth, which horse is yours?"

"The bay gelding."

"He's a bit long in the tooth, isn't he?"

"I just bought him. He was all I could afford."

"Why don't I saddle one of the outlaw horses we took, and we'll use your old one as a pack horse?"

"I won't complain. He has a horrible, jarring gait, too. I'm sure the liveryman was glad to be rid of him."

"Okay, so I'll set up the horses in the morning and get underway right after breakfast. Does that work for everyone?"

They all nodded.

After he joined them at the kitchen table, they shared coffee and just talked, beginning with Luke's getting lost in the blizzard while Laura provided more details of her captivity.

After they finished, Luke asked, "Laura, can you give me a description of each man?"

"Sure. Charlie Bassett is the biggest. He's about three inches shorter than you but weighs probably thirty pounds more, and it's not fat, either. He has brown hair and eyes and doesn't shave too much, so he always has some scratchy beard.

"Philly Henderson is a lot thinner, but a little shorter. He looks like Charlie. He likes women a lot, but he's really creepy. He wears his hair slicked back and has a lot of silver stuff on his holster.

"Mack Johnson is about the same size as Henderson but has black hair that he wears long and has a mustache that he keeps waxed. He fiddles with it all the time. He only wears one gun, too.

"Joe Pendleton is the youngest, I think. He's also the shortest, around my height. He's the easiest to spot, too. He has bright red hair and blue eyes. He's the meanest of them after Charlie. He's even mean to his horse."

"Thanks, Laura. That helps a lot," Luke said, astonished at Laura's eye for detail.

Then he turned to her mother and asked, "Ann, is it alright if I sleep on the couch?"

"You really didn't think I'd make you sleep in the barn, do you?"

"It wouldn't bother me very much."

She laughed and gave Luke permission to sleep on the couch.

Two hours later, he found that didn't work because it was too short, so he stretched out on the floor and went to sleep on the bare wood. He'd slept in worse places.

CHAPTER 3

For the second day in a row, Luke was up well before dawn and did the same things in exactly the same sequence. He washed, shaved, started two fires, put the coffeepot on the cook stove, and left the house to start getting the horses ready.

He had them all saddled including the pack horse and had the others trail roped by predawn, then returned to the house and sat down with his cup of coffee. He expected Laura to be the first one to pop out of her room but was wrong. Beth showed up first and waved as she pulled on her light boots and trotted out the door. She returned a few minutes later and found a cup of coffee waiting for her on the table.

"That looks good," she said as she smiled.

"I didn't know if you added anything, so it's black."

"Black is fine," she replied, taking the cup in her hands as she sat down.

"How accurate are you with that Spencer, Beth?"

"I haven't shot it in a few months, but I was pretty good. Are you having second thoughts about bringing me along?"

"And having to surrender again? Nope. I'm thinking about how best to position you if we find them. Remind me before we go to have your mother write a note and put it on the door."

"A note?"

"Sure. I figure even if they can't trail us here, and I don't think they can now, they'll show up looking for Laura. If your mother leaves a note on the door that says something like, 'Laura, if you get home, I've gone to town for more supplies. The door is open, Mama'. That will make them believe that Laura never made it here."

"That's a brilliant idea."

He smiled at Beth and said, "It's been known to happen on rare occasions."

She smiled back and took a sip of coffee before asking, "How are we going to find them?"

"After we drop Laura and your mother off with Hal, the next day we come straight back here and don't go through town. We won't care about them seeing our trail. They'll either still be here, or they'll head into town to get some more supplies before they return to their cabin. If we get here and find them here, we wait until they go one place or the other."

"What if they stay here?"

"We didn't leave them enough food for them to stay here. I think they'll stop, find no Laura, and go into town for some supplies. Then they'll come back to your house but take a different trail back to see if they can find Laura's body."

"You sure think like they do. You weren't a criminal, were you?" she asked with a grin.

"No, ma'am. It's just that when you're a sniper, you have to think what the other guy will do before he does it. Where would I go if I were him? That kind of thing. You try to stay one step ahead, then you get into position and wait. Now when you're dealing with high-ranking officers rather than other sharpshooters, it's a whole different thing. You need to know how they act.

"The peacocks were always the easiest to target. They wanted everyone to see them and know they're a general, much like our General Custer. The Rebs had their fair share, too. The hard ones to track are like Grant. He blended in too well with the other soldiers because he didn't wear any braid or stripes. If a sniper had to find Grant, he'd better know what he looked like."

"I never thought of that, but you're right. Is that why you asked Laura for the men's descriptions?"

"Sort of. The odds of four men riding around in the deep snow together who aren't crooks are kind of slim. But once they're separated, I don't want to shoot an innocent man. Did you listen carefully to her descriptions?"

"I did, but they reinforced the descriptions I had already gotten from my mother. She just didn't know the names."

Luke smiled and said, "You'll do."

Beth grinned at the best compliment she'd ever had.

Laura popped out a few seconds later and mimicked Beth's arrival with a wave donning of boots and a rush outside.

Luke prepared a cup of coffee for Laura and had it ready when she skipped back into the kitchen.

"Thank you, Luke. Just like a real gentleman," she said as she smiled and took the coffee.

"What no curtsy?" he asked.

Laura put her cup on the table, curtsied, then picked up the cup again and intentionally slurped loudly as she drank.

Beth and Luke laughed as she smiled.

Ann appeared with the laughter and after her trip outside, joined them for some coffee.

"Ladies, I'll get breakfast going while you finish your coffee. I'll just scramble the eggs to make it fast."

"I can live with that," said Ann.

Laura replied, "Not me. I want my eggs poached."

"Of course, Milady. Perhaps garnished with a pinch of paprika and a touch of cloves?"

"That will do, I suppose. I shall suffer the indignities of your rather poor efforts. Your last food preparation attempts caused me great distress."

"I do beg your pardon, Madam. I will endeavor to poach your eggs to your satisfaction. Perhaps you could direct me to the source of these eggs, whereby I may poach them from their rightful owner?"

Laura grinned, finished her coffee, and said, "You do make some good scrambled eggs, Luke."

"We had a bunch too, but we didn't finish them all, did we?"

"No, but they're not getting eggs for breakfast, either."

Beth and Ann had witnessed the repartee between the two with some degree of amazement. Neither could recall Laura being quite so witty and animated. Beth was surprised when she felt a twinge of jealousy toward her younger sister.

They all headed for their respective bedrooms to dress for the trip while Luke went to work in the kitchen. Luke had set aside some bacon and a dozen eggs for breakfast and began slicing the bacon, tossing them straight into the frypan. By the time Beth returned wearing pants and a shirt and looking not at all like a man, Luke had the bacon cooked and was whipping the eggs. He took one look at Beth and almost dropped the fork he was using to mix the eggs. Beth noticed and smiled; her momentary bit of jealousy forgotten.

She set the table while Luke dumped the eggs into the frypan and began his ritualistic scraping and flipping as the eggs cooked. Beth walked over and handed him a plate for the eggs, so he dutifully began scooping them out of the frypan and flipping them onto the plate until there was a giant stack of scrambled eggs. He placed the plate on the table, took the coffeepot from the warming side of the cook stove, and poured four more cups of coffee.

Beth took a seat as did Luke before Ann and Laura trotted out just after Luke sat down. Laura only had on one shirt but two pairs of pants and was wearing a jacket now.

Each of the women added some eggs and bacon to their plates, leaving what amounted to a half-dozen eggs still piled on the plate.

"You three don't expect me to eat all these eggs, do you?" Luke asked.

"Of course, we do," replied Beth. "Laura told us how much you love eggs."

"Cooking. Not eating," he muttered as he scooped some eggs onto his plate.

Beth laughed and took some more eggs.

Luke mentioned to Ann his idea about the note and she agreed it was a wonderful idea, so as soon as they finished cleaning from breakfast, she scrawled a quick note.

Luke left the house, headed to the barn then led the horses to the back of the house and tied them at the hitching rail. When he returned to the kitchen, he began lugging the stuffed panniers onto the packhorse and then tied them down. After he put his guns back into their scabbards, including the newly cleaned and oiled Spencer, and put his heavy saddlebags in place, all he needed to do was to let the women mount their horses. The sun was up and the weather was pleasant for mid-December in Colorado.

All three of the heavily bundled women walked out together and made quite a sight as they walked stiffly onto the porch.

"Does anyone need any help getting aboard?" he asked.

"I do," replied Laura with a grin.

"I'm sure you do, Laura," he said, smiling back at her.

He scooped her up again, set her left foot into the stirrup, then she stood and put her right leg over the horse and took the reins.

"I really didn't need any help, you know," she said as she giggled.

"I never would have guessed," he replied and smiled back at her.

After Beth and Ann mounted, Luke stepped into his saddle and then took the lead away from the house. When they reached the road, he found a broad path already cut through the snow. It was still cold, but with the sun returning in all its glory and little wind, it was almost a comfortable ride. They made good time and reached Colorado City just two hours after leaving.

Charlie, Philly, Mack, and Joe had a much harder ride as they plowed through the lower, but still heavy snow. Charlie had decided that they'd ride straight for the girl's house to see if she had made it that far. None were in a good mood after having had a breakfast of just beans with no coffee.

"What if she ain't there, Charlie?" asked Mack loudly.

"We head into town and get some more grub, then when we head back, we swing a bit more north to see if she tried to get back that way."

"Why don't we just take over that ranch?" asked Joe.

"It's too close to town."

"But your cousin ain't gonna do nothin'."

"No, but he's worryin' about his job. He's got an election comin' up in April, and he said the rumors are already hurtin' his chances and doesn't want us hittin' any more places so close. He was kinda mad after we killed that farmer and snatched the girl. The wife was in his office the next day whinin' about it and he had to make like he was lookin' for us."

"We shoulda killed her too, Charlie."

"Yeah, I know. She just looked so pathetic on the floor."

Philly said, "It's too late now unless I do something to her this time."

"We play the hand that's dealt, Philly."

———

Ann had deposited the money, and Luke had already returned with the second pack-saddled horse. The pack saddle came with four used panniers as well, so Luke felt ready to load. He brought the panniers inside the general store and found the women already loading the counter with food and other things they'd need, some of which hadn't been on his Circle S ranch in years.

Luke made sure that Laura had a heavy coat and a warm pair of gloves before Beth showed him the rubberized boots and her other cold-weather clothes, including a slicker. Luke walked back into the clothing section and picked out a nice Stetson and walked back to Beth and popped it onto her head. She grinned and pulled the brim down creating an impressive image.

Then he turned back to the same spot where he had found her Stetson and picked up two very un-cowboy-looking hats, brought them up front, and added them to the pile.

He bought four boxes of cartridges for the Spencer and decided a compass might be a wise idea after his debacle in that blizzard. He also picked up two pocket watches, planning on giving one to Hal.

Then, because he thought it might be handy, he added another Winchester '66.

After Luke settled the substantial bill using the outlaw cash he hadn't deposited, Frank Salk helped Luke pack all the food, clothes, and other purchases into the panniers and load them onto the pack horse. Once everything was tied down, Luke and the three ladies mounted and then headed out of town taking the southwest road.

The road had an even wider path than the westbound road, and the temperature was getting warm enough to turn the snow under their horses' hooves into slush.

"Luke, when are we leaving?" asked Beth as they plodded along.

"Tomorrow morning. I don't want to let them get holed up in that cabin again. We couldn't touch them once they get inside there."

"Why did you buy another rifle?"

"For you. The Spencer is a good gun, but it's difficult to reload and takes time. The Winchester carries a lot more rounds, can be reloaded easily, and the hammer is cocked when you lever in a new round. It doesn't have the range or the stopping power of the Spencer, but it's an impressive rifle."

"Will you be able to show me how to shoot it when we get to your ranch?"

"I will. If you can shoot a Spencer, this one will be easy. I'll probably clean and oil it before I give it to you because they're not usually as clean as they should be when you first get them."

"Are we taking a pack horse?"

"I'm not sure. What do you think?"

"You're really asking my opinion?"

Luke turned to look at her and replied, "Of course. Why not?"

"It's just unusual, that's all. It's not like you're asking about making an apple pie or something."

"No, but you understand the situation as much as I do, so I thought I'd listen to what you think."

"I'm not too sure about having one either. How much food can we carry?"

"Enough for a couple of days if we don't take a pack horse. We don't need all that ammunition. We'll each have two long guns, and a pistol. The pistol is really for close-in defense anyway. Have you ever shot a pistol?"

"No. Just the Spencer."

"I'll give you a quick lesson on that as well."

"You're turning me into a regular soldier," she said as she smiled.

"I don't recall seeing many soldiers that looked like you when I was in the army. I'd probably still be wearing the blue if they had."

Beth blushed under her new Stetson, surprising herself. She usually just caused blushes.

Just after noon, Luke spotted his ranch ahead and saw the smoke from the fireplace in the main house and the heat stove in the small house and wondered where Hal was staying.

Beth spotted it as well and said, "You have a nice house, Luke."

"It's not as big as some, but it's solid and stays warm."

"It's not so bad right now."

"No, but I don't think it's going to last."

Beth nodded as they turned onto the access road.

As they were riding down the access road, Charlie and his boys were sitting on their horses watching the Harper ranch house from eight hundred yards away.

Philly said, “There’s no smoke comin’ from the fireplace, Charlie. I don’t think there’s anybody in there.”

“Maybe.”

Charlie Bassett didn’t live the life he led without being cautious, and he smelled a trap. There should have been some movement somewhere. They’d been watching the place for twenty minutes and hadn’t seen a glimmer of movement.

Philly, with noticeable irritation in his voice, said, “Charlie, there was only that one woman livin’ there when we left. She’s probably still all hunkered down from the last time we visited. Maybe she froze to death, too.”

Charlie rubbed his stubble-covered chin and said, “Alright, we’ll go down there. When we get close, me and Joe will pull our Winchesters. Philly and Mack, you’ll have your pistols ready. Keep an eye on the windows, Philly. Joe and Mack, keep an eye on the barn.”

They nudged their horses forward slowly toward the house, Charlie and Joe Pendleton with their Yellow Boy Winchesters cocked and ready, Philly and Mack with their pistols. Their eyes were busy as they neared the front porch, but there was still no sign of movement.

They drew up to the porch and Joe pointed at the house and said, “There’s a piece of paper on the front door.”

"Go get it," Charlie said.

Joe hopped down and trotted to the house, grabbed the note, read it, and laughed.

He waved it at the others and shouted, "It's a note to her frozen kid telling her that she had to go to town to get some supplies. Like she was expecting her to come home."

He jogged back down from the porch and handed it to Charlie, who read the short note quickly.

"So, she didn't make it back after all. That means our money is somewhere between this house and our place. She headed north so she probably turned east when she figured out where she had to go. Let's go in the house and see how many supplies we can roust out of there."

The three mounted outlaws stepped down and all four entered the unlocked house then headed straight for the kitchen and found little in the way of food.

"She didn't have much left," said Mack.

Charlie said, "Makes sense, I guess. She'd been here almost a month by herself."

"That means we gotta go and get some food ourselves, boss."

"You're brilliant, Mack. I never woulda figured that out for myself," Charlie replied with a sneer.

This whole thing was getting him riled and he didn't see an end to it.

"Alright, Mack, go out to the barn and see if she took the other horse. I'm gonna start a fire. At least there's some coffee and enough food so we can scratch together somethin' to fill our bellies."

"Okay, boss," replied Mack as he left the house and trotted to the barn.

Philly and Joe headed for the kitchen while Charlie started the fire in the fireplace. Philly filled the coffeepot and put it on the cold cook stove, tossed some kindling into the firebox, lit the small scraps of wood shavings and twigs, then once the flame was strong enough, he added some split, dried logs. With the fire blazing, he held his hands close to the firebox to enjoy the heat for a minute before closing the cast iron door.

Mack returned, using the front door and found Charlie bent over the fireplace, adding wood to the new fire.

"Boss, there ain't no horses out there. She musta used one as a pack horse."

Charlie stood up, smiled, and said, "That's the first good news we've had all day."

Mack looked at his boss with a puzzled look on his face and asked, "Why's that good news, boss?"

"Because, Mack, it means we don't need to go into town at all. We just sit back and let the woman bring us our food and a couple of spare horses to make up for the ones her bitch of a daughter stole from us."

Mack smiled, nodded, and said, "That's good, boss."

"Alright, let's see what we can scrounge together for lunch and wait for her to return."

Hal was in the main house and heard Luke's shout as he reached the front of the house. He trotted to the front window and was mildly stunned to see Luke with three women. There were several reasons for his surprise: Luke went looking for rustlers, not women, Luke rarely even talked to women and he seemed to be smiling when he talked to these women. He hustled to the door and swung it wide as the women all walked up the steps and Luke called to him from horseback.

"Hal, this is Ann Harper and her daughters, Beth and Laura. Take care of them while I bring the horses around the back, so we can unload the supplies."

"Okay, Luke. You've got some serious explainin' to do!" he shouted back.

Hal ushered the three women into the house and closed the door while Luke led the pack horses to the back of the house and tied them off at the hitchrail. He began unloading the food-laden panniers first, carrying them one at a time onto the back porch. Hal, after showing the ladies where they could leave their outerwear trotted to the kitchen unlocked the back door, then began moving the weighty panniers into the kitchen as Luke continued to unload them from the horses.

Once the supplies were emptied, Luke began unloading the four heavy panniers of clothing and other things that the women had packed. Luke knew which pannier belonged to which Harper woman, so he could carry them directly to their assigned bedrooms.

Hal hadn't said a word yet as he began unloading the food panniers into the larder, pantry, or cold room as appropriate.

"Hal, I'm going to go and put the horses in the barn after I talk to the ladies."

"I'm sure you've got a story or maybe a dozen of 'em for me, Luke."

"A continuing story, Hal, and it's not over yet. Not by a long shot."

"I'll be waitin' to hear it when you get back."

Luke walked out to the main room and found the women all sitting in chairs waiting for more information.

"I brought your things inside. Ann, I put yours in the first bedroom. Beth's things are in the middle and Laura's is on the end. There's a bathroom across the hallway from Beth's room that has a big tub. I'm going to go and take care of the horses while Hal's putting away the food. He may have a problem when he gets to the items you bought, though."

Ann replied, "Then I guess we'll go out there and help him."

"I'd appreciate it. Just to let you know, Hal can be a little uncomfortable around women."

"Even more than you, Luke?" asked Beth with a wry smile.

"Even more than me."

Luke trotted back down the hallway and stopped momentarily to tell Hal that help was on the way before heading back outside. He led the two packhorses into the barn and then returned for the others. Once they were all inside, he unsaddled and brushed them down before putting them in stalls. There weren't enough stalls, so he had to leave two just loosely tied so they could get food and water.

He finally took the two Winchesters, the Spencer, and the shotgun from their scabbards and headed back to the house. As he neared the door, he could hear laughter, so he stopped and listened. He was almost shocked to hear Hal talking and laughing. Hal laughing wasn't new, but Hal laughing with women was most assuredly different.

He toed the door open and stepped inside, kicking the door with his heel to close it behind him.

"Can I get some help with these weapons?" he announced.

Beth popped up and took the shotgun and a Winchester from his arms and Luke set the other two against the outside wall before Beth did the same with the others.

Luke looked at a grinning, red-cheeked Hal and raised his eyebrows, and received a milder shock.

Hal said, "Luke, Ann was just tellin' me about what happened. Just the quick version, though. We was all laughin' about the pepper that Laura spread over their beds. That musta been a fun night's sleep for those thievin' bastards."

Hal called Ann by her first name? What was coming next? Was he going to ask to move into the main house?

After the minor revelation, Luke said, "We sure didn't leave them much to eat, either. They must've been mighty put out by the time they finally broke into their cabin."

"Are we gonna do anythin' about them?"

"We have to, Hal. Aside from dispensing justice, those four will be a plague on the area unless they're stopped. They think they can do anything as long as it's away from town."

"Am I comin' with ya?"

"Nope. I need you here to protect Laura and Ann. Beth is coming along."

"You're takin' a woman along to hunt outlaws?"

"Not just any woman, Hal. I'd take Laura along too if she was older. They're pretty strong ladies."

"I hope so."

The two strong ladies smiled, but it was only after Luke announced his decision to bring Beth with him and Laura if she had been older.

"I see you got another Winchester. What's with the Spencer?"

"The new Winchester is for Beth. The Spencer belonged to her father. It'll give us two long-range guns and two repeaters. It'll offset their numbers, and we'll have the advantage of surprise. That reminds me. I've neglected one critical piece of information. Laura, do you know what kinds of guns they have?"

"Yes, sir. Charlie and Joe have Winchesters like yours. Philly has a repeater, but it has a tube for the bullets. Mack only has a pistol. The other three all have pistols too."

"Very good, as usual, Laura. So, Philly has a Henry and they have two Winchesters. Nothing that'll reach out much beyond a hundred yards."

"What are these?" Hal asked as he held up the two odd-looking hats.

"I picked those up for me and Beth. They're fur-lined and the flaps fold down to cover your ears. They just looked really warm to me and after getting trapped in that blizzard, I don't want to be caught like that again. I also bought a compass. If I had one the last time, I wouldn't have been blown off course like some wayward sailor."

"But you wouldn't have found me," Laura said softly.

"Which is why I'm very happy I didn't have it with me then," he said as he smiled at her.

"Alright, after we get the things put away and you ladies get settled into your rooms, we can have some lunch and figure out how to get this thing done. I've got to empty out my room for Ann."

"This means I get a housemate for a while, Luke?" Hal asked as he grinned.

"For a while, Hal. You'll be entertaining Ann and Laura for at least a day or two. Oh, and I picked this up for you," Luke said as he handed him a box.

Hal opened the box and took out the pocket watch.

"Why, thank you, Luke. That's right thoughtful."

"I thought it might be a good idea to know what time it is. I have one as well. They have alarm chimes built in, so you don't oversleep."

"Well, that ruins one of my best excuses," he said with a grin.

They finished unpacking and Luke moved his things out of Ann's new bedroom, took them to the small house, and put them into the second bedroom.

While he was moving out, the women were moving their things into their rooms. Beth noticed that she was in the largest bedroom and shortly afterward, when she pulled open a drawer, discovered that it had been Luke and Emma's room.

In one of the drawers was a collection of woman's things: hair pins and combs, a hairbrush and mirror set, and some inexpensive jewelry, and wondered why Luke had kept them. They weren't particularly valuable, and he hadn't kept her clothes or shoes, yet he had kept these items. She didn't use that drawer but put her things in the other drawers, nor did she pack her newly purchased trousers, long johns, or heavy shirt. She set them aside with her rubberized boots, her new Stetson, and the fur-lined hat and gloves.

Luke left the rifles at the house but needed to get the extra pistol and gunbelt for Beth when he returned. He'd have to fill the ammunition pouch for the pistol as well. He had an extra flask of gunpowder for filling the pistol's chambers, too. He guessed he had enough percussion caps, powder, and balls for fifty or sixty rounds. That was more than enough. With the outlaws' six boxes of cartridges for the Winchesters and his modified Remington, the four boxes of Spencer rounds, and two boxes of cartridges for his Sharps, it should be more than enough to deal with the problem.

He walked back to the bigger house and found it filled with the aroma of good food. He headed for the kitchen and was again surprised to find Hal and Ann engaged in conversation. She was cooking and Hal was helping. He glanced over at Laura and Beth and raised his eyebrows. Both smiled and Laura added a shrug.

He stepped over to the kitchen table and sat between them before he quietly asked, "This is interesting, don't you think?"

"Very," replied Beth succinctly.

"Tomorrow, I'll come over around seven o'clock. We can have breakfast and then start out right away. Does that sound alright to you?"

"Are you still planning on riding cross-country or have you changed your mind?"

He smiled and said, "Read my mind again, didn't you? I've been giving it some thought and probably came to the same conclusion you did. We won't save any time because we'll be going slower, and we'll leave a trail straight back to this house. So, after we leave, we'll pass through Colorado City again."

"I thought you might reconsider."

Laura just sat back and watched them. She still had that little pang of jealousy but knew it was for the best. She loved her sister and thought she loved Luke, too. But she was honest with herself and knew it could be hero worship or just an infatuation. But either way, she was very fond of him. She liked Hal too and noticed how much her mother seemed to like him as well. Her being kidnapped may well be the best thing that ever happened to the women in her family, except for herself, of course.

After lunch, everyone adjourned to the main room where Luke and Laura filled Hal in on the events that led to the current situation. Once he had been fully informed, Hal agreed with the decision to go after them. These men should not be allowed to live.

Once the stories were done, Laura went to her new room for a nap. She was already tired and hadn't fully recovered her energy after being deprived of food for so many days.

Luke moved all the guns into the main room, then went to his gun closet and removed his Sharps and the extra Remington New Army and its gunbelt. He returned to the main room, passing Hal and Ann who were headed for the kitchen and some private coffee time.

"So, that's your Sharps," said Beth as Luke leaned the rifle against the sofa.

"Yes, ma'am. I grew very fond of the weapon during the war. Mine was getting a bit tired, so I bought a new Army surplus weapon when I mustered out. I stopped in Denver on the way home and found a gunsmith who was modifying the rifles for hunters. He modified the breech and firing mechanism to handle cartridges that didn't use percussion caps. He also refined the already very well-made rifle, so it was even more accurate and smoother to operate. I had to stay in Denver almost two weeks waiting for the gun to be finished. I also bought a full cover for the rifle to keep it dry and free from dirt and dust. The rifle has been very accurately sighted and balanced as well. I need to get the ammunition from him, so I wire him once every few months and he sends me a couple of boxes. They're a little pricey, but well worth it. I should order some more soon."

"So, can you show me how to shoot the Winchester and the pistol?"

"The Winchester is very simple to use. You fill the tube with up to fifteen cartridges by sliding them into the loading gate on the right side here. When you finish, you need to bring a cartridge into the chamber by using the loading lever. You can actually have sixteen rounds available if you fill the magazine tube after you put one in the firing chamber."

Luke showed Beth how to cycle the lever of the new, still unloaded repeater.

"Now, when you do that, notice how the hammer is automatically cocked. All you need to do now is to pull the trigger. After it fires, just lever in a new round and pull the trigger again. The expended brass is tossed out of the rifle. If you have one already in the breech, you just cock the hammer."

"Okay. Can I try it?"

Luke handed her the rifle and she quickly cycled the lever and pulled the trigger. After the hammer snapped, she grinned. "That was easy. Can I try it with live ammunition later?"

"Absolutely. I want you to feel the kick, which is nowhere as much as the Spencer. Now I'm not going to show you how to load the pistol, at least not yet. You'll have five of the six cylinders loaded. To fire the pistol, you pull back the hammer and then the trigger. I'll let you fire it in a little while as well."

"Alright. What else are we bringing with us?"

"A couple of tarps, two slickers, a couple of blankets, maybe a bedroll, some food, and those goofy hats."

"They didn't look goofy to me. They looked warm."

"That's why I bought them."

"Luke," she asked quietly, "are you scared?"

"Sure. I'd be stupid not to be scared."

She smiled and said, "Then I don't feel so bad."

"Beth, you can always back out of this. I wouldn't think any less of you."

"No, no. It's alright. I just wondered why I was scared. I've never had to shoot at a man before."

"If it makes you feel any better, you don't have to shoot them. You can just shoot near them to distract them and cause confusion."

Beth thought about it before asking, "Do I have to decide now, or can I wait?"

"You can wait right up until you have to pull the trigger."

"How bad was it when you had to shoot someone?"

"After that first one, I was so sick that I wretched. But two days later, one of my friends was hit by one of their snipers and killed, so I didn't feel bad again. It was war and I felt I had to stop them from killing my friends."

"This is war, too. Isn't it?"

"It is. It's actually a more righteous war than that other one. These men are causing pain and suffering among the innocent and must be stopped. They deserve punishment for what they did to your family and others. I haven't one concern about killing them all, Beth."

She nodded, but Luke thought he saw some doubt beneath the determination in those deep blue eyes and hoped she would be all right. He also recalled seeing his friends as they lay injured or dying. *Could he bear seeing Beth that way?* Luke was beginning to question his decision to bring her along.

After telling Hal and Ann that they'd be doing some practice shooting, they took Luke's Winchester out to the front porch and closed the door.

Once they were on the edge of the porch, Luke handed Beth the Winchester and had her pick out a target about fifty to sixty yards away. She found a depression in the snow, cocked the hammer, took aim, and squeezed the trigger. The rifle cracked and the snow around the depression exploded.

"Good shot, Beth!" Luke exclaimed.

"This is much easier to shoot than the Spencer. It's so balanced."

"It is. Want to try the pistol now?"

"Alright."

She leaned the Winchester against the porch rail and Luke handed her the revolver, showing her how to use the two-handed style of firing because of her smaller hands. She picked out a closer target, cocked the hammer, aimed, and fired, missing low by about three feet.

"Can I try again?" she asked.

"Go ahead and empty the pistol if you'd like. I've got to clean and reload it anyway."

She smiled and after her second shot, continued until the Colt was empty, getting better with each successive shot. When she finished, she handed the pistol back to Luke.

"It's pretty heavy and a bit awkward at first, but I got used to it."

"You did very well, Beth. Let's go get warm again. I've got to clean and reload the pistol and my Winchester, then clean and oil your new repeater, too."

Luke picked up his Winchester and they went inside. Laura must have been very tired because the nearby gunfire didn't awaken her.

Beth watched as Luke cleaned the two Winchesters and oiled them both. Then he cleaned and reloaded the pistol. Finally, he added one more cartridge to his Winchester and loaded Beth's with fifteen cartridges.

"In this weather, it's important to keep moisture away from the rifles. The Sharps has its own case, but the Winchesters and the Spencer will be in open scabbards. I'll bring some towels that we can stick around the stocks and into the scabbards to keep that flying snow from getting into them."

Beth nodded and asked, "So, are we all ready?"

"Except for the food and getting dressed. Are you really sure you want to come, Beth? I can do this on my own. Really."

"Why are you trying to get rid of me all of a sudden? Is it because you think I'm just a woman?" she asked defensively.

Luke shook his head and replied, "You know better than that, Beth. That was beneath you to even think it, much less say it. I had two reasons for asking. I was concerned that you might feel bad for killing those men and I didn't want to see you like I saw my friends during the war. There were missions that really only needed one shooter, but a friend would want to come along. I'd try to talk him out of it just as much as I'm trying to talk you out of it. That's all it was."

Beth did feel bad immediately after the words had been blurted out.

"I'm sorry, Luke. You're right. I shouldn't have even thought it, much less said it. But I do want to come along. I think I can help."

"You can help, I never denied that. It's just that, well, I didn't want to see you that way."

"I understand, and I appreciate it. But I'd feel better going."

"Alright. I won't bring it up again."

"Good. Now that we've gotten that out of the way, can you tell me anything else I need to know?"

"The most important thing is to move a few feet after you fire. You'll leave a large cloud of gunsmoke overhead and it makes it easier to target the shooter."

"Even if we're outside their range?"

"Range is an iffy thing. It's called effective range for a reason. A pistol's effective range is a lot higher than most people think. It's just not as accurate or as powerful because of the shorter barrel. My Remington has been modified to use the same cartridges as the Henry or Winchester, but its range is lower because the hot gases that push the bullet down the barrel stop pushing earlier.

"The Winchester's effective range is a hundred yards, but I've hit targets from two hundred yards with one. It doesn't have the same lethal power at that range but having a .44 caliber bullet hit you at that range isn't going to feel good, either.

"Now, the Spencer has a longer barrel and the cartridges have more powder than the Winchester, and even though the bullet is much bigger, it has both a longer range and more power than the repeater. The Sharps is actually a musket version with a longer barrel and even more powder in its .45 caliber cartridges. That gives it even more range and power.

"So, remember to move after you fire, but don't expose yourself, either. If you're firing from cover, say some rocks, just slide a bit to a new position. Sometimes, with the Sharps, I had to fire from virtually no cover at all, but the range of the rifle gave me some measure of protection. Some of those Johnny Rebs were pretty good with those muzzle-loaders, too. I got into some ticklish situations with only Confederate infantry to deal with."

"Did you ever get shot?"

"Twice, but neither of them was too bad. I only missed a couple of weeks."

"Where did you get hit?"

"One was in my left forearm, and the other is between me and my horse."

Beth laughed and said, "That must have been embarrassing."

"Only after it was well on its way to being healed. Nobody ever joked about where we took a bullet right after we got hit because there was much chance of infection. Only after a week or so when it looked like we'd be okay did my nicked behind become a good joke."

"Luke, what happens after?"

"After they're gone?"

"Yes."

"I don't know, Beth. There are a lot of things to think about. In this case, I really think we need to worry about one thing at a time. Let's get rid of these men and then we see what we can do about the rest."

"That's probably the best thing to do," she replied, wishing he had given a different answer.

Beth was already concerned about her future. She didn't want to move back into town and knew that the ranch was lost as well. She knew what she wanted but didn't dare think about it too much. She wanted to go with Luke as much to get to know him better as she did about seeking vengeance.

At the Harper ranch house, Charlie Bassett was stewing as his sixth sense was tickling his brain. There was something wrong in this whole damned mess. *Why did the woman leave a note up for a daughter she hadn't seen in a month?* As he dwelled on the situation, he began to re-examine Laura's escape. *How did she get out and why seal the barn back up? How did she get so high to cut the bar rope?*

He then looked at his partner who was sitting across from him at the table and said, "Philly, I think we're bein' set up. I don't think that girl got out on her own at all. Somebody helped her."

"Who? You think somebody rode there in the blizzard and let her out?"

"Not during the blizzard, the day after we left. The weather was okay, and she'd still be alive. If he waited until the blizzard arrived, she'd probably already be frozen to death. It makes more sense."

"But who even knew about that place?"

"Nobody that we knew, but what if old McCaffrey and his wife had relatives that got curious after not hearin' from them for a while?"

"Okay, say that's true. Why come out in the winter to check on them?"

"Yeah, I know. That's wrong, too, but I still think we're bein' set up. I can feel it. We got enough time to go into town and get some grub and get back here, then we can light out first thing in the morning. I don't think whoever is doin' this is gonna come back tonight."

"Okay, boss. You want me to get the guys mounted?"

"Yeah, let's go."

An hour and a few minutes later, they rode up to Salk's dry goods and went inside. Charlie noted that the woman who left the note wasn't anywhere to be found which reinforced his belief in his theory. They bought four bags of food, hung them over their saddle horns, and quickly rode out of town heading back to the Harper ranch.

As they trotted west, Charlie was still deep in thought about either setting up the ranch house to defend against those who had set up the trap or heading back to the cabin. At the hideout, they'd be on their home ground and the cabin was much easier to defend, but it was a tossup.

Luke and Beth returned to the kitchen and again found Hal and Ann chatting as they jointly prepared dinner. Laura was sitting at the kitchen table with a slight smile on her face and when Luke glanced her way, he received another wink.

Beth had seen the wink and looked at Luke's smiling face with curiosity thinking that surely there wasn't anything between them. She thought she'd ask Laura, but realized she'd be spending the whole day tomorrow with Luke, so she could ask him. Either way, she felt the sudden burn of jealousy, and this time, it didn't dissipate very quickly.

After dinner, Luke and Beth finalized their preparations in the main room while Laura looked on. Hal and Ann stayed in the kitchen having more coffee.

Luke finally felt he was getting comfortable with Beth and not having any more sudden lapses of distraction. He didn't doubt she was capable of sending him there if that was her intention, but this was business and they needed to get ready.

Luke and Beth picked each other's brains to make sure they hadn't missed anything but couldn't come up with much. Luke packed their saddlebags with their necessities then Laura suggested wrapping some matches in a waterproof tea canister along with some short candles, which Luke and Beth agreed was a wise precaution.

Satisfied that they were as ready as they could be, Luke went out to the kitchen and told Hal that he'd be going back to the small house, but Hal just waved to him and Luke left the house grinning. There was one more trick left in the old dog after all.

Charlie and the boys were back in the Harper house and had made themselves a decent supper but didn't bother to clean up. Charlie was sipping coffee at the kitchen table still deep in thought, convinced that the place was a trap.

Finally, he set the cup down and said, "Tomorrow morning, we head back to the cabin. I don't like this place for defense. Our place is much better, and nobody can shoot through those walls."

"I'm with you, boss," replied Philly, "This place gives me the creeps."

"Alright, we turn in early and lock the doors in case someone tries to sneak in, but I don't think anyone will. They'll be comin' tomorrow, but we ain't gonna be here. We'll be back in our cabin before noon, I think."

"Who's comin', boss?" asked Mack.

"I figure that after that woman went to see the sheriff and nothin' happened, she went and found some more family and they're the ones who got the kid loose. After she told 'em what we did, they're all hankerin' for revenge, too. That's who."

"We still gonna swing north to see if the girl's body is there?" asked Joe.

Charlie snapped, "*What did I just say?* She ain't there, Joe! That's why we bought the food and are headin' back to the cabin early. Now, when we get back to the cabin, we set up a little ambush of our own for her kin that show up. We shoot these bastards when they try to get us, but we'll be able to get one of 'em to tell us where the money is."

They all nodded. It was a good plan and it was why Charlie was the boss.

CHAPTER 4

Luke's alarm startled him when it went off at five o'clock. It was louder than he thought it'd be, but he quickly pushed in the alarm button, silencing the dinging bell. He swung his legs from under the cozy blankets, then sat on the edge of the bed, rolled his shoulders, and stretched before winding the watch per the instructions. As he stood, he realized that he hadn't even heard Hal come in and wondered if he had come in at all. He had a flash of suspicion but quickly shook his head.

He left the room then began his daily routine and found Hal sound asleep in his bed, so much for that wild thought. He had the cookstove and heat stove fired up and the coffee water heating as he washed and shaved, pulled on his two pairs of socks, his long johns, his heaviest wool shirt, and then his rubberized boots.

After he made the coffee, Hal began stirring and wandered out, quickly moving past Luke and out the door to answer nature's call. When he returned, he gratefully accepted Luke's offer of a cup of coffee.

"Any sign of life from the main house?" Luke asked.

"Nope. Not yet. I been meanin' to ask you about bringin' along Beth. Are you sure it's the right idea?"

"I'll admit to some concerns, Hal, and I'd feel better about leaving her here. I argued with her about it in the beginning, but I just couldn't win. I think if I left without her, she'd follow after me anyway and not be prepared. At least this way, I know she's at least minimally ready."

Hal nodded and said, “I’m only askin’ ‘cause Ann was worried about it.”

“You two seemed to hit it off.”

“Yep. She’s a mighty fine woman, Luke. Kinda makes a man think.”

“Well, whatever you’re thinking about, you know I’ll back you up.”

“I appreciate that, Luke. I surely do.”

“Well, whether they’re up or not, it’s time for me to start moving. I need to get our horses saddled.”

Luke pulled on a sweater and then his heavy jacket and gloves before leaving the small house for the barn. He noted that smoke was coming from the chimneys of the main house, so the ladies were awake. He reached the barn and had both horses saddled in twenty minutes and added a bedroll to Beth’s horse. He added the two rolled-up tarps and blanket to his instead then headed for the house. After he stepped onto the back porch, he tapped his gloved knuckles on the door and waited.

Laura opened the door with a smile a few seconds later and Luke stepped inside.

“Good morning, Laura.”

“Hello, Luke. All ready?”

“Pretty much. I need those bangy things from the main room, though,” he replied as he smiled before walking past her.

He entered the main room and hefted the two full saddlebags then lugged them out to the kitchen and set them down, returned to the main room, and picked up the two Winchesters. He was carrying them out to join the saddlebags and almost ran down Beth who was exiting her room.

"Oops! Excuse me, Beth," but that was before he really saw her.

He was glad he got that much out because he knew he wouldn't get any more. She may have been dressed warmly, and maybe it was because the added layers increased her curves, but the reason didn't matter. Beth simply overwhelmed his senses.

"Good morning, Luke. Are we almost ready to go?"

Luke nodded and smiled as Beth smiled back and walked in front of him to the kitchen. It made everything worse as he watched her walk away. Luckily, she'd be on horseback most of the day.

Breakfast wasn't ready, so Luke began moving the guns and saddlebags out to the horses. The saddlebags were first, and the long guns took two more trips. By the time he finished getting everything where he wanted them and returned, the table was filled with bacon, eggs, biscuits, and coffee. He really wasn't that hungry, but he knew he had to eat. It was the same every time he had gone out on missions during the war; he couldn't eat as his stomach refused to be bothered.

After a subdued breakfast, it was time to leave. Beth received hugs and kisses from Ann and Laura. Luke wasn't surprised when Laura gave him a big hug as well, but when he looked at Laura, he couldn't help but read her deep blue eyes and was surprised by what his eyes told him.

Beth was preparing to don a sweater when Luke reminded her of her other accessories that she needed to don first and held out her gunbelt. She smiled, then after wrapping it around her waist, he helped her adjust the belt to fit properly before she put on her sweater. After she put on her heavy jacket and a scarf, she pulled on her new Stetson and she was ready to ride.

Luke opened the door and held it as Beth stepped out quickly before Luke followed, closing the door behind them.

"Well, Beth, it's time. Are you all right?"

"I'm fine, Luke. Really."

"Good," he replied but still had those lingering doubts.

They headed to the barn and Beth mounted, but Luke led his gelding from the barn, and once outside, he closed the barn door before quickly climbing into his saddle. They rode out of the ranch and turned left toward Colorado City as the sun's early morning rays were creating long shadows across the snow-covered ground.

Charlie had to wake them all up just before dawn, so they could get out of there early. They had a hasty breakfast and had to pack up their supplies again, so they didn't get out of the house until after sunrise. But half an hour later, they were riding west to get to their cabin, so there would be enough time to set up the ambush.

As Luke and Beth passed through Colorado City almost two hours later, Luke asked her if she could think of anything else that they might need. She couldn't, so they continued through town and headed for the ranch.

"Beth, have you been watching the west?" he asked.

"It's hard not to. It's beginning to cloud up and the temperature is dropping."

"Yes, ma'am. I don't know how bad it's going to be, but I think we're ready for it this time. We have our hats."

Beth laughed and said, "You make fun of them, Luke, but I think we'll be grateful we have them."

"I know we will. Luckily, the only ones who can see how goofy we'll look will be us."

"You may look goofy, but not me."

"No, I'm sure you'll be very cute. But you're right, we'll both be a lot warmer."

They continued to ride and watch the menacing skies. It looked like snow, so the questions were how much and how it was going to be delivered. The wind was negligible now, but that might not mean much in a few hours.

They were almost to the ranch when Luke slowed them down.

"Beth, your ranch doesn't have any fence, so I think it might be a good idea to cut across to the west here and see if we can take a look at the house. They could still be there."

"Alright."

They cut across the pasture, both watching to the north as the ranch house appeared in the distance.

"No smoke, so that reduces the chance that they'll still be there, but if they suspected that someone might be coming, they'd want to stay low."

"What do you want to do?"

"I'm not sure. Let's ride toward the back of the barn. It'll cut down their vision if they're in there. They'd only be able to spot us from the front room's side window."

Beth nodded, then they turned to the north and walked their horses directly toward the barn. When they reached the back of the barn, they dismounted.

"Beth, stay here and hang onto the horses. I'm going to walk up there as if I live there. I don't think they'd shoot until they think there was a threat and they can't see if I'm armed. I'm going to move my pistol to my jacket pocket in case I need it."

Beth simply nodded and took his horse's reins. Luke unholstered his Remington, slid it into his large jacket pocket then slipped around the eastern edge of the barn and walked calmly toward the house, keeping a sharp eye for any motion.

He was tempted to look for tracks but knew he couldn't afford to peel his eyes from the house. His heart was pounding as he drew closer, so he willed it to slow down, a technique he'd learned when he'd been a sniper. His head told him that the house was empty, but his stomach disagreed.

He finally stepped up on the porch, half expecting a hail of gunfire from the windows or having the door slam open and see Charlie Bassett standing there with a grin on his face and a cocked pistol in his hand. But nothing happened, so he reached for the door, pulled the screen door open, and then opened the main door. He took a deep breath and walked in, his Remington now in his hand. He was met with silence and quickly scanned the house and found nothing except a mess. They'd been here but had already gone. He walked to the cookstove and touched the surface, feeling the heat, so they must have gone just a couple of hours ago.

He returned to the porch closed the door jogged down the steps and headed for the barn.

"Beth!" he shouted, "It's empty."

Beth felt a rush of relief as she began walking around the east side of the barn, leading the horses. She spotted Luke smiling broadly as he saw her. She matched his smile and walked quickly toward him.

"So, what do we do now?"

"We head for the house, tie off the horses and look around. I want your opinion of what I found in the house before I give you mine."

"So, you want me to go into the house?"

"You go ahead. I'm going to look around out here for a bit."

"Alright."

Beth handed Luke's reins to him then led her horse to the hitch rail and tied him off before walking inside the front door.

Luke mounted his horse and began to check for their tracks, and it wasn't long before he found them. The four horses had departed the barn and headed west, and Luke was curious about their direction after they cleared the yard. *Did they head west or northwest?*

After following their trail for a couple of hundred yards, he found that they didn't alter their direction at all, so he continued to follow for almost a mile before he realized that they were heading straight back to their big cabin, which told him a lot.

He wheeled his horse and set him to a medium trot to return to the ranch house. Once he reached the house, he stepped down and tied off his horse next to Beth's, then hopped onto the porch.

Luke entered the house and closed the door behind him, catching a glimpse of Beth at the other end of the house in the kitchen, so he just walked down the hallway and soon entered the kitchen.

"What do you think?" he asked.

"They're pigs. They left the house a mess."

"I can see that, but there's more to see here. Look past the mess and what do you see?"

She scanned the kitchen, then spotted the broken eggshells and exclaimed, "Food! They went into town and bought some food. They had eggs and we didn't leave any."

"Right. Now, when you were in here looking around, I took a short ride to follow their trail. What if I told you they rode straight west? What would that tell you?"

"That they were heading back to the cabin. Isn't that what you expected them to do?"

"Yes, but the direction they took is significant. They rode due west, straight to their cabin."

Beth thought about it for a few seconds.

"They aren't looking for Laura anymore," she said slowly.

Luke grinned and said, "Nope. We know they didn't find her, but they've given up looking. Why?"

"Because they know she's not dead."

"So, if they know she's not dead, why aren't they out hunting for her anymore? They sure aren't going to just forget about the money."

"Okay. Now you've got me. Why not?"

"Because they finally figured out that she had help. They got here, and something triggered them to look at all the clues at the cabin again and they figured out that she had help. It really wasn't hard and I'm a bit surprised that it took them this long. Now if they know she's had some help, then they know they could be targets. Look at a few other things, Beth. They didn't exactly race out of here, but they sure did leave earlier than they would have if they thought they were safe."

"That means that they're probably expecting us to show up."

"That's what I think, too."

"So, what do we do?"

"We stay in the house tonight, ma'am. They're expecting us to follow them today, so they might be more relaxed by tomorrow. It's hard to stay vigilant for very long. We're going to stay out of their range anyway, but if we go today, they'll be watching for us."

"So, we stay here and leave early tomorrow morning?"

"Very early. A lot depends on the weather, though. If it's lousy, we may wait another day. Is that alright with you?"

"I think you're right. They rushed out of here. I don't think they'd clean up even if they stayed another day, but they did ride out of here very early."

"So, I'll put the horses up and bring the saddlebags and rifles in."

"Being the woman, I'll do the cleaning up. Is that right?"

"Well, if you'd rather take care of the horses and guns and have me do the cleanup, that's fine, too. I've always prided myself on my domestic skills."

Beth laughed and waved him away as she began to clean up their mess.

Almost an hour later, Luke was helping Beth make beds and straighten out the house.

"My husband was a mess maker, too," she said as they worked, "I was surprised to find out how neat your house was."

"I wasn't kidding about my domestic skills that much. It's just a lot easier to keep things neat than it is to let things turn into a disaster and have to fix the mess."

"My goodness, what is the world coming to?" she said after she laughed again.

After they finished the cleanup, Luke asked if she wanted him to make lunch.

"Another surprise, or are you just trying to impress me?" she asked.

"Maybe. Laura liked my cooking."

"Luke, on the subject of Laura, may I ask you something?"

"Sure."

"When we were in the kitchen yesterday, Laura gave you a wink, and you smiled. What was that all about?"

"Um, that's a good question. I think I know what she meant. It was about Ann and Hal."

She noticed that the question had an unsettling impact on Luke, so she continued.

"How would you know that?"

"Well, it was obvious, really. They'd been talking a lot since she arrived. I've never seen Hal talk to any woman that much."

"You're holding back again, aren't you?"

"Lordy, Beth, am I that much of an open book to you? It's not fair if you ask me. Or can you do that to everyone?"

"Not everyone, but you're very easy to read. So, what was it?"

"Can I just tell you that it might embarrass you and let it go at that?"

"Embarrass me? But she was winking at you."

Luke really didn't want to tell her what Laura had said. He'd only known Beth for a short time and things just didn't happen this fast.

"Beth, I've only known you for two days and I've only known Laura for three days, yet I already think that each of you as being very special. You'll have to trust me on this one."

"Luke, you know how Laura feels about you. I don't want to see her hurt."

"Beth, I know about Laura. She told me already and she'll be all right."

"Are you going to tell me, or do I have to really put the pressure on?"

Luke sat down, took a breath, and said, "Alright. I'll tell you, but don't tell me I didn't warn you."

"Alright, I'm ready," she replied and took a seat across from him at the kitchen table.

"When we first arrived at this house, she winked at me in the kitchen just like she did yesterday. I asked her about it later and she told me. She said that when she saw me look at you, she felt jealous at first, but then she told me that she loved you very much and it was all right."

"What was all right?" she asked softly.

"It was all right for us to be together. She said that you needed me as much as I needed you because we were both lonely. Then she told me what had happened to you."

"Meaning my marriage and my baby?"

"That and the circumstances leading to your marriage."

"Oh. All of it?"

"As much as necessary."

"Did she say how I got pregnant?"

"Yes."

"Does that bother you?"

"Why?"

"My being so soft-headed that I let that creature have his way with me?"

"You're many things, Beth, but soft-headed isn't one of them. Soft-hearted, probably, but not soft-headed."

"How do you know? You weren't there."

"No, I wasn't. I haven't a clue why it happened, and it doesn't matter."

"Why doesn't it matter? Are your standards so low that you'll take any woman regardless of her morals?"

Her answer startled him but he replied, "Beth, this isn't about my standards, it's about yours."

"Meaning my slutty decision to give into Richard?" she asked quickly as she fumed.

"No, the way you punish yourself for a mistake you made years ago. You're letting that mistake control your whole life. You need to step back and look at yourself honestly and stop focusing on that one mistake. I know about the mistake and yet when I look at you, I see an extraordinary woman. You're smart, witty, a good person to talk to, and yes, you're beautiful. I don't see a single negative about you. So, if you're really honest about yourself, you shouldn't think of yourself that way."

"But you know what I did, so now you think I'm just one of those women you can have your way with any time you wish."

"No, I don't. Besides, even if I did, it wouldn't matter."

Beth stood and glared at him as she said, "Really? So, if I offered myself to you right now, you'd turn me down?"

"Yes."

"I don't believe that for a second."

"Beth, you can believe what you want, but I know I couldn't."

"Why not?"

"Because it's one of my many faults. I can't do it with just any woman. I have to be in love with her."

She sat back down slowly and asked, "Wait a minute. Are you serious? You mean you never had relations with another woman other than your wife?"

"That's right."

"I find that hard to believe."

"I can understand that. I'm not joking when I say it's a fault. I just can't."

"You must never have had the opportunity then because I find that still hard to believe."

"Yes, quite a few, in fact. Many from women that I would classify as slutty."

"Meaning?"

"Women who seek the company of men and try to lure them into their beds. In their case, they are the aggressors. With Richard, were you that way? Did you try to talk him into your bed or was it the other way around?"

"The other way around," she answered quietly.

"Beth, you made a mistake, that's all. It's not worth beating yourself for the rest of your life."

"Were you serious about your fault with women?"

"Yes. Remember you thought it was funny when I was shot in my behind? I took some ribbing for that, as you might expect. But I took a lot more for my other problem. Some guys thought I didn't like women."

"But you were married."

"That wasn't until after I got home and married my Ella."

"Is that why you prefer to call me Beth instead of Ellie?"

"In a way, but not the way you probably think."

"What way?"

"Laura probably told you about Ella. How she was and how she died."

"Yes, she did."

"And she probably told you about the two promises she asked of me."

"Yes."

"What I didn't tell Laura was that Ella, after she had my promise to remarry, told me that I should never try to make my new wife into another Ella. I should love her as herself, not as another Ella."

"Laura told me that you had been cheating on that second promise."

Luke smiled and said, "Yes, I told her that, too. I've been avoiding women for years. Laura was the first woman that I've exchanged more than three sentences in three years. You're the second."

"You loved her that much."

"Terribly."

"Was she pretty?"

"Yes, but cute more than pretty."

The whole conversation had evolved into a much deeper exploration than Beth had expected, but she felt better now that her dark secret was out and didn't seem to be of importance to him.

"Luke, I apologize for some of the things I said. It's just that ever since that night, I've been disgusted with myself. Then I found out I was pregnant and had to marry Richard. My whole life was over, then the baby died when he was born. I know you lost your son, so you understand how devastating it was. If that wasn't bad enough, Richard then emptied our bank account and left with my brothers. It was like God was punishing me for what I did."

"It wasn't God who was punishing you, Beth, it was Richard. Now stop blaming yourself. You're better than that. You're an amazing woman, and that's the woman I want to see from now on."

Beth smiled and replied, "Alright. It's a deal."

"Good. Now, the last time I recall, I had offered to make lunch."

"And I'm holding you to that offer," she replied, feeling enormously better.

Luke smiled back at her then stood and began to prepare their lunch.

As Luke was lighting the cookstove, the boys reached their cabin. Charlie and Philly unloaded the food while Mack and Joe took care of the horses. They had fires going in the fireplace and the cookstove shortly and less than thirty minutes later, Philly began cooking.

When Mack and Joe returned, Charlie had them both go right back outside and keep an eye out for any visitors. They complained and asked if they could wait for lunch first, but Charlie was insistent. He told them that he and Philly would relieve them after lunch.

After they'd gone, Charlie groused to Philly, "I'm gettin' mighty fed up with this mess. I feel like shootin' somebody and wish whoever did this would just show up."

"What do we do when they do?"

"I'm still thinkin' about it. They ain't about to come ridin' in with bells on. Comin' in at night would be stupid. No, they'll show up today or tomorrow in the daylight. I don't know how many. I'm guessin' no more than four. They'll have to get close, though, so I'm thinkin' of setting up pickets further out and pickin' 'em off when they show up."

"I don't know, boss. The weather's lookin' like it's gonna turn bad. If we hold up here for a few days, there ain't nothin' they can do except freeze."

Charlie blinked, then stared at Philly and said, "That's probably not too far wrong, Philly. This place is built like a fort. We lock it up, and they're stuck outside."

"What about the barn?"

"I'm thinkin' about the barn. How can we lock it up, too?"

Phil grinned and said, "Why don't we let them move into the barn and think they're safe. Then while they're in there, we lock 'em in like we did with that girl."

"Philly, what's got into you? That's two good ideas in a row. Let's leave the barn doors open as a temptation. We can see the doors through the shutters in the main room window. You know, that might work. When Mack and Joe come back, let's set it all up."

Philly was proud of himself. He just figured out something that Charlie couldn't. Maybe he should be the boss.

"This is pretty good, Luke. I'm impressed."

"When you spend years avoiding women, you need to learn certain skills," he said as he smiled.

"Can you sew too?"

“Yup. I can’t knit, though.”

Beth laughed and said, “I’ll make a deal. I’ll show you how to knit and you can show me how to shoot.”

“We’ll work on your shooting, but I’ll pass on the knitting. Guys can understand the need to fix clothes, but they’d frown on some other guy picking up a pair of knitting needles.”

“So, what will we do this afternoon?”

“That’s a good question. I had planned on doing some shooting at bad guys, so I’m at a loss. I don’t want to do anything with the guns. They’re ready to go and we’re keeping them warm and dry. Our supplies are good, so I guess we could do something really daring.”

“Such as?”

“Talk. Tell me about your brothers and Richard. Why steal from family and run off to someplace that has such a small chance of success? I’ll bet not one out of twenty miners finds a good amount of gold.”

“Honestly? I have no idea. My brothers, John and Rob, were almost twins. John is older by a year and Rob treated him like a hero. He did everything that John did. They were supposed to help out around the ranch, but they never liked the work, so they did as little as possible to get by. My father was angry with them all the time when they were teenagers. Richard was their friend in school. That’s how I met him because he was always hanging around the house.”

“So, he was older than you.”

“By four years. I was so stupid. He acted so nice when he was around me that I thought I loved him. Then he convinced me that it would be all right to do things. I had boyfriends in school, but Richard was different. He was a man and not a boy and I thought I could keep what I was doing with Richard a secret, but he told John. One day, my father was yelling at John for leaving his horse outside for too long and he decided to deflect my father's wrath and told him that his older daughter was a tramp and had been giving herself to Richard. That's how I got married."

"Do you think they'll all come back someday?"

"I'd be surprised if they didn't. We haven't heard anything from them since they left, but the money that my brothers got for selling the cattle and what Richard took from me is probably almost gone by now."

"What do you think they'll do when they get back?"

"Before my father died, I'd think that they'd just stay away, but now, they may come back and try to bully my mother and take over."

"They'd do that to your mother?"

"Yes, I think so. My father was the boss. He was in charge and no one argued with him."

"So, your mother had no say in what happened."

"None at all."

"So, I guess that you and Laura got your backbone from your father."

"I guess. Is it that noticeable?"

"Very. You're both very strong women. I didn't see that in your mother, though. She's a very good woman, I'm sure, but she needs someone to lean on."

"She does. I think Hal will be very good for her."

"I think she'll be very good for Hal, too. He's never had anyone to really share his life with. He's just lonely, I think."

"How about you, are you lonely?"

"I'll confess to that. I was so used to having Ella always there, that to have her suddenly yanked away was hard. If it hadn't been for my promise, I'd probably be a lot worse. I imagine it's been bad for you, Beth. I had Hal to keep me going, but you had no one."

"No, I didn't. I just went through the motions. I was living in Harken's Boarding House after he left. Then my mother showed up a few weeks ago and told me what happened, and I moved back into the house."

"Things will be different now, Beth. Neither one of us has to be lonely anymore."

Beth was startled and asked, "Are you asking me to marry you?"

"No, I'm saying that you can live on my ranch with Laura in the main house. I'll live in the small house. I think Hal won't be living at the ranch much longer. I enjoy having you around, Beth, and I'd like to get to know you better."

Beth didn't know whether she should be relieved or disappointed, but it was a wonderful solution.

"That does sound nice, Luke."

"We can plan more as we spend more time together, Beth."

"I'd like that, Luke," she said softly.

"So, would I. Now, let's do some planning for tomorrow."

"Alright."

Luke took out two coffee cups and set them on the table before sitting back down.

"This is the cabin, and this is the barn. There's a copse of trees to the southwest on a rise overlooking the cabin and barn," he said as he put a fork where the trees were.

"There are some more trees to the east, but they're behind the barn and pretty useless."

"How far away are the fork trees?"

"About four hundred yards or so."

"That means that we can hit the house from there."

"Yes, ma'am."

Laura then said, "So, we should get into those trees tomorrow morning and then take a look at what they're doing."

"That's what I'm thinking. Once we're in the trees, we'll have cover and they can't do anything without exposing themselves."

"But they can go out the back door."

Luke smiled and said, "Yes, they can. They can go out the back door."

Beth saw the smile and then saw the obvious, "But they can't go anywhere."

"No. They can't. I had originally thought about getting them in a crossfire, but there's no need. Our only problem is time. We'll be outside, and they'll be in the cabin with enough food to last a while. They'll be warm, and we'll be cold. That's something we'll have to deal with."

"So, we ride over there in the morning and get in the trees, set up, and start shooting?"

"One shot to let them know we're there and then we wait to see what they do."

"Won't they see our smoke?"

"If they do, it doesn't matter. They can't hit us from the cabin, and they aren't about to leave the cabin to come after us. Knowing that we have the weapons to reach them at distance should get them nervous and they might make a mistake."

"So, what if they just stay inside and wait us out?"

"I'm working on that. Do you have any ideas?"

"Can we smoke them out?"

"I was thinking along those lines. We can't go down there and throw something over the top of the chimney, but we might be able to collapse the chimney which would have the same effect."

"Can we do that?"

"I'm not sure. From a quarter of a mile, I'm not sure the rounds would have the power to blast apart the stones. I'd have to get closer, maybe within a hundred yards. Then I'd need you to keep them inside with your Spencer. I'd take my Winchester with me as well to provide coverage if they suddenly pour out of there."

"We're going to have to wait until we get there, won't we?"

"Yup."

Beth thought about the problem and soon concluded that she couldn't come up with a better way.

Mack and Joe had returned for lunch and were a bit irritated that Charlie and Philly weren't going to go out and do guard duty, but after Charlie told them of the new plan, they were pleased because they knew they wouldn't have to spend more time outside.

After Mack and Joe had been briefed, Charlie and Philly left the house to open the barn doors. The wind was minimal, so Charlie thought that the horses wouldn't be impacted much. Then they checked to make sure they could see the barn from the main room and were satisfied with the angle of fire it provided. They had set their bait, and now they needed to spring the trap.

The rest of the day was spent getting their three rifles and four pistols ready. It was only then that they noticed the missing six boxes of cartridges.

"Son of a bitch! That leaves us pretty damned short! How many rounds do we have for the rifles?" Charlie exclaimed.

They did a quick inventory and found each of the Winchesters was fully loaded as was the Henry and Philly had a spare box of cartridges.

Charlie was somewhat mollified knowing they had more than sixty rounds available and said, “That should be enough. After we’re finished with this, we each carry a couple of boxes of cartridges in our saddlebags. Mack, we need to get you a rifle, too.”

Mack nodded. He wanted to get one when they were at Salk’s but was afraid to ask again. Charlie had really taken him down a notch the last time he had asked for one.

“Alright, we keep an eye on the barn. One of us needs to just check on it from time to time. If we spot ‘em or if the doors are closed, we move.”

“Sounds good, boss,” said Joe.

Charlie set up a schedule for checking the barn doors. It was much more pleasant than staying outside, so Mack and Joe didn’t complain. They knew that they’d be warm and whoever was coming to try to kill them would freeze their butts off.

———

Luke and Beth were sitting on the couch, talking about things not related to tomorrow’s task. Luke had just given Beth a more in-depth accounting of discovering Laura and their first day in the cabin.

“It makes me shiver to think that she wanted to die, Luke.”

“But you can understand it from her perspective, Beth. She was utterly alone and at the mercy of those four vicious men. She thought she was going to have a baby and that they were going to kill her. She may have hoped for a rescue for the first few days, but after two weeks that hope had disappeared. Laura had nothing to live for."

"I can't imagine the despair she must have felt."

"Nor could I, which is why I'm still amazed at how quickly she recovered. Laura is a remarkable person."

"She is," Beth agreed, then asked quietly, "Luke, could we both sleep in the big bed in the first bedroom? I don't want to sleep alone tonight."

Luke had to come up with some way of preventing anything from happening. It was much, much too soon and he was not about to rely on his fault to hold him back, not with Beth.

He came up with a reasonable solution and replied, "We can, but I'll sleep on top of the blankets."

Beth smiled, not altogether pleased with his answer, but said, "Thank you, Luke."

They had to get to sleep early because of their anticipated departure in the wee hours of the morning. Beth had no nightdress, so she just removed her boots and heavy shirt and slipped under the blankets. Luke did pretty much the same and stretched out on top of the bed. He had borrowed another blanket from a different bedroom and pulled it over him, adding another layer of warmth for Beth.

She had her eyes closed and Luke glanced over at her relaxed face, wondering how she would do tomorrow. His earlier doubts had grown into more serious doubts about his decision to bring her along. She may be a strong woman, but how would she react if she had to kill a man?

He hoped that if she did have to fire, she'd just do as he had advised her and shot high, so she didn't hit anyone. Shooting those bastards for effect was his job.

Luke slid out of bed early to let Beth sleep a little longer, then took one more look at her peaceful face, and his decision to include Beth seemed even worse. He left the bedroom with his boots in his hand and headed for the kitchen.

Twenty minutes later, while Beth prepared breakfast, Luke went out to the barn and saddled both horses. He led them to the house, tied them at the back hitchrail, then looked at the sky and saw the three-quarters moon, but there were clouds passing in front of its face. It was understandably cold too, but at least the wind wasn't too bad.

He returned to the house and closed the door, but only removed his gloves and hat. It was still chilly in the house, despite the cookstove's heat.

Beth had breakfast ready ten minutes later, so they took a few minutes to sit together at the kitchen table and just enjoy each other's company. Beth seemed to have recovered from her anxiety the night before, so Luke set his concerns aside.

Thirty minutes later, two heavily bundled riders departed the Star H ranch wearing funny-looking but warm hats.

There was more than enough moonlight to follow the trail left by the four men, and because they could follow the path through the snow, it was easier going than if their horses had to make their own way.

Beth had thought she'd be colder than she was. The warm hat, gloves, and layers of clothing coupled with the heat from the horse kept her reasonably comfortable.

Luke was concentrating on the task at hand and didn't say much. In less than an hour now, they'd be set up in the trees overlooking the cabin. He still recalled that slippery descent from the trees to the barn and wasn't sure about the distance from the trees to the cabin because of the conditions when he first found it. He'd find out soon enough how accurate his first estimate had been.

Forty minutes later, Luke spotted the outline of the barn in the moonlight, so he waved to Beth and they shifted their track to the south to climb the ridge to the trees overlooking the cabin and barn. Ten minutes later they reached the trees and entered the small forest as the predawn began to lighten the sky.

Once hidden by the trees, Luke stepped down before Beth dismounted and walked next to him.

"Did you see the cabin and barn?" he asked.

"Yes."

"I'm still not sure about the distance, but it didn't appear to be as far away as I originally expected. I'll get a better idea when there's some more light. Right now, I'll build a shelter with one of the tarps and set up for a fire. As soon as it's light, I'll start the fire, so you can have some heat."

"What are we going to do after that?"

"I'll set up the sights on the Sharps and Spencer as soon as I get the range, then we wait until someone comes out and I'll take the first shot. Even if I miss, that'll chase them back inside and keep them there. Then I'll go down to about a hundred yards or so and start working on the chimney. I'll need you to cover me."

"Alright."

Luke pulled out one of the two tarps and selected a spot near a large pine with dry ground on the side of the clump of trees away from the cabin so the smoke from their fire could dissipate.

He attached the peak of the tarp to an overhanging branch and spread it out on the ground. He used some of the nearby dead branches to fashion stakes to hold the corners in place and a large rock to anchor the bottom of the tarp near the trunk of the tree. It wouldn't hold up to any strong winds, but it would keep the heat in and the breeze out. He began piling up kindling and then heavier branches until he had built a good-sized pyramid of wood.

Beth had been busy removing the saddlebags and putting them on the ground under the shelter. Luke checked his watch, which read 7:12, so the sunrise would be arriving soon.

"I don't think they'll be getting up this early, but I think we should head over to the other edge of the forest and watch. We'll see smoke from their chimneys before we see them."

"Won't they have to leave to pee?"

"They'll just go outside the back door because the front door has that goofy rope opener. They won't even bother going to the privy."

"I should have guessed that."

"It's a man thing. We go where we feel like it," he said as he grinned.

"Yes," she replied, "one of the many advantages of being a man."

Luke opened his saddlebags, took a dozen of the long Sharps rounds, put them in his right pocket, and then a full box of cartridges for the Winchester and dropped it into his left pocket before grabbing his Sharps and Winchester. Beth added the same number of cartridges for her Spencer and her Winchester and followed. They reached the edge of the forest and leaned their weapons against a tree. The sky was noticeably lighter and the air above both chimneys was clear.

"Beth, let's set up some shooting positions. Find a tree with a low branch to use as a support and make sure it has a clear line of sight to the cabin."

"Okay."

Luke found his tree quickly and used his knife to cut the branch, so he had a shorter support that wind wouldn't move.

Beth took a little longer but found a suitable tree thirty feet away.

"Are you comfortable, Beth?"

"As well as I could hope to be, Luke."

Luke moved his Sharps to his selected firing location, and after leaning it against the trunk, he advised Beth to do the same as it could be a while before there was any movement from the cabin.

Once they were settled into their positions, he watched the cabin but would glance over at Beth to get a gauge of her mood as the time for action drew near. She seemed all right but would shift her eyes away from the cabin often as if she didn't want to see what was going to happen and that gave him concern.

The sun came up at 7:47 and there was still no sign of life in the cabin.

"Are you sure they're in there, Luke?" she asked, looking at him, and not the cabin.

"They're in there. Nobody wants to get out of their warm beds and do the work of starting the fire. Charlie Basset will have to get one of them to do it."

That was exactly the situation inside the cabin. Each of the men had to go outside, but none wanted to be the first, or leave the warmth of their beds. Finally, Charlie, who shared the doored bedroom with Philly, snarled, "Get your ass out of bed, Philly, and get that fire started."

Philly grumbled as he slid out of bed and into the cool air of the fireless cabin. He quickly slipped on his boots and scrambled to the back door, then hesitated, half-expecting a gunshot but opened the door. He glanced at the open barn doors then went outside, returned seconds later closed the door, and started the cookstove fire. Once it was going, he headed to the main room and took ten minutes to get the main fire going. As he was returning to fill the coffeepot, Charlie raced past and went out the back door, knowing no one was out there. Mack and Joe followed three minutes later.

"There's the smoke, Beth. They're awake now. They've already probably taken care of business out the back door, so they'll go and have breakfast now. How much time do we give them?"

"Not much, I don't think. The longer we give them the warmer they get and the colder we get."

"Good call, Beth. Let's go and wake them up. Shall we?" he said as he grinned.

Beth nodded and watched as Luke picked up his Sharps.

Luke noted her drop in enthusiasm for the mission and came close to asking if she wanted to just return to the tent but didn't. He wanted to put a round through the door to get the range set properly.

Luke had left the chamber empty to make sure the cartridge wouldn't be frozen in position, so he pulled one out of his pocket, opened the breech, and slid the long cartridge inside. He closed the breech, but before he cocked the hammer, he checked the range. He set the sight for three hundred yards then adjusted the setting on the ladder sight, taking into allowance the temperature and the altitude.

Once he was satisfied, he set the barrel of the big rifle on his branch support, aimed his sights at a point dead center on the big front door let out his breath, and squeezed the trigger.

Inside the boys were all anxiously awaiting breakfast when there was a sudden crash at the front door followed by a large boom. They all ducked automatically, and Charlie jumped from his chair, then trotted a few feet down the hallway toward the main room and saw the splintered door.

"They're here!" he shouted, "Must be close, too! That round punched a big hole in the door."

Philly and Joe grabbed their Winchesters and Philly asked, "What do we do, boss?"

Charlie was at a momentary loss. If the shooter put a round through the front door, he probably wanted them to come out the back door where his brothers were probably waiting. But the size of the hole in the thick door and the loud report bothered him, too.

"Hang on. Let me think," was his delaying reply then he turned and jogged to the back door and peered through the small crack between the shutters but didn't see anyone.

Charlie turned to the boys and said, "I think there's only one of 'em. We can bull rush him if we were all moving in different directions. That hole wasn't made by a Winchester or a Henry. He's got a big gun, maybe a Spencer. He can't fire as fast as we can and if he's a long way off, he's in worse shape against moving targets. Everybody get a jacket on. Don't bother with hats or gloves. We've got this bastard!"

They all scrambled to pull on their coats as Charlie began to think about the best way to avoid taking a bullet.

Luke had anticipated a mad rush from the cabin, but he didn't know which direction it would take.

He looked over at Beth who was looking at him and not the cabin.

"Beth, I want you to get ready to fire at the left side of the house. Just aim a couple of feet past the edge. As soon as I fire, count one, and then fire."

"Alright," she replied and shifted her Spencer's sights to the left edge of the house.

Luke sighted to the right of the house. He knew more would be coming out the other side as well, but he would be Beth's target. Even if she didn't hit anyone, it would force them back.

Then they just waited with their sights set on opposite sides of the cabin.

Inside, the boys had their rifles except for Mack, who had his pistol drawn feeling helpless.

"Ready?" shouted Charlie, who was conveniently in the back of the four men.

"Ready!" answered Joe who was at the front of the short line.

The bar had already been removed from the door and his hand was on the latch handle.

"Go!" shouted Charlie.

Joe yanked open the door, letting it crash into the kitchen wall, then shot through the doorway and turned right, Philly was second, then dashed out, turning left. Mack followed, and after a moment's hesitation, followed Joe.

The sound of the door slamming open was what Luke had been waiting for. Luke counted to one and squeezed the trigger. The Sharps belched a large cloud of smoke at the same time as it belched a large .45 caliber missile. It had only eight hundred and sixty-two feet to travel, so the bullet arrived just as Joe Pendleton passed the outside of the house, meeting the round with his right shoulder.

It blasted him off his feet as it quickly passed through his upper humerus, shattering the bone. The bullet, its energy greatly diminished by the bone, lodged in his right upper lung. He screamed in agony as he hit the ground. He was still alive but wouldn't be for long as he hit the snow and blood began to turn it bright red.

Mack, directly behind Joe, dug his bootheels into the snowy boards of the porch, but slid right past the edge of the porch and landed flat on his back next to Joe, who was still screeching. Mack had enough presence of mind to grab Joe's repeater and crawl back to the porch, his feet wheeling to gain purchase on the slippery surface.

As Mack was crawling for his life, Philly cleared the left side of the house. Beth had seen Luke's bullet strike Joe Pendleton and watched as he flew sideways. Her stomach reeled, as she closed her eyes and jerked the trigger. She hadn't intended her shot to hit anything, and it didn't. It was off to the left fifteen feet and high and exploded the snow nearby. Philly saw the snow volcano, then mimicked Mack and tried to stop with the same results, except he buried himself in snow as he slid into the white blanket.

Luke quickly reloaded the Sharps and cursed silently as Mack escaped his second shot, but then he caught sight of Philly desperately trying to regain his footing. Luke quickly swiveled his rifle the few degrees of arc to the left, took a quick aim, and fired.

Philly was just getting to his feet when Luke's second shot arrived. In his haste to get the shot off, Luke was low, but the round ripped through Philly's right calf as he began to run. The round had enough energy to spin him around and he found himself in the snow again but this time, he was in agony as he wailed. There was so much blood pouring from his leg he knew he didn't have much time on his earth and Philly Henderson, killer of three men and defiler of many women, began to sob.

Charlie never made it past the doorway. Now he knew there were at least two shooters. Mack joined him several seconds later as Philly's screams still rebounded across the frozen ground, but Joe had gone silent.

Once inside, Charlie barred the door and screamed, "Son of a bitch! There are at least two of 'em out there!"

Mack looked at his furious boss and knew that he had sent them all out as targets. Part of him wanted to shoot Charlie Bassett right then and there but knew that Charlie was his only chance of survival. He'd kill Charlie once he was safe.

Charlie nervously said, "Mack, we're okay inside here. They can't shoot through those walls. Stay away from doors and windows, though. Once the sun goes down, we'll go and get 'em. Right now, they're cold and we're warm."

As he nodded, Mack noticed that Philly's screams had ended.

Luke leaned his Sharps against the tree again and trotted over to Beth, who was leaning against the tree, obviously upset. Her eyes had remained squeezed tightly shut through the whole ordeal yet the screams of the two wounded men still echoed in her mind.

When he reached her, he put his gloved hand on her shoulder and asked, "Beth, are you all right?"

She shook her head violently but didn't reply.

"Let's get you back to the shelter," he said but received no response from Beth.

He led her quickly back to the shelter and set her down on the tarp. The fire was still going but was low. He tossed on some more dry branches and watched as it flared to life.

"I have to go, Beth. You just stay there."

Beth didn't respond at all, not even a nod as she kept her eyes tightly closed.

Luke took one more look at Beth then turned and jogged back to his two rifles, cursing himself for not being firm in his original decision to go alone.

Luke began trotting down the long, gentle slope, angling to the right slightly, heading for the back of the barn. It was then that he first noticed the open barn doors, wondering why they had left them that way.

Inside the house, Charlie was getting even more fidgety and despite his earlier advice, was peering through the crack in the shutters. But the angle was very limited, and he was focusing on the southwest where the first shots had originated, but Luke was already due east and still moving. After not seeing anything, Charlie stepped back.

"Mack, you see anything on your end?" he shouted.

Mack was in the kitchen, turned to Charlie, and yelled, "Nothin', boss."

If he hadn't turned to respond to Charlie's question, Mack would have seen Luke trotting by. But when he returned to peek through the crack, the narrow viewing angle showed him nothing.

Luke had found a very good position to take out the chimney. He had no cover but thought it was unimportant, at least until they realized what he was doing. At least there were only two of them now.

He had brought the Winchester's scabbard with him, so he slid the repeater into the scabbard before he set it on the nearby snow, wedging it in so he could grab the stock quickly. Then he reloaded his Sharps. This was going to be drudge work for the big gun as he aimed at a specific rock on the chimney but didn't even bother adjusting the ladder sight for the short distance and the size of the target. Not three seconds after letting his sights settle, he pulled the trigger.

The bullet, at less than fifty yards, had enormous power when it hit and exploded the rock into flying shards and dust.

"Christ Almighty! What the hell was that!" shouted Charlie as a large cloud of dust flew from the fireplace.

Mack had thought about moving to look out another kitchen window to see what had happened but quickly changed his mind and dropped to the floor instead.

Luke reloaded and took aim at an adjoining rock and fired again then watched as the rock disintegrated into pieces, many of them falling into the fireplace.

"What the hell is he shootin' at?" screamed Charlie.

Luke fired a third shot, shattering two more rocks as the hole grew and the upper part of the chimney began losing its support. Luke fired a fourth time and the chimney suddenly sagged just an inch or so. He knew the next one would do the job.

Inside, Charlie finally figured out what Luke was planning on doing and ran out to the kitchen to grab a bucket of water to extinguish the fire quickly before the chimney collapsed into the flames scattering the burning wood across the room.

Luke fired his fifth and final shot and after another rock blew apart, the chimney wobbled twice and then collapsed. It didn't topple to one side or the other, it just imploded and fell straight down into the fireplace.

Luke leaned the Sharps against the barn and grabbed the Winchester, then levered in a fresh round to make sure everything was working properly as the unused cartridge spat from the rifle and disappeared into the snow.

Charlie was waddling back to the main room with his bucket when the chimney dropped into the fire and the effect in the cabin was devastating. There was a huge cloud of dust and rock that slammed into the fire, causing flaming logs and debris to blow out across the room.

Charlie Bassett had a catastrophic problem to deal with and didn't meet the challenge well as he panicked. He looked wildly around the already burning room and decided his best bet was to escape through the kitchen. He began running, but Mack had already reached the same conclusion, and quickly opened the door and ran straight out, remembering what had happened to Joe and Philly by running left or right.

Luke fired as soon as Mack appeared, the .44 taking a small fraction of a second to catch Mack flush in the right side of his chest. His momentum kept him going including his feet, as he appeared to be running but he was really flailing as he left the porch and flew four feet before landing face-first into the snowbank. The bullet had ripped through a rib, then his right lung before stopping in his heart's left ventricle. He died before he felt the cold snow on his cheeks.

Luke kept his aim on the door as he levered in a new round, waiting for the last man.

Charlie had seen Mack take the dive and almost fell onto the porch when he tried to stop. He quickly regained his balance before he slammed the door shut as his panic level increased with each second. He was in a burning house and his only escape was under someone's rifle. He anxiously looked around the room and then hurried to the kitchen-side window. It was on the eastern wall, but the shooter might not be ready for that, so he decided to open the window and take a shot.

He unbarred the window cocked his Winchester then slowly opened the right-side shutter. When nothing happened, he calmed down, thinking he might be able to get out of this after all.

Luke was concentrating on the back door, but when he heard it slam shut, he shifted his gaze and rifle sights to the closest window and was rewarded seconds later when the shutter opened. His patience as a sniper was rewarded when he spotted a Winchester barrel begin to slide from the windowsill, and he set his sights along the top of the protruding repeater.

Charlie Bassett stuck his head up to pick up his target and just as he spotted Luke's rifle barrel pointing in his direction, he saw the muzzle flash and a large cloud of smoke bubbling from the muzzle.

Everything was in slow motion for Charlie as he watched Death approaching. He didn't see the bullet, but the last thing his mind ever interpreted before the .44 caliber slug plowed through the bridge of his nose was the distinctive crack of a Winchester. The energy from the bullet threw him onto his back on the cabin floor and after a few seconds of consciousness, he slid into perpetual darkness.

The smoke was building rapidly as the front of the house became engulfed in flames, so Luke had to act quickly.

He ran to the house and set his Winchester on the porch but before dragging the bodies of the three outlaws into the burning cabin he removed their gunbelts and dropped them on the porch. The flames hadn't reached the cookstove when he finished, so he took a few seconds to grab Charlie's gunbelt and

Winchester but had to run from the smoke-filled cabin out into the back yard.

After spending a few seconds clearing his lungs and taking in fresh air, he hung the four outlaw gunbelts over his shoulders and grabbed the three Winchesters and one Henry and headed for the barn, and leaned them near his Sharps. Then he went through the open barn doors and found their horses. They were already saddled, maybe for a quick getaway, so he stepped back outside, picked up the repeaters, carried them into the barn and slipped their rifles into the scabbards, then hung their gunbelts over the saddle horns before making a quick trail rope and leading the horses from the barn. He had to slide his Winchester and the Sharps into their bedrolls as he led them slowly to the trees as the cabin burned violently behind him.

Luke's biggest problem had been eliminated, but now there was the problem with Beth. He blamed himself, not Beth, for her distress. He should have stood firm and told her to stay home but he'd given in.

Luke had forgotten about the almost full keg of gunpowder near the inner wall and was still thinking about Beth as he led the four horses up the slope when the fire finally reached the bedroom and touched off the gunpowder.

The blast blew out the windows first and then part of the roof, making Luke lose his footing and lose control of the horses. But they didn't go far as he scrambled to his feet and quickly regained control of the animals. The already damaged and flaming wood scattered over the area and soon the barn was ablaze.

Luke shuddered when he realized how close he had been to being obliterated.

He soon crossed through the trees and when he reached the shelter, he found Beth still sitting with her arms wrapped tightly around her knees as she sat.

She had her eyes open and was glaring at him as she snapped, “Did you blow them up, too?”

Luke was startled, but asked, “Beth, are you all right?”

She stood and said tersely, “I’m fine. I want to go home now.”

“Alright.”

Luke knew whatever hopes he had with Beth were over but wasn’t sure why. He left the shelter in place around Beth as he hitched the trail rope to his horse.

“It’s time to leave, Beth. Can you get on your horse, or do you need help?”

“I don’t need your help. Now, or ever,” she snapped then stormed to her horse.

Luke pulled down the makeshift shelter and folded it until it was compact enough to fit behind his saddle. Once it was stowed, he tossed some snow onto the fire, then mounted his horse and angled it south.

Luke knew it would be a long, silent ride, especially as Beth had decided to stay behind the last of the outlaw horses, leaving a fifty-foot gap between them. Luke thought the real gap was much wider than that.

As they rode south, the smoke from the burning cabin and barn reached high into the sky. A giant funeral pyre for men who Luke hoped would be experiencing much greater pain by now.

As Luke and a sullen Beth were returning, Hal and Ann were worried, but Laura wasn't. She seemed positively ebullient, which was in sharp contrast to her mother and Hal.

Ann finally asked, "Laura, how can you be so cheerful? Beth and Luke are in danger. They should have been back yesterday."

"Mama, Luke promised me he'd kill those men on the day he found me. Luke would never disappoint me."

"But this is very different, dear."

"No, Mama, it's harder but not different. I'm going to get lunch started. They'll be cold and hungry when they arrive."

Laura bounced into the kitchen, having decided to make some Luke stew, as she called it after he'd told her how to make it when they were together in the cabin. She began adding ingredients and had everything in the pot when Hal exclaimed, "Somebody's comin'!"

Laura trotted back to the main room and joined Hal and her mother as they peered through the windows.

"It's them," said Hal then asked, "I wonder why Beth is bringing up the rear like that."

"I don't care, as long as they're safe," Ann said with a sigh of relief.

"They have four more horses, Mama. I wonder where Luke got them," Laura said as she grinned.

Luke turned down the access road trying not to dwell on Beth's obvious rejection. Why she had suddenly found him repulsive was obvious. She had seen him kill a man and knew he had killed three more. Why she had so quickly decided that bringing justice to those men was reprehensible was beyond him. He looked at his house and saw a smiling Laura pop out of the front door and wave. Luke waved back and wondered what Laura would think about what he'd done. *How would she feel after Beth told her what had happened?*

He reached the house and passed by, heading for the barn to take care of the horses.

Laura knew there was something wrong immediately. The outlaws' horses were there, all four of them, but when she saw Luke's solemn face pass by, she then quickly turned to her sister and Beth's face was much worse. It was a combination of loathing and shock. *What had happened?*

She then realized that Beth and Luke had probably spent the night together and it must have been the root of the obvious falling out. She simply couldn't imagine that Luke would have done anything to her sister.

Beth stepped down, wrapped her horse's reins around the trail hitch then walked past Laura into the house leaving the door open. Laura glanced back toward the barn, seeing Luke dismount then turned, trotted back inside, and closed the door.

Once inside, Ann rushed to Beth and hugged her but hadn't noticed the look on Beth's face.

Ann stepped back then saw the look of horror on her daughter's face and asked, "Are you alright, Lizzy?"

She answered in a monotone, "He killed them all, Mama. He shot them without a word of warning. They never even got a shot off. He murdered all four of them. Take me home, Mama. Now."

Laura was shocked. *Beth was calling Luke a murderer?*

"Alright, dear. I'll get dressed. Laura, you'll need to get dressed as well."

"I'll escort you home, Ann," said Hal despite being deeply angered about Beth's comment about Luke. *What did she expect Luke to do?*

Ann turned her eyes to him and said, "Thank you, Hal."

Hal pulled on his jacket, hat, and gloves and left the house through the back door, needing to get the story from Luke. Hal was more than just a little angry with Beth for saying that about Luke and couldn't have been prouder of what he had done.

He reached the barn and found Luke unsaddling the third of the five horses.

"Luke, what happened to Beth? She's in there callin' you a murderer."

"I'm not surprised, Hal. I saw it in her eyes after I took out the first two. They were holed up in the cabin and after I put a warning shot through the door, they tried running out the back. I took two out with the Sharps. Beth shot the Spencer, but she probably shot high intentionally or had her eyes closed. I went down and shot their chimney to pieces with the Sharps and waited. I shot them as they came out. The cabin caught on fire and I dragged the bodies inside to go up with the house. Beth simply looks at me as a killer and that's that."

"Luke, I gotta tell ya, that kinda puts me in a bind."

Luke looked over at Hal and asked, “Why’s that, Hal?”

“Well, while you were gone, me and Ann decided to tie the knot.”

“Congratulations, Hal. That’s really good news,” he said as he smiled.

“But this changes everything, Luke,” Hal said in obvious distress.

“Nonsense, it doesn’t change anything at all. You and Ann are wonderful together. You make each other happy. Beth will live in the house, and she’ll get past what she witnessed in a day or two. She’ll get on with her life and so will I. I’ll be fine, Hal.”

“Are you sure, Luke? I don’t wanna hear her sayin’ bad things about you.”

“If she does, just let them go like someone complaining about the weather. It’s her opinion and she can express it anytime she’d like.”

“You are the most forgivin’ man I’ve ever met, Luke Scott.”

“Not so much forgiving as understanding, at least in this case. I understand how she feels and why. It’s really my fault for giving in and letting her come along. I should have known better. Anyway, that problem is solved. What can I do for you, Hal? When are you and Ann going to get married?”

“We were gonna do it today after you got back. Do you think it’d be all right?”

“You’re asking the wrong person, Hal. You should ask Ann.”

"Beth wants to go home right now, Luke, so I've got to saddle all the horses."

"Doesn't everyone have to pack?"

"Ann already packed her things and Laura did too. My stuff is all packed in the small house. We just need to get the packhorses ready."

"I'll help you with that, Hal. I just need to get these last two unsaddled. Beth's horse is already saddled, and you just need yours, Ann's, and the packhorses."

"Yup."

Hal started saddling his horse while Luke unsaddled the last two outlaw horses, before helping Hal with the pack horses. When the animals were ready, he and Hal led them outside and hitched them to the rail, then Hal trotted to the small house to get his things while Luke walked into the house.

It was like a mausoleum when he entered, and he wouldn't let it stay that way. He owed it to Hal.

He looked at Ann, smiled, and said, "Ann, Hal tells me that you're getting married. Congratulations!"

Beth whirled to her left and looked at her mother but didn't say anything.

Ann smiled and said, "Thank you, Luke. We were planning on doing it today."

"That's a good idea. You'll be passing through town anyway. It shouldn't take long."

"Hal was hoping you'd be a witness."

"I'd be honored, Ann. I'll go and load your things. The pack horses are outside."

"Thank you, Luke. Hal will be very happy to hear that you're coming."

Luke smiled at her and replied, "Ann, you make him very happy and that's what matters."

She nodded with smiling eyes as Luke left to go to her room where he picked up her two bags then carried them out to the packhorse and hooked them in place. He returned and picked up Laura's things and had them hung and strapped down a few minutes later.

When Luke returned to the kitchen, he found Laura staring at him and it was very disconcerting.

"I've got to get my horse saddled again. I'll be right back," Luke said.

As Luke was leaving to saddle his horse again, Hal was loading his single bag onto the pack horse. It wasn't much.

"I've got to saddle my horse again, Hal. I'm going to be a witness at your wedding."

"Ann says it's okay?"

"She did. She said you were happy to have me as a witness."

Hal cheered up and said, "Say, Luke, I was wondering. Next spring, do you think I could buy about twenty head of cattle for Ann's place?"

"No, Hal, you can't buy one. You just come and take as many as you want come springtime. Do you need any cash?"

Hal laughed and said, “Hell, no. You and your pa been payin’ me all these years and I ain’t been spendin’ much. I probably got more money in the bank than you do.”

“Glad to hear it, Hal. You head on in and get the ladies ready to go. I’ll get my horse saddled.”

“See you in a bit, Luke.”

Hal jogged back up the porch steps and went inside as Luke headed to the barn.

As he saddled his horse Luke exhaled sharply. It had been an incredibly difficult day and he tried to put it all behind him to make Hal, Ann, and Laura comfortable. He knew he’d never be able to make Beth comfortable.

He finished saddling his horse and then led him back outside as Hal and the ladies walked out. Hal carried Beth’s bag of clothing and hooked it onto the pack horse.

Beth refused to even look at him as they mounted their horses. Laura did though, and smiled at him broadly and pointed at her stomach, and shook her head.

Luke got the message and grinned back at her and nodded. Laura wasn’t pregnant after all, and it made the morose feelings that Beth had created melt away.

They set off to Colorado City just around one o’clock and arrived an hour and a half later then went straight to the courthouse where Hal and Ann completed the necessary forms before being ushered into the chambers of Judge John Stevens. It was a sweet ceremony as Hal and Ann just seemed right for each other. After they had been pronounced man and wife, Luke noticed a small smile on Beth’s face, and Luke knew that she’d be all right in a few days.

They had to stop in the outer offices to sign more forms, and as Beth and Luke were the witnesses, they had to stand closer. Luke noticed that she wasn't as distant as she had been before. She didn't smile at him, but she didn't look at him with disgust, either.

"We're gonna get some lunch, Luke. You'll be comin' along, ain't ya?" asked Hal.

"I'd like to Hal, but I have business with Mister John R. Kingman. He'll be leaving in another hour, so I've got to get over there. Congratulations to you both," he said as he shook Hal's hand then leaned over and kissed Ann on her cheek.

After his congratulations, he simply turned and strode out the door, knowing that he didn't belong there. He stepped down into the street, mounted his horse, then wheeled him back to the east and rode to the railroad stockyards.

The wedding party had just left the courthouse and Beth watched him ride off already fighting a building sense of guilt, now that the morning gunfight was fading into her memory.

Luke reached the railroad stockyards and stepped down, looping his horse's reins over a corral fence. He stepped into the office and caught John Kingman clearing off his desk. When the stock manager looked up and saw Luke Scott, he blanched.

"Good afternoon, Mister Scott, how may I help you?" he asked.

"Good afternoon, Mister Kingman. A few days ago, I had twenty-eight head of cattle stolen from my ranch and I trailed them here. Did you happen to ship any Circle S cattle in the past few days?"

"Why, um, yes. I believe we did."

"How could that happen when the only two people authorized to sell Circle S cattle are me and my foreman, Hal Rawlings?"

"I believe the gentleman had an authorization letter from you."

Luke paused, then asked, "Was the gentleman named Charlie Bassett, perhaps?"

Kingman turned another shade whiter and choked, "I'm not sure I'm familiar with the name."

"Mister Bassett was very familiar with your name, Mister Kingman. It seems he was complaining about your attempt to give him less than the agreed price. He mentioned something about paying you back."

Kingman collapsed into his chair as he asked, "How do you know Charlie Bassett?"

Luke stepped closer and said, "He kidnapped a young lady last month ago. I rescued her, and she told me what he said."

Mister Kingman, despite the chilly temperature in his office, produced a polka-dotted handkerchief and began wiping his brow before he spoke.

"You must understand, Mister Scott, these are violent men. If I cross them, they'll kill me."

"What if I could make the four men disappear, Mister Kingman. Would that help you to see the error of your ways?"

Kingman's eyebrows peaked as he said, "Most definitely."

"Well, it's your lucky day, Mister Kingman. A few hours ago, I shot and killed all four members of the Bassett gang. They'll never bother you again."

Kingman smiled and said, "Halleluiah!"

"So, Mister Kingman, about my cattle. I'm sure that you'll be operating on the up and up now, but there is the issue of my stolen animals. Now, I'm a forgiving man, but I'm not sure if the railroad is of the same ilk."

"No, no. I understand. So, I'll just make out a draught for your stolen fifty head of cattle. The current price on cattle is $23.15 a head."

Luke didn't bother mentioning that he was being reimbursed for almost double the number of critters that had been stolen, but he was sure that the stock manager was well aware of the difference.

With a surprisingly steady hand, John R. Kingman wrote out a bank draught for $1157.50 and handed it to Luke.

"I'll be forever grateful to you for getting me out of this mess, Mister Scott. And I'm sure I can count on your discretion."

"You can. I'll see you in the spring with more cattle."

"And only you will ever sell them to me again."

"That's true now. My foreman is gone now."

"Oh? Did he die?"

"Sort of. He got married."

Kingman enjoyed a full belly laugh as Luke left the offices, then boarded his horse, and headed back into town, and stepped down before the bank. He still had the money he liberated from the Charlie Bassett fund as well, so when he deposited the draught and most of the cash, it gave him an all-time high balance of $4674.34.

He left the bank, stepped up on his horse, and left town at a good pace as the sun was setting. He didn't get back inside his empty house until well after sunset and had to start lighting lamps. After he had the fireplace going strong again, he headed into the kitchen and found a pot on the cook stove. He had to add some wood to the cook stove fire as well, then stuck his nose over the pot and the aroma made him smile. It was the same stew he had made for Laura that first day, so he stirred the stew and scooped out some of the still-warm concoction.

He sat down at the table with his stew and found it to be at least as good as the stew he had cooked for Laura.

He had a lot of work to do now, so after he finished the stew, he went back out to the barn and collected all the guns. Three repeaters and four pistols in addition to his own weapons. He had to clean and oil them, even if they hadn't been fired recently because they were an unknown. He really needed to clean his rifles, too.

After all the firearms were in his house. He cleaned his Winchesters, including the unfired one he'd given to Beth, and the Sharps, then put them away. He'd clean the others tomorrow, knowing none had been fired today anyway. He needed to check on the cattle tomorrow too, then suddenly realized that had to do everything now. His ranch had become a one-man show.

At the Star H ranch, Hal felt a little awkward when he arrived. It was his first night away from the Circle S in a long time and more importantly, it was his first night with a woman and his wife at that.

But Ann suspected he might be uncomfortable and made every effort to make him feel more at home. As it was their wedding night, they both knew what was expected of them and neither was shy about meeting those expectations.

They had already snuck off to their bedroom, leaving Laura and Beth alone in the main room.

"What happened, Beth?" Laura finally got a chance to ask.

"It was horrible, Laura. I had to keep my eyes closed. Luke just shot them."

"Didn't he tell you what was going to happen before you volunteered to go?"

"Yes, but it wasn't what I expected. It was just terrible."

"Now you've got me confused, Beth. Luke tells you he's going to go and shoot these four men. He shoots those four men and you hate him now."

"No, I don't hate him. I just thought I knew him. He was so gentle and so nice. But when he was shooting them, he was so cold and calculating. He didn't even look human."

"It was what he was trained to do, Beth. He was a sniper in the war. It was his job. He didn't like it, but it was necessary. He told me that when he was in the war, he didn't fight for a cause, he fought for his soldier brothers. Then he said that this war, the war to stop those men from harming innocent people, was a much more righteous war."

"But he just killed them, Laura!" she exclaimed.

Laura looked at her older sister and asked sarcastically, "Oh. You'd rather that they just killed Luke, then."

“No, of course not, but he could have just let them be.”

Laura was incensed and exclaimed, “*To do what? To come and take me back so they could rape me a few more times? To go and kill other girls’ fathers?* These men should have been arrested and hanged, but the law turned away, Beth. Luke knew he had to stop them because no one else would.”

“Just let me be, Laura. Please?”

“Okay. We’ll make a pact. You don’t talk about Luke and I won’t either. Alright?”

Beth smiled weakly and said, “Okay.”

Laura then stood and gave her older sister a needed hug and Luke Scott slid from a conversation in what was now the Rawlings household.

CHAPTER 5

Luke was determined not to let the Beth incident drag him down because of his promise to Ella. The next morning, he had more stew and then rode out to check on the cattle. They needed some hay, so he returned to the barn and hooked the sled behind his horse and piled three bundles of hay on top, returned to the pasture, and just forked it out of the bed onto the snow. The cattle began grazing on the gift, but not one of them thanked him either, he noted.

As he was riding back to his house, he wondered if this wasn't his opportunity to make a break from his past. He thought that come springtime, he'd just let Hal take as many animals as he wanted, and then he'd take the rest to Colorado City and start fresh.

He didn't have any hands to pay and his only real costs were food and taxes. He needed direction, but he had no idea which direction it would be.

He had more stew for lunch and figured he'd finish it off for dinner, grateful that Laura had made such a large batch.

He cleaned and oiled the outlaw guns after his stew lunch and then decided to clean the house now that he was the sole occupant. He went from room to room, making the beds and making sure the drawers were empty of anything that wasn't his.

He walked into the room Beth had used and could smell her presence as his mind reminded him of those deep blue eyes. He shook his head and continued cleaning.

At the Rawlings ranch, Hal and Ann couldn't have been happier. Everything was going so well. Beth had come out of her bad mood and seemed cheerful again. Laura, of course, had never stopped being cheerful. Both girls also made Hal feel welcome. He made a point not to bring up Luke anymore, but it bothered him. He still thought Luke Scott was the best man he had ever met, but he was the new man here and needed to keep the peace.

A few days passed, and Luke was returning to a routine. Both houses were immaculate, and the cattle were content. The horses were all brushed down and in fine fettle. Luke hadn't been paying attention to the calendar until he was in his bedroom one evening, stretched out on his bed, and saw snowflakes gently falling past his window. He stood and walked out to the porch. There was no wind, and the snow was just wafting down like small white feathers. It was a marked contrast to that hellish blizzard that had sent him so far off course.

But as he watched the snow, he looked at his watch. In a small window was the number 24. It was Christmas Eve, and he'd never felt lonelier in his life.

He gazed up at the snow and said quietly, "Ella, I know I cheated on my promise for years, but I really did try this time. I thought it would work, but it just wasn't right. She rejected me for her own reasons. If I didn't know you better, I'd swear this was a bit of spite. But you'd never do anything like that, would you? I'm awfully lonely now and don't even have Hal to talk to. But you knew that, didn't you? I think the least I can do is go to church tomorrow. I'll see you there, my love."

Luke smiled at the snow, then turned and walked back into the house.

Luke was on the road at sunrise, riding along through the soft white blanket that made the world seem clean. He could have ridden faster, but it was such a beautiful day. It was Christmas morning and it felt like it. He hadn't had a Christmas that felt like Christmas since he'd lost Ella. Luke's loneliness seemed to be a creature of the night as he felt alive and in good spirits.

He reached town and turned toward the Methodist church, already seeing a line of worshippers heading for the door, as he expected. Luke entered the church, removing his Stetson as he passed the doors, and took a seat in the back pew. He wasn't a regular churchgoer, so he felt if he sat any closer, it might put him in danger of being struck by lightning.

He was sitting and staring ahead when he glanced to his right and saw the stream of worshippers entering. Among them were Hal and Ann, followed by Laura and Beth. They didn't see Luke, and he was grateful for that. They found a pew across the aisle and three rows in front of him.

The service was joyful and well received by the congregation, the lack of fire and brimstone was appreciated and as soon as the Christmas service ended, Luke slid out of his pew and left the church quickly. He practically ran to his horse, mounted, and had him at a medium trot as he passed the church.

As he passed the door, he took a quick glimpse at the entrance and caught a pair of dark blue eyes staring at him. He quickly turned his head back to the front and accelerated the horse to a fast trot. It was only after he had turned onto the southwest road that he felt like a coward. He hadn't even done anything wrong except to take Beth along but knew he'd pay for that decision for the rest of his life.

He returned to the house and decided he'd move to the small house because it was easier to heat, so he moved some clothes to the small house and made himself a Christmas meal of ham and beans.

Despite his early morning high spirits, as he sat at the table, he poked at his food and mumbled, "Merry Christmas."

At the Star H ranch, there was a true Christmas feast and shared presents. Ann was very grateful for having her daughters with her, Hal was happy to be part of the family and everyone seemed in a good Christmas spirit. Even Beth was smiling and cheerful. But it was Laura, of all people, who seemed a bit somber. She tried to keep a smiling face, but it wasn't working.

As soon as the meal was finished, she smiled and returned to her room, closed the door behind her, then lay on her bed and was soon convulsed in silent tears. It was her deep blue eyes that had seen Luke riding away after church, and she knew he was going back to an empty ranch and had no one to share the joy of the day.

The others in the kitchen thought she had gone back to her room to admire her gifts and continued with the merriment of the day.

Two days after Christmas, another blizzard struck. This one, if anything, seemed worse than the last. Luke knew he'd have to go and check on the cattle but thought it would be pointless until the storm passed. There was no place on the ranch any better than the other. The bad news wasn't even the weather's impact on the herd, it was that the blizzard forced Luke to spend long hours indoors hunting for things to do to keep his mind occupied.

He decided that he'd add a bookcase to the main house and stock it, so he'd have something to do while he was alone at night. Unfortunately, he couldn't do anything about it now. All he could do was sketch out designs for the bookcase, maybe bookcases. Then he had another revelation when he decided to turn the small house into a private library. He had all that money sitting in the bank, and if he was going to get rid of all the cattle, he had no other use for it. He began wandering around the house and looking at the construction. He'd leave the kitchen sink, but if he took out the dividing bedroom walls, he could have a full wall of books on the north side and another on the west. The more he thought about it, the more he liked the idea. He'd buy hundreds of books and no matter how long he lived alone he'd have friends on shelves everywhere.

After the blizzard subsided, he was finally able to check on the herd. He found that he'd lost one steer and one cow to the storm, but it could have been worse. He took some more hay out to the cattle and returned to the house. When the weather cleared enough for a trip to Colorado City, he saddled a pack horse, rode into town, then stepped down at Salk's and after entering the store, brought his list to Frank Salk.

As Frank did a quick scan of the list of supplies, Luke asked, "Say, Frank, can I order a whole bunch of books from here?"

"Sure 'nuff. How many you lookin' for, Luke?"

"At least a couple of hundred."

"A couple of hundred?" asked an astonished storekeeper.

"Uh-huh. But I don't want to sit here and go through title by title. That would take hours."

"Well, they offer library packages. You know, for setting up whole new libraries. It's kinda pricey, though."

"How much is pricey?"

"Including shipping, a hundred and thirty-two dollars."

"How many books are in the package?"

"Two hundred. They have three different packages. One for children's libraries, one for adults, and one is mixed."

"I'll order the adult version. How long does it take to get here?"

"I have no idea, Luke. Nobody had ever ordered one before. I'd guess at least a couple of weeks."

"Will you deliver it to my place?"

"Sure."

"Alright. Add that to my bill, will you? I'll be back in a few minutes. I need to do something first."

Frank waved Luke's list in the air and said, "It'll take me a while to get this stuff ready anyway. Do you want this all packed in those panniers?"

"If it'll all fit," he replied as he grinned.

"I'll make it fit."

Luke waved and left the store. When he had been riding in, he had passed the livery and had been intrigued by a horse in their corral.

He walked to the livery and walked inside, shouting, “Hank! You in here?”

Hank Akins popped out of his dry room and said, “Luke! I haven’t seen you in ages. What you up to?”

“Like everyone else, trying to keep from freezing.”

“It’s been a bad winter already and it’s just gettin’ started. What are you needing?”

“What’s the story on that little filly in the corral?”

“She’s a beauty, isn’t she?”

“She surely is.”

“She’s four years old and fully grown, just not that big.”

“Can I go look at her?”

“Sure. Let’s go.”

They walked out to the corral. The filly was only about fourteen hands, but she was a solid, deep black with a coat that appeared blue in the sunlight when she turned the right way. She was almost iridescent, but just as importantly, her demeanor was peaceful as she calmly looked at Luke while he rubbed her neck.

“She seems pretty smart.”

“She is. Has a really pleasant gait, too. She’s a bit too nice to use to move cattle, Luke.”

"I know. She'd be a gift."

"Who's the lucky lady?" Hank asked as he grinned.

"Just a young lady that would enjoy having her."

"Then I'll make you a good price on her, Luke."

He did, too. Luke paid for the horse and then led her back to Salk's. He didn't want to buy a used saddle, so he stopped at Cheatham's leather shop and bought a complete set of new tack, but had to have the saddlebags modified, so he'd pick them up in a week or so. He saddled the mare and was pleased with the effect. The saddle was a dark, reddish hue, which blended perfectly with the little mare's exquisite coat.

He led the saddled horse to Salk's then after tying her off to his gelding, walked inside and wrote a draft for the large bill, then he and Frank loaded the packhorse, and he looked at the small filly.

"That's one handsome young lady, Luke."

"She is, isn't she?"

Luke untied his gelding, then mounted and turned back down the main road and was soon out of Colorado City and heading back to his one-man ranch.

When he returned, he put the filly into the nicest stall in the barn and spent some time moving his supplies into the small house.

Over the next week, Luke began working on his library as the weather bounced from nasty to decent and back again. He knocked down two of the bedroom walls and used the lumber to construct the bookshelves. It took another week to finish the project, sandwiched around his other routines. He had almost completed it when a freight wagon with wide wheels rolled into his ranch with his books. He was surprised by how many were in the back of the wagon and helped the freighters unload the heavy crates into the small house. If it was dependent on weight alone, he had gotten a bargain.

After the freighters left, Luke left the books in their crates until he finished building the shelves.

Four days later, he was finished and was unloading the crates, smiling almost constantly as he read the titles. It was like an early birthday present for himself. His birthday wasn't until June when he'd turn twenty-seven years old on the 29th of the month. He placed the last volume in his bookshelves and then looked at the six empty crates. He'd find some use for them later, but for now, he just dragged them all out to the barn and hoisted them into the loft.

He returned to the small house and after he cleaned up all the loose excelsior and splinters from the shipment, his library was almost finished. There was a smaller crate that he had left unopened until everything else was done. He knew what was in the crate because of the invoice. He pried open the top and took out the large globe. It was included as part of the library package as was a large calendar. He hung the 1872 calendar on the wall as the last finishing touch. He needed some more lamps, but otherwise, his library was done.

He spent the next two weeks reading and doing his jobs. Tomorrow would be the 26th of the month and had a job to do tonight. He was lucky that the weather was holding.

———

The next day, right after supper, he walked out to the barn and approached the filly. He'd grown fond of the small horse since he'd bought her a few weeks ago, and spent a long time saddling her as he talked to her. He linked her to his horse with a trail rope and it was well after sunset when he led the small horse out of the barn and down his access road toward Colorado City, passing through town around eight o'clock and continuing west.

It was after nine o'clock when he reached the Star H ranch and noticed just a single lighted window before he dismounted. He kept his eyes on the house as he led the little filly into the barn. After unsaddling her, he put her in a stall, made sure she had water and grain, then put the saddle and saddlebags on the stall divider before he approached the filly and rubbed her nose.

"You be a good friend to Laura, sweetheart," he said as he smiled into those big brown eyes.

He gave her one more pat on the side of her neck before leaving the barn silently, mounted his horse, and walked him quietly into the night, returning to his ranch after midnight.

———

The next morning, Laura was treated to a cake and gifts from Hal, her mother, and Beth. She smiled and thanked everyone profusely, but her eyes weren't as bright as usual.

"Laura, what's the matter?" asked Ann when she followed Laura to her room while she put away her gifts.

Laura was fighting back tears as she said quietly, "I thought he'd remember."

"Who?"

"Luke. I told him that first day that I was turning sixteen on the 27th of January, and I thought he'd remember, that's all."

"Laura, you couldn't expect him to remember something from more than a month ago."

"I suppose, Mama, but it would mean so much to me if he had."

"Well, we still want you to have a special birthday. We're going to take you to a nice lunch in town in a little while."

"Thank you, Mama," she replied as she forced a smile.

Ann left her bedroom and walked to the kitchen, debating about asking Hal to go and talk to Luke.

An hour later, a still hopeful Laura was standing on the porch scanning the road to Colorado City hoping to spot Luke as Hal went to the barn to get the horses ready. He had been gone for just a minute when he popped back out of the barn and shouted, "Laura, you need to come and get your horse."

"Okay, Hal," she replied then hopped down the steps and walked carefully across the icy ground.

She looked at Hal who had a giant grin on his face and wondered why she needed to get her own horse and why he seemed so happy about it. She was still looking at Hal curiously when she stepped inside and turned to take her horse's reins.

When her eyes left Hal to look into the barn, they revealed the beautiful filly and her mouth popped open. Laura was awestruck. For a short second, she believed Hal had given her the horse and almost turned to hug him, but then almost immediately knew who had given her the horse.

She was wiping joyful tears from her eyes as she approached the horse, and was so caught up in her new horse, she almost missed the note on the nearby saddle. But once she spotted it, she quickly pulled out the small piece of paper and stared at it. All it said was, 'Happy 16th birthday, Laura'. She tucked the note into her pocket and went back to exploring the most precious gift she would ever receive.

She noticed the beautiful leatherwork of the dark saddle and then saw the matching saddlebags. Her hand flew to her open mouth as she stared. Each one had *Laura* pressed in flowing script on the flap.

"He didn't forget, did he, Hal?" she asked quietly as her fingertips slid slowly across her name carved into the leather.

"No, darlin', he didn't, and I don't think he ever will."

"I'm ashamed for ever doubting him, Hal. I won't do it again."

"You just ride that pretty little horse and be happy. I'm sure that's all he wants."

"I'll do that," she replied as she smiled softly.

Hal helped her saddle the filly, and when they were finished, Laura led her outside.

Once she reached the sunlight, Laura saw the effect on the horse's coat and gasped.

"Hal, look at her! She's glowing!"

"Well, I sure ain't seen the like before. That's one special little horse."

Beth and Ann exited the house and saw the effervescent Laura leading her new horse.

"Laura, where did you get that horse?" asked Ann.

"She's a birthday gift. Isn't she beautiful?"

"She's amazing," Ann replied as she and Beth neared the filly.

"Can I guess who gave her to you?" asked Beth.

"I'm sure it was Luke. Look, it even has my name on the saddlebags."

"Even the stirrups are adjusted for me. Are we ready to go?" she asked as she grinned widely.

Hal led three other horses out of the barn then they all mounted to ride to Colorado City. Hal and Ann were in front with Beth and an ecstatic Laura trailing. The filly rode so smoothly, and she was a gift from Luke.

Next to Laura, Beth watched her sister's joyful expression and felt a mix of jealousy and remorse. Her guilt for what she had said and how she had acted after the cabin shootings had almost evaporated. The only thing that kept her from apologizing to Luke was her pride.

Back at the Circle S, Luke could only imagine the joy on Laura's face when she saw the horse. The saddlebags had been an inspiration when he went to the leather shop.

He had found a workable routine. He'd do the housework in the early mornings, take care of the cattle and outside work during the day, clean up after dinner, and then read the rest of the night. He found that because he had ordered the library startup set, there was a wide variety available on his shelves. There were many works of fiction, of course, but there were also books on science, history, and other subjects. There was even a Bible. He guessed the inclusion of the Bible accounted for his count of two hundred and one books.

Luke was alone, but he wasn't as lonely as he expected to be because as he had hoped, the books became his friends.

———

Three weeks later, he was out in the near pasture, just beyond the back of the house when he had his first visitor since the book delivery. He knew who it was when he caught sight of the horse trotting down his access road. It was late morning, and the sun was reflecting off the glossy black coat shimmering between purplish blue and black.

His stomach did a quick flip as he saw Laura waving to him. He waved back and smiled, which was never hard when he saw Laura. She did look spectacular when riding her black filly.

Luke set down the pickaxe and began to walk toward the yard. He hadn't even saddled a horse for the morning's work as it was so close to the house. The ground was soft enough for his latest plan to add a vegetable garden this spring.

He was still sweating when Laura trotted close and he smiled up at her as he said, "Good morning, Laura. You're a marvelous sight to behold this beautiful morning."

"Hello, Luke. May I step down?"

"You know you don't have to ask, Laura. Would you like something to drink?"

"Do you have something other than coffee?" she asked as she smiled.

"I have some lemonade if you'd like."

"That sounds wonderful," she replied as she dismounted.

Luke rubbed her filly's neck and asked, "How are you doing, lady?"

The small horse nickered and nodded her head at the sound of his voice.

Laura laughed and said, "She knows you, doesn't she? You didn't sign the note, but I knew she was from you."

"I didn't want to start any trouble, Laura."

"They all knew, Luke. Hal knew the second he saw her."

"Well, as long as you like her, Laura. That's all that matters."

"I love her, Luke. She's perfect. Could I have some lemonade now?"

"Sure. Let's tie her off and go inside. Does she have a name yet?"

"I was waiting until I could come and talk to you," she replied as they walked up the steps.

Laura noticed the rocking chairs on the porch and said, "Those are new."

"Yup. I got them just a week ago. I'll show you the biggest change after we get the lemonade."

Laura trotted into the main room finding it as immaculate as she expected. They reached the kitchen and Luke walked into the cold room and walked out with a glass pitcher half full of lemonade.

“When did you start making lemonade?”

“When I was at Salk’s I found a tin of dry lemon mix. You add sugar and water and have lemonade. It’s quite good, really.”

He poured two glasses and before she could sit down, he said, “Let’s go out to the porch, Laura.”

“Why? It’s warmer inside.”

“It is, but proprieties, Miss Harper. You’re a young, single woman and I’m a bachelor.”

“We spent a lot of time alone before, Luke.”

“That was forced on us, Laura. I don’t want your reputation sullied, so out we go.”

Laura turned and headed down the hallway toward the porch with Luke following. After they were seated in the rocking chairs, Laura took a sip of the lemonade and found that Luke was right, it was very refreshing.

“Luke, why are you worried about my reputation? You know what happened to me. It’s probably all over town already.”

“Laura, we’ve had this conversation before. Any young man that shows an interest in you and takes what happened to you into account isn’t worth a second of your time. But coming to see an old unmarried bachelor is something else.”

“You aren’t that old, Luke.”

"I'll be twenty-seven in June, Laura. But enough of that. Why did you come out to visit? Is something wrong?"

"No, everything is fine. Well, mostly. I think Beth regrets what she said to you and how she acted. How close was it, Luke?"

"Pretty close. But letting her come along was my decision, Laura. I screwed up by letting her join me. I was already seeing some doubt in her eyes and even that last night when she showed all the indications that she was getting tense, I didn't change my mind. I should have told her to stay at the house and I'd take care of it. Then maybe things would have been different."

"I think she's past that now, Luke. Are you going to come by and visit so she can at least apologize and see where it goes from there?"

"No, Laura. She doesn't have to apologize at all. I made a bad decision, but she sees me differently now. If I married her, what if I had to kill another bad man in the future, would it all come back? Or would she simply hold that view of me deep in her mind and someday just let it slip out again? No, I believe that my coming to visit would only make her feel bad."

"So, you're giving up on her that quickly?"

"It was far from quick, Laura. After you had all gone, I was lonelier than I had ever been in my life. I had no one, not even Hal. But all of that time alone gave me the opportunity to do a lot of honest thinking and I knew that door had been slammed shut and locked."

"You shouldn't have to be lonely, Luke. That's not right."

"It's all right, I have hundreds of friends now, and we meet every night."

Laura looked at him with a tilted head and asked, "Hundreds?"

"I'll introduce you to them after you finish your lemonade."

Laura replied, "Okay," then upended her glass, gulped down the last of her drink, and set the glass on the porch.

"I'm done," she said as she smiled at him.

Luke smiled back, downed his lemonade just as quickly then set his glass onto the porch and said, "Let's go, ma'am."

He stood and she walked alongside as they left the porch, then headed to the small house. He opened the door and gave her a sweeping gesture to enter.

Laura walked in and stopped as she saw his friends lining the walls.

"Luke! Look at all these books!" she exclaimed in wonder as she walked along the bookcase reading the titles.

Luke smiled as she wandered along and said, "You're the first one to see them other than me, Laura."

"I assume you've read some?"

"Quite a few, really. One of them might help you with naming your horse."

Laura looked back with a smile and asked, "How can we do that?"

Luke found the volume he needed and handed it to her. It was a book on ancient mythology.

"If I were naming that beautiful filly, I'd name her after an ancient goddess, wouldn't you?"

Laura was still wearing her smile as she accepted the heavy tome and set it on one of the two tables that Luke had built using the wood from the crates. She sat down and began thumbing through the pages.

Luke took another chair and sat across the table from Laura.

She scanned page after page and suddenly stopped.

"This will work. What do you think of Nyx?" she asked.

Luke smiled and said, "The Greek primordial goddess of the night."

She looked up at his smiling face and asked, "Did you read that much already, or did you know about this one?"

"It is what I would have named her."

Laura closed the book stood and slid it back to its home on the shelf, then returned to her chair.

"Luke, what happens if you see Beth again?" she asked.

"I still like Beth, Laura. Nothing will change that. I'll be friendly with her as I should be."

"You don't think that there's a chance you could put that behind you?"

"No. It's not just a question of forgetting it ever happened, Laura. She saw it as a defect in my character, and maybe it is. To Beth, it was a critical defect, one that isn't easily forgotten."

"I told her that you had to stop them from raping and killing other innocent people and I think she's beginning to understand, Luke. I wish you'd try again. She needs you."

"No, Laura. She needs someone that will treat her well and love her. She needs someone that she can be with and not worry about what evil is buried deep in his soul. She'll find someone else."

Laura was going to continue the argument yet couldn't come up with a valid point but said, "I still think it's a waste, Luke, you shouldn't be living out here by yourself."

"It's my fate, I think, Laura. Even Ella couldn't see that."

"Fate is what we make it, Luke."

Luke's eyes popped wide and he asked, "Are you sure you just turned sixteen, Laura?"

"Positive. Someone gave me a birthday gift of a beautiful horse I'll name Nyx," she replied as she smiled back.

"Well, Laura, I'll go and saddle my horse and escort you back home. I'd feel better knowing that you didn't ride alone."

"I'd like that, Luke."

They left the small house and walked to the barn where Luke saddled a horse with Laura watching.

"Luke, why haven't you bought a horse just for yourself, like you bought Nyx for me?"

Luke stopped and looked over at Laura then replied, "You know, maybe I will. I've always looked at my horses as work animals, like smarter cattle, but after talking to Nyx for those weeks before your birthday, maybe it's time I had one for a friend."

Laura smiled but thought that Luke needed much more than a horse to talk to.

When he finished saddling the gelding, he led the horse out to where Nyx was standing, then Laura led Nyx to the trough to drink before they set off to the north and straight to the Star H rather than pass through town. It saved a good two hours on the trip. They talked continuously on the way back, never mentioning Beth again.

During that long conversation, Luke found he had to avoid thinking of Laura as a young woman. She was ten years younger than he was and needed to find a young man.

———

A month later, Luke hired two drovers to help him move some cattle to Hal's place and then the rest of the herd to Colorado City.

Luke had never seen his friend since his wedding day more than three months earlier. In fact, his only real visitor had been Laura. She'd come out twice more since then to try to convince him to see Beth again but to no avail. He began to think that maybe it would be a good idea to just put the whole issue behind him. Moving the cattle to Hal's ranch would be a good excuse to start the conversation.

The two drovers, Al Feinstein and Chuck Miller, were in their early twenties and were good at the job. They helped Luke carve out thirty head, including a bull and eighteen cows to help Hal get going. After they had them culled, they drove them due north to Hal's ranch which only took them four and a half hours now that the snow was temporarily gone. It was technically spring, but that didn't mean the snow couldn't return with a vengeance.

Hal caught sight of the small herd while they were a mile out, and by the time they were close, Hal was waiting near the barn as Luke, Al, and Chuck approached after having left the cattle in the greening pastures.

"Luke!" he shouted, "Where have you been! I haven't seen you since I got married."

"Working, Hal," he answered as he grinned then stepped down and embraced Hal in a giant bear hug.

"I brought you some critters, so you could get some work done. This is Al Feinstein and Chuck Miller, Hal. Boys, this is Hal Rawlings. He knows more about these dumb cows than all of us put together."

They both shook Hal's hand before Hal said, "Why don't you boys come on in and get some coffee. I think Ann and Beth can rustle up some quick vittles for ya, too."

The four men all turned toward the house, three leading their horses.

"Hal, you need to get this place fenced off," Luke said.

"I know, but I gotta hire a couple of hands. I need to make some improvements, too."

"Al and Chuck are looking for work. I have one more job for them and then they might want to talk to you about filling those spots."

Hal looked back at the two smiling cowhands and asked, "Is that so? Well, Luke, I'm even happier to see ya."

They reached the porch and climbed the three steps, then Hal opened the door to the kitchen, and they all walked inside.

As Ann turned, Hal said, “Ann, look what the cat just dragged in.”

“Luke!” she cried before running over to give him a hug.

“Hello, Ann. How have you been?” he asked as he smiled at her.

“You wouldn’t believe it if I told you,” she replied with a giant grin that could mean only one thing.

“You’re kidding! You’re having a baby?”

Ann blushed and nodded before saying, “Isn’t this amazing? I thought I was, well, too mature for such a thing.”

“Ann, that’s wonderful. Who’s the father?” he asked with a grin.

His little joke earned him a smack in the head from Hal, but it wasn’t unexpected.

Beth heard Luke’s voice then bounced from her bed and hurried out to the kitchen. Laura was in her room but wanted Beth to greet Luke first.

Beth quickly walked into the kitchen and smiled at Luke.

“Hello, Beth,” he said as he smiled back, “You look wonderful.”

“Thank you, Luke. How are you doing?”

Then he surprised her by stepping forward quickly and embracing her softly. After he released her, he continued as if it hadn't even happened.

"I'm fine. I just dropped off some cattle for your ranch. I've probably dropped off a couple of hands as well. Beth, this is Al Feinstein and Chuck Miller. Boys, this is Beth Harper."

The two drovers were stunned by Beth as Luke knew they would be recalling his first sight of her.

Beth made it worse by smiling and saying, "Hello."

They both quickly yanked their Stetsons from their heads and replied, "Hello, ma'am."

Beth returned her gaze to Luke and said, "Laura is very happy with her horse. She said she'd visited you a few times."

"She has. Where is Laura?"

"She's in her room. She'll be out shortly, I'm sure."

Almost on cue, Laura bubbled from her room, walked into the kitchen, and said, "Hello, Luke. I see you've brought help this time."

"Hello, Laura. Yup, I couldn't move that many cattle on my own. This is Chuck Miller and Al Feinstein. Gentlemen, this is Laura Harper."

They were both equally impressed with Laura and smiled as they passed their, 'hello, misses'.

"Hello. It's nice to meet you both," Laura said with her usual smile.

Hal asked, “Ann, can we fix Luke and the boys up with something to eat kinda fast?”

“Of course, Hal.”

Beth and Laura helped their mother prepare a quick lunch as the men went into the main room.

“Luke, Laura told me about the books. You tellin’ me that you have a bunch of paper to take my place?” Hal asked.

“If it makes you feel any better, Hal, it took about three hundred and fifty pounds of books to do it.”

‘Luke, why haven’t you stopped by sometimes? I kinda missed ya.”

“There were a couple of reasons, Hal. The easiest is that I’ve been busy. You know about the second reason.”

“I know. But I think that’s all over now. I reckon she’d be mighty pleased if you visited.”

“No, Hal. Even if she says it’s all over, it won’t be. It’s all my fault, too.”

“Laura told me that, too. Dammit, Luke! You can’t go on livin’ by yourself. It ain’t right.”

“It is what it is, Hal. For once, I didn’t cheat on my promise to Ella, and look what happened when I did. I can live with it, Hal.”

“That promise is still holdin’, Luke.”

Luke shrugged.

Al and Chuck were totally confused by the conversation but suspected it had something to do with Beth Harper.

"Hal, I'll send Al and Chuck back to you in a couple of days. If you want to hire them both, you'd be a smart man. They're hard workers."

"I'll probably take you up on that suggestion, Luke. I had the bunkhouse fixed up, so it's in good shape now."

"You need to order the posts and wire."

"Already have. They're sitting over at Salk's warehouse in back."

"Then you're on your way to a proper ranch, Hal."

"You need to do the same, Luke. And it ain't no proper ranch without a woman."

Luke shrugged again but before it could go any further, they were summoned into the kitchen for a quick lunch.

After lunch, Luke thanked Ann, Beth, and Laura for the food and stood to leave. Al and Chuck decided to stick around for a while and said they'd see him tomorrow morning for the last job, so Luke waved and left the house beginning to think he smelled bad.

He was preparing to step down from the porch when he heard, "Luke, could you wait a minute, please?"

He turned and smiled at Beth before replying, "Sure, what can I do for you, Beth?"

"Laura told me that you said you didn't have to forgive me and that it was your fault for taking me along, but could you please forgive me for what I said. They were horrible, mean things for anyone to say."

"Of course, I forgive you for what you said, Beth. I'm not sure that they weren't accurate, though. I owe you a much bigger apology for putting you into that whole situation. I had a feeling about it the night before and I'll never forgive myself for not taking my own advice. I caused you a lot of pain."

"But it was my fault for asking to come with you."

"No, it wasn't, Beth. You had no idea what to expect, even if I told you. Hearing about it and experiencing it are totally different. I had experienced it many times before, so I should have explained it to you in greater detail to make you so disgusted that you wouldn't go. I didn't do that, Beth, and for that, I beg your forgiveness."

"I forgive you for that with all my heart, Luke. I just don't want to have such animosity between us."

"I have no animosity for you at all, Beth. I still admire you and wish nothing but the best for you."

She asked quietly, "Can you never love me, Luke?"

Luke gazed into those hurt blue eyes, and answered softly, "I will probably love you for the rest of my life, Beth, but sooner or later, I may be forced to do something like that again. There is too much evil out there. Then you'll see me as a murderer without a soul again. I want you to be happy, Beth. I honestly do. You are an incredible woman, but I just don't think you'd ever be happy with me."

"Can I come and visit your ranch sometimes?"

"Of course, I'd love to see you."

Beth managed a smile nodded and said, “I’ll do that, then.”

Luke smiled then softly touched her face with his fingertips before turning and hurrying down the steps to his horse not daring to turn around. He mounted wheeled his horse and headed him for home.

Beth stood watching him leave in a tumult of emotion. *What could she ever do to change his mind?*

All the way back, Luke wondered if he had made the right decision. He had been truthful when he told her that he would love her until he died. He knew that on the night before the shootings. He had every intention of courting Beth and marrying her and everything had been so very close. Then he had done what needed to be done and he had lost everything. He didn’t regret doing it just having allowed Beth to join him.

———

Al and Chuck returned after five o’clock and joined Luke for dinner. The next day was their big move to drive the remaining cattle to the railroad stockyards and Luke would be out of the cow business.

———

They started early and drove the hundred and eight head of cattle the twelve miles to the pens in Colorado City in a little over six hours. Luke paid off Al and Chuck, thanked them for their work, and visited Mister Kingman. He left with his bank draught and deposited it in the bank, swelling his balance to an impressive $7,379.45.

He returned to his ranch the same day, arriving just before dusk. He made himself some dinner then took a much-needed bath and hoped Al and Chuck worked out for Hal. Oddly enough, he was jealous of them both. They would be taking his place with Beth and Laura as they'd be spending much more time with them and he wondered if he had unintentionally played matchmaker.

Beth was still younger than either man and both were still within six years of Laura's age so when she turned eighteen, she could marry either one unless Ann and Hal gave her permission to wed earlier. She could marry the one that would be left after the first one married Beth. He knew that many girls married earlier than eighteen and some much earlier, but he was worried about Laura.

After he finished his dinner, he stared into the empty bowl as the image of Beth and Laura in the arms of Al and Chuck flared in his imagination, then he suddenly stood, grabbed the bowl, and hurled the innocent dinnerware against the far wall, watching it explode into hundreds of sharp pieces and shards.

"That was stupid," he said aloud as he reached for the broom and dustpan.

CHAPTER 6

APRIL 16, 1872

In a mining camp, sixteen miles southeast of Pike's Peak, John and Rob Harper and Richard Swanson sat in the small shack they had built when they had arrived to find gold in the claims they had purchased.

Richard had abandoned his played-out claim three months earlier and wasn't even getting half an ounce of dust a month when he just walked away, and John's wasn't much behind. Only Rob's was still producing but not enough to put away any money, not with the prices charged at the camp's store.

"I ain't gonna put up with another winter like that last one again," complained Richard.

"Same here," agreed Rob.

John then said, "Look, that character Angus McGill who's been snooping around offered to buy our claims, Rob."

"How much?"

"Two hundred and fifty dollars."

"Two hundred and fifty? That's not even half what we paid for 'em."

"That's for both claims, Rob, so it's not even a quarter, but I think we should take it. Mine's just about played out and yours isn't much better. We aren't making any money here. I say we take the man's money while we can along with the dust we've got and head back to the ranch."

"What'll that do for us? The old man will still think he's the boss."

"Well, things have changed, Rob. We're not kids anymore. We're tough now. This mining has made us stronger. Hell, either one of us could take the old man. We make him do what we want now."

"Okay, we go back to the ranch, and then what?"

"He probably has more cattle by now. We only took half of 'em. We can always grab the other half and skedaddle to California. They got a lot of gold out there and it doesn't get cold, either."

Rob grinned as he said, "Now, you're talkin'! What about the women?"

"You mean Laura and Mama? They don't matter. They always did what Pa told 'em to do. Now they'll do what we tell 'em."

Richard piped up and asked, "What about Lizzy? I'm kinda gettin' lonely for her. She sure was put together good."

Neither John nor Rob thought too highly of Richard and it showed in their reply.

Rob finally answered, "Who invited you along, Richard? McGee wants to buy our claims, not yours. You never worked the ranch, anyway. If you wanna go back to Lizzy, you figure out your own way back."

"That ain't right, John. I helped build this place and used my money to help stake your claims, too. You didn't get enough from the cattle for both of 'em."

"Hell, Richard, it wasn't even your money. It was Lizzy's money you stole."

"Well, it sure wasn't your cattle you stole, either, John."

They glared at each other for a few seconds, but John began to think that having Richard along might not be a bad idea. Three would be better than two and if their father had hired a couple of hands, they might need the extra pistol.

"Alright, you can come along. If we take McGill's offer, we can get horses and enough supplies to ride out of here. I've got my Henry and we all have pistols. We can do this."

Rob was excited and said, "Okay, John talk to McGill."

Three hours later, the transfer of the claims completed, John, Rob, and Richard began making their plans for the eighty-mile journey to their ranch.

Luke wasn't finding a horse he liked at the livery, so he asked Hank at the livery where he got his horses and was directed to Pearson's Horse Farm east of Colorado City. He was headed there now and hoped he could find something he liked. He might buy more now that the weather was nice and was already thinking big. He would hire a building firm to construct a proper stable for the horses, the cruel winter still looming large in his memory.

He found the horse farm an hour after leaving Colorado City and was already impressed with the quality of the animals in the corrals. Some were well beyond just handsome.

He approached the house and saw two men talking near the entrance. One turned and stepped away from the conversation.

“Good morning. Can I help you?”

“Yes, sir. My name is Luke Scott. I’m looking for a horse for myself and maybe some others for my ranch.”

“Well, step down and I’ll see what we can do.”

Luke dismounted and hitched his horse to the rail as Mister Pearson stepped down from the porch.

“I was just talking to my son. So, what are you looking for, Mister Scott?”

“I want a solid horse for myself and maybe a stallion and four or five mares for my ranch.”

“You don’t need any working horses?”

“No, sir. I have six horses right now for that, but I just got rid of all my cattle.”

“So,” he grinned and said, “you’re going to be competition.”

“If I am, it won’t be for ten years and never at your level. You have some incredible horses.”

“Thank you. We try to keep the good ones for breeding. Let’s see what we can find.”

They walked to a large corral containing over twenty horses, and he pointed at them as they walked.

"These are all saddle-broken and are either geldings or mares."

Luke noticed a large, chestnut gelding with four white stockings and a star that struck his fancy.

"I like the chestnut gelding with the stockings. What's his story?"

"He's five years old now. I've kept him around a little longer than I would most geldings because he's such a pleasure to look at and ride. He's got enormous staying power and can leave most of the other horses in the dust. He's an exceptional animal, and he won't come cheap, Mister Scott."

Luke smiled at him and replied, "I'd be ashamed of you if you did let him go cheap, Mister Pearson."

Eli Pearson nodded with a smile and said, "You can have him. Let's go and find you the others."

Two hours later, Luke was waving goodbye to Eli Pearson, trailing the chestnut gelding, a black stallion, and five mares. Pearson hadn't been joking about the horses not coming cheaply. He had laid out almost a thousand dollars for the horses, but as he looked behind him, he was pleased with his purchase.

He returned to his ranch in the early evening and released the horses into his own corral, then walked over to the big gelding.

"You need a name, big boy. I could call you something stupid like 'Boots', but that would be demeaning, wouldn't it? Seeing as how Laura's mare is named Nyx after the goddess of the night, I'll name you Apollo, the Greek god of the sun and light. Of course, you can't exactly father any little gods or goddesses, can you? That's his job," Luke said, pointing at the black stallion, "but you've got a better name."

As if he knew he was being addressed, the gelding plodded over to Luke who then reached over and stroked his long nose. He was an impressive horse.

He tossed in a bunch of hay and pumped the trough full before heading into the barn and unsaddling his horse. He'd head into town and see about getting the new stables built tomorrow.

He returned to the house and slipped back into his daily routine. Now that he didn't have to care for the herd anymore, it gave him more flexibility.

The Harper brothers and Richard Swanson were saddled up and glad to be leaving the mining camp. It had been almost three years of hard labor with little reward. They could have done better in the state prison.

"How long do you think it'll take us to get there, John?" asked Rob.

"I'm thinking three days. We have some rough country that we have to get around, but once we get within thirty miles, it'll be all right."

"What do we do when we get there?"

"We get a read on the place first. I figure we just walk in like we're happy to be back and see what's going on. A lot might've changed in the time we been gone. Pa might be dead and ma, too."

"Then it'll be your ranch, John. Wouldn't that be a hoot?" Rob asked.

"That would work. I'd sell the place and we'd be off to California."

Since they'd decided to leave, Richard's thoughts had all been centered on Lizzy. He'd been too long without a woman and Lizzy may have been annoying, but she was all woman. Just a few days in the saddle and he'd be able to exercise his husbandly rights.

Luke had arranged with Taylor Construction for the stables and headed to Salk's for some more supplies. He didn't need a lot, just some eggs, bacon, and other essentials, and hadn't even bothered making a list or bringing a pack horse.

He walked through the store piling his items into his arms and waddled to the counter.

Frank Salk snickered as he lowered them all gently to the counter and had them spread, roll and tumble all over the place.

"I need some eggs, too, Frank," he said as he grinned.

"Lucky they weren't in that pile, Luke," Frank replied as he smiled, then took a full basket of eggs and put it near Luke's mountain.

As he totaled and placed the items in a heavy, handled bag for him, Luke's eyes traveled to the gun case, as a boy's eyes would always wander to the penny candy.

"Say, Frank, what's that small pistol over there near the Colts?"

Frank Salk stopped and looked over.

“That’s from England, I just got two of ‘em in two days ago. Want to look at one?”

“Sure. What does it shoot, .36 caliber?”

“Nope. It uses the same ammunition as your Yellow Boy, the .44 rimfire.”

“You’re kidding! That pistol is a .44 caliber?”

“Yup. It only has five cylinders, but it’s well made and getting all sorts of good press back East. It’s even a double-action, so you don’t have to cock it before pullin’ the trigger.”

He handed the Webley Bulldog to Luke. It may have been smaller than the other pistols he had, but it sure felt good in his hand. He liked the pull of the trigger too, as he tested the double-action. He’d only read about double-action pistols.

“Does it need a special holster? It seems like it’d be lost in mine.”

“I think you could use a Pocket Navy holster, but I ordered them with these shoulder holsters, so you can wear it under your vest. It doesn’t need a hammer loop either, because the clothes hold it in.”

“You say you have two pistols and two shoulder holsters?”

“Yup. You aren’t gonna buy ‘em both are you?”

“I’m leaning that way, Frank. Go ahead and add the two pistols and shoulder holsters. I’ll play with them when I get back to my ranch. I suppose I should buy a vest or two as well.”

He turned, walked to the back of the store, found two gray vests, returned to the counter, and added the vests to the pile.

Frank packed the two Bulldogs and holsters into the bag, then carried the eggs while Luke lugged the heavy bag out to his horse. He had ridden one of the other horses because he thought hauling groceries was beneath a Greek god.

He mounted, accepted the basket of eggs from Frank, and wheeled his horse to the east and then rode in that direction until he turned onto the southwest road. He was anxious to try the new pistols. Why he decided to buy them both was beyond him, but he was grateful that Frank didn't have a dozen. He'd have a lot more weight to carry on his way home if he had.

When he returned to the house, he put the food away and took the Bulldogs into a bedroom where he stored all his guns and ammunition. It wasn't a proper gun room, but it served its purpose.

He dry-fired the guns and smiled. His only question was the accuracy with those short barrels, so he'd find out tomorrow. He still had plenty of .44 caliber ammunition courtesy of Charlie Bassett's crowd.

The next day, Luke was pleased with his self-control as he took care of all his daily chores before he went to the gun room and picked up the two Bulldogs. He put on a shoulder holster and slid a loaded Webley snugly inside, donned one of his new vests, and was impressed that the pistol and holster were invisible. He knew he didn't need it, but he still liked it.

He took the other Webley, loaded it, and headed out the back door. One of the first things he had done since disposing of the cattle was to set up a shooting range. He had targets at fifty feet, a hundred feet, a hundred yards, and two hundred yards. The target for the Sharps he didn't step off, he simply walked for ten minutes, which put it at around nine hundred yards.

He started his test-firing at fifty feet, and after firing all five chambers, he was definitely impressed, so he moved to the hundred-foot target and used the second Bulldog. He found a wider pattern but discovered that the pistol was almost as accurate as his Remington. He had reloaded his first Bulldog and reinserted it into the shoulder holster and was reloading the second one when he heard hoofbeats, then turned with a smile on his face. He knew the sound of Laura's horse by now.

She waved as she rode toward him and he waved back. He was finishing loading the second pistol as she stepped down.

"I got you at a good time, I see. You never did show me how to shoot," Laura said as she led Nyx to him.

"I apologize, Madam, for my failure to honor my chivalrous offer."

"I accept your apology, sir, and shall foreswear my orders to my headsman."

Luke bowed deeply, and said, "Thank you, Milady. I have, over the years, grown rather fond of my head."

Laura laughed, looked at his pistol, and asked, "Is that new?"

"It is. I bought two of them yesterday and just finished test-firing them both. They shoot very well."

"Where's the second one?"

Luke smiled and opened his vest.

"Well, that's sneaky," she said as she grinned.

"It's nice to have a weapon when someone doesn't know you do."

"So, can I try to shoot one?"

"Sure. It's small enough but let me empty the chambers so you can fire it while it's empty."

After removing the cartridges, Luke handed the pistol to Laura. He explained how to fire the pistol and use two hands to hold it. After she dry-fired the pistol and said she was comfortable with the gun, Luke loaded the five chambers and they walked to the fifty-foot target.

"Laura, see that target. Just point the pistol like you're pointing at something with your finger. Don't spend a long time aiming."

"Okay."

Luke stepped back and watched as Laura aimed and squeezed the trigger. The small pistol jumped in her hands and Luke watched the target. She was low but in line.

Without further instruction, Laura fired the remaining four rounds and hit the target on the last three.

She turned, grinning at Luke as she handed him the pistol.

"How'd I do, Mister Teacher?"

"Very well, Miss Student. A few more sessions and you'll be a genuine pistolero."

"Thank you, Luke."

“Laura, come on inside for a few minutes. I’m going to clean this gun and give it to you.”

“Really? Why?”

“For one thing, I promised you a pistol. For a second reason, I’d feel more comfortable if you were riding over here with some protection.”

“Where can I put it? I surely can’t wear that holster.”

“No, I don’t think so. It’s small enough for you to keep in a pocket or in a purse, though.”

“Okay. Can we shoot a rifle, too?”

“We’ll do that the next time you visit. I didn’t bring any with me today, but I can give you one for your scabbard if you’d like.”

“Then that will be another promise you fulfilled. You still have that big one hanging over you.”

“I seem to be reminded of that often. I thought Beth said she wanted to come with you.”

“She did, but she was busy talking to Chuck Miller.”

“Well, see, I was right. She’s doing better.”

“Maybe. I know Chuck sure wants to get to know Beth better.”

“And Al would like to know you better, I assume.”

“It doesn’t matter, Luke,” she said as she blushed, surprising Luke.

“Too old for you, Laura?” he asked with a smile as they reached the house.

"Age is unimportant, Mister Scott," she replied seriously.

"Oh, before we go in, I have something else to show you."

"Not another gun, I assume?"

"No, ma'am," he answered as he turned back toward the barn. They passed the barn and Luke showed her the corral full of horses.

"Look at them! Luke, those are beautiful horses. That stallion is a bit scary, though. Is he your new ride?"

"Nope. The big gelding is. If he thinks I'm talking to him, he'll come over."

Luke turned to the gelding and said loudly, "Come on over here and introduce yourself to Laura."

He was halfway through his request when the gelding's ears perked, and he began trotting over.

Laura grinned as she rubbed his neck. "I can see why you like him. He's very handsome and looks like he has a good personality."

"Want to guess his name?"

"Is it from the same book you found Nyx?"

"Yes, ma'am."

"Then you'll have to enlighten me."

"He's Apollo, the Greek god of light and the sun."

Laura smiled and said, "Well, it's too bad he's a gelding. No little gods or goddesses from him and Nyx."

“Nope. Keep Nyx away from the stallion too, unless you want to be walking in a few months.”

“So, why the horses? Are you going to start raising them?”

“Sort of. With all the cattle gone, I decided to try a different direction.”

“With the horses and the library, I’d say you’ve done that.”

They returned to the house and Luke cleaned and reloaded the pistols while they talked, laughed, and had a very enjoyable hour as Luke stretched the cleaning.

When he finished, he handed her the Bulldog.

“Luke, when are you going to come and visit the ranch?”

“I don’t know, Laura. Things seem to be settling down over there now. Beth is doing better, and Chuck seems to have filled her needs. I don’t want to disrupt anything.”

“Beth told me that you told her that you’d always love her, so why are you letting her go so easily?”

“It’s anything but easy, Laura. But I know that despite what she may feel now, I could never make her happy. There would always be that memory hiding in her mind. Even if I never fire another gun, it’ll be there. One day, she’d be angry with me for something else, and that cast-aside memory will emerge with a vengeance. With someone else, she can be happy and not have to worry about that happening.”

“So, does that mean you’re going back to your cheating ways and hiding out on the ranch?”

Luke smiled as he stared at the tabletop.

"I talked with Ella on Christmas Eve about that. I confessed to my sin of not living up to the spirit of my promise and explained that it had been close with Beth but look what happened when I did what had to be done. I don't want to go through that again."

"It wouldn't always have to be painful, Luke," Laura said quietly.

"I don't know if I can take that chance again, Laura. I lost Ella to disease and lost Beth to me just being me."

Laura didn't say what she wanted to tell him but said, "Just promise me that you won't completely give up hope."

Luke looked up at her concerned blue eyes and smiled as he said, "How could I ever deny you anything, Laura? I promise."

"I'll hold you to that promise, Luke," she said as she smiled back at him.

"So, now I have promises to keep for Ella and to you."

"Yes, but at least I'm here to make sure you keep it."

"Oh, I think Ella is still watching to make sure I keep the first one."

"I suppose I need to be getting back."

"I think so. Do you want me to escort you to the ranch?"

"Always."

"I'll go and saddle Apollo and then we'll get you home. And let's get that Winchester into your scabbard, too."

"Okay."

Luke stopped in his war room, picked up a Winchester and they left the house.

Luke handed the Winchester to Laura who slid the repeater into Nyx's empty scabbard and then walked to the corral, called Apollo over, and led him out of the corral. After saddling the gelding, he mounted Apollo for the first time, and they rode away from the Circle S.

"This is the first time I've ridden him," Luke said as he looked down at Laura.

"How is he?"

"Maybe not as smooth as Nyx, but I can feel the power. He's holding back and wants to run."

"Let's go, then!" she shouted, and Nyx spurted forward.

Luke grinned and released Apollo. The big chestnut gelding sprang away like a coiled spring, churning up the earth and throwing large clumps into the air as his hooves dug deep for purchase. Luke was exhilarated as he quickly gained on Nyx and shot past Laura, waving as he did.

Laura saw the look on Luke's face and was happy for him. She knew that Nyx was going to be no match for the big horse, but she knew that Luke needed to free himself from dwelling on his loneliness. He may not acknowledge it, but she could see and hear it in every word he had spoken.

Luke let the gelding run for five minutes before finally slowing him down, then had to bring him around to wait for Laura. He'd be a terrible escort if he left her miles behind.

He rejoined Laura after another minute then set Apollo at a slow trot to match her smaller horse's medium trot.

"He's a very fast horse, Luke."

He turned and grinned at her as he said, "It's more than that, Laura. It's the sheer power. I don't think that was as fast as he could go, either. He seemed to revel in the speed, too."

"I know poor little Nyx didn't stand a chance when you shot past us."

"It really wasn't fair anyway, Laura. It was good to let him run, though."

Laura just enjoyed riding with Luke.

Of course, he enjoyed every second he could spend with Laura at least as much.

When they were close to the ranch, Luke saw Charlie and Al putting up posts for the fence. That would be a two or three-week job and putting up the wire would take a week after that.

"Laura, could you mention to Hal it might be a good idea to put in a gate on the southern fence line?"

"He already told them that, Luke."

"Good. Well, I'm going to get back now, Laura. I really enjoyed your visit, as always."

"Thank you for the pistol and the Winchester, Luke. You just remember that last promise you made to me."

"I don't forget promises, Laura."

"And no cheating on this one, either," she said as she smiled up at him.

"No cheating," he said as he smiled back before wheeling Apollo to the south and waving as he set the big gelding off at a medium trot.

Laura watched him ride away for almost a minute before riding Nyx the last half mile to the barn.

After he'd taken care of Apollo, he returned to his house and made himself something to eat. He wasn't sure if it was lunch or dinner, but it would be the last meal he ate for the day, so it was larger than normal.

He went to the small house, picked out a book, and then returned to his bedroom in the main house.

As he started to read, he stopped and then closed the book, set it on the table beside the chair, and just stared at the front door, cursing the years that separated him and Laura. He always thought of Beth as an old version of Laura but now, months later, he began to realize why he had viewed her that way. Beth may be closer to his age in time, but Laura was much closer to him in everything else.

At the Rawlings household, Beth cornered Laura after she returned.

"So, Laura, how is Luke?"

"Lonely, I think. With no more cattle, he bought a stallion and some mares. I don't think he's going into the horse business, though. I think it just gives him something to do."

"Laura, honestly, do you think that he'll ever forgive me for what I said? I know he said he did, but I'm not sure."

"Yes, I'm sure he has, Beth. He blames himself not you, for what happened."

"Have I lost him, Laura?"

"I'm not sure. He really does want you to be happy, but he doesn't believe it will ever happen with him. He thinks that what you saw that day will always haunt you when you see him."

Beth sighed and said, "I'll admit that he may be right, Laura. Chuck Miller has been talking to me and has asked if he could visit. I like Chuck, but he's not Luke. He's not even close to being Luke. Should I settle instead of trying to convince him that it doesn't matter?"

"It's up to you, Beth. You should have come with me today instead of talking to Chuck."

"He just kept talking and I thought it would be rude to break it off to go to visit Luke. Al was asking about you, too. He's only twenty-one and I think he wants to see you more often."

"He can see me all he wants, Beth. It won't matter."

Beth was startled and asked, "Laura, you can't be serious. You're only sixteen. Luke's five years older than I am."

"I know. So, I'll spend two years talking to young men and measuring them against Luke. How do you think that will go?"

"Laura, it's probably just an infatuation for saving your life. You know that."

"Maybe. I have the time to find out, though. Don't I?"

Beth threw up her hands as Laura smiled, then returned to her room.

After she entered her bedroom, Laura closed the door and then took a seat on her bed. Let Beth and anyone else believe she was a silly, infatuated teenage girl, but she knew better. She loved Luke Scott and didn't care how long it would take for her to convince him that eleven years didn't matter to her at all. She always thought she was older inside than Beth was anyway, even when she was Lizzy.

———

Richard was trying not to whine about the cold, but it was in his nature and he had to vent about his inability to stay warm, even in the bedroll.

"Why is it so damned cold!" he groused.

"Because, Richard, we're in a pass and it's even higher than where we were in the gold fields," snapped John.

"Why didn't we just continue another three miles into the valley?"

"Because it was too dark, remember? Just shut up and we'll be getting an early start. We've only got two more days of this."

"I thought you said it was gonna be four days?"

"We made better time than I thought we would."

"That's good," Richard replied, trying to curl up inside his bedroll. He was still cold.

———

The next day, the construction team from Taylor Construction arrived. He showed them where he wanted the stable built and the foreman, Grover Wilson, agreed that it was a good site on good, level ground. He told Luke it would take about a week and a half to get it done.

The design included pumps on both sides of the stable to keep water in the long troughs along the walls. There would be sixteen stalls, two large tack rooms for storage, and plenty of wall storage as well.

He got out of their way to let them get to work and while they began to unload their supplies, Luke decided to increase the size of the corral, thinking of doubling its area. It would be good, hard work, so he soon had his shirt off on the still-cool April day as he dug post holes and split rails. He estimated he'd get the expanded corral finished tomorrow if he didn't give himself too much time off.

———

John had them moving faster than Richard thought wise because his horse wasn't as good as either John's or Rob's.

"John, can we slow it down some? My horse is laboring."

"We're almost there, Richard. We could make it tomorrow if we keep going."

"Not at this pace, John. We can still make it tomorrow if we slow down a little."

John didn't tell him that he was hoping that Richard's horse broke down, but the pace wasn't doing his horse any good, either, so he really didn't have much choice and they slowed.

Rob shot John a look and his brother shrugged. They didn't know how to get rid of Richard short of shooting him, but they had talked while he slept and decided to wait until they discovered the situation at the ranch.

Luke finished his first day of work on the corral as the construction team left for the day. They had done a remarkable amount of work that first day, and because they were working off a standard design and each man knew his job well, he doubted if it would take ten days.

He decided he needed to clean all of his body's nooks and crannies, so after heating some water, he took a long bath and felt human again when he finished. After dinner, he chose another book from his personal library and finished off the first day of construction reading a book about raising horses. As it turned out, it was a lot more than just leaving a stallion with some mares.

The next morning, Luke headed back outside, splitting rails for his new corral shortly after sunrise, and by the time the crew arrived, he had already completed one whole section of rails. They waved to Luke as they began their much more impressive construction.

John, Rob, and Richard had started early and despite Richard's flagging horse, were getting close to the ranch, and were already seeing recognizable landmarks. John estimated they were just five hours out.

"Do we stop for lunch or ride straight through, John?" asked Rob.

“I think we just grab some jerky and keep going. The horses can rest as much as they want when we get there.”

Richard didn’t comment as he was already getting excited about seeing Lizzy again.

———

Luke finished the corral in mid-afternoon, then returned to the house to clean up and have some late lunch. It felt good to do something constructive and was pleased with the enlarged corral and the progress the crew was making on the stables.

He went back to the corral and saddled Apollo, just needing to take a fast ride. Once he was saddled, he mounted the chestnut gelding and set off to the north into the pastures. He knew there was nothing there, but he had to let Apollo stretch his legs. When he neared the northern border, he slowed down and turned west.

He had ridden two hundred yards when he pulled Apollo to a stop, then grinned. Trotting toward him was a young calf. Somehow, they must have missed the little guy when they cleared out the herd, so he stepped down and walked to the calf.

“Well, little feller, it looks like you don’t want to be eaten for a while, so I’ll return you to your friends tomorrow. Right now, you stay out here and have all this grass to yourself,” he said as he smiled and rubbed the calf’s head.

He stepped up on Apollo and headed back to the house, glancing back at the lonely calf a few times wondering if he’d still be there when he returned in the morning.

———

The Swanson brothers and Richard crossed a rise and saw their father's ranch before them. They pulled to a stop on the rise and examined the ranch.

John said, "Looks like pa put in a fence finally. He couldn't have done that without help, Rob. There are at least a couple of hands in the bunkhouse we gotta deal with."

"How are we gonna handle this, John?"

"We ride in like we belong here. Hell, we do belong here. We act really friendly and get a read on what's happening. We make our play after I figure out what we need to do. Richard, you need to rein it in. Don't go getting Lizzy angry. You can act like you're sorry for doing what you did and tell her that you only did it to make her life better or some other nonsense."

"Alright."

"Okay, let's go."

They began the long ride down the decline and twenty minutes later, arrived at the access road, turned toward the house, and were spotted by Al Feinstein.

He turned to his partner and said, "Riders comin' in, Chuck."

Chuck glanced at the riders and said, "Go and let Hal know. I'll go and see who they are."

"Got it," he replied as he began trotting to the back of the house while Chuck walked to the front to greet the strangers.

Rob said, "Someone's coming, John. Looks like a hired hand."

"Remember we're just returning prodigal sons," he said as he grinned.

As they approached Chuck, they pulled up and waved.

"Howdy! I'm John Harper. This is my brother Rob and Lizzy's husband Richard Swanson. Who are you?"

"The name's Chuck Miller."

"My pa hired you?"

"No, Mister Rawlings hired us. He's the boss."

"My father died?" John asked in surprise.

"I don't know the details, but go ahead and step down and I'm sure the missus will fill you in."

They all stepped down and trotted up the stairs followed by a still-suspicious Chuck Miller.

"Mama! We're home!" John shouted exuberantly as he threw open the front door and crossed the threshold.

Ann heard the shout just as Hal learned of their arrival from Al, and she wasn't pleased. Everything was going so well. She was happy and pregnant, and Hal treated her like royalty. Now her wayward sons had returned to cause her problems as that was all they had done before they left.

Laura and Beth were in Beth's room talking about their favorite subject, Luke, when they heard boots entering the front door followed by John's shout.

Curiosity compelled them to leave the room to see what John and Rob looked like. If Beth had known that Richard was there, she would have bolted out the back door, jumped bareback on a horse in her dress, and ridden to the Circle S, but she never even suspected that he would have the nerve to return. She would discover the error in her assumption shortly.

Ann passed her daughters as she walked quickly to the main room. Hal followed right behind her and after Laura and Beth cleared the doorway, Al walked behind them.

John was pleased that the whole crowd was there. Now everything depended on the welcome that they received from their mother.

He saw her walking sternly toward him and guessed that the welcome would not include hugs and kisses.

"Mama! You look wonderful!" he said with a broad smile as he reached out to hug her.

Ann stopped a few feet short, put her hands on her hips, and said, "John, what are you and Rob doing back here? You have a lot of gall to come here after you almost bankrupted our ranch by taking more than half the cattle."

"Mama, you know we only did it so we could make more money and make you more comfortable."

"John Harper! You know I could always see through you. You are lying now like you always did. You and Rob came back because you failed and thought you could rob us again. Get out! And take that poor excuse for a man with you," she railed as she pointed at Richard.

Beth had spotted Richard standing beside Rob and a wave of nausea struck her. He was looking at her and had a sick smile on his face, making it worse. She turned to run away when she heard the loud click of a pistol hammer being cocked, stopping her cold.

"Everybody stay right where you are," said John in a steady, commanding voice.

"Now, here's what's going to happen. You three men, drop your pistols to the floor. Now."

Chuck glanced at Hal, who nodded. Rob and Richard already had their pistols drawn and cocked now, so there was no chance for heroics.

Three gunbelts clunked to the floor before John smiled and said, "Very nice. Now, I want you three gents to step forward and stand over to the right."

Hal was the first to move and walked to the right of the room by the fireplace. He was thinking of a way to attack them but there was no chance at all. Al and Chuck followed.

"Mama, you, Lizzy, and Laura all take seats. Richard, you keep an eye on them while we take care of these three."

"With pleasure, John," he grinned, meaning every word.

John and Rob marched Hal, Chuck, and Al out of the house and headed toward the bunkhouse. When they arrived, John had them all stop.

"Rob, go in there and make sure there aren't any weapons inside."

"Okay, John."

Rob spent five minutes searching the bunkhouse and found it clear of weapons of any kind.

"It's good, John," he announced when he reappeared.

“Now you three get in there. If you want those women to be safe, you stay put and just take a nice nap.”

Hal glared at the brothers as he entered the bunkhouse. Once all three were inside, John closed the door and walked back to his horse. He pulled off his rope as well as Rob’s, returned to the bunkhouse then ran two full loops around the small building using his rope and tied it off. He repeated it about three feet off the ground with the second rope and they holstered their pistols.

John looked at his brother and said, “Let’s go and have a chat with our mother.”

Rob grinned before they headed for the house then stepped up onto the porch and entered the main room.

“Well, Mama, that takes care of those three. I didn’t kill them yet, so you’d better behave. What happened to pa?”

“He was killed a few months ago when four men came and rustled the last of our cattle and took Laura away to their cabin.”

“So, she’s ruined?”

Laura snapped, “What I am is obviously no concern of yours, John. I see you haven’t changed at all. You’re still looking for easy money.”

“You’d better watch your mouth, sister. I’ve gotten a lot meaner since I left.”

She glared at him and said, “I find that hard to believe. You were a mean bastard then and still are.”

John was ready to slap Laura but held off for now.

"So, who's the old man? The foreman?" he asked his mother.

"No, he's my husband."

"You got married again? Well, isn't that cute? Two old people getting together. Well, it doesn't matter much. Do you love him, Mama?"

"Very much."

"So, you wouldn't want to see him die, then, would you?"

"You wouldn't dare!"

"How do you know? In that mining camp, men died every week, either protecting their claim or trying to take someone else's. Killing doesn't bother me much."

"What do you want, John?"

"I need money, Mother. As much as I can get. How much money do you have?"

"Not much. We have the cattle and Hal had to hire Chuck and Al to put in the fence and mind the herd."

"How big is the herd?"

"Only thirty-four animals."

"That's something. That'll get us to California without a problem. Maybe even buy us a stake, but it isn't enough. I think we might want to sell the ranch, too. Now to do that, we'll need you to come along and sign over the ranch to me. I'll let you and Hal live here until it's sold. I haven't decided on what I'll do with the other two. Lizzy will be happily reunited with Richard, I'm sure. Laura is another wild card. I'll figure out what to do with her later.

"For now, we need to eat. So, Mother, if you please, I'll watch you make us some food while Rob keeps an eye on Laura. Richard has been aching to see Lizzy again. So, get going."

Ann glared at her firstborn before she turned and walked to the kitchen. Rob sat down and indicated with his pistol for Laura to take a seat across from him.

Richard looked at Beth and grinned as he said, "Looks like I get to exercise my husbandly rights."

"You're not my husband, you, worthless bastard. I divorced you months ago for deserting me. I should have had you arrested for stealing my money, too."

Richard advanced on Beth with his pistol pointed at her gut.

"I didn't steal nothin'. I was entitled to that money 'cause I was your husband. Now I'm entitled to some favors, wife."

Richard reached over with his left hand, grabbed a fistful of Beth's hair and walked her into the first bedroom, and kicked the door closed behind him.

Laura could hear him slapping her around to get some measure of control. After that, the sounds became less violent, at least to everyone else, but not to Laura. The sounds of what Richard was doing to her sister rekindled those horrible memories that she'd worked so hard to suppress.

After they finished eating, John had the three women bound and locked in Beth's room. Beth already had bruises and cuts on her arms and face, but she wasn't crying. She was much too angry for that. She wanted to kill Richard Swanson.

John had decided that he would ride with his mother to the land office in the morning and get the deed transferred. Then when they returned, they would kill everyone and bury them in the pastures. It would take a lot of digging, but they were all used to handling pickaxes and shovels.

It would be a long night for everyone at the ranch.

CHAPTER 7

Luke was up early as the construction crew had a habit of arriving early themselves. How they managed to drive down from Colorado City and get here that early was a mystery. They'd have to leave around six in the morning.

He had breakfast and pulled out his pocket watch. It was 7:10, so he finished his breakfast and walked out to the corral. He was wearing his Remington and had grown accustomed to wearing the Webley under his vest finding that he liked having a concealed pistol. He saddled Apollo and trotted out to the pastures to find the lone calf. He wasn't hard to find, and still wondered how he'd been missed the first time. Luckily, he was old enough that he didn't need his mama.

Ten minutes later, he was leaving the ranch with the calf across his pommel. He had spread an extra horse blanket over the pommel to give the calf more comfort. He was a cute little guy.

At the Rawlings house, the three men had eaten breakfast and John had allowed Ann to clean up before their trip to the land office. He threatened to kill Hal again before they left, just to make a point. Ann had no choice. Her only thoughts were how she had managed to carry such a monster for nine months.

They left as Luke passed the halfway point between the two ranches.

Luke spotted the ranch and smiled as he saw the gated fence ahead.

"You're almost back, little feller, and maybe your mama is waiting for you," he said as he patted the calf on his noggin.

He reached the gate, opened it from the horse, and trotted inside then turned Apollo and kicked it closed. He found the herd easily enough and set the calf down and watched him trot off to join the other bovine creatures wondering if one really was his mother. It was certainly possible.

He was going to turn back but glanced at the farmhouse and felt something was wrong. It wasn't anything specific, it was just something. He stood in his stirrups and looked around at the cattle. They seemed content, so he set Apollo at a walk toward the house wondering what was itching at him.

He realized it was the quiet. It was nine o'clock, and there should be some noise somewhere. Those two hands should be out and working and horses should be moving. Something should be making noise, but nothing was.

He kept Apollo walking toward the house and decided to head behind the barn and hadn't noticed the roped-off bunkhouse as he was concentrating on the house. He parked Apollo behind the barn and left him standing, trusting that the gelding would stay put. Then he did something he thought was crazy. He unbuckled his gunbelt and hung it over his saddle horn. He wanted to look like an unarmed, non-threatening visitor. If nothing was wrong it wouldn't matter one way or the other. If there was a problem, he'd have the Bulldog.

Inside the house, Laura was sitting in the chair with Rob across from her. She had thought she could talk Rob into letting her go, but Rob seemed to be as hard as John now. Maybe he was just afraid of John. She knew that there was nothing she could do. It was like the cabin all over again. She also knew without a doubt that John and Rob would have to kill everyone for their plan to work. She only prayed for one thing. She wanted Luke to find them but the chances of that happening before John returned with her mother were almost zero. He rarely visited the ranch and there was no reason for him to show up now.

Beth was in her bedroom again, with Richard having finished his morning 'husbandly rights'. She was getting dressed as Richard smiled at her.

"You're gettin' used to me again, wife."

She glared at him and said, "You're not my husband. You're nothing more than a rapist."

"It don't matter what I am. I still took you and I'll take you a few more times before we leave."

She was going to reply when there was a knock at the front door startling her and just about everyone else. Richard pulled his pistol and cocked the hammer.

Luke had walked as quietly as he could across the porch, but when he reached the door, he pounded loudly.

Laura may have been startled but then immediately felt a surge of relief. She knew who was on the other side of the closed door. It had to be Luke. Someone had heard her prayer after all.

Rob stood and said in a threatening voice, "You'd better behave, Laura, or I'll shoot you and whoever is knocking."

Luke heard every word and unbuttoned his vest as he heard footsteps approaching the door and before it opened, put on his most disarming face. If it had been just one man, he'd shoot him when the door opened, but he didn't know how many he'd have to deal with, so he went the 'aw shucks' direction.

Rob yanked open the door and asked brusquely, "Who are you?"

"Mornin'. I'm Luke. Luke Scott. I've been callin' on Miss Elizabeth. She told me to come by today."

"She ain't here. You go away."

Luke caught a glimpse of Laura when Rob opened the door but had to focus on Rob.

"Well, if you don't mind, I'll wait. I can talk to Miss Laura, though. She's a good friend, too. Hi, Miss Laura!" he said as he grinned and waved to Laura.

Laura held up two fingers when she waved.

Luke got the message. *Thank you, Laura!*

When Rob took a second to look at Laura, Luke winked at her.

"Good morning, Luke. Come in, please." Laura said.

Rob glared at her, but Luke wasn't armed, so he thought there was no problem.

Rob snarled, "Alright, come in, but you ain't stayin'."

Luke stepped past Rob, took off his hat and looked at Laura, and asked, "Miss Laura, when do you think Miss Elizabeth will be comin' back?"

"I'm not sure, Luke. She's been tied up recently."

Luke was steamed by that hint but maintained his calm demeanor.

"I guess she's been plannin' our weddin'. I don't know if I can wait much longer. Miss Elizabeth kinda gets me all steamed up, you know."

Richard was standing just inside Beth's bedroom and had heard Luke's comments and wanted to step out into the hallway to shoot the bastard. He also wondered why Rob had even let him inside. He was a danger to John's plan anyway, but he didn't know if Luke was armed or not. He might get off a shot at him and Richard didn't like the idea of being shot, so he grabbed Beth by the arm.

"We're gonna go see your new boyfriend. You keep your mouth shut and I may not kill him."

Beth had been listening to Luke and wondered why he was talking that way and saying those things about calling on her and that they were going to get married.

But Beth nodded in agreement to Richard's threat, terrified of what was going to happen. She knew that Luke was good with guns, but Richard already had one cocked and ready to fire. She assumed that Luke's would still be in his holster if Rob let him inside, or maybe Rob already disarmed him.

Luke heard noise from the hallway pulled his gaze away from Laura and saw Richard standing behind Beth with a cocked Colt pointing in her direction. This was getting harder by the second.

Then Laura helped again.

"Luke," said Laura, "I forgot to introduce you. That is my brother Rob, and the gentleman holding a gun to my sister is her ex-husband, Richard Swanson."

"Oh. Normally, I'd say pleased to meet ya, but I don't know why Dick's got a gun to Miss Elizabeth's head like that. She's my fee-yan-say."

Richard was already annoyed with Luke and was getting angry now. Nobody called him Dick. Nobody.

Rob heard Luke call him Dick and snickered. He knew Richard's aversion to the name and thought that this might be funny to watch.

Richard snarled, "Don't call me that if you know what's good for you."

Luke saw the horrified look on Beth's face and had to get through to her to assist in the takedown.

"Now, Dick, you shouldn't oughta be pointin' that hogleg where it don't belong. Miss Elizabeth and me, we get along right nice. Why, the other night, when we was kissin', she passed out. Fell right outta my arms. I'd hate to see her do that again 'cause she's all excited right now."

Beth was listening to Luke and wondering what he was talking about. She had never kissed him at all and much less passed out.

"Well, she ain't gonna be seein' you no more. You ain't callin' on her again."

"Dick, are you tellin' me that she's done dropped me for the likes of you? I don't why she would drop me. That's worse than gettin' plugged with a .44."

"I told you to stop calling me Dick. My name is Richard!" he shouted.

Beth had finally understood what Luke wanted her to do, and just as she was figuring it out, everything else came into play.

Rob was beyond snickering, but when Luke said his next line, he lost control and began laughing ...hard.

"Shucks, Dick, I wasn't callin' you by your name, that's just a title."

Richard was so enraged, he turned the pistol away from Beth, who suddenly dropped to the floor before him.

When Luke saw the pistol start to move, he joined Beth and dropped as well, reaching behind his vest and clutching the Webley's grip.

Richard pulled the trigger of his Colt and would have hit Luke square in his chest if he was still there, but he wasn't. Luke was on his left side, aiming up at Richard as he pulled the trigger and immediately rolled to his back and took aim at Rob.

Rob's laughter had cost him. His pistol, while still cocked, was facing straight down at the floor. When Richard had fired, his finger involuntarily jerked, firing his round through the floor and into the damp earth beneath the house.

Luke fired from eight feet and his .44 caught Rob in the chest, just above the notch of the breastbone. His sixth and seventh vertebrae shattered and his spinal cord all but severed, Rob Harper dropped back three feet and crumpled to the floor. Luke turned his sights back to Richard Swanson, who was still alive but wouldn't be for long. His first bullet had ripped through his right shoulder, mangling bone and tissue.

Beth scrambled to her feet and was looking at Richard with wide, hate-filled eyes as he writhed, cried, and bled on the floor near her feet.

Luke looked to Laura and gestured to her, telling her to get Beth into her room or someplace else where she didn't have to see this. Laura hopped up from her seat and trotted to Beth and then guided her away, steering her into her room before closing the door.

Luke walked close to Richard and watched him die when he stopped bleeding as his heart failed. Luke's shot had obliterated his right shoulder and severed the brachial artery. The amount of blood he lost was massive as it pooled across the floor at the end of the hallway.

In Beth's room, Laura sat with Beth and asked quietly, "Beth, are you going to be all right?"

"He was going to kill me, Laura," she whispered as she shook.

"I think they were going to kill us all, Beth. They had to."

Beth looked at her younger sister, blinking as she asked, "Why?"

"If John was selling the ranch, he couldn't very well leave us tied up here, could he?"

The certainty of Laura's observation hit her like a runaway bull as she put her hand to her mouth and then gasped, "Our own brothers were going to murder everyone. What kind of bastards had they become?"

"The worst kind, Beth. Those are real murderers, Beth, not Luke."

"I know. He saved us, didn't he?"

"Yes. He saved us. He saved me a second time."

"I've been so wrong, Laura. So very wrong."

"Yes, you have, Beth."

There was a quick sequence of light taps on the door before Laura stood and opened the door.

"Laura, could I talk to you for a minute, please?" Luke asked.

She nodded, glanced back at Beth, and stepped into the hallway, closing the door behind her.

"You need to know what's going on, Luke?"

"Very much."

"My brothers and Richard returned yesterday afternoon. They disarmed Hal and the hands and shoved them into the bunkhouse. This morning, John took my mother to the land office to transfer ownership of the ranch to him, so he could sell it."

"He could only do that if you were all dead."

"I know."

He nodded and said, "Okay. I'll get Hal and the boys out of the bunkhouse to clean up my mess in here and I'll ride into Colorado City and see what I can do for Ann."

"Luke, thank you for saving me again," she said quietly.

"I had to, Laura. You have to make sure I keep my promise," he replied as he smiled at her before walking quickly out of the house and trotting over to the bunkhouse as Laura returned to Beth's room to talk to her.

Luke reached the bunkhouse but before he started to cut the ropes holding the door shut and avoid being bull rushed by the trapped men inside, he shouted, "Hal, this is Luke! I'm going to cut these ropes to open the door."

They had all heard the shooting and wondered what was happening believing they had shot the women, so Hal was immensely relieved to hear Luke's voice.

"Glad you made it, Luke!" he shouted back before he turned and grinned at Chuck and Al.

It took five minutes to cut through the ropes and get the door open.

Once they stepped out into the bright sunshine, Luke said, "Hal, Rob Harper and Richard Swanson are dead in the main room. Laura and Beth are in her room. They're all right, but Beth is in a state of shock because she was standing right next to Richard when I had to shoot him. John took Ann to Colorado City to get the ranch's deed transferred to him, so he could sell it."

"But he'd have to…"

"Yes, he would. My horse is behind the barn, so I'll go find Ann."

"I'll come with you, Luke."

"No, Hal. I have a big advantage. John doesn't know me from Adam. I'll be able to get close."

"Yeah, you're right. We'll take care of your mess. Go and bring me back my Ann."

"Count on it, Hal," Luke replied before jogging to the back of the barn.

Apollo was still there and eyed Luke as he jogged around the corner.

"Apollo, you're a keeper," he told the horse as he grabbed his gunbelt and strapped it on, stepped into the stirrup, and was headed down the access road just seconds later.

John was riding with his mother about four miles out of Colorado City. The deed transfer had raised no eyebrows, which surprised Ann. She had just added Hal to the ranch and had her name changed to Ann Rawlings, but she had behaved to keep Hal safe, although the more she rode with this monster who called himself her son, the more she was convinced that all she had done was to buy them some time. She didn't even mind dying herself if Hal was gone because she wanted to be with Hal always. It was the loss of the baby that plagued her. She had been so anxiously awaiting being a mother again but now she knew that it wouldn't happen. Her baby would die with her and she felt tears welling up in her eyes.

John didn't notice. He had the modified deed in his pocket and all he had to do now was to get rid of the evidence, meaning his family and those ranch hands. He should get over five thousand dollars for the ranch and the cattle. Then they'd go off to California, minus Richard, of course. He'd be in the ground with the rest of them.

As wet as Ann's eyes were, she still made out a rider coming toward them. She should know who he is as there weren't a lot of ranches beyond hers. She wiped the tears from her eyes to get a better look and when she recognized the rider now just a hundred yards away, an explosion of hope erupted inside her. *It was Luke!*

She failed, however, to make one vital deduction. He was riding from her ranch, not to it, which meant that he had already been there and may have already set things right. But Ann had been so happy to see him that she stopped thinking and just waited for him to get close.

Luke saw them coming but didn't remove his hammer loop as the motion would be spotted by John. He already thought he'd be able to talk his way in close, but he hadn't counted on Ann who was desperate to gain his attention and warn him about John.

John had been watching Luke suspiciously for five minutes. He knew that there weren't many more ranches to the northwest of theirs and he knew most of the men on those ranches, and this guy wasn't one of them. He had never put his hammer loop in place in case his mother tried something stupid and was glad of that decision which now gave him the edge.

Ann made up her mind about what to do. It would be dangerous, but Luke needed to know what was going on.

When they were a hundred feet apart, she kicked her horse. It surged forward and Ann shouted, "Luke, stop him!"

John had his Colt out of his holster and cocked before Luke could react, as he was momentarily stunned by Ann's sudden rush and cry.

As Ann raced toward Luke, he saw John taking aim and knew Ann was in the line of fire. He kicked Apollo who leapt forward right at her horse, causing Ann's mount to veer away.

John fired, and Luke felt the bullet strike his chest on the left side. He slumped forward but managed to get his pistol out of his holster and cocked. He had to bring Apollo to a sudden stop, then wheeled him around to fire at John, who was already aiming at Ann.

Ann's horrified face was still staring at her son when Luke's shot ripped past John after nicking his horse's right ear, making him rear. John had to grab his horse's mane to keep control, and his pistol flew out of his hand as he looked back at Luke. He had thought that he had killed Luke, but he was defenseless now as Luke was cocking his hammer. He dropped to his horse's neck as Luke fired, missing again at close range then John wheeled his horse to the north and exploded cross country. Luke fired once but was already feeling light-headed and missed yet again.

Ann trotted up to him and asked, "Luke, are you all right?"

"No, but everyone is safe at the ranch. You need to get back there. Hal is worried. I'll get into town and get patched up. I'll see everyone later."

"Are you sure?"

"Go," he said so he could ride quickly to Colorado City.

Ann hesitated but then turned and rode quickly toward the ranch. She knew that Luke was badly hurt, but also knew that she wouldn't be able to help him. She also had her unborn baby to worry about.

Luke watched John's dust trail still heading north and he knew Ann would be safe, so he gave Apollo a nudge and the horse set off toward Colorado City at a canter.

He arrived at Doc Spanner's office before Ann reached the ranch, stepped down, and flipped Apollo's reins over the trail hitch. He was getting woozy as he climbed the steps and it was like someone else's hand was turning the doorknob and someone else was being looked at by all the other patients waiting to see the doctor. He took three steps toward the receptionist and started to say, "I've been shot," but never got a word out of his mouth before he fell face forward to the floor.

Hal had been on the porch watching the access road since he'd cleaned himself after being held captive overnight. The boys had removed the bodies and cleaned up the blood. They were in the back yard right now but would be buried later.

He heard the distant gunfire and was worried about Ann as he paced the porch. He kept looking toward Colorado City and kept debating about just grabbing a horse and riding bareback to find her.

Laura had fixed them all something to eat and was waiting with Hal as he finally spotted Ann appearing on the road and felt tears of relief rise in his eyes.

"That looks like Ann!" Hal said excitedly and wiped his eyes.

Laura, with the sharp eyesight of youth, confirmed his identification and said, "Yes, it's my mother. But where's Luke?"

"Huh?" asked Hal then said, "That's right. Luke should be with her. Maybe he just went home."

"I don't think so, Hal."

Ann turned down the access road saw Hal and waved with a giant smile on her face. She and her baby would live, and Hal was alive, too.

Hal waved back and was happier than he'd ever been. His Ann was coming back to him and she was safe.

Laura was happy for both of them, but asked herself again, *where was Luke?*

Ann trotted up to the house and stepped down quickly as Hal rushed to her and held her close.

"Are you all right, Ann? What happened?"

"I think I messed up, Hal. I saw Luke coming and I shouted his name and John pulled his gun. I think he was going to shoot me, but Luke put his horse in between us and got shot. John was going to try to shoot me again, but Luke shot at him and he dropped his gun and ran off."

"How bad was Luke hit?" Hal asked with deep concern.

"I don't know. He was bleeding a lot from his chest and rode to Colorado City. I asked if he wanted me to come along, but he said I needed to come here to see you."

"That's just like the boy. Let's go inside."

"I'll get your horse, Mama," volunteered Laura.

"Thank you, sweetheart. I'm a bit shaken," said Ann as she and Hal walked inside.

Laura quickly led the horse to the barn and unsaddled him. Then she just as quickly saddled Nyx, mounted, and left the ranch, turning toward Colorado City.

Luke woke up after forty minutes, surprised that he felt such little pain. He knew he was bleeding when he left Ann, so he felt his chest and could feel the sutures. There were only ten or twelve.

He tried to sit up but was a bit dizzy then after a minute, tried a second time and managed to sit up. He was still on an examination table, and his shirt was a mess, but he still put it on. His Webley which was sitting on the table nearby was, well, different.

There was a large gouge in the leather. When he pulled the pistol out, he saw the gouge corresponded to a large crease in the cylinder. He put his vest on and looked at the holes. The bullet had come in at an angle more from the back, had hit the Webley, ricocheted slightly, and then ripped a chunk of flesh off his ribs before leaving through the second hole. If he hadn't been wearing the pistol, the bullet would have punched a hole right into his heart.

He vowed never to go anywhere without the Webley after he made sure that it was still functional, but the crease looked superficial.

He put on his Stetson and stepped out of the examination room.

"Doc! Are you around here somewhere?" he asked loudly.

Doctor Nathanial Spanner walked into the hall from the kitchen and glared at his patient as he said, "What are you doing walking around? You should be resting."

"I'm all right, Doc. You did a great job. How much do I owe you?"

"Five dollars, but you need to rest."

"I'll head home and get all the rest I need. Did you see where that slug hit?"

"I noticed. Did you know you'd be dead if that pistol hadn't deflected it?"

"Yup. I figured that out," he answered as he handed the Doc a five-dollar gold piece then said, "Thanks a lot, Doc."

The doctor just shook his head in disbelief as Luke went outside into the sunshine, but knew the doc was right. He needed to get some sleep and was already pretty tired.

He stepped up on Apollo turned him east and then when he hit the southwest road, he turned in that direction. It was a pretty day to be alive.

Laura arrived in Colorado City twenty minutes after Luke had gone and reached the doctor's office where she quickly dismounted and trotted up the porch steps and then into the doctor's office.

She spied Doctor Spanner walking toward his kitchen and asked, "Doctor Spanner, is Luke here?"

"He was. I sewed him up and he left. I told him he should rest for a while, but I can't keep them here if they want to leave, so he headed for home."

"How bad was his wound?"

"It could have killed him if he hadn't been wearing that pistol under his vest. If he makes it to his house, he'll be fine, but he still needs to watch out for infection and come back in two weeks to have those stitches removed."

"Thank you, Doctor. I'll go and make sure he's all right."

"Miss Harper, should you be out on the road unescorted? It's going to be dark soon."

"I'm armed and dangerous, Doctor," she said as she grinned before leaving his office.

The doctor shook his head again and mumbled something about the town going to hell in a handbasket as he continued to the kitchen to have some tea.

Laura was up on Nyx and riding out of Colorado City two minutes later.

Three miles ahead, Luke was riding easily. He noticed a bunch of riders coming his way, and he knew who they were. It was his construction crew, so he pulled out his pocket watch, but when he tried to focus on the watch, he found it difficult. He blinked and finally read the hands. It was almost five o'clock. *Where had the time gone?* He thought it should be around two o'clock.

The riders passed and waved as he rode in the other direction. Luke waved back and was going to pass a howdy to the foreman but couldn't remember his name. Oh, well. No problem.

He kept riding thinking he was doing fine as he passed the halfway point.

Laura had been gaining on the big gelding as she had Nyx running at a canter. The construction crew had been more than a bit surprised to see her but had seen her on the ranch a few times before, so they just waved as she passed by, and she returned the waves.

After another forty minutes, Luke turned onto his access road, happy with his return, and was looking forward to getting to sleep. He reached the barn and stepped down and managed to get the saddle off and pull off the blanket. He ushered Apollo into his stall and tossed in some hay. He left the tack on the floor then headed for the house lazily walking to the front of the house and up the steps. He was having the same out-of-body experience he had at the doctor's office as he entered the house leaving the door open. He just tossed his Stetson on the floor and walked into his room, took off his gunbelt, and let it fall as well. He was going to take off the Bulldog but never got that far. He finally just gave up trying to take it off and sat on the edge of the mattress before flopping down and pulling his booted feet onto the bed.

Laura reached his access road as Luke crawled onto his bed, stopped at the front of his house, dismounted, and then saw the open door and was worried. She trotted onto the porch, entered the house, and closed the door behind her. She lit a lamp, found Luke's Stetson on the floor, picked it up and walked slowly to his bedroom and found him sprawled face down on the mattress. After a few moments of terrified panic, Laura saw his chest move and sighed.

She picked up his gunbelt and hooked it over the bedpost before walking over to Luke and saw the bloody shirt and vest with the holes from John's bullet.

"What am I going to do with you, Mister Scott," she whispered.

She needed to take care of Nyx, so she left the house and walked the filly to the barn. Before she unsaddled her filly, she moved Luke's gear to their proper locations then stripped Nyx and brushed her down.

After putting grain into both horses' feed boxes, Laura returned to the house, closed the door behind her, and walked to Luke's room. He was still out, so she walked to the kitchen, fired up the cook stove, filled the coffeepot, and set it on the hotplate.

She returned to Luke's room, pulled a chair near the bed, and sat down near his head. She stared at him and wondered what she should do. It was too late to leave the house and go home, so she'd have to spend the night and didn't mind in the least, aware that her disappearance would generate talk in her home.

What did concern her was when she wondered how Beth was doing. She had seen Beth's face after Luke had killed Richard. There was hate there, but she thought it was directed at Richard, not Luke.

John had ridden north for half an hour after the encounter with Luke. He eventually stopped and was debating about returning to the ranch. His mother probably returned, but she would run into Rob and Richard. She'd be in bigger trouble if they found her, but he was beginning to wonder if they were there after all. That rider had been coming from the northwest and may have been at the ranch earlier. *But what could one man do?* Then his mother seemed to know him, so his uneasiness grew as he sat in his saddle.

He decided to go and see what was going on at the ranch before he made up his mind about where he should go, so he turned his horse and headed southwest.

An hour after John had made the turn, he was sitting on his horse looking at the ranch and didn't like what he was seeing. The bunkhouse door was open, and the two hands were digging a hole. He thought about taking them out with the Winchester but knew that it would be difficult to do. He might get one but then he'd have the other two. He snorted with disgust, then turned his horse east and headed back to Colorado City for the night.

It was a good decision because on the ranch, Hal was scanning the road for Luke, had spotted a rider watching the house, and assumed it was John and had his Winchester ready if he rode toward the house. When he saw the rider heading back to town, he watched closely until he was out of sight.

He returned to the kitchen and said, "Ann, I think John was lookin' the house over and decided to go into town."

"What can we do, Hal?"

"Our best bet is to stay here. We lock up the house and he'd have to make noise to get in."

"Alright."

Beth came wandering into the kitchen and asked, "Where's Laura?"

Ann turned and asked, "Isn't she in your room?"

"No. The last time I saw her was when she was outside with Hal waiting for you to return."

Ann said, "That's right. She took my horse and said she'd take care of it."

Beth then said, "I think I know where she went. She heard that Luke had been shot and she rode into Colorado City to make sure he's all right. I should have gone along, too."

"No, dear, you were too upset. It's all right."

Beth asked, "But what will Laura do? She needs to come back before it gets too dark."

Ann replied, “She’ll be all right if she makes it to the doctor’s office. It’s not that far.”

“What if Luke is already home and she followed?” asked Beth.

“Then she’ll be safer if she’s with Luke,” replied Hal.

Beth nodded but still wished she had gone with Laura.

Charlie and Al came inside and told Hal that the job was done, then Ann thanked them and invited them to dinner. They accepted and cleaned up outside before returning.

Charlie sat next to Beth and Al looked around for Laura.

“Where’s Laura?” he asked Hal.

“We think she followed Luke after he was shot.”

“He was shot?”

“By John. He was aiming for Ann and Luke took the bullet instead. I don’t know how bad it was, but he told Ann to head home and he rode into Colorado City.”

“And Laura chased after him? Why?”

Beth replied, “Luke saved her before and she’s kind of infatuated with him.”

Al raised his eyebrows and asked, “Really? Isn’t he a little old for Laura?”

Beth answered more out of hope than honesty, “I’m sure it’s only hero worship. She’ll get over it.”

“Good,” Al replied with a smile.

LUKE

Luke stirred and felt his Webley irritating him under his chest. *Where was he?* It took him a few seconds to recall that he had made it to his house and was in his own bedroom. He rolled onto his back and almost missed Laura sitting three feet away.

"Laura?" he asked hoarsely.

"Luke? How do you feel? You left the doctor's office and I think you barely made it home."

"What time is it?"

"Almost eight o'clock at night. Do you want some coffee?"

"That sounds perfect."

"I'll bring you some."

"No. I'll join you."

"Are you sure?"

"I'm fine. Let me get my shoulder harness off."

"Do you need a clean shirt?"

"I'll get it."

"That's alright, I'll get it for you. Which drawer?"

"The top right."

Laura opened the door and was impressed to see the shirts all neatly folded. She pulled one out and handed it to him.

"You really are a domestic god," she said as she smiled.

"I have the time now," he replied as slowly sat up, then took off the vest and the shoulder holster.

Laura examined both and was shocked at the damage.

"The doctor said the pistol saved your life."

"It looks that way," he said as he peeled off the shirt.

For the first time, Laura saw Luke shirtless and flushed as she looked. Luke was nothing like those monsters that had abused her. He was younger and more muscular, then she hunted for an appropriate adjective and decided that 'sleeker' was correct. Then she saw the wound and gasped.

"Does it hurt, Luke?"

"It stings more than hurts," he answered as he put on the new shirt and tucked it into his pants then stood.

Laura willingly accepted his arm as they walked into the kitchen, where Luke took a seat as Laura poured the coffee.

"I have cream in the cold room if you'd like some, Laura."

"No, I'm okay with black."

She took the two cups to the table, set them down, and took the chair next to Luke.

"I owe you again for saving me, Luke," she said as she looked into his eyes.

"No, you don't, Laura. They had to be stopped."

"That was a gutsy thing to do, Luke. To come into the house without your Remington. They could have just shot you straightaway."

"I know. I would have come in with a pistol drawn and cocked, but I didn't know how many were there until you told me. Thank you for that, by the way. You are a special person, Laura. You saved everyone as much as I did."

"Don't be silly. I knew what you were trying to do when you launched into your hayseed suitor routine. You wanted to draw Richard out, didn't you?"

"Yes, but I didn't think he'd have a gun to Beth's head. I had to change my angle a bit."

Laura laughed and said, "I almost started laughing myself with that whole 'call me Richard' routine. Did you do that to get Rob laughing?"

"That was an unexpected bonus. I just wanted him distracted."

"It did that and a lot more."

"How was Beth when you left?" he asked.

"She was better. I think she finally understands the difference between murderers and what you needed to do."

Luke just took a sip of coffee rather than open that can of worms again.

"It's too late for you to go back, Laura. You'll have to sleep in the next room."

"I know. It's alright."

"I'll escort you back in the morning."

"As you always do," she replied as she smiled.

Luke smiled back. He didn't see any problems for Laura because the only people who knew that she was here were her family, and they knew he wouldn't do anything. Tomorrow was Sunday, so the contractor crew wouldn't be outside to see her leave the house in the morning either.

Luke and Laura spent two more hours just talking. As usual, Luke enjoyed every second. There was nothing phony about Laura, and the longer they chatted, the more he cursed that decade-long gap that separated them.

He finally said, "I suppose we need to get some sleep, Laura."

"I suppose."

"Thank you for looking after me, Laura," he said as he smiled and stood.

She rose and smiled before saying, "I had to, Luke. I needed to make sure you keep that promise."

They adjourned to their rooms and closed their doors.

Luke told himself he had to stop thinking about Laura and found it didn't work. He still drifted off to sleep thinking of what an amazing young woman she was.

Next door, Laura had no qualms thinking about Luke whatsoever. He was the center of her life. Beth can say that it was hero worship or gratitude for saving her or anything else. She knew she loved Luke Scott with every fiber of her being and would wait as long as she needed to convince him that the age between them didn't matter because she was convinced that he loved her just as much.

———

When Laura hadn't returned by nine, the family assumed she was at Luke's or back in town. The only two that seemed perturbed by the assumption were Beth and Al.

Al thought he had a chance with Laura and Beth thought she had turned a corner in her view of Luke. She had almost died until Luke arrived. She had wanted to kill Richard, but Luke had done it instead. *How could she think poorly of someone who did what she wanted to do?* Yes, she had been shocked seeing Richard dying in a pool of blood but had recovered quickly. She began to think that something was wrong with Laura because she seemed to be unaffected by all the violence that she had experienced in the past six months. She had been kidnapped, raped, beaten, and left to die, yet she didn't seem scarred at all.

Laura's chase after Luke had inflamed her jealousy, and she was concerned that Al might give up his attention to her believing she was only interested in Luke, so she decided to tell him why Laura was simply infatuated with Luke and that there was really no reason for him to stop his pursuit of her sister.

They were all sitting at the kitchen table having coffee when Beth looked at Al and asked, "Al, could I speak to you for a few minutes in the main room, please?"

Al glanced at Chuck and could tell his partner wasn't pleased, but he was curious, and partner or no partner, if he could slip in first with Beth, he'd do it in a second.

"Yes, ma'am," Al replied then stood and followed Beth down the hallway leaving a fuming Chuck at the table.

Hal and Ann paid scant attention to their departure as they discussed Laura's decision to chase after Luke.

Al was a bit disappointed when Beth sat in a chair rather than the couch, but he sat nearby and looked at her expectantly.

"Al," she began, "I know that you're fond of Laura, and deservedly so, but I thought you should understand why she chased after Luke Scott."

"I was kinda wonderin'," Al said.

"You heard the story about how he saved her from those four outlaws, didn't you?"

Al nodded then said, "Only part of it, though."

"Then let me tell you the whole story, so you can understand my sister better."

Beth then narrated an abbreviated version of the story, including the multiple assaults by the four men, but not the details of the escape or how Luke had found her.

After telling her view of the tale she said "Well, ever since then, she's looked at him as some legendary white knight that rescued her from a dragon, but it's only an infatuation. She's still young and her only experience with men was, well, never mind. I don't believe you have anything to worry about with Luke. He's so much older than she is, but she needs some time to understand that."

"Okay, I understand," Al said, "I ain't gonna give up on her, Beth."

Beth smiled, stood, and said, "Good. Now, let's head back to the kitchen."

Al rose, grinned, and let Beth walk first as he followed behind, watching the show.

Chuck was glaring at Al when he entered, and Al just tilted his head slightly toward the bunkhouse.

Chuck then stood and said, "Well, me and Al are gonna head out and get some sleep. We'll see you in the mornin'."

Hal and Ann both waved as Hal said, "See ya, boys."

Once they were in the bunkhouse, Al explained what Beth had told him and Chuck's short duration of anger at his partner evaporated when he realized that Beth had steered Al back to Laura and interpreted that to mean she was interested in him.

Al was just titillated with the idea that Laura wasn't some inexperienced girl.

After leaving his horse at the livery, John had eaten at the café before taking a room at the hotel. When he was eating, he was listening for any gossip about the ranch and heard none, which had struck him as odd. No one seemed to know a thing about what had happened at the ranch or even about the shootout just a couple of miles out of town. Hell, the gunfire could have been heard in the streets of Colorado City.

When he had returned to his room, he lay down and began to think about his next move. He didn't have a lot of money left, less than sixty dollars, and had to get out of the area by tomorrow. Sooner or later, he'd be marked as an outlaw, probably sooner. He needed cash, maybe a new horse too, but knew better than trying to knock off the bank. He knew that some of the ranches nearby had a good amount of cash on hand. Tomorrow was Sunday, so they'd all be home, and he recalled that there was a horse ranch east of town, which would be sure to be flush with cash. He couldn't remember the name but didn't matter. He could get a horse, cash, and buy some time in the process.

He smiled. It was a good idea.

CHAPTER 8

Luke, despite his wound, woke up before Laura, snuck into the kitchen, and started the cook stove before running out onto the porch and relieving himself off the northern edge. He returned to the house went to the bathroom where he washed and shaved and then cleaned the bathroom, returned to the kitchen, and put on the coffeepot.

He had the water boiling and the coffee made before Laura made an appearance. Her hair was a disaster, but she still managed to look very perky.

"Good morning, Luke," she said as she quickly sped out the door for the privy.

When she returned three minutes later, she closed the door and said, "The coffee smells good."

"I'll be making breakfast in a minute, ma'am, help yourself to a cup."

"You don't, by chance, have a hairbrush, do you?" she asked.

"In the room you used last night, in the top drawer in the dresser."

"Really? I'll have the coffee when I return."

Laura trotted back to the room and opened the top drawer, where she found what Beth had discovered months before: hair pins and combs, the hairbrush and mirror set, and inexpensive jewelry. She looked around and realized that the room had been

Luke and Ella's room before she took the hairbrush and began to brush her long, sandy brown hair. It took a while, but she was pleased with the results as she used the hand mirror in the set. She returned the hairbrush and mirror to the drawer and walked back out to the kitchen.

Luke had the bacon made but was holding off on the eggs until Laura returned.

"Now that you're back and looking as pretty as ever, how would you like your eggs?"

"If I can't have them poached, I suppose over easy would be nice. Can you do that?"

"I could go and steal some more eggs and you could have poached eggs over easy," he said as he smiled.

Laura laughed and settled for eggs over easy.

Luke cooked her eggs and slid them out of the pan onto her plate.

Laura had poured herself some coffee and was sitting down as Luke put her plate on the table. She waited to eat until Luke had his eggs cooked and joined her.

After he set his plate down and took a seat, she asked, "Luke, are the hairbrush and things in the drawer Ella's?"

"Yes, they are. You're the first person to use the hairbrush since Ella. Would you like to take it and the mirror with you?"

"Why? Don't you want them anymore?" she asked before she began to eat.

"No, it's not that. I just want you to have them."

"Are you sure, Luke? They must mean a lot to you."

"They do, but I don't want anyone else to use them, Laura. You're special."

"Then, I'll keep them with me," she replied.

"Good."

"How are you feeling, Luke? You were shot less than twenty-four hours ago."

"Pretty sore, but I don't have any of those other effects, which kind of surprises me."

"Do you want my pistol to replace the one that was hit?"

"No, ma'am. You keep yours. I'm sure mine was just creased on a part that doesn't matter, but I'll try it later. I owe the gun that, at least."

Laura smiled and said, "I owe it a lot more, Luke. It kept you alive."

"Your brother's .44 could have missed me altogether, you know."

"Don't remind me about him. Do you know where he went?"

"No, but I'm not going to let him get away, Laura. He'll cause you nothing but trouble until he's gone, one way or the other. The sheriff surely isn't going to care."

"Don't get shot again, Luke. Please?" Laura pleaded.

"I have no intention of it, ma'am."

Laura tried to smile but failed, so she just continued to eat.

After breakfast, Luke and Laura went out to the barn to saddle Apollo and Nyx, chatting about less-worrisome topics as they walked.

As they prepared their animals, Laura placed the hairbrush and hand mirror into her special saddlebags. As she did, she spent some time thinking about just how much Luke had given her and feeling somewhat guilty about it. He had given her Nyx, the beautiful saddle and saddlebags, the hairbrush, and, most importantly, her life. But he had given her more than just her life, he had given her a reason to live. Those first few hours they had spent together had changed her life more than he could ever know and she felt even then that she could never repay him.

Yet her guilt stemmed from the fact that she had never given him anything at all, not realizing just how much pleasure she had given him just by being with him. She would have been surprised to think that Luke thought he got the better part of the deal.

They rode back as they always did, chatting amiably and laughing often, as usual. Unfortunately, the ride had to end when they reached the gate.

Luke leaned down, opened the gate, and let Laura ride through before closing it behind him. They continued to talk as they crossed the pastures to the house. Luke was scanning the landscape to make sure that John hadn't shown up unexpectedly.

They reached the front yard, stepped down, and tied off their reins.

Ann had been knitting baby booties in the main room, heard the approaching hoofbeats set her needles down then stood, walked to the window, and after peeking outside, broke into a big smile.

"It's Laura and Luke!" she shouted to Hal.

Hal came trotting in from the kitchen with a cup of coffee still in his hand.

He reached the main room as the door opened and Laura walked in with Luke trailing.

"How are you doin', Luke?" Hal asked.

"Just a bit sore, Hal. I only came in to find out what happened with John."

"I saw him watchin' the ranch from beyond the access road an hour or so after you went into town. I couldn't leave with Ann and Beth here. I think he might have headed to Colorado City about two hours after Laura left."

"She found me passed out in the house. I guess I was pretty stupid to ignore the doc. It's a guy thing."

Hal laughed as he nodded and said, "Don't I know it."

Ann said, "If it's stupid, it's definitely a guy thing."

Luke then asked, "So, he went into town last night?"

"I ain't sure, but he mighta."

"I'm going to find out where he went. I don't want him showing up here again."

"Luke, I'll come along."

"No, Hal. You're going to be a proud papa in a few more months. Besides, I owe him for this."

"How'd he miss hittin' you square at that range?" Hal asked.

Luke was heading for the door and just answered over his shoulder, “He didn’t.”

Luke trotted down the porch steps and was mounting when Laura popped out of the house, not surprising him at all.

“Luke, would it do any good if I told you to be careful?”

Luke grinned and replied, “No, ma’am.”

He tipped his hat to Laura, wheeled Apollo to his right, and then rode out of the access road and turned toward Colorado City as she watched him ride off.

Laura sighed and then returned to the house.

———

About the same time that Luke was leaving the ranch house and climbing aboard Apollo, John was riding east out of Colorado City to find that horse farm, keeping the horse to a slow trot as he scanned the landscape. He had to spend eighteen dollars of his precious cash reserves to buy a new pistol and ammunition before he left but didn’t bother with a gunbelt as he already had an empty one when he entered the store.

Ten miles behind him, Luke had Apollo at a fast trot, eating up the miles with each stride. Luke had his Remington, his damaged Webley, and his Winchester ’66 with him as he rode. He reached Colorado City less than an hour later and his first stop was the café, figuring that if John was in town, he’d have to eat. He pulled up to the café, dismounted, and walked inside, spotted the waitress, and strode quickly to where she was picking up payment from a customer.

"Morning, Susan. I'm looking for a guy that tried to kill a few folks yesterday."

"Really?"

"Yup. He's about four inches shorter than I am, with light brown hair, and blue eyes. He'd probably have an empty holster."

"I noticed the empty holster. He was asking me about a horse ranch, but I didn't know one."

"That's a big help, Susan. Can I give you a tip even if I didn't eat anything?"

"I don't see why not," she answered as she smiled.

Luke pulled a silver dollar from his pocket handed it to her then waved before he quickly left the diner and mounted Apollo. He turned him east and set him off at a medium trot in town, then picked it up to a fast trot once he passed the last building. He needed to get to Pearson's before John did anything, knowing he must be desperate.

———

John had spotted the horse ranch easily and was riding down the access road examining all the good-looking animals with satisfaction, knowing that would be money here. He just didn't know who was in the house.

The Pearsons had just returned from church and were having their traditional after-church large, late breakfast. Eli Pearson, his wife Mary, and his two sons, Michael and John, were sitting in the kitchen enjoying each other's company. None were armed, of course. Sunday was a day of peace and family.

John decided to play it safe as he rode up to the house and then stepped down. It was a business, so he didn't need permission. He climbed the four porch steps and then after crossing the expansive, wrap-around porch knocked on the door.

Eli Pearson looked at his wife, stood, and said, "I'll get it, Mary," then left the kitchen and walked to the front door. After swinging it wide, he was greeted with the sight of John standing on the porch smiling.

"Good morning, son, what can I do for you?"

"Sir, I hate to bother you, but I need a horse to replace mine and noticed you had a lot of nice animals and I'd like to purchase one."

"I'm having breakfast with my family right now. I can help you when we're done."

"I can wait. I'll just sit on the porch if that's alright."

Eli was getting ready to close the door but felt guilty as it was Sunday and Reverend Ellison had preached about Christian charity, so he changed his mind.

"If you'd like to join us for breakfast, I'm sure there's more than enough food."

John couldn't believe his luck and said, "Why, thank you, sir, I appreciate it."

He walked into the house, and after Eli closed the door, followed him down the long hallway.

Before reaching the kitchen, Eli asked loudly, "Mary, could you set another plate for our visitor?"

"Yes, dear," she replied before standing to prepare another place setting at the table.

She was reaching for some plates when Eli and John walked into the room.

It took John less than three seconds to see that no one in the room was armed and there was no reason for him to waste any time, so he quickly pulled his new Colt and pointed it at Mary.

"Alright, all of you sit down. I need some things. You'll give me money and a horse, and I'll let you live."

Everyone was shocked by the sudden change in the atmosphere. Just seconds before, it had been a cheerful, family get-together and now this had happened.

"I don't keep much money here," protested Eli.

"Don't lie to me, old man. I see those horses out there. You're making a lot of money."

"I am, but I get paid almost entirely in drafts. I drop them off at the bank on Fridays. All I have here is about a hundred and twenty dollars in cash and eight hundred dollars in bank draughts from yesterday's sales."

"Give me the cash. Now."

"I'll get it. Don't do anything rash," Eli said as he held out his palms.

John put his back against the wall and said, "I'm keeping this pistol on your wife, mister. If you come into this room with anything other than the money in your hand, she dies."

"Alright. Alright. I'll get the money."

Eli left the room to go to his office to get the cash, furiously trying to think of some way to disarm the bastard. He didn't believe for a minute that he'd leave peacefully after he had the money.

Just after turning down the access road, Luke spotted John's horse tied out front and assumed John had bought another gun because his Winchester was still in his scabbard.

He stepped down well short of the house and pulled his Winchester, not sure of what he'd find. He decided to go around to the back to do some reconnoitering first. This may not be a long-range shot, but his ingrained sniper skills were still vital to getting the job done. He bent at the waist to keep a low profile as he trotted along with his Winchester in his left hand, passing the corner of the house less than two minutes after dismounting.

Eli knew that the odds of him or his family living much longer were slim. This man was a killer, and he thought of trying to shoot it out with him as he looked at the Colt in his drawer but knew it would mean his wife would die. He couldn't let anything happen to his Mary, so he took the cash and returned to the kitchen, still trying to come up with a solution. Maybe he would be able to take one of the kitchen knives without him noticing.

Luke had cleared the house, then stopped near the back porch and studied the back of the house. There was one window on the opposite side of the back door, but the door had a glass panel as well.

He leaned the Winchester against the porch, removed his Stetson, and set it on the ground before tiptoeing up the porch steps with his eyes glued to the windows. He set his left foot softly onto the porch, hoping there were no creaking boards, then once he had his right foot on the porch, he began to place each foot heel-to-toe slowly forward until he was just five feet away and peered inside.

He saw the family sitting at the table, and all of them were focused on something or someone to his left, so Luke shifted very slowly to his right with patience only a sniper could manage as sudden movement would catch someone's eye.

He had his cocked Remington in his hand and was fortunate that Eli arrived with the money bringing everyone's attention to him as Luke finished his slow slide to his right, then stopped and saw John's profile through the window. His Colt was cocked as well and pointed at Pearson's wife, yet no one had noticed Luke yet, but that was about to change. He could have taken the shot, but not with the pistol pointed at Mrs. Pearson. He needed to get John's attention.

He kept his pistol at waist level, aiming at John through the door. It wasn't a heavy door, so it shouldn't affect the short-range shot that much. When he was satisfied with the pistol's direction, he smiled reached up with his left index finger, and tapped on the glass door.

John was startled by the tap, then turned and saw Luke's smiling face looking at him from just six feet away.

He shouted, "Son of a..." and began to swing his Colt toward the new, much more dangerous adversary.

As soon as Luke had seen the gun shift even slightly, he pulled his trigger. His Remington blasted a hole in the door and caught John flush in the chest just as he brought his gun into position to fire. When Luke's .44 caught him in the chest his finger squeezed closed, sending his shot through the glass just inches above and to the left of Luke's head. The glass exploded, sending shards everywhere.

Luke had several pieces punch into his arm, chest, and face, but luckily none hit his eyes.

At such a short range, Luke's shot was devastating. Even after passing through the wooden door, it knocked John backward against the wall after drilling into his chest, exploding ribs before it ripped through his aortic arch, killing him instantly. John then simply slid to the floor with his eyes still wide open in disbelief.

Luke holstered his smoking pistol and began picking the largest glass splinters and shards from his body.

It had happened so suddenly that none of the Pearsons could comprehend what had just happened. One second the killer was there in total control and three seconds later he was dead and there was a hole in the now windowless door. Ira recovered first, quickly walked to the damaged door, and opened it, looking at the man still pulling glass from his shoulders and face.

He recognized Luke and asked, "Mister Scott?"

"Hello, Mister Pearson. I'm sorry I had to shoot through your door, but I had to get him to take his aim from your wife before I could shoot."

"You know him?"

"He tried to shoot his own mother yesterday and wound up shooting me. I found out he was heading here and knew he was going to do something bad. I had to stop him."

Eli Pearson, stunned by what Luke had just said, replied, *"He tried to shoot his own mother?"*

When Luke nodded, Eli realized just what kind of soulless creature had just been threatening his family and shuddered. Mary had heard the exchange and just wrapped her arms around herself tightly as she began to cry softly in relief while her sons both stared at the dead man on the floor.

Then Eli asked, "Are you all right?"

"I've got some glass splinters in my hide, but I should be able to get them all."

"Why didn't you get the sheriff?"

"Aside from the fact that it's Sunday and he'd be impossible to find; I have some issues I have yet to resolve with the sheriff. He was letting Charlie Bassett and his gang get away with a murder and kidnapping without even investigating. I wasn't about to trust him with this."

"You don't say. You'll have to tell me about that later. What will we do with the body?"

"If you or your boys could help me, we can put him on his horse. I'll take him into town and drop him off at the sheriff's office. I think I'll have a chat with him about resigning while I'm there."

Mary Pearson wiped her eyes then stood and walked to stand beside her husband.

"If you weren't covered in glass splinters, I'd give you a big hug, Mister Scott."

"Call me Luke, ma'am. Do you have an old towel I could use to get this blood off my face?"

Mary turned, walked to the sink grabbed a towel then pumped some cold water and soaked the towel before returning to the doorway and handing it to him.

Michael and John Pearson finally tore their eyes from John's body, bounded out of their chairs, and walked to the doorway.

"We'll get the body loaded, Mister Scott," said Michael.

"It's Luke."

"I'm Michael and this is my brother, John."

"Good to know you Michael, John."

They turned, grabbed John Harper's body, slid it past Luke across the porch, then carried it around the house and disappeared around the corner.

After watching his sons leave with the body, Eli said, "Luke, I can never thank you enough. He was going to kill us all, wasn't he?"

"He had planned to kill his whole family, so I would think he'd do the same here."

Eli asked, "Is everyone there all right?"

"They're all fine."

Ian smiled, and asked, "Can I guess you had something to do with that as well?"

Luke smiled back, and replied, "Yes, sir," as he continued to pull glass splinters.

He had his face cleared, but bloody, so Luke wiped his face and held onto the towel as he began working on larger shards in his arm and chest. His heavy jacket had protected him from the annoying splinters, but the bigger shards that had penetrated the thick wool would make more blood under the jacket. After another minute or so, he had pulled the last of them out and tossed them onto the porch to join the other, less destructive pieces.

"Maybe you should be the sheriff," Eli suggested as he watched.

"No, sir. I'm happy with my ranch, and I'm getting tired of getting shot."

"How are the horses doing?" he asked.

"Really well. I'm having a new stable built to keep them warm. It even has a heat stove."

"I didn't even go that far," he said as he smiled.

"I was caught in a blizzard late last year and grew to appreciate the value of heat."

The boys returned to let Luke know that the body was tied down on the horse, so Luke made his farewells and returned to Apollo as they stayed behind to begin cleaning up the mess.

He made a trail rope and led the horse out of the farm and headed back to Colorado City. He hadn't been joking about getting tired of being a target for bad men. He didn't know any more of them though and was more than ready to hang up his role as rescuer. But he had saved Laura and that made it all worthwhile.

He reached Colorado City and turned for the sheriff's office. The sheriff may not be in on Sunday, but one of his two deputies should be. He knew one of them from school but hadn't seen him in a while. He stopped at the office and dismounted, tying Apollo's reins to the hitchrail then crossed the boardwalk, opened the door, and smiled as he entered.

"Afternoon, Larry."

The deputy was grinning as he said, "Luke Scott, I haven't seen you in ages. What do you need?"

"I have a body outside."

Larry Talbot was startled, then stood and asked, "What happened?"

"I had an incident with this man on the road yesterday and he put a bullet into my side. This morning, when I got into town looking for him, I found out he was heading to Pearson's. I knew he was up to no good, and when I got there, I found that he had the entire family in the kitchen under a cocked Colt. I tapped on the glass and when he turned to shoot me, I shot him first."

"Holy cow, Luke! *Any of the family hurt?*" he exclaimed.

"Nope, but I made a mess of their door. They didn't seem to mind too much, though."

They left the sheriff's office and crossed the boardwalk to the body-draped horse.

Larry asked, "Can you write up a statement for me, Luke. I'll get the mortician to take care of this mess."

"Sure. You'll probably want to contact the Pearsons and get them to write their statements, too."

"I'll do that. You go ahead and write the statement and I'll be right back."

"Thanks, Larry."

He went into the offices and found a small office with paper and pencils, then took a seat, pulled out a sheet, and began writing.

Larry returned before he finished and walked into the small room, then asked, "Do you know his name?"

"John Harper. His family has a ranch west of town. You should know them."

"I knew Elizabeth, but I thought the brothers were gone with her husband, Richard Swanson. When did they get back?"

"They showed up a couple of days ago and put the men on the ranch in the bunkhouse and kept the women in the house under threats to kill the men if they didn't cooperate. John had his mother put his name put on the deed, so he could sell it."

"How could he sell it if they were all there?"

Luke looked at him and raised his eyebrows.

"You're kidding! *They were going to kill their own family?*"

"Yup. Then I found John riding back after he got the deed transferred and he tried to shoot his mother, but I wound up getting hit, but missed with three shots and he escaped."

"How many of the family are dead?" he asked quietly.

"None of the good ones, but John, Rob, and Richard are no longer with us."

“I’ll need statements from them too when they can come in.”

Luke finished his statement and set down the pencil, then handed the statement to a bewildered Larry Talbot.

“Larry, how much do you know about Sheriff Crenshaw?”

“He’s about the laziest man I’ve ever met, why?”

“Do you know the name Charlie Bassett?”

“Who doesn’t? We just don’t know what he looks like.”

“Why? Don’t you get wanted posters on him?”

“Nope. Not on any of his gang.”

“Doesn’t that seem odd?”

Larry scratched his chin and replied, “Now that you mention it.”

“Would it make any sense if I told you that Charlie Bassett was Sheriff Crenshaw’s cousin?”

“You’re kidding! No wonder there aren’t any posters. We’d get rumors of him operating around here, but we didn’t go out after him.”

“Do you know he killed Ann Harper’s husband, kidnapped her daughter, Laura, and took her to a cabin fifteen miles west of her place?”

Larry was getting to the point of disbelief as he mumbled, “No. Not a word.”

“Well, I got blown that way in the blizzard and found the place. I got Laura out of there and took her home before I went back. I killed them all, Larry. Burned their cabin to the ground with their bodies inside."

"Did you know there were rewards on all of them?"

"No, and I don't care. They hurt Laura and that's the only reason I needed."

"What can I do, Luke?"

"Get the sheriff in here. You don't have to be in the room, but I want you to hear what we say. I want him out of here and have a decent sheriff in his place."

"I know where he is. I'll be back in a few minutes," he said before he turned and left the jail.

Luke spent the time going over what he would say to the sheriff. He didn't know John Crenshaw that well, which was downright astonishing since he'd been the sheriff for so long. He had been elected sheriff twelve years ago and stayed on the job almost as if no one else seemed to want it.

Five minutes later, Sheriff John Crenshaw came storming down the boardwalk with Deputy Larry Talbot trailing, entered the office, and let Larry close the door.

"What's so damned important that I had to have my one day off ruined?"

Luke stood and said, "Sheriff Crenshaw? I'm Luke Scott. I own the Circle S ranch, southwest of here. I was wondering if you have heard of Charlie Bassett."

The sheriff licked his upper lip, then said, "Of course, I've heard of him."

"Have you ever seen him?"

He slipped into a defensive posture and replied, "No, I haven't. What is this all about?"

"It's about your cousin, Charlie Bassett, Sheriff."

Sheriff Crenshaw suddenly felt sick. He didn't think anyone knew because Charlie had grown up in another state and moved to Colorado fourteen years ago.

"Who told you that?" he snapped.

"He did. Did you know he was hiding out in a cabin about twenty miles northwest of here, in your county?"

"No, of course not. If I'd known, I would have chased him down and arrested him."

"Why didn't you do that after Mrs. Harper told you that he had killed her husband and kidnapped her daughter?"

The sheriff snapped, "She never did any such thing."

"You deny that?"

"Of course, I deny it."

"Well, I guess I'll just have Ann and Laura Harper tell what happened to the newspaper. They'll love the story."

The sheriff knew he could no longer keep up the front, but decided if he couldn't deny Charlie, he may as well use him.

He glared at Luke and said in a low voice, "I think that would be unwise, Mister Scott. Charlie Bassett would take a dim view of someone blaming him for something he didn't do."

"I'm not the least bit afraid of Charlie Bassett, Philly Henderson, Joe Pendleton, or Mack Johnson, Sheriff."

"Be careful what you wish for, Mister Scott. My cousin will be very angry, and you don't want to see him angry."

"Why? Have you ever seen him angry?"

"Several times, and it's an ugly thing. You're also getting me angry. Between my cousin and me, you're making some powerful enemies."

"So, you know he's operating in this area."

"Yes, he's here and he'll do what I ask. He owes me."

"For covering up all his rustling, murders, and kidnapping?"

"I've had it with you, Scott. Get out of my office. If you ever set foot in this office again, I'll toss you in jail and throw away the key."

"Sheriff, the next time I set foot in this office, you will be long gone or in jail. I killed Charlie Bassett and his whole gang. You're dangling all by your lonesome now. You have no bullies to protect you anymore. If I tell the newspaper this story, then you are in jail. It's that simple. One of two things is going to happen, you resign your office and go back where you came from, or I walk right across the street to the newspaper and have them run you out of town on a rail."

"You? You think you could kill Charlie and his boys? You're lyin'!"

"Last December, I rode out of the Harper ranch with my Sharps rifle. I'm a sniper, did you know that? Anyway, if you go out there now, you'll find nothing but ashes where the cabin and barn were. Buried in those ashes are the four skeletons of Charlie Bassett, Philly Henderson, Joe Pendleton, and Mack Johnson. I'd be happy to give you a tour, Sheriff.

"You can ask Mister Kingman over at the stockyards if he's received any more stolen cattle from your cousin. You haven't even heard a word from them either, have you? You never will, Sheriff, so you'd better accept my offer."

Sheriff Crenshaw had been getting more and more anxious as Luke went on as his story smacked of truth. He hadn't seen his cousin for a long time and thought he might have moved on, but Scott's story made a lot more sense, and the thought of them being burned to death scared the daylights out of him. Luke hadn't mentioned that they were all dead before the cabin went up in smoke for that express purpose.

The sheriff knew he was finished and needed to get out of town quickly, but luckily, he had his healthy bank account from his kickbacks and bribes.

Luke had watched the sweat bead on the sheriff's forehead and knew the sheriff understood his predicament, so he wasn't surprised at his response.

"Alright. I'll leave, and good riddance to this hell hole!" he snarled as he turned then stormed out of the office.

After the door slammed Larry walked into the room and whistled.

"Wow, Luke. He's really gonna get outta town."

"Yes, he'll leave, but you have to do something. Write up what you heard. Tomorrow morning, as soon as you can, go and see Judge Stevens and have him freeze the sheriff's bank account. His money is mostly illegally gotten. Tell him to let him have a hundred dollars or so to finance his way out of town."

"I'll do that. I really appreciate your help, Luke. We'll clean this place up now."

"Good luck, Larry," he said and shook Larry's hands, then turned and left the jail.

Once outside, he mounted Apollo and turned west. He had to tell Ann that John was dead and that they needed to go into town and see Larry Talbot about writing their statements. He still had the towel in his hand and would pat it on his face as he rode to clean up the diminishing blood from the glass splinters.

At the ranch, Hal and Ann were having coffee and talking about Luke's chase after John. Laura and Beth were in Beth's room talking about other things.

"Do you think he'll catch him, Hal?"

"I'm sure he will, Ann. That boy's got no quit in him."

"Hal, what do we do about Beth? I know she loves Luke terribly, but I think she fears him as well."

"I know. I'll talk to Luke about it, but he knows that, too. What makes it harder is that I think Laura is the same way, but with no fear attached."

"I know, and I can understand it, too. Luke is an amazing man, but with Laura, I think it's more of an infatuation for all he's done for her."

"I ain't so sure, Ann. That Laura is a mighty mature filly. She knows herself a lot better'n most."

"She is remarkable in so many ways, isn't she? To go through all that she has at her age and still be the sweet person that she was before this all started is astonishing."

"Luke had a lot to do with that, Ann. I swear that boy would make a helluva preacher if he wasn't such a good rancher."

"So, will you talk to Luke if he returns?"

"I will."

An hour and twenty minutes later, Luke pulled up to the back of the ranch house and dismounted, thinking that they'd be in the kitchen about this time of day. It was almost four o'clock when he walked up onto the porch and knocked on the door.

Hal opened the door and smiled at Luke, saying, "Come on in, Luke. What happened to your face?"

"Glass splinters. It'll be all right in a couple of days," he replied as he crossed through the doorway.

"Hello, Ann," he said as he smiled at her.

"Welcome back, Luke. Did you find him?"

"Yes, ma'am."

"Have a seat and tell us what happened. I'll get you something to eat, too. Can I guess you haven't eaten since you left?"

"No, ma'am," he replied as he sat at the table.

Laura and Beth heard him enter, then just after he'd taken his chair, they walked into the kitchen.

Luke smiled at them and said, "Good afternoon, ladies."

"What happened to your face, Luke?" asked Laura.

"I'll explain in a minute, Laura."

Ann brought him a cup of coffee and a ham sandwich.

He bit into the sandwich quickly and then started on the coffee.

As he ate, he started explaining what had happened at the Pearson farm. When he finished, he added that because of John's connection to what happened earlier, they would all have to go to the sheriff's office and write statements.

"But that bastard knew about what happened and did nothing!" steamed Ann.

"That particular bastard resigned his office and is leaving town before he goes to jail," Luke added before he took a sip of coffee.

"*He's gone?*" exclaimed Ann.

"Not as gone as I'd like, but he's leaving. Deputy Sheriff Larry Talbot will probably take over until the next election. He's a good man. He'll take your statements. I don't know how far back he'll need to go, but I wouldn't mention the money. The state will probably want it, just because they can take it."

"What money?" asked a grinning Laura.

"Exactly," he replied as he smiled back at her.

“Anyway, I’ve got to get back to my place before it gets dark. Thanks for the coffee and sandwich, Ann.”

“You’re welcome,” she replied then caught Hal’s eye and he nodded.

Luke stood, grabbed his towel and his Stetson then headed for the door as Hal followed.

Laura started to leave but was stopped by her mother. Laura looked at her curiously but stayed in the house.

Luke wondered what Hal wanted to talk about but so far, he hadn’t said a word, but when he reached Apollo, Hal asked, “Could I have a word, Luke?”

Luke turned to an obviously uncomfortable Hal and replied, “Sure, Hal.”

“Let’s walk,” said Hal as he began to step towards the eastern pastures.

Luke got in step with Hal and commented, “This must be serious, Hal. You’re not happy about the subject.”

“I’m not. It’s just not somethin’ that I know too much about, Luke.”

“Can I guess it has to do with Beth?”

“It is. Ann asked me to talk to you about her and Laura both, but mostly Beth.”

“I’ll help you out, Hal. I’ll just explain and if I miss anything, you can ask, alright?”

“That would be much easier, Luke.”

"Now, I'll say right up front that I love them both dearly. With Beth, it was so close to where I was ready to ask to court her, just before the shooting incident at the cabin. I'm not sure if I explained it to you or not, so I'll tell you again. Bear with me if you heard this all before.

"You had to be there, Hal. It wasn't just what she said about my being a murderer, it was the way she looked at me right afterward. I knew right then that I had lost her. It's easy enough to say you'll shoot someone, but for Beth, the reality was a total shock to her.

"Once I took that first shot, and she saw a man being struck by a bullet, things changed. I was now a killer. I'm sure she'll say that it doesn't matter anymore and that she understands now, but deep down inside Beth, she'll have that image of me pulling that trigger causing a man to lose all he had in this life. Then, she magnified that image three times with the other deaths. It was made worse because she knew none of them even got a shot off.

"She may say it's alright and she can live with it, but she would never be able to forget that day. It's burned into her memory. I don't blame her at all, Hal. It's entirely my fault. I should have simply ignored her requests to come along and left on my own. She never would have seen it and it would just be some abstract event that wouldn't sit simmering in her soul. I'll never forgive myself for that, Hal. I ruined what could have been a wonderful life for both of us."

They continued to walk away from the house as Hal simply listened.

"Now, Laura is a totally different person. I used to think that Laura was just a younger version of Beth, but she's not. Laura is simply Laura. She's the most extraordinary person I've ever met. If she were a few years older, I would have proposed to her that first day. Laura simply overwhelms me sometimes, but I'm far too old for Laura. She needs to grow into that remarkable woman she'll become. I'll be honest with you, Hal. It hurts a lot when I think of Laura with someone else. I know it's the right thing to happen, but it still hurts a lot.

"Beth can be happy with someone else. Maybe not as happy as we could have been together, but she can be content. Laura is the problem, Hal. It's like I need to wean myself from her. I've become addicted to having Laura stop by, but I need to break that addiction if she's to enjoy a good life."

"I didn't know it was that bad, Luke."

"Bad is what it is, Hal. As much as it will hurt, I've got to stop seeing Laura, so she can meet young men her own age and find one who can make her happy."

"Are you sure this is the way you want to go, Luke? I'm nine years older than Ann, you know."

"But Ann wasn't a teenager when you met her, Hal. Laura has so much more life to experience."

"If that's the way you want to go, and I think it's all wrong, I'll talk to Ann."

"It's not the way I want to go at all, Hal, but it's the only way for Laura."

"Alright," Hal replied before they turned to head back.

The walk back was silent, each man with his own thoughts. Luke found himself already slipping into depression over his decision but believed it was the only one possible for Laura, and she was all that mattered.

They reached the house and Luke mounted then looked down at Hal.

Hal was looking up at his dearest friend as he said, "You take care, Luke."

Luke nodded then replied, "You too, Hal."

Luke turned Apollo to the south and headed back to his ranch in a foul mood.

———

When he returned, he walked Apollo into the barn and freed him from his gear before brushing him down and wondering if he had done the right thing. It would be harder than anything he'd done before, which would be difficult to understand for those who knew what he had done in the past. But to not be able to experience the uplifting joy of seeing Nyx trotting down the access road and Laura's smiling face was devastating.

He needed to find focus. He wished he could just get away but didn't want to take the coward's way out. But to Luke, the true coward's way out would be to marry Beth but that would be an unmitigated disaster, and he knew it. Aside from that lingering, but very real concern of Beth's deep wounds, was his own very real concern. He knew he'd never be able to make love to Beth because he loved her younger, too much younger, sister.

———

Hal had explained what Luke had said to Ann, and she believed what Luke was doing was the right decision.

Hal asked, "Do you want to tell her, Ann? Or do you want me to do it?", hoping she'd handle it.

Ann thought about her reply for almost a minute before answering, “I think I’ll need your support on this one, Hal.”

“Alright. Did you want to talk to her here or in her room?”

“I think her room might be better. She’s in Beth’s room right now. I’ll meet you in her room.”

Hal nodded and his stomach was twisting in knots as Ann rose and he followed her down the hallway. He turned and entered Laura’s room, found a straight-backed chair, and sat down, kneading his hands as he waited for Ann and Laura.

Ann tapped on Beth’s door before opening it, then spotted her daughters and asked, “Laura, could I see you for a moment, please?”

“Okay, Mama,” she replied then bounced up from Beth’s bed where they had been talking about Luke’s latest adventure.

She followed her mother into her room and saw a very nervous Hal sitting there, making her more than a bit concerned. Something was brewing, and she didn’t like the looks on Hal’s or her mother’s faces.

“Have a seat, dear,” Ann said as she closed the door.

Laura sat on her bed and looked expectantly at her mother, who then took a seat next to her on the bed. The closed-door had just kicked up her level of concern a notch.

Ann took in a deep breath before she looked into her daughter’s deep blue eyes and decided to get this over quickly.

“Laura, I asked Hal to talk to Luke about Beth. He did that just before he left to return to his ranch, and Luke told him how he felt about you as well and asked that you not see him anymore.”

Laura had been expecting many things but not that as her entire world crashed inside her.

"He told you that, Hal?" she asked quietly as she looked at him.

Hal nodded and answered just as softly, "Yes, Laura, he did."

"Why would he say such a thing? We enjoyed each other's company so very much."

"I know, dear," replied Ann, "but that was the problem, you see. Luke wants you to experience the joy of having the life of a young woman. He thinks you should meet young men of your own age."

Laura was on the verge of exploding in tears but quickly controlled herself and asked, "So, I'm not to ride to his ranch again?"

"No, sweetheart. You must honor his request. You need to go to socials and dances. I know Al already has his eye on you."

"I know that, Mama. What did he say about Beth? Can she go and see him?"

"He didn't put any restrictions on Beth going to visit him, Laura," answered Hal.

"So, he wants to marry Beth?" she asked then added, "I suppose that would be alright," but not meaning a single word.

Ann replied, "No, Laura, he doesn't want to marry Beth. He just didn't say she couldn't visit."

"So, he's going to turn into a hermit again."

Hal nodded and said, "It looks that way."

Laura's head was filled with conflicting plans and schemes even as she replied, "Alright. I'll do as Luke wishes."

Ann was relieved to have it over and done but not at all pleased with Luke's decision because she knew how much it hurt Laura.

Hal and Ann left her room closing the door behind them assuming that Laura would be breaking down in tears, but they didn't know Laura as well as Luke did. And Laura knew that she understood Luke even better than Hal did and was certain she knew why he had made the prohibition. It was that damned concern about the difference in their ages.

Laura then set her mind to one goal: she'd wait until she turned eighteen, then once she was an adult, she would ride to the Circle S and have Luke tell her to her face that he didn't love her.

She'd go to their damned dances and other soirees, but none of those boys would come close to matching the man that she loved.

CHAPTER 9

The next day was a momentous day for the citizens of Colorado City, whether most knew about it or not.

Sheriff John Crenshaw had left his badge and letter of resignation on his desk before returning to his room at the boarding house to finish packing. The train to Denver wasn't due to depart until 1:40 that afternoon, so he had time. He needed to get his money from the bank first, so at about half past ten, he left his room to go to the bank.

Deputy Larry Talbot had seen Judge Stevens earlier that morning and shown him his statement about the conversation between Luke Scott and the sheriff. The judge was appropriately outraged and immediately issued not only a freeze on the sheriff's bank account but a warrant for his arrest as an accessory after the fact in the murder of Les Harper. *The man had never even gone out to the Harper ranch!*

Deputy Talbot, willingly accompanied by Deputy James Marsden, gave a copy of the judge's order to the bank president who happily froze the large account. The deputies waited in the bank for the ex-sheriff to enter the bank and quickly put him under gunpoint, removed his pistol, then marched him to the jail and locked him in a cell. John Crenshaw was too stunned to protest as he thought he'd been promised free passage out of the town.

Just after the sheriff was tossed into the slammer, Hal, Ann, Beth, and Laura arrived to write their statements and Ann noted with gleeful satisfaction that the ex-sheriff was behind bars. It took them over an hour to write out their statements. Laura's and Beth's took longer because Laura wrote about her capture and treatment at the cabin and also wrote glowingly about her rescue.

Beth also included a detailed description of the shootout at the cabin. It was then, as she was writing, she realized that Luke was right after all. She would always have that image in her mind. It hurt her enough even as she wrote her statement that the sheets were sprinkled with blurred words that had been caused by dropped tears.

But they all finished their statements and gave them to Larry Talbot less than ninety minutes after entering the offices.

An hour later, after lunch at the café, they left Colorado City to return to the ranch.

Luke was out with his horses, looking at the mares when he spotted a rider approaching, then walked toward the front of the house and waited for Deputy Marsden to get close.

"Mornin', Luke," the deputy said loudly as he pulled his horse to a stop.

"Howdy, James. What brings you down here?"

He leaned over and handed Luke a folded piece of paper as he said, "You've been subpoenaed by the prosecutor for John Crenshaw's trial in two days."

"That's a bit of a surprise, isn't it, James?" he asked as he glanced at the legal paper.

"It was to us, too. I guess the judge was mighty put off with Crenshaw, especially when he heard that the sheriff hadn't done anything when Mrs. Harper told him that her husband had been killed and her daughter had been kidnapped."

"How come neither you nor Larry were around when things like that happened?"

"The sheriff kept us busy with small things. The only time anyone would ever be able to talk to us about anything was on Sundays, and then we needed to get the sheriff if it was serious. She must have come in during the week."

"I wondered how he was able to keep all of Charlie's crimes quiet."

"You also have some rewards coming your way for the Charlie Bassett gang."

"How is that even possible without the bodies?"

"You told Larry about the incident and it was confirmed by Elizabeth Harper in her statement."

"Oh. How is she doing?"

"She seemed mighty broke up when she was writing her statement."

Luke nodded then said, "So, it'll be on Wednesday morning at ten?"

"Yes, sir. The prosecutor wants to see you tomorrow sometime to prepare your testimony."

"Alright. I'll visit him then. Thanks for stopping by, James."

"It's been a real pleasure talking to you, Luke," he said before he smiled, then reached down and shook Luke's hand.

Luke waved before the deputy wheeled his horse around and headed back down the access road

After Deputy Marsden left, Luke returned to his house and fixed himself some lunch. He hadn't counted on a trial because he thought that the sheriff would just hightail it out of town. This might present some problems for him. He had shot those bastards without warning unless you included the warning shot through the door. He might even be hanged for murder and wondered if it would provide any solace for Beth if they did. But even if they did charge him, he didn't for one moment regret what he had done.

The next day, he met with County Prosecutor Morris Ralston just after noon. It took him over an hour to go over his testimony with the attorney. Satisfied with Luke's story, the prosecutor assured Luke before he left the office that the sheriff would be convicted. As he mounted his horse Luke smiled, knowing that he was sure that the prosecutor said that to everyone, but doubted if he won all his cases.

He returned to his ranch and found his stables nearly complete. They were doing interior work now and told him they'd be finished late tomorrow. There was a large quantity of boards remaining and the foreman asked where he wanted to store them. Luke had them put them in the barn loft and began to wonder what he would use them for. There were a lot of straight, knot-free boards.

At eight o'clock the next morning, he mounted Apollo and headed northwest toward town. It was a beautiful spring morning, and Luke didn't know how it would turn out. Would he even make it back to his ranch or would he find himself in jail for four murders?

He reached the courthouse just after nine o'clock and stepped down. He was wearing his surviving gray vest and if he walked out of the trial a free man, he'd go over to Salk's and buy a replacement Bulldog, assuming he had a new order. His Webley, as it turned out was unusable. It didn't look bad, but the cylinder would no longer align with the barrel. Rather than having it repaired, which would be almost the cost of a new one anyway, he had mounted it on a piece of walnut and hung it on the wall in his library. He'd get a new pistol but still use the damaged holster. He still had the other holster from the pistol he'd given to Laura but was superstitious enough to keep using the 'lucky' holster.

He took a seat in the back of the already crowded courtroom and could see Hal, Ann, Beth, and Laura in the front row. Just seeing Laura when he entered had made him smile inside at the same time his stomach turned creating a very peculiar sensation. He could see her turning her head to look for him, but she would only be able to spot him if she stood and turned completely around.

A few minutes later, John Crenshaw was led into the courtroom by the two deputies. He wasn't cuffed or shackled.

The judge entered at exactly ten o'clock and everyone stood. Then, after he took his seat, court was in session and the trial began with opening statements.

Crenshaw was represented by Ralph Somerset, although he preferred the British pronunciation of his name: Rafe. For some reason, that line of thought reminded him of how angry Richard had gotten when Luke called him Dick, and Luke smiled.

The first witness was Deputy Sheriff Larry Talbot. His testimony was straightforward and minimally challenged by Mister Somerset.

Luke was called next, so he rose and walked to the witness stand then turned, was sworn in, and took his seat. He made a mistake by glancing at Laura and found her deep blue eyes boring into him.

He was so caught up in Laura's eyes, he fully missed the first question by the prosecutor and had to ask him to repeat it. He gave the same testimony to the prosecutor that he had given to him the day before, so his examination was finished without any surprises. Now it was Mister Somerset's turn as he approached Luke like a wolf stalking a newborn calf. Luke swore he was salivating.

He began by asking about how he had learned of the alleged connection between the sheriff and the outlaw, Charlie Bassett, and Luke made his second mistake by glancing again at Laura. She was still focused on him. It was highly disconcerting, and Luke stumbled through his answer.

Somerset knew he had him now. He was going to destroy the prosecutor's star witness with his next line of questioning.

"So, Mister Scott, without ever meeting Mister Bassett or the sheriff, you made this connection based on the ramblings of a terrified, confused teenage girl. Is that right?"

Luke snapped back into the present and said, "No, sir. I made this connection based on the calm, descriptive statement of an incredibly brave and resilient young lady."

"Regardless of the source, just based on that information, you told her that you would kill the four men, did you not?"

"I did."

"Are you above the law, Mister Scott? Do you believe that God almighty has appointed you his avenging angel and that allowed you to ignore the laws of the land and act as judge, jury, and executioner because of this one statement?"

"When she told me of the connection between Charlie Bassett and the sheriff, I saw no other way of setting things right."

"So, you took your big rifle and stood hiding behind some trees, shot all four men without warning."

"Not exactly. I put one round through the door to let them know I was there. When they started running out of the house, I shot two of them. Then I went down to the cabin and collapsed their chimney with my Sharps and waited for them to come out with my Winchester. One did, and I shot him. The last one, Charlie Bassett, tried to shoot me from a window and I shot him before he could pull the trigger."

"And then, Mister Scott, you coldly dragged them into the house and left them there to burn to hide your murderous act."

"I wouldn't call it coldly, Mister Somerset. The house was already on fire when I dragged them in there. I didn't drag them into the house to hide what I had done. I dragged them into the house, so they could experience what was waiting them for eternity."

"Since then, you have killed another three men, is that right?"

"Yes, sir."

"Why, Mister Scott, that puts you in a class with Mister Bassett, whom you claim to be a murderer."

"There is a difference, Mister Somerset. All the men I shot were armed."

Somerset got a look of disgust on his face and sneered, "I'm done questioning this murderer, Your Honor."

Luke looked at the prosecutor who still smiled at him but was obviously not going to ask any more questions in cross-examination, which bothered Luke. *Was the prosecutor satisfied with his star witness being called a murderer?*

He stepped down from the witness box and leaned over and asked the prosecutor if he needed to stay around. The prosecutor told him he could leave, which Luke thought was just as well.

As he was leaving, he stopped and said softly to Larry Talbot, "If you need to come and get me, Larry, I'll be at my ranch. I'll come along peacefully."

Larry looked up at him like he'd just swallowed a June bug as Luke left and walked out of the courtroom.

Next to be called was Laura, who had been following Luke's exit. She finally heard her name called a second time and walked to the witness stand.

Luke mounted Apollo and rode back to his ranch much faster than when he had left the ranch.

Back at the trial, Mister Somerset had run into a very hard time of it when he thought he'd make mincemeat of Laura. *What sixteen-year-old girl could withstand his questioning?*

The tables were reversed on the astonished defense attorney when Laura not only answered his questions accurately and with complete, unabashed honesty, but had managed to twist two of his questions into attacks on him.

The first was when he questioned the accuracy of the information that she had heard considering how she had been subjected to almost unrelenting abuse. Laura asked him quietly what kind of abuse he was asking about. Somerset had to stumble and finally replied with a convoluted, "Abuse of a sexual nature, Miss Harper."

Laura had glared at him, the intensity from her dark, foreboding blue eyes startling the defense attorney. "You are talking about rape. Are you not, Mister Somerset?"

"Yes," he croaked.

"Yes, they did that many times. They also beat me, Mister Somerset. For some women, I believe it would cause them to shrink into a shell and I can understand that. But Mister Somerset, it made me angry. I concentrated on every word they said and stored it in my memory in case I ever escaped."

"But you admitted in your statement that you contemplated suicide."

"I did. After I thought I was pregnant and had been with them for almost a month, I believed I never would get out of that cabin. When they locked me in the barn with no heat or food for two days, I decided to let myself go. I wanted to die because I saw no way of escape. But Mister Scott found me. He brought me into the cabin and brought me back to life. He told me a story that made me want to live every moment and savor life. Mister Scott did much, much more than just save my life, Mister Somerset. He gave me a reason to live, to really live, not just exist."

"And you were alone with Mister Scott for an entire day in that cabin, Miss Harper. Are you telling me that nothing happened?"

“Many things happened, Mister Somerset. Mister Scott fed me and helped me to recover so that he could get me home the next day. But in order to satisfy your lascivious mind, no, nothing happened of a romantic nature, which seems to be the focus of your attention.”

Somerset opened his mouth to ask another question, but then just said, “No more questions,” before letting Laura leave. The prosecutor was giddy with Laura’s testimony.

Then the defense attorney called Beth to the stand. Beth knew she would be questioned about that day. She knew that if she was honest, Luke could be arrested for murder, but she saw no way out.

“Miss Harper,” Somerset began, “you were there on the day of the fatal shooting of Charlie Bassett, Philly Henderson, Mack Johnson, and Joe Pendleton, were you not?”

“I was.”

“Did Mister Scott give these men any warning before firing on them?”

“He fired a warning shot into their door.”

“But once these frightened men began running from the cabin, did he warn them? Did he shout at them to surrender?”

“No.”

“And when he went down to the cabin to murder the last two men, did he give them an opportunity to surrender?”

“I don’t know. I was on the other side of the trees in a shelter.”

"Why was that, Miss Harper?"

"I wasn't feeling well."

"Was it because you were nauseated by the execution of these men?"

Laura thought for a second before answering, "Yes."

Somerset smiled at his victory and said, "No more questions, Your Honor."

Beth started to rise from the witness chair when Marsden stood. "Just a moment, Miss Harper. I have a couple of questions."

Beth sat back down, already devastated by what she had just done. She thought she had put a noose around Luke's neck.

"Miss Harper, I have in my hand four wanted posters. They are for Charlie Bassett, Philly Henderson, Mack Johnson, and Joe Pendleton. I want you to look at them and see if you recognize any of them."

Laura looked at the pictures. She recognized Joe Pendleton and maybe Philly Henderson.

"I recognize this one, Joe Pendleton. I think this is the second one, Philly Henderson. I never saw the other two."

"Your Honor, I'd like to have the jury advised that these wanted posters for the four men supposedly murdered by Mister Scott are all listed as 'Wanted: Dead or Alive'. Even if Mister Scott had not had cause to shoot them, as he obviously did, his actions do not merit condemnation or arrest, but deserve our thanks for ridding the area of these wanted criminals."

He handed the judge the wanted posters.

"I believe you have already advised the jury, Mister Marsden. I need take no further actions."

"Thank you, Your Honor."

"No more questions, Miss Harper," he said as he smiled at Beth.

Relieved would be a gross understatement for how Beth felt about the introduction of the wanted posters.

The two attorneys gave their closing remarks, and the defense attorney's only real chance was to deflect attention to Luke, which had failed, so he had to modify his closing statement to paint the sheriff in a positive light.

When the case went to the jury, they spent more time gossiping about the rescue of Laura and the subsequent punishment meted out by Luke Scott than they did about the actual case itself. They handed down a guilty verdict thirty minutes later.

The judge sentenced John Crenshaw to twenty-five years in the state prison, and in a surprising move, awarded the money in his bank account to be held in trust for Laura Harper until she came of age. The trial was gaveled closed and everyone went home murmuring.

Luke, of course, had heard none of this. After he had returned to his ranch and taken care of Apollo, he had gone to his library and found a lawbook. Whether it would help him or not was doubtful.

The stables were finished, so he could move the horses in at any time, but there would be no point if he was going to prison or walking up the gallows steps. He was sure that the prosecutor would call Beth as she was the only one there when he had done it. He wouldn't expect her to lie and in fact, would be disappointed if she did. But still, it would be another nail in his coffin.

The book had nothing remotely useful in his case and brought it back to the small house before he decided to inspect his new stables. He needed to sign off on its completion anyway.

When he stepped inside, he was immediately struck by how well-built it was with no cheap hammer and nail construction. All the stalls were mortise and tenon construction and built using thicker than normal boards. The two tack and storerooms were more spacious than he had expected and the two pumps on the ends poured water into the stable-length troughs. He noticed a ladder in the back of the stables that he hadn't noticed on the plans and climbed up, reached the attic area, and found a full, stable-sized storage area. He could put anything he needed here. At the end was a hoist, probably for hay. He got to the hoist and found two doors he had missed when looking from the outside, swung open the doors then swiveled the hoist on its base until the pulleys were outside the doors. He was very pleased with his new stables as he brought the hoist inside, closed the doors, and went back down the ladder. Once down on the floor, he took a quick look at the heat stove and then left. He'd move the horses into their new home tomorrow.

———

Hal and his ladies rode back to the ranch an hour after the trial's conclusion, having eaten at the café before they left. Ann drove the buggy while Hal rode alongside.

"You'll have quite a bit of money waiting for you when you turn eighteen, Laura. It'll make you even more of an attraction to the young men in the area," she said as she smiled.

"Mama, what will make me more attractive will be the stories that they'll tell about my being taken so many times. They'll think of me as fair game."

"No, they won't, dear," Ann said even as she knew the opposite to be true.

"I feel terrible, Mama. If Mister Marsden hadn't brought those wanted posters, I would have gotten Luke hanged for murder," Beth said with a tremor in her voice.

"I doubt that, Beth. They were wanted men, and everyone knew it."

"He's going to hate me, even more, when he finds out what I said."

"You're so very wrong, Beth. Luke loves you. That's what he told Hal on the day they talked."

Beth's head whipped around to her mother as she asked, "He told Hal that?"

"Yes, he did. He just feels that the shooting incident will always stand between you. That's why he told Hal he could never marry you. He blames himself completely for that day, by the way. He said it was he who had ruined what might have been, not you."

"Then he doesn't hate me?"

"No, dear."

Laura wanted so much to ask what Luke had said about her but thought it would be better if she asked Hal when she could get him alone.

When they returned, Ann drove the buggy toward the barn, following Hal.

"I'll take care of the horses, Ann. You ladies can go inside."

Laura saw her opportunity and offered, "I'll help, Hal. I need to see Nyx anyway."

"Alright, Laura."

She clambered out of the buggy and trotted over to the barn as Beth and Ann climbed out of the buggy and walked into the house.

Laura began unharnessing the buggy horse while Hal was unsaddling his horse. She quickly had him free of the harness, then led the buggy horse into the barn to begin her planned questioning.

"Hal, while we were riding back, Beth was worried about her testimony."

"I can see where she would. For a few seconds there, I thought Luke was a goner."

"Anyway, she told mama she was worried that Luke might hate her even more and mama said that Luke had told you that he loved her."

"He did."

"But he told you that he didn't want to see me at all. What did I do to make him hate me?" she asked, knowing that Luke didn't hate her at all, but she hoped it would trigger the release of more information which it did.

"No, Laura, that's not even close. He loves you more than he loves Beth. He just thinks that you're too young and needed to be happy with someone else. That's all."

Laura felt her heart race. It was a better answer than she could have hoped for.

"So, he wants me to go to dances and things and meet young men?"

Hal looked at Laura and sighed, put down the saddle, and replied, "Laura, I don't know if I should be tellin' you this, but I think he's all wrong about this. When Luke described how he felt about you, he called it an addiction. He said it was the right thing to do, but he said it would hurt somethin' fierce not to see you anymore."

Laura was soaring inside as she asked, "Don't you think it's silly?"

"I think so, and so does your mother. She's been actin' the way she is to try and do what Luke wants."

"Thank you for telling me that, Hal. I'll think of what I can do."

Hal smiled at Laura and said, "You do that, Laura. I think what we need to do is to make Luke happy, even if he doesn't want to be."

"So do I, Hal. So do I."

The next morning, having not been arrested, Luke moved the stallion and mares into the stables and then Apollo. He decided he'd name the other horses and went out to the small house and picked a god and goddesses from Greek and Roman mythology. The black stallion had to be Zeus. He was going to father a bunch of gods and goddesses. He went down the row and named each mare as one of the goddesses. Luke took some of the excess lumber and carved their names into the wood. It wasn't as good as the calligraphy used in Laura's saddlebags, but it was reasonably nice.

After lunch, he did odd jobs around the ranch and then walked back to the small house, wondering what he could do with the extra lumber. It was enough to add another room, but to what purpose? He was still thinking when he heard the unmistakable sound of hoofbeats. A lot of hoofbeats.

He trotted out of the house and saw Ira Pearson riding a magnificent gelding and leading a string of seven more horses, all equally beautiful. His son Michael was with him.

He saw Luke and waved. Luke returned his wave and stepped out into the yard.

When he was close enough, Ira shouted, "Where do you want them, Luke?"

"I didn't order any more, Ira."

"I know you didn't. I did."

"Ira, you don't owe me anything."

"Oh, no. You save me, and my entire family, and I owe you nothing."

"I shot a hole in your door."

Ira laughed and said, "That's why I only brought seven. Six mares and one gelding."

Luke could protest more, but the horses were even more magnificent than the ones he had purchased.

"Put them in the corral until I make some new signs. I'll be running out of Greek gods and goddesses, so I'll probably have to add Roman gods now."

Ira waved and led the horses to the corral. Michael grinned at him as he passed. Luke couldn't help but grin back as the parade of handsome mares passed.

After the horses were all in the corral, Ira and Michael stepped down, tied their horses to the corral fence, and walked over. Ira handed Luke a bill of sale for the horses, which Luke folded and put in his vest pocket.

"Do you want to see the stable?" Luke asked.

"Of course, I want to see the stable. It looks great from out here."

Luke gave them a tour of the interior and Ira commented on the name signs. He admired the quality of construction and the size of the stalls. There was enough room for even the largest animal to turn around. When they were leaving, Luke asked if they wanted something to eat.

"No, thanks, Luke. We've got to be going back. But it did remind me. Mary sent these along as her contribution."

He opened his saddlebags and pulled out a large bag.

"I hope it didn't crush too many," he smiled as he gave the aromatic bag to Luke.

"Oatmeal raisin cookies," he explained as Luke peered inside.

He snatched one from the bag and offered the bag to Michael who took one, followed by his father who also took a cookie.

"Better than the horses, I think," mumbled Luke as he chewed the tasty treat.

"You mean I could have gotten away with just some cookies?" asked a laughing Ira.

"Not if you baked them," Luke replied as he laughed back.

They each enjoyed another cookie before Ira and Michael mounted.

"Don't be a stranger, Ira. Come on by so you can see some of the foals."

"I will, Luke," Ira said before he waved then he and Michael wheeled their horses and trotted away.

After they turned onto the roadway, Luke returned to the corral and looked at the new horses, finding each one perfect in its own way. He decided he'd give one to Beth to make her feel better and picked a cream-colored mare with a blonde mane and tail. He'd take her to the ranch tomorrow, hopefully avoiding Laura.

He returned to the small house and pulled out the mythology book again and took it and the bag of cookies to the house. He needed to find someplace to put the cookies that was airtight to keep them from getting crunchy. He liked them soft like they were now.

He found a sugar tin that was almost empty and emptied the sugar into the sugar bowl and filled the tin with the cookies and sealed them with the top lid.

He decided to build a second corral adjacent to the first for the stallion and his new covey of mares. He should be a happy horse with ten mares to keep satisfied after he gave Beth the eleventh.

He didn't want to waste the rest of the day, so he took off his shirt and began to dig the post holes for the new corral. His gunshot wound gave him some grief, but he ignored it, as well as the stings from his glass cuts once he began to sweat. It was still cool outside, as it should be. He had the post holes dug by six o'clock and knocked off for the day. He kept his shirt off as he walked into the house and poured himself a bath. An hour later, he felt better and had a new shirt on. After a quick dinner, finished off with two cookies, he was sitting in the main room reading a book just for pleasure when he heard hoofbeats.

Sighing, he stood and walked to the door. *Two visitors in one day?*

He opened the door and his heart stopped. So much for his good mood.

Deputy Larry Talbot was walking up the steps with a piece of paper in his hand. Luke was sure it was his arrest warrant.

"Evening, Larry. Here to do your duty?"

"Yup," he smiled and handed the sheet of paper to Luke.

"They should be in within a couple of days. Do you want to have Western Union hold them for you to pick up?"

Luke was confused until he read the paper. It was authorization by Acting Sheriff Larry Talbot for release of the rewards for Charlie Bassett, Philly Henderson, Mack Johnson, and Joe Pendleton to Luke.

"It totals $2250. They were some nasty men, Luke."

"So, I'm not facing a murder trial?"

"They were all wanted dead or alive, Luke. Besides, the stories are already running all over. The paper put out some stories of the trial, too."

"How did Laura do, Larry?"

"Laura emasculated Mister Somerset. Elizabeth kinda hurt you a bit, and I think she felt really bad about it."

"She told the truth, Larry. It's what she was supposed to do."

"She did that."

"Good. You gotta go back?"

"Yup. Just needed to run this down to you. Just swing by Western Union in a couple of days and show them this paper."

"Thanks a lot for not throwing me in jail, Larry," Luke said as he smiled.

Larry laughed gave him a short wave and then turned, climbed back on his horse, and headed out of the ranch.

Luke looked at the sheet of paper. Two thousand dollars for something he would gladly do again for free. Hell, he'd have paid for the privilege.

LUKE

The next morning found Luke shirtless again putting the posts into position and tamping them down. He'd split some more rails tomorrow and he'd have the basic corral finished by the end of the day and put in a proper gate the day after.

He was heading for the house when he saw dust to the west out of the setting sun, so he shielded his eyes to try and pick out the riders. Someone was coming from the Rawlings ranch, he guessed, so he just continued to watch the two riders. He didn't recognize either horse, which meant neither was Laura. It took five more minutes before he recognized Al Feinstein and Chuck Miller. Luke wondered what they were both doing away from the ranch and coming to see him.

He stood waiting for them, his axe still in his hand and his shirt thrown over his shoulder. Chuck and Al approached Luke and waved. Luke waved back, still curious about their reason for coming all this way.

"Afternoon, Luke," said Chuck, "Buildin' somethin'?"

"Yup. Adding a second corral. What can I do for you boys?"

"Mind if we set and talk to you for a bit?"

"Come on in," he replied before he turned and walked to his house.

They both stepped down and hitched their horses before following him inside.

"So, what can I do for you?" Luke asked as he buttoned his shirt and took a seat.

They each sat and then glanced at each other before Chuck spoke.

"Luke, we're kinda wonderin' about Beth and Laura."

"What about them?"

"Well, I'm kinda fond of Beth and Al likes Laura and we were wonderin' what your view is on all that."

"My view is my own, Chuck. I have no hold on either of them. They're free to make up their own minds, as they should."

"Well, Beth, I think, doesn't mind my payin' attention to her, but Laura is kind of pushin' Al away."

"Al, Laura's only sixteen. She needs time."

"Hell, Luke, lotsa girls get married when they're only sixteen," complained Al.

"Laura isn't 'lotsa girls', Al. Laura is very special."

"We just wanted to make sure you weren't gonna object," said Chuck.

"It's not my call, Chuck. It's their call, but I will tell you something that you need to keep in mind. Any man who hurts either Beth or Laura, whether physically or any other way, will incur my wrath, and that's not something to ignore."

"No, we wouldn't ever hurt 'em, Luke. We just want to be sure we're not steppin' on your toes."

"You're not stepping on my toes."

"Okay. That's all we needed to know. We've gotta get back. Thanks, Luke."

"You're welcome," Luke replied as both men stood.

They hustled back outside as if Luke were going to shoot them then trotted to their horses, mounted and waved as they quickly rode west.

Luke may not have wanted to shoot them, but he surely wasn't happy with the idea. It felt as if they were dealing in women. *Why didn't they just let Beth and Laura decide?* They knew what they wanted and needed and was sure that neither Chuck nor Al had a clue.

Their visit put Luke in a foul mood. The more he thought about it the more he slipped into a sullen demeanor. He pulled out his mythology book to get some Roman names but was in such a sour mood that he named the big gelding Mars, the god of war. It was a good name anyway, as the gelding was a deep red with no markings and a black mane and tail. He still backed off somewhat with naming the mares, though. They all had to have pleasant goddess names.

He set the book aside and made himself some dinner before turning in. Tomorrow, he'd move them into their stalls and make their name signs before finishing the new corral.

———

The next day, he followed through on his plans, and now that he had a good look at Mars, he liked him even more and thought the name was totally appropriate. In addition to his color, he had a fiery look in his eyes. He led Mars into his stall and then all the mares into theirs. That left just one empty stall after the stallion, Apollo, and Mars were present. One open stall, but he'd get one back when the cream mare was given to Beth. That left six stalls in the barn for the other horses and two open in the stables.

Once his pantheon of gods and goddesses were in their new home, he went to work on the name signs. He'd leave Beth's horse's name blank, but on the spur of the moment, he carved 'Nyx' into the last sign, then hung it on the last empty stall and laid the blank sign on the stall rail.

After he was finished with the job, he had lunch, cleaned up, and then returned to the stable. He brought out Mars and the unnamed mare, took them to the barn, and saddled Mars. He didn't have a fancy saddle to give Beth, but she had her own anyway. He left his ranch at just after two o'clock and headed to the Rawlings ranch.

As he was riding, he had second thoughts about his request to have Laura stay away. The visit by Chuck and Al made him realize just how stupid it was. He enjoyed Laura's visits immensely. *Why should he deny himself that enjoyment just to satisfy some misguided sense of nobility?* He decided as he rode to trash the whole idea and hoped that he'd find her there.

Forty minutes later, he arrived at the fence line and opened the gate. After he had crossed through, he closed the gate and began trotting toward the house. He spotted Chuck and Al with the herd, where they should be, and not riding all the way to his ranch to ask him if they could see Beth and Laura. He stopped in the front yard and stepped down, tied off Mars and walked up onto the porch, and knocked. The door popped open ten seconds later and he was rewarded with the still breathtaking sight of Laura's blue eyes.

"Hello, Laura," he said as he smiled.

"Hello, Luke. I thought you didn't want to see me anymore."

"That was pretty stupid, wasn't it, Laura?"

She smiled and replied, "I thought so. Does this mean I can visit again?"

"As often as you'd like. I have more horses to show you, too. Is Beth in?"

"Sure. Come on in."

He followed Laura into the main room, suddenly aware of Laura's sudden shift from young woman to just a woman. It had only been five months since he'd found her in that barn, and she was already filling in. Maybe it was because she was eating more regularly.

Laura stuck her head into Beth's room and said, "Beth? Luke's here to see you."

"Luke?" she asked quickly.

"Either that or someone doing an excellent impersonation."

Beth popped out of her room with an insecure smile, saw Luke, and asked, "Luke, how are you?"

"I'm fine. How are you doing, Beth?"

"Okay, I guess. What do you need?"

"I brought you a present."

"Are you serious? You brought me a present? Why?"

"For being a good friend and an honest person."

"I didn't act like it on the witness stand."

"Did you lie?"

"No, but I almost got you hanged."

"No, you didn't. As it turns out, your honesty led to my being over two thousand dollars richer. They took your statement as corroboration for the rewards on those four. That really didn't matter to me. I was just proud of you for telling the truth even though it would be hard for you."

"You're not mad at me?"

"Not a bit. Do you want to see your present?"

"Is it in the main room?"

"I hope not," he answered as he smiled.

He turned and ushered both women out to the porch.

"The red gelding is Mars. You'll have to name your mare."

Beth looked at the beautiful mare and smiled as she asked, "Luke, you're giving her to me?"

"I didn't ride all the way over here to show you and bring her back. I was given a few more horses, but when I saw her, I thought you'd like to have her."

She stepped down slowly and rubbed the mare's neck. It meant a lot more than just a gift. It meant that Luke really didn't hate her. Hal and her mother could tell her anything, but the mare told her so much more.

"You and Laura will have to come over and see the new stables and all the new horses someday soon."

"I'd like that, Luke," said Beth, still admiring the mare.

Luke leaned over to Laura and whispered, "I still like Nyx better."

She smiled, leaned back, and whispered, "Me, too."

Hal and Ann finally appeared from the kitchen and saw Luke. They were surprised but pleased. Then they saw the mare and Hal looked over at Luke with raised eyebrows.

"Eli Pearson brought some more horses by two days ago in thanks for saving his family. That's Mars, right there and I brought the mare for Beth."

"She's very pretty, Luke," said Ann.

"I also told Laura how stupid my last request was and rescinded it. Actually, I incinerated it, so the odor didn't linger."

"You had to," said Laura, "it was a horribly stinky idea."

"It was, and the less we speak of it, the better."

Laura's eyes sparkled as she said, "I may remember to bring it up occasionally."

"Laura, there's something I've been meaning to ask you that I keep forgetting. That day when your brothers returned, where was your pistol?"

Laura's impish expression changed in a flash to one of utter embarrassment as she replied, "Um, in my saddlebags."

Luke raised his eyebrows, and said, "You don't bring up my stinky idea and I won't counter with the pistol in the saddlebag."

She smiled back and said, "Is that a deal?"

He held out his hand and they shook, cementing the pact.

This is what Laura and Luke would have missed most of all if he had tried to keep her away; the simple joy they had in each other's company.

Beth returned to the porch smiling. “Thank you, Luke. She's beautiful.”

“You're welcome, Beth. I'm going to head back now and take care of her sisters.”

“Won't you stay for dinner, Luke?” asked Ann.

“I appreciate the offer, Ann, but I really need to get back.”

Luke really didn't have anything going on but knew that Chuck and Al ate with the family and knew his presence would cause some uneasiness, especially after their recent visit.

He returned to Mars, stepped up, and waved to everyone as he wheeled the red gelding back toward his ranch.

As he passed the herd, he waved to Chuck and Al. They didn't return the gesture, and Luke knew he had just stepped on their toes after all.

He returned to his ranch, put Mars away in his marked stall, and brushed him down, then went into his house, made a quick dinner, and called it quits for the day just doing some reading before turning in.

CHAPTER 10

The next day started out easily enough: wash, breakfast, and a ride to Colorado City for his reward money. He showed the letter to the telegrapher who gave him the Western Union vouchers, which he deposited in his account.

He made a quick trip to Salk's and found that he had ordered and received four more Bulldogs. He had already sold two, and Frank was grateful that Luke only needed one. Luke told him what had happened to the last one but wasn't surprised that the proprietor had already heard the story as most of the town had.

Things began to get odd after that. People would see him, approach him, and shake his hand. Young women that he didn't know would smile and wave. The first two times he'd received the waves, he had turned around to see who was behind him.

It got worse when he stopped at the café for lunch. Folks he knew in passing were coming up to his table to congratulate him or tell him how great he was. It wasn't until one of his admirers gave him a copy of the newspaper that he understood what was going on. They had published the full story of his actions in saving Laura and the two families. Where they had gotten the information remained a mystery until he found out that most of the information came from the trial followed by some not-too-strenuous digging.

After he left the diner, he boarded Mars and set him to a trot back to his ranch. Luckily, he had plenty of supplies, so he shouldn't have to repeat the visit anytime soon. It should die down by the time he had to return.

He had finished putting Mars away and was getting ready to add the gate to the new corral when he wasn't surprised to hear riders approaching. He didn't even bother looking down the access road before he turned to the south and saw a black horse and a tan horse kicking up dust as they neared the yard. The Harper ladies had come to visit.

He waved to them and they waved back and noted how much Laura was catching up to Beth again as they approached the house. Luke stepped over to the front of the house and waited for them to get close enough to carry on a normal conversation.

"Hello, Luke. Laura and I decided to take you up on your offer. Your stable looks wonderful!" Beth exclaimed.

"Hello, Beth. Step down and I'll show it to you unless you'd rather have some lemonade first."

"Stables first and lemonade second," Laura answered.

They both dismounted tied off their horses then each took one of Luke's offered arms and they headed for the stable.

After he opened the doors, he stepped aside so they could each walk down one row of stalls as he walked down the center between them.

Laura walked down the left side and said, "Luke, these horses are amazing."

"They are pretty special. I'm going to have a whole crop of foals next year, I think. What I'll do then, I don't know."

"We'll take some when they're weaned," added Beth as she walked down the right.

Laura reached the last stall and saw ‘NYX’ carved into the wood and ran her fingers over the letters with a smile. Luke may have said he wanted her to stay away, but she knew he’d been thinking of her.

After Luke had given them the tour, they adjourned to the kitchen and Luke made some lemonade which they carried to the kitchen table.

“So, is there any reason for this visit, or am I just lucky?” he asked.

“Actually, there is, Luke,” replied Beth, “It has to do with Chuck and Al.”

“I’m not surprised. They rode out here a few days ago to express their desires to get to know you both better.”

“I didn’t mind talking to Chuck at first, but he’s getting overbearing. It seems like he’s always there.”

Laura said, “Al’s worse. He leaves me little notes on Nyx and other places, and I’ve never shown the slightest interest in him at all. I’ve even told him to leave me alone.”

“What does Hal say about it?”

“We haven’t told him or our mother yet. We wanted to see what you’d say.”

“They work for Hal. If Hal knew, I’m sure he’d let them have it and fire them if they didn’t behave themselves.”

“When they asked you, what did you tell them?” asked Laura.

“I told them that the decision of who you would see belonged to each of you and not to me or anyone else. But I also told them that if either of them hurt you in any way, there would be serious consequences, and I wasn't talking about just physical hurt. I meant it, too. If they continue to bother you after you tell Hal, let me know and I'll deal with them."

"Luke, when we leave, could you escort us back and kind of act like you're enjoying yourself?" asked Laura.

"I wouldn't have to act, Laura. I thoroughly enjoy being with you both. When I bring you back, we'll just be ourselves, alright?"

The sisters glanced at each other, then looked back at Luke and smiled.

"Oh, by the way, Laura, look what I picked up earlier today," he smiled as he pulled back his vest.

"Is that a new one?"

"It is. The old one's cylinder had been moved and wasn't worth repairing."

"Where is it now?"

"Mounted on a plaque in the library."

"Can we see it, Luke? I've never seen your library," Beth asked.

"Sure, let's go."

When they reached the small house, Luke opened the door and ushered them inside where Beth was amazed at the collection.

"Could I borrow one to read at home?" she asked.

"As many as you'd like. That's what they're here for."

Laura selected two books as did Beth before they admired his Webley plaque and the globe as well.

"This is a wonderful place, Luke. You need some easy chairs scattered about, then Laura and I could come over and read here."

"I'll do that. It has a kitchen right there as well."

They returned to their horses slid the books into their saddlebags then led them to the barn and waited as Luke saddled Apollo for the return ride. When he returned, he'd have to finish the new corral and gate. He needed to let the new mares get some exercise and meet Zeus as well. They already knew he was there but hadn't had a face-to-face introduction or one of any other kind, either.

He rode between Beth and Laura all the way to their home and told them of the experiences he had in town and how disconcerting it was. Both were curious about all the young women that seemed to want to get to know him better and he assured them that he'd become a hermit again if it got too bad.

They were all having a grand time as Luke took care of the gate and they rode to the house. Luke spied Chuck and Al off to the side staring at them as they rode past. Luke, as he had told Beth and Laura, didn't have to act as if they were enjoying themselves at all. Beth was acting more like her normal self again and ribbed him several times and laughed often, so maybe she'd be all right now.

They arrived at the house and stopped at the hitchrail near the back porch dismounted and tied off their horses. Beth and Laura took out their books and they all walked into the house.

Back in the pastures, Chuck and Al were feeding off each other's jealousy.

"That son of a bitch said he didn't have any interest in either one of 'em, and here he is paradin' like he owns 'em."

"And he goes and gives Beth that fancy horse, too," groused Chuck.

"Yeah, he gave Laura the horse and saddle and even had her name carved into the leather."

"I think he's playin' us for suckers, Al."

"What can we do about it?"

"He lives alone out there in that ranch house of his, Al."

"What you figurin', Chuck?"

"Oh, I don't know. Accidents happen, you know."

"We ain't talkin' a .44 caliber accident, are we, Chuck?"

"Maybe. If he suddenly just disappeared and no one knew what happened to him, maybe things would change."

"I'll bet he's got some cash lyin' around, too. He always seems to have some."

"Well, let's just wait until we see how things go."

"Alright."

Everyone was gathered around the kitchen table as Laura and Beth explained the situation with Chuck and Al to Hal and Ann.

Hal turned to Luke and asked, “What do you think I oughta do, Luke?”

“How much work are you needing to get done right now?”

“Not much. We’re in good shape and the herd isn’t that big yet.”

“I’d let them both go. Tell them that there isn’t enough work to keep them busy. Don’t bring up Beth or Laura.”

“That sounds like a good idea. Ann, what do you think?”

“What happens when we need more work?”

“If it’s not much, I’ll come over and help. If you need to hire more hands next year, hire one.”

Hal nodded and said, “That sounds good.”

“Maybe you should look at hiring a blind cow hand or hide Beth and Laura away in the attic.”

They all laughed, but Luke wasn’t far removed from his belief that it might be an ongoing problem with two women as pretty as Beth and Laura, and Laura was growing prettier and shapelier almost daily.

“Did you want me to stick around while you tell them, Hal?” Luke asked.

Hal had to think about it before replying, “No, Luke, I think it’ll look more like just a work decision if you’re not here. They’re both mighty jealous about you, you know.”

"That was my impression when they stopped by as well, so I'll head back. Hal, until they're gone, keep your Colt handy."

"I was gonna do that, Luke."

"I figured as much," he said as he stood with a smile, "Everyone knows where to find me if you need anything."

He waved as he left the kitchen and headed for the door with Beth and Laura following, so they could take care of their horses.

Luke untied Apollo, stepped up, gave them a final wave, wheeled the gelding to the south, and began the ride back to his ranch. As he passed by the herd, he saw Chuck and Al not doing anything, just watching him ride past. Luke pretended he didn't even see them and rode on, but he really wished he was with Hal when he told them.

Chuck and Al wasted no time returning to the house. It was close to mealtime anyway, so that was their excuse. That, and it was payday.

Chuck caught sight of Beth admiring her new horse and seethed. Laura had already led Nyx into the barn, so Al was just jealous.

Beth heard them coming and decided to bring her new horse into the barn as well. She wasn't afraid, just nervous. Once inside the barn, she began unsaddling her mare, but she and Laura kept glancing outside keeping an eye on the two ranch hands. Laura pulled her Webley from the saddlebag and slipped it into her pocket.

Chuck and Al stopped at the house, tied off their horses, and stepped up onto the porch. Chuck knocked once and then just walked in, not waiting for a response. Ann was preparing dinner and looked at them.

"Dinner's not ready yet, boys. It'll take another thirty minutes."

"That's alright, Mrs. Rawlings. We'll just take a seat."

Hal heard them enter and blew out a breath. He had never fired anyone before, so he was decidedly uncomfortable as he headed to the kitchen and found them drinking coffee at the table.

"Boys, I have your pay envelopes already done," he began, and slid the two envelopes onto the table, "I included another ten dollars each because I'm gonna have to let you go. There just ain't enough work to have two ranch hands here anymore. The herd's just too small. I appreciate all your help, though."

"You're firin' us?" Chuck snarled as he snatched an envelope.

"Sorry, Chuck. You know how the business goes."

"It ain't about work, either, you, old lyin' bastard. It's 'cause that pretty boy from next door don't want us hornin' in on his plans."

Hal was expecting a bad response and said, "If you're talkin' about Luke, then you may as well pack your gear and get out. I don't want either of you on this ranch in ten minutes."

Al was going to say something but just grabbed his envelope and Stetson and stormed out of the room with Chuck trailing closely behind.

Hal walked to the door with his hammer loop removed and watched them climb back onto their horses and head to the bunkhouse. They went in and five minutes later emerged with their saddlebags threw them over their horses and mounted. They set off at a fast trot down the access road and turned toward Colorado City.

Hal exhaled then turned to Ann and said, "That went better'n I expected."

Beth and Laura had seen their faces when they left the house, then stepped out of the barn and stood in the doorway waiting until they watched the two irate cowhands ride down the access road before they walked to the house.

Chuck and Al kept up the fast trot as they rode under a dark cloud to Colorado City. Forty minutes later when they arrived, they rode straight to the Golden Saloon as they normally would do on payday. This time, they were going to drink with a vengeance.

Luke made his return trip without incident which surprised him a bit. He had been watching his backtrail since he left the Star H ranch. He supposed it had been all those gunfights he had fought recently that made him think every disagreement had to result in a hail of bullets and there was no love lost now between him and those two. He wondered how he could have read them so wrong when he'd first hired them and recommended them to Hal, another error in judgement, but not as bad as letting Beth join him that day.

Once he returned, routine overtook the issues caused by Chuck and Al as he fixed himself something to eat and then went outside and began to tackle the delayed construction of the gate for the new corral. He had more than enough wood and had bought some large hinges at Salk's.

It took him three hours to hang the gate and then another hour to move Zeus and his goddesses into the corral. They all seemed anxious to get some exercise of one form or another, so he left them to their exercising and returned to the house.

———

At the Golden, Chuck and Al were already deep into their alcoholic haze. Their ire directed at Luke had been pushed deep into their minds, and they not only blamed him for their failed attempt at romance but had also cost them a good job. There hadn't been much work after the fence had been put up and even though they knew that Hal's explanation had been accurate, it didn't make what had happened right.

After an hour with the two of the ladies on the second floor, they took rooms at the boarding house for a week. They'd find another job and then they'd see about Mister Scott.

———

When nothing had been heard from the boys after a couple of days, Luke relaxed and settled into a pleasant routine. Luke would work in the morning and entertain Beth and Laura most of the afternoons.

Beth had seemingly returned to the Beth that Luke had known before the cabin shootings and Laura was still the same extraordinary Laura. Everything seemed to be just as good as possible with no angst from any quarter.

———

But ten days after Chuck and Al were fired, angst reared its ugly head again from an unsuspected direction.

Laura and Beth had just arrived for their visit and all three were in the small house. Luke had ordered four easy chairs for his library, but they hadn't been delivered yet.

Luke had noticed the more somber mood of both women, especially Beth when they arrived. He knew something was wrong and waited for them to bring it up. He knew something was seriously wrong when Laura said she needed to go and check on Nyx, so Beth could talk to Luke. It looked as if she was ready to break into tears as she left, giving him even greater concern.

After she left, Luke looked at a very worried Beth and asked, "Beth, what's wrong? Laura looked like she was almost crying and you're even worse."

"Luke," she began, her voice trembling, "I…I have a problem. When Richard and my brothers took over the ranch, Richard claimed to still be my husband and took what he called his husbandly rights. He did it twice and now I'm pregnant."

Luke felt so bad for Beth that he stepped over and held her as she began to cry convulsively. She was shaking as the tears coursed from her face and soaked Luke's vest.

"Beth, it'll be all right. You'll be fine. You're a strong person. It's not the end of the world, you know."

She stopped sobbing long enough to ask, "Luke, do you still love me?"

"Of course, I love you, Beth."

"Would you marry me, Luke?"

Her question jolted Luke to the depths of his soul. He did love Beth, but that one wall that he knew still existed would have a big effect on them both.

"Beth, you don't want to marry me. I know that you're fond of me, but that's not enough. I know that deep down, you'll always see me as a killer and I'll always feel guilty for bringing you into that whole situation. It's a terrible thing to have between us."

She looked up, her deep blue eyes still moist, and Luke felt himself weakening and didn't like it.

"But I do love you, Luke. I always have from that first day. I know how wrong I was to think and say those things. When you shot Richard, I was happy. I would have done it myself if I'd had a pistol. I learned, Luke."

Luke felt enormous pressure and felt backed into a corner of his own making.

"Beth, you stay here, would you? I need to talk to Laura."

"I know. I thought you would have to. I'll be a good wife to you, Luke."

"I know, Beth."

She took a seat and began wiping her eyes and face as Luke left the small house, his mind jumbled as he walked past the house where Nyx was still hitched. He walked to the stables, rather than the barn because he knew where Laura would be.

He entered the stables and found Laura in the back, her fingers sliding over the Nyx nameplate. She had been crying herself, then when she heard him enter, she turned and looked at Luke with reddened eyes.

Looking at the perpetually happy, confident Laura in tears had a crushing impact on Luke and only added to his horrible conundrum.

Laura tried a smile but failed as she managed to squeak, "Hello, Luke."

Luke stepped close to Laura and said quietly, "Laura, you know what Beth asked of me, don't you?"

Laura just nodded and when she began to cry softly, he knew how much she was holding back.

Luke took one long step and pulled Laura close, and she gripped him like she never would let go. He felt her head softly laid across his chest, and he laid his hand on her hair.

"Laura, I'm really not happy about this at all. I think what Beth is asking is unfair."

Laura spoke softly, her face pressed against Luke's chest saying, "I know it's not fair. You didn't do anything but help her and now she's asking you to give up your freedom."

"Laura, it's not my freedom that I'd be losing. It's you."

"Me? I thought you kept saying I was too young."

"Another one of my stupid thoughts, Laura. Yes, you're young, but I had already made the decision to wait for as long as it took until you could marry me, Laura. You must know how much I really love you, don't you?"

"Yes."

“Then I’ll confide in you again, Laura, when I tell you my secret, and why a marriage with Beth just won’t work. Oddly enough, I already told her.”

“Alright, Luke, I’m ready.”

Luke took a deep breath, feeling Laura’s head rise and fall against his chest.

“I was in love with my Ella since we were very young. When I went off to war, I was eighteen and, like all young men, thought of women a lot. Yet during those three years, whenever the opportunity presented itself to enjoy the comforts of a woman, I couldn’t do it. Even though I wasn’t married to Ella, I felt as if I was cheating on her. I just couldn’t make love to a woman who I didn’t love. The word got out and I took a good share of ribbing, but I never had a problem making love to Ella. After she died, I had other opportunities, but again, I couldn’t do it. I felt as if I was still cheating on Ella. I have to love a woman to make love to her, Laura.”

“But you said you loved Beth.”

“I do, but not like I love you, Laura. I’d feel like I was cheating on you now, not Ella. It’s a defect somewhere in my mind or something, but it’s there.”

They continued to stand in the stables, locked in each other’s arms for three more silent minutes before Laura spoke.

“Luke, knowing that makes me feel much better. What will you do?”

“Tell her the truth. I think it’s the best. Do you think that’s the right thing to do?”

"I suppose I should be noble and tell you to marry her anyway to help her with her problem, but I'm not that saintly. Tell her the truth and I'll be with you when you do."

"Thank you, Laura. As usual."

She looked up at him with a genuine smile and Luke couldn't resist. He leaned down and kissed her softly. Laura quickly moved her arms to his neck and pulled herself closer. It was Luke's first kiss since Ella had died, but he was surprised at how much more passion he felt than he had ever felt with Ella as he held and kissed Laura.

They mutually ended the kiss and Luke sighed before saying, "Let's go and talk to Beth."

Beth had been sitting in the chair wringing her hands as she waited. She had never missed her monthly, and this one was already a week late. She hadn't told anyone about her suspicions until she had confided in Laura earlier today. It was while she was talking to Laura that she decided to ask Luke to marry her, then everything would be better. She never suspected for a moment that Luke would say no, nor did she even pay attention to the dramatic impact her decision had on Laura when Beth had told her of her idea to ask Luke to marry her.

She heard the door open and saw Luke holding the door for Laura before entering himself, then taking seats nearby.

"Beth, I can't marry you," Luke began but was interrupted by a sudden rush of tears from Beth.

She quickly asked in a shaking voice, "Why not?"

"Because it's just the wrong thing to do. It's that simple. Now, you won't show for another three or four months. It gives us plenty of time to come up with a better solution than a rushed marriage."

She continued to cry, but was getting angry before she snapped, "What better solution is there? I don't want this baby. It's that bastard Richard's baby!"

Even Laura was shocked by her anger and her vehemence.

Luke was momentarily stunned but soon said, "Beth, it's not the baby's fault. It's your baby now. It's you. It could be another cute little girl. Never blame the baby for the parent's problems. I told Laura the other reason why I couldn't marry you, Beth. I told you about it before that day at the cabin. It's my problem and I've known about it for a long time. If Laura wants to tell you why it affected my decision, I give her my permission."

"But what about the baby? I don't want to raise the baby by myself."

"You forget that Ann will be having her baby in a few months. There will be two babies in the house."

"But I'll still be tied down until I'm an old maid."

Laura glanced at Luke and then back to Beth before she said, "I'll raise your baby, Beth."

Beth looked at Laura and asked, "You'd be willing to do that?"

"Yes."

Behind Beth, Luke smiled. He knew why Laura was making the offer. She wouldn't be alone when she was raising the child, nor would she be living on the Star H ranch.

Beth had recovered from her initial shock at being denied and thought about Laura's proposal. If she wasn't tied down to the baby, she could get back to a normal life.

"Luke, can I still visit?" she finally asked.

"Of course, you're always welcome, Beth. Besides, ask Laura, these things sometimes work out all by themselves."

Beth smiled, at last, sniffed, and said, "Alright. We'll see what happens. I'm sorry I asked such a thing. It was a bit of a shock for you, wasn't it?"

"That, Beth, is the granddaddy of all understatements."

She laughed and smiled at Luke as Laura smiled as well, but for a much better reason.

"So," asked Luke, "who wants to go and shoot guns?"

They both agreed, so the next, much happier hour was spent on the shooting range.

After they had gone, Luke had to do some serious thinking about the future. The sudden shift in the relationship between him and Laura, coupled with the possibility of Beth's pregnancy loomed large on the horizon. He was sure that he had made the right decision in denying Beth's request and telling Laura about everything. He had known for longer than he cared to admit how much he needed Laura. He just had let that age difference stand as an impenetrable barrier.

If she hadn't been sixteen, it wouldn't have bothered him. He knew she was extraordinarily mature for her age and that Al had been right in that many young women married at that age, but he was still bothered by it, and he knew why. It was that image of finding her in the hay. She seemed so childlike, so much in need of protection. But looking at Laura today, just a few months later, he could see Laura, the woman. But it was everything else about Laura that had fascinated him. She was simply the most exceptional person he'd ever known.

Satisfied that the problem had at least been delayed, Luke was finally able to relax and return to his interrupted daily routine.

After returning to their home, Laura sat with Beth and tried to explain Luke's decision. It was difficult because she was worried that if she told Beth the real reason, that he would have failed her in the bedroom because Luke loved her, she might create a permanent rift between them, so she modified his reason.

"So, he thinks he'd still be cheating on Ella?" Beth asked.

"It really embarrassed him to tell me, Beth. A man who can't perform isn't well-regarded by other men. He said that during the war, he was the butt of a lot of jokes by the other soldiers. He said even after Ella was gone, he felt like he was cheating on her."

"That explains a lot then, like why he never went to town looking for a new wife. It's really a waste, don't you think? I imagine he's something under that shirt."

Laura smiled and said, "I saw him without his shirt when he was shot."

Beth grinned and like a giddy schoolgirl excitedly asked, "*You did? What was he like?*"

“Spectacular. I felt all warm inside just looking at him.”

“That makes it more of a waste, then, doesn’t it?”

“I suppose so, or it will make some woman very happy when he’s finally able to get past it.”

“If that ever happens,” Beth replied before she sighed.

Laura felt guilty about her misdirection but hoped things would work out. Now all she could think about was that one kiss they had shared in the stables and even then, she was well aware that Luke would have no problem performing after they were married if they could hold off that long.

———

Two days later, Beth discovered, to her eternal relief, that she wasn’t pregnant after all and woke up Laura to give her the good news. They’d go and visit Luke later that day to tell him.

Both women were in fine fettle as they fixed breakfast, and both Ann and Hal noticed and appreciated the change from the moody daughters of just forty-eight hours earlier without understanding the reason.

———

In Colorado City, Chuck and Al were angry and frustrated. They had been looking for a job and hadn’t found anything available. That problem and their rapidly dwindling funds caused by their nightly excursions to the saloon were putting them in a permanently sour disposition.

They had all but forgotten about Beth and Laura as their sole focus was now Luke Scott. He had ruined their lives and with no money and little else before them, they decided to rectify the perceived injury.

At nine-thirty, Laura and Beth mounted their horses. Beth had named her mare Sandy because of her tan coat, and they departed cheerfully as they headed south to visit Luke.

Chuck and Al headed southwest just fifteen minutes later in anything but a cheerful mood. They were out to settle the score with Luke Scott.

Luke was out doing his morning chores and was currently moving hay out of the stable's loft to the floor of the stable and was unarmed. He'd normally wear his Bulldog in its shoulder holster but when doing heavy manual labor, like moving the hay, it chafed something fierce. Besides, all was right with the world.

He was in the loft with the doors open wide to the beautiful Colorado May morning and spotted the two riders coming from the north. He easily identified Laura and Beth, so he halted his job, then climbed down the ladder to the stable floor and was brushing hay from his shirt as he saw them ride to the stables. They both wore giant smiles, and Luke could tell there was good news in the offing but didn't have a clue what it could be.

They both stepped down and Beth leapt at him and embraced him tightly, then gushed, “I'm not pregnant, Luke! I'm not!”

Luke hugged her back and said, “That's wonderful news, Beth. So, things worked out after all.”

She stepped back and brushed back a wisp of her sandy brown hair from her eyes as she said, “Yes, they did. I’m glad you stopped me from doing something stupid, Luke.”

“It would have been a disaster, wouldn’t it?” she asked, mildly referencing his ‘problem’.

“Yes, but it’s not a disaster any longer. Can you both stay for a while?”

“Sure. Let’s unsaddle the horses this time. Did I tell you I named her Sandy?”

“No. That’s a nice name. It matches her coloring.”

“It does, doesn’t it?” she smiled as she led Sandy into the stables.

Laura followed and smiled much wider at Luke, who grinned back at her and winked. Laura returned the wink and Luke helped her unsaddle Nyx.

“Are you going to make a name sign for Sandy now?” Beth asked as she was stripping her mare.

“I’ll do that,” he said, even though it would destroy the naming scheme in the stables.

They had the saddles off and sitting on the tack shelf when Luke’s stomach twisted at the sound of a pistol’s hammer being pulled back. He whirled around and spotted Chuck and Al standing in the doorway. Neither had shaved or bathed in days and looked filthy. Filthy they may be, but they were both armed and their pistols were drawn and cocked, and he had nothing. Laura’s Winchester was nearby, but getting a rifle out of a scabbard, levering in a round, and bringing it to bear would be impossible before one or both got shots off. He was annoyed that he hadn't even heard them approach. He'd just been too focused on Laura.

"What are you two doing on my ranch?" Luke asked, trying to bluster his way out.

"What does it look like we're doin'?" Chuck replied with a sneer, "We're comin' to pay you back, Scott. You really had to get in the way of everything didn't you?"

"I didn't get in your way. You two just screwed everything up. Now, leave my ranch and I'll forget all about it."

"Oh, you're gonna forget alright. But first, you're gonna get us some money."

"Just how much do you think I've got here? I don't think it's more than two hundred dollars."

"Well, that's a start. Where is it?"

"In the house in my bedroom."

Chuck looked at Beth and said, "I'll bet Beth and Laura know where your bedroom is, don't they? You've been havin' 'em both, haven't ya?"

"Don't be absurd. I would never dishonor either of them."

"There you go with all that high-handed talk. I'll bet you get 'em both goin' at the same time, too. I think after we get you out of the way, we'll have a go with 'em ourselves."

As he'd been blustering, he'd been frantically thinking of a way out, and it was Laura who bailed him out.

"Luke, I'm ashamed," she began sadly, "I already broke our deal. The one I gave you my right hand on? I'm so sorry."

Luke knew instantly what she meant as she'd only made one deal with him. She didn't have her pistol with her, and he knew if she was telling him, then it had to be close. He was sure that her Bulldog was in her right saddlebag where she kept it when she wasn't carrying it in a pocket.

Al finally asked, "What are you talkin' about, Laura? What deal?"

Laura said, "The one I made with Luke about not letting anyone else ride my horse. I let Beth ride her this morning."

"Why the hell would you be ashamed about that? It ain't nothin'."

Laura was impressive as she worked up some tears, and said, "Because you said you were going to kill Luke and I broke a promise."

Beth was stunned by Laura's sudden emotional outburst and was also confused about the horse. She had never ridden Laura's horse.

Al released his hammer and replaced his pistol in his holster. Chuck could handle Luke. He wanted to comfort Laura as an excuse to get to hold and feel her.

Luke was standing next to Laura's saddlebags and watched as Al stepped over to Laura. Chuck was more than just a bit disappointed in his partner's actions.

"Get away from her, now, Al! Get that pistol out!"

Al turned and was going to argue with Chuck but thought better of it and was reaching for his pistol when Laura took a step forward and hugged Al.

Chuck turned his head to see what was happening and Luke took that brief distraction and simply bent his knees, flipped open the saddlebags, pulled out the Webley, and was grateful for the double-action as he quickly brought the sights onto Chuck.

The sudden movement brought Chuck's attention back to Luke, but it was too late. Luke was only seven feet away when he fired. The .44 punched through his abdomen and just passed right through without hitting any vital organs, then exited and left the stable before losing its energy and finally digging into the dirt in the front yard. But as the bullet passed through Chuck, the very edge of the bullet nicked his abdominal aorta. Then the shock wave of the bullet's passing popped the aorta, causing the small slice to rupture, and Chuck collapsed when his blood pressure disappeared.

Al, seeing Luke fire, tossed Laura aside and pulled his Colt, but it was not only stupid, it was much too late. Luke fired a second round at point-blank range and his second bullet did much more extensive damage to Al's chest than the first had done to Chuck's abdomen, and he dropped where he stood, his eyes still wide open.

Luke didn't care about either dead man but rushed to Laura and picked her up from the floor of the stable.

"Laura, are you all right?" he asked anxiously.

Laura stood and said, "I think so. I was just surprised when he threw me down."

He hugged her closely and said, "Thank you for the clues, Laura. I thought we were all dead."

"So, did I."

He released Laura and turned to see how Beth was doing. No bullets had gone her way, but the sight of seeing two more men killed in front of her might be too much. He was surprised to see her picking up Chuck's pistol from the floor.

"This thing's still cocked, Luke. I don't know how to release the hammer. Can you do it, please?" she asked calmly.

"Sure," he replied as Beth handed him the pistol with her thumb and fingers gingerly holding the grip. He took it by the barrel and released the hammer.

"You forgot to show us how to do that, Luke."

"My error. I'll get these two on their horses and bring them back to Colorado City. You'll both have to come along as witnesses."

"Okay. I'll go in and make some coffee. Is that okay?" asked Beth.

"I'd appreciate that, Beth."

Beth smiled and left the stables to make the coffee as Luke collected Al's gunbelt and stripped off Chuck's. He put both pistols in their respective holsters and slipped the hammer loop over them before setting them aside, then dragged them both out of the stable before he quickly grabbed a bucket and scooped some water from the trough, then dumped the water on the pools of blood. It took three buckets to get the floor clean.

After setting the bucket down, he finally turned to a silent Laura and said, "Laura, I can't tell you just how impressed I was by everything you did. You were amazing, as usual."

Laura stepped through the still-wet floor and asked, "Enough to earn another kiss?"

"I suppose."

She smiled, and Luke took her into his arms, kissed her, and then added a bonus by sliding his lips to her neck, giving Laura a thrill that she never had experienced before as she felt goosebumps erupt over every inch of her skin. She put her hand on the back of his head, so he'd keep kissing her, but after another thirty seconds, he pulled back and she just sighed.

"Luke, when we're finally together, will you be able to make love to me?" she asked quietly.

He looked into those deep blue eyes, smiled, and said, "I'm sure that you understood that when I kissed you the first time, but I'll tell you now that I'll never stop making love to you, Laura."

"I'll never want you to stop either," she replied, before they both turned and left the stables.

An hour and forty minutes later, Luke rode into Colorado City, escorted by Beth and Laura, trailing the two horses with the bodies.

After dismounting and tying off their horses, Luke held the door to the sheriff's office as they entered.

"Elizabeth, how are you?" asked a smiling Larry Talbot.

"I'm fine, Larry. I haven't seen you in a while except for that short time at the trial."

"That's my fault, I'm afraid. I was always a bit afraid of you."

"Afraid? Why?" she asked with a wry smile.

"Come on, Elizabeth. You're, well, you're Elizabeth. I'm only Larry."

"Larry, don't sell yourself short. You're the sheriff now and you're a very handsome man."

Larry blushed as Luke cleared his throat and said, "Larry, at the risk of breaking this up, I have two more dead bodies outside."

"Again?"

"This one I didn't see coming. Their names are Chuck Miller and Al Feinstein. They were hands at the Star H until they were let go a couple of weeks ago. They seemed to have blamed me for getting them fired and came to get revenge and take my money.

"They had me, Larry. I was unarmed, and Beth and Laura were visiting in my stables when they came in with their pistols drawn and cocked. I'll tell you how we got out of it when we write our statements. You'll find their gunshot wounds in the front."

"They had you under their cocked pistols while you were unarmed and got them both? That's a story I've got to hear."

"All because Laura forgot to keep her end of our deal," he said as he grinned and looked at Laura, who grinned right back.

While they wrote their statements, Larry led the two horses to the mortuary, then returned fifteen minutes later.

After all the statements were finished and read, Larry sat back.

"That's an incredible story, Luke. What are you going to do now?"

"I'm going to escort Beth and Laura to the diner for lunch before escorting them home. You're more than welcome to join us for lunch, Larry. My treat."

Larry didn't have to be asked twice as he snatched his Stetson and eagerly agreed as he smiled at Beth.

She smiled back and took his arm as they left the office. Luke glanced over at Laura, who winked back at him.

It was a pleasant lunch considering why they had to come to town in the first place. Larry shifted to calling Elizabeth, Beth, which he admitted was much more fitting. Beth, for her part, seemed to be thoroughly enjoying Larry's company, and as they were preparing to leave, he asked Beth if he could visit her. Beth told him she'd be disappointed if he didn't and Larry returned to his office on a cloud.

After returning to the Star H, Luke, Laura and Beth filled Hal and Ann in on the incident and aftermath.

"That'll teach ya to go about naked," Hal admonished him.

"Never again, Hal."

Luke stayed around for dinner, now that things were much more settled. He told Hal the whole story, including the previous visit and Beth's request, and his time with Laura.

"Bout time you figgered that out, son. Time ain't the problem. If it's right, it's right."

"It did take me a while to come to grips with that, Hal. I still want to wait until Laura is ready. I'm not going to push her."

"Hell, Luke, you aren't pushin' her at all. You're holdin' her back."

Luke smiled and replied, "I know, Hal. Maybe it's me that I'm holding back, too."

"As long as you make this thing right."

"Oh, I will."

For such a strenuous week, it turned out amazingly well. It would be the beginning of a long stretch of quiet for everyone.

CHAPTER 11

Over the next three months, Laura and Beth would visit the Circle S often, but Beth's visits began to drop off after a month when she began spending more time with Larry. His initial visits gave way to calling on Beth and things seemed to be progressing smoothly.

That meant that Luke and Laura spent more time together alone. Luke intentionally kept from going much beyond the kissing stage with Laura because he wanted to do everything right with her.

Laura was getting frustrated. She had continued to blossom and now matched Beth, curve for curve. The change was not lost on Luke, but he persisted in treating her as he thought he should.

In October, with the trees still clinging to their remaining leaves, Ann Rawlings went into labor. Because of her age, Doctor Spanner was with her. He was concerned that she was too old to have a normal birth and had told Hal of his worries.

They turned out to be unnecessary as Ann gave birth to a beautiful, healthy baby girl at 4:11 in the afternoon on October 12th. They named her Martha after Ann's mother. Ann had always wanted to honor her mother, but Les Harper had insisted on honoring his mother and aunt first. Beth and Laura were the first visitors to see their new sister.

Luke and Hal were outside on the porch enjoying cigars when Doctor Spanner told Hal he could go inside. Hal tossed his cigar thirty feet to the ground and bounded inside.

Luke looked at the grinning physician and pulled a cigar from his pocket, then offered it to the doctor, who took the smoke, bit off the end, and puffed away as Luke held a match to the end.

"I never thought I'd see any of this, Doc. Hal, married and now a proud papa. Just a year ago, he thought his life was pretty much at an end. Now, he's happily married and has a baby."

"What about you, Luke? Are you going to go through life unmarried?"

"No, sir. Just waiting on Laura."

"Waiting for what? Are you expecting her to sprout wings or something?"

"Doc, she's only sixteen."

"So? I've delivered a lot of babies to sixteen-year-olds. It's a lot less stressful than delivering them to a forty-four-year-old, I'll tell you."

Luke looked at the doctor and digested his words. *Was he the only one with this age fixation?* He puffed the cigar and let his mind wander as he let the smoke fill his vision. *Why was he waiting?* Laura was surely a fully developed woman. She was much more mature than most of the older women he knew, and more than anything else, he loved Laura totally. *Why waste the time?* Everyone else seemed to think he should marry Laura, including Laura.

He took another puff as the doctor waved then stepped down to his buggy and clambered inside. He turned the buggy back to the access road, then Luke watched it roll away leaving a series of tobacco clouds, looking like a small locomotive.

Luke waved one more time and finally tossed his cigar away.

Almost on cue, Laura stepped out onto the porch next to Luke and asked, "Is Doctor Spanner gone?"

"Yup. He headed back to town before it got too dark."

"Have you seen my new sister yet?" she asked as she smiled.

"No. Not yet. I'll do that in a little while," he said as he turned to Laura, saying, "Laura, I've been doing some thinking."

"Which is usually a lot better than the opposite."

"That's true. What everyone seems to think is that I'm being silly about this age thing. Can I guess that's your opinion as well?"

"You need to ask?"

"No. I knew better. But it's still there and I can't shake it, so I was wondering if we could wait until spring."

"To do what?" she asked, trying to draw it out of him.

"To get married."

"I didn't recall you asking, Mister Scott. You're making quite an assumption, are you not?"

"I am, madam, and I apologize profusely. It is beneath your dignity for such a wayward fellow as I to assume to be worthy of an esteemed personage as yourself. Please allow me to withdraw my inappropriate comment."

"I shall grant you this boon, Mister Scott, only on the provision that you restate your declaration using a more acceptable format."

"Ah! I am most grateful, milady. Perhaps this would suffice to your satisfaction. Laura Harper, next spring, would you please marry me?"

Laura broke into tears and a giant smile at the same time as she hugged Luke and kissed him.

"I suppose I can wait that long," she replied when she finally managed to speak.

"I just want everything to be perfect for you, Laura."

"You're perfect for me, Luke," she replied softly before Luke kissed her again.

After they ended the kiss, Luke and Laura walked into the house holding hands and headed for Ann's birthing room. Beth and Hal were still there with Ann and the newly arrived Martha.

Ann took one look at Laura's ecstatic face and her grip in Luke's hand and she knew. Luke had finally realized what everyone else, except maybe Beth, had known for a while.

Laura looked at her mother's smiling eyes and said one word, "Spring."

Ann nodded as Luke had his first look at his future niece.

"She's perfect, Ann. She's almost the prettiest girl I've ever seen."

"I can guess who number one is, can't I?"

"I think so."

Beth finally did understand and quickly hugged Laura.

After he returned to his ranch that evening, Luke began to make his plans. He had plenty of money in the bank, a stallion, and ten mares but decided that he wanted to make the house even better for Laura's eventual arrival. How he could make it better was the question. It was very well built. Their bedroom would be the same one that he had with Ella, but maybe that was it. Maybe he should make a new bedroom just for him and Laura, one that would be for them alone.

His plans were made, he would ride to Colorado City tomorrow and order the furniture for the new bedroom and stop at Taylor Construction. He'd add a new heat stove for that side of the house as well. He mustn't forget all the necessities either: the lamps, rugs, and curtains. He smiled to himself as the room became almost an obsession.

He left early the next morning and stopped at Taylor Construction first and outlined what he wanted. Because it was cooler weather, they had plenty of manpower and little work, so they said they'd start tomorrow, and they'd need him there to answer any questions. He paid for the work and then went to Salk's. He found Frank and told him what he needed to order. It was going to be a large bedroom, so he added two easy chairs in addition to a large, four-poster bed. He remembered all the lamps and things, but while he was going through the catalog, he found a mirrored table with drawers for perfumes and things with a matching table. It even came with an assortment of scents and soaps for milady, according to the sales sheet, and added it as well. Satisfied that it was complete, he paid for the order and left Salk's.

After he returned to his ranch, he quickly took care of his daily duties, including seeing to the health and fitness of the mares. All but one were in foal, so he knew that it was going to be a busy spring.

Laura arrived right after lunch as normal and, of course, noticed his ebullient mood.

"What has you so bouncy today?" she asked.

"I wanted to start getting the house ready for your arrival in the spring."

"Luke, the house is perfect. Why would you change anything?"

"Well, I was thinking, Laura. I wanted this to be your house as much as mine. I wanted something to be uniquely for us, so I'm having a new, much larger bedroom added to the south side of the house. It'll be ours, Laura."

Luke was surprised that Laura didn't seem nearly as excited as he was, in fact, she almost seemed sad.

"What's wrong, Laura? Did I screw up again?" he asked.

"Luke," she asked quietly, "are you doing this because you don't want to use the same bedroom that you shared with Ella?"

"Sort of. I wanted you to know that I love you as you, not as a replacement for Ella."

Laura smiled softly and caressed his face with her fingers, "You, silly man. You great big, silly, wonderful man. I would never worry about that. I know you too well, Luke. I was only a bit concerned that you didn't think me worthy of using the same room."

"Now, who's being silly, Laura? I didn't want to say anything about this because I felt bad about it, but I'm going to tell you. Remember when we shared our first kiss? That one in the stables?"

"I'll never forget that, Luke. It meant everything to me."

"Well, when I was kissing you, Laura, I felt a passion that I had never come close to feeling with Ella. Since then, I've thought about it often. I still get that feeling when I kiss you and I realized what it was. I loved my Ella very much. I thought it was impossible to love another woman like I loved Ella, and I was right. I never have and never will. And that was part of the problem, you see. We grew up together. We were rarely apart as we reached our teenage years. She was just so comfortable to be around.

"But when I met you, Laura, I was terribly confused. I found you to be the most fascinating person I've ever met. I wanted to be with you all the time, but I thought the age difference was too great, and when I met Beth, I thought she was an older you, which was a horrible mistake. There is no other you. There is just one Laura. Then I had to deal with trying to understand my feelings for you. They were nothing like what I felt with Ella. With Ella, it was all about comfort.

"With you, it was everything. It took me a while to recognize love for what it was, Laura. You inspire me in every way a woman can inspire a man. When I kissed you that first time, I felt an explosion of passion inside me. You, Laura, are the only woman I will ever love like this."

"Then I guess we'll get to make good use of that new bedroom," she said softly.

He hugged Laura close and kissed her even more passionately than he had ever done before.

Laura felt the love and passion and it curled her toes, so she pressed herself against him and slowly slid back and forth to let him know that she was ready.

Luke was beginning to think that spring was much too far away, but he still managed to end the kiss and the close contact before he put an end to his self-imposed celibacy.

Then they headed to the couch and spent over an hour talking about the new bedroom and other changes she'd like to make, so it turned out to be a wonderful day.

Over the next week, Laura would stop by and see how the room was progressing and add her input. On the last day, she brought Beth along.

Beth was grinning as she stepped into the house and announced that she and Larry would be getting married on November 15th, so Luke gave her a hug and kissed her on the forehead.

Luke had his own news of a sort. He had been reading a three-day-old copy of the Rocky Mountain News from Denver when he was in town getting a haircut and came across the story of a big gold strike near Pike's Peak. He had saved the paper for them on their next visit. So, when they stopped by, he pulled out the paper and showed the story to Laura. She read it and started to laugh before handing it to Beth, who also laughed.

The article was about a miner named Angus McGill, who had bought out two claims and after one stick of dynamite, had uncovered one of the richest veins ever found in the area. He named the mine the Golden Harp after the two Harper brothers who had sold him the claims. They returned to the Star H with the paper to show their mother.

The next visit was only by Laura, and Luke was happy about it. The house modifications were completed, and Laura was in awe of the size and completeness of the room. Luke had intentionally not mentioned the dressing table. She was so impressed by the four-poster bed that she failed to turn to the right and see the dressing table until Luke revealed its presence when he stepped aside.

When she saw the table, she whirled around and looked at Luke with wide eyes.

“Luke Scott, where did you get that idea? It’s beautiful! I can’t get over how thoughtful you are.”

“Open the drawers.”

Laura trotted over and opened one drawer after another, seeing the bottles of perfumes, colognes, bars of scented soaps, and even an atomizer.

She pulled a small bottle of rose scent and touched it to her finger and then to her neck before returning the stopper to the bottle and the bottle to the drawer.

She put on a devilish look and beckoned Luke to approach, which he did willingly and was rewarded appropriately. It seemed to add yet another month before spring arrived.

For the next two weeks, Luke would be rewarded with a visit by Laura right after lunch every day. He'd escort her home and share dinner with the Rawlings. The routine was only interrupted when Beth's wedding day arrived.

They all were present when a very happy Beth married an even happier Larry Talbot. They moved into a house purchased by Hal and Ann. Luke had paid for most of the furnishings.

The next big event was Christmas. Luke bought a pipe and tobacco tin for Hal, who had expressed an interest in going that route, a brooch for Ann, and a new rattle for Martha. Beth and Larry arrived late, and Luke gave Beth a necklace watch. He held off giving Laura her gift until they were alone.

After Beth and Larry had gone, Martha was napping, and Hal and Ann were in the kitchen when Luke lured Laura into the main room by the very obtuse method of beckoning to her with his index finger.

Laura sat down with him on the couch and curled under his arm.

"Laura, a few weeks ago, I took a train down to Denver."

"When did you do that? I don't recall you being gone a day."

"Take the evening train down and the morning train back. It doesn't give you much time for shopping, but if you know what you're looking for, it can be done."

"And what were you looking for, Mister Scott?"

"This," he replied handing her a small box.

She opened it carefully and saw a beautiful sapphire ring. It was a dark blue stone and had a single small diamond on each side on the band.

She slowly pulled the ring from the box and slid it over the ring finger on her left hand.

"Luke, I…it's so, so stunning."

"It's the only thing that comes close to the marvelous blue of your eyes, Laura. I also bought a matching wedding band set for us."

Laura snuggled in closer and said, "Luke, I didn't even get you anything."

"Sure, you did. I had the joy of seeing your face when you opened it, Laura."

She leaned across and kissed him. It was a wonderful Christmas.

Luke rode back to the Circle S with darkening skies knowing it was the last Christmas he would be alone. He wished he hadn't been such a prude as he wanted to be with Laura every second now.

He made it back to the ranch as the snow began to fall, brought Mars into the stables, unsaddled him, and then put him into his stall. He fired up the heat stove for the horses, as he had every night for the past month. It kept the stables above freezing, which was what they needed.

He returned to his house and after getting the fireplace and the new heat stove going, soon had the house nice and toasty.

He walked into the new bedroom, which he hadn't used yet as he wanted that first night to be with Laura. When she had noted its lack of use, she had asked him about it and was touched by his explanation. She promised that their second night alone together would be much more memorable than their first when he had laid in his bed with his fresh gunshot wound. He reminded her that this would actually be their third.

He opened the top drawer which was empty except for a single box. It was similar in appearance to the small box he had given her earlier. He opened the box and admired the matching sapphire necklace and earrings. They matched her ring in design, except that the earrings were smaller, round sapphires surrounded by smaller diamonds. He closed the box with a smile. It was her birthday gift. He'd follow the Nyx tradition and ride in at night and leave the box in a leather satchel by her door. He wanted every one of her future birthdays to be a reminder of that first birthday gift.

Laura still visited over the next few weeks, despite the weather worsening. Luke would hurry Nyx into the stables and then rush the bundled Laura into the house to warm her up in ways that heat stoves could never replicate. The more time he spent with Laura, the more he became addicted to her, but it was the best form of addiction he could imagine.

Then it was the eve of her seventeenth birthday. She came to visit as usual, despite the ominous clouds in the sky. Luke suggested that she start being more careful because of the weather, but Laura reminded him of her funny hat that Luke had given to her and her warm jacket and gloves that he had bought for her as well. Luke knew better than to argue, besides, he knew he wouldn't want to go a day without Laura's visits.

Laura told him that Beth was pregnant, and this time it was for real. She was due in June, she told him with a grin before Luke did the math.

“Really?”

She nodded with a smile and laughing eyes.

Luke laughed before he pulled her close and kissed her.

Two hours later, he escorted her home as usual. He had decided that he’d be smarter this time because of the weather. In his saddlebags were the small satchel and Laura’s birthday present.

He escorted her all the way to the barn and helped her unsaddle Nyx and get her into her stall before he walked her to the porch.

“Are you coming in, Luke?”

“No, sweetheart, I’ve got to get back before the weather falls apart. I’ll just give you an early birthday kiss and head back.”

After the kiss, Laura smiled and went back inside. After she closed the door, Luke trotted out to Apollo and pulled the satchel from his saddlebags, and set it near the door. He felt like an elf as he trotted back to Mars, mounted, and headed back home. An hour later, he was back in his house and making his dinner.

Early the next morning, Laura was up first. She was happy because she knew it would be the last birthday she would have away from Luke and wasn't expecting a birthday gift from him.

She was still warmed by the memory of finding Nyx waiting for her in the barn.

But she had to make a run to the privy. She had her coat and funny hat on with her rubberized boots that Beth had given her as she left the back door and trotted out quickly to the privy. It was on her return trip that she saw the satchel leaning against the door.

Attached to the case was a note that was fluttering in the swirling wind being blocked by the house. It just said, "Happy 17th birthday, Laura".

Laura smiled, held back some tears, and picked up the satchel saying quietly, "Thank you, Luke."

She went inside started the cook stove put on the coffee pot and got the fireplace and heat stove going before she went to her room with the satchel. She knew it couldn't be as special as Nyx nor as glamorous as the sapphire ring, but when she pulled out the familiar-looking box, she wasn't so sure.

She opened it and her hand flew to her mouth. She thought the ring had been spectacular as she fingered the necklace and touched the earrings. She carefully closed the box and carried it with her to the kitchen before she made the coffee and started on breakfast.

Hal popped out and waved on his way outside, then Ann entered the kitchen as Hal returned.

"How bad is it out there, Hal?" she asked.

"Not too bad. I think it's gonna get worse, though."

She donned her jacket and hurried outside.

"Hal, look what I found by the door," Laura grinned as she handed him the box.

He opened the box and whistled, "That Luke surely does care for you, Laura."

"I knew that, Hal, and it didn't take things like this to tell me."

"You seemed kinda fond of last year's gift if I recall."

"And I always will be."

Ann returned, and Laura showed her Luke's gift. Ann was pleased as much for the gift as further evidence of Luke's deep love for her daughter. She could see the happiness on Laura's face and remembered that she had the same look over a year ago when Luke had brought her home and wondered if Laura had already been in love with Luke. Then she thought it was a silly question. Of course, she was. She and Beth were the only ones who didn't understand it then.

After breakfast, Laura returned to her room, admired her new jewelry, and compared it to her ring. They were a matched set but were all beautiful individually and she knew she had to thank Luke personally. She could feel the wind buffeting the house but wasn't worried. She had made the ride hundreds of times by now and knew it by heart. More importantly, so did Nyx. She'd just dress warmly as usual and make the hour-long ride and spend the rest of her birthday with Luke.

Luke may have thought Laura was perfect, but she had one weakness; Laura was stubborn. Once she set something in her mind, it was difficult to dislodge, if not impossible.

Around ten o'clock, while Hal and Ann were in Martha's room, Laura bundled herself into her long johns, pants, rubberized boots, a sweater over her heavy shirt, and then her heavy jacket. She wrapped a scarf around her neck and face and pulled on her funny hat, then stepped outside and fought her way across to the barn. He had to remove her gloves to saddle Nyx but managed to finish after ten minutes and was ready to go. She donned her gloves and led Nyx out the door. After closing the barn door, she mounted and set her trotting south. The wind was fierce, but she wasn't deterred.

She had made the run before in an hour but that was in good weather. With the wind, she had to set Nyx to a walk rather than a trot and Nyx had to fight to keep from drifting to the east from the force of the western wind.

Twenty minutes and one mile after she'd gone, the snow started. Hard, icy pellets pummeled Laura and Nyx as Laura pulled the scarf more tightly around her face. An hour later, she was only three and a half miles from the Star H and even further from the Circle S. She knew she should turn back but her stubborn streak won the day, so she and Nyx pressed forward.

The snow kept increasing as she fought the wind and it was almost an hour later before she passed the halfway point and began to be afraid that she had lost her way, but she trusted Nyx because she had no choice. It was another hour before she began to sense a growing panic welling deep inside. The ride to the Circle S didn't have a lot of landmarks. It was nine miles of shallow hills, but nothing that would tell her where she was.

Just as Luke had discovered over a year ago, the wind's direction and having to lean her horse into that wind was pushing her in the wrong direction.

At the Circle S, Luke had the fire roaring and both heat stoves going to keep the house warm. Then he fought the wind to go outside and light the heat stove for the horses and while he was in the stables, he looked down at the empty stall for Nyx and smiled. He missed his daily visit from Laura. It was her birthday and he wouldn't see her today, so he walked to the stall and ran his fingers over the sign. It was a year ago today that she had first seen Nyx and he hoped she liked her new birthday present. It was elegant, but he was convinced that nothing would hold a candle to Nyx.

He walked to the end of the stables and was reaching for the door when an image of Laura fighting the storm just popped into his mind. Surely, she wouldn't be riding today, but he still began to feel uneasy. It made no sense at all, but it was already nagging at him. Common sense told him she was safely at home in a warm room, looking at her sapphires, but common sense sometimes has little weight when love is thrown into the mix.

Luke walked back and saddled Mars. This was stupid, he kept telling himself. *She can't be out there.* But he didn't want to take the risk. He had his compass and had tested it a few times on the ride to the Star H. It wasn't perfectly north, but a few points to the east. He had the compass in his pocket as he returned to the house and began to add more layers of clothing. He still had the funny hat that now wasn't so funny any longer. He trotted back to the stables and led Mars outside before closing the door mounting then heading north.

———

Laura was in serious trouble and knew it. Nyx was beginning to stumble from the exertion of fighting the wind with the added trouble of treacherous footing. She began to worry about her horse, so she finally stopped and stepped down. She began to walk with her shoulder into the wind, leading Nyx. She was still three miles from the Circle S, but it may as well be a thousand. She was so tired and wanted to sleep, but kept her feet moving. Nyx wasn't stumbling as much with the load no longer on her back, but Laura was tripping as her toes began to catch icy grass patches and breaks in the frozen soil. She finally felt the reins slip from her fingers and fell to the ground, then curled up into a ball relieved to be able to rest. She just wanted to sleep.

Nyx stopped and waited for Laura. She turned to the small, huddled shape and nudged Laura with her nose. Laura could feel Nyx and smiled. Nyx, her first and greatest gift from Luke. When she thought of Luke, she began to cry. She knew how horribly she would miss Luke. She didn't want to die, not now, not this time. She wanted to live but didn't have the strength. She tried to move but was too stiff, so she began to pray.

She kept repeating, "God, help Luke find me, please."

It was a silly prayer, she knew. No one would find her until she was a lifeless lump on the frozen ground covered in snow.

———

Luke was moving much faster than Nyx had been able to manage. The extra weight of Mars and his two hundred pounds of man on his back gave the horse much better traction. The visibility was horrible, and Luke still thought he was losing his mind for making the trip, but he wanted to be sure. He could ride all the way to the Star H with the compass and when he arrived, he'd find Laura safe and warm, and he'd feel like an idiot, but he'd know that she was safe.

———

Laura was losing her battle to stay alive. She should be warmer with all the clothes she was wearing. *Why was she so cold?*

Luke was only half a mile away, but Laura had been fighting the wind and had been swerving ever so slightly to the east, so she was no longer on the straight path between the two ranches. Luke was going to pass to her west by two hundred yards and the visibility was less than fifty. He would never see her and the little light that was clawing through the clouds was fading as the sun was nearing the unseen horizon.

Luke knew that she may not be out there, but the fading visibility was drastically reducing any possibility of finding her even if she was.

He reached the closest point to the freezing Laura less than five minutes later and didn't see her, but Nyx picked up the scent of Luke's big red gelding. It was a familiar scent and she whinnied loudly. Mars perked up his ears and turned his head to the east. Luke hadn't heard the whinny in the wind but knew better than to ignore his horse, so he turned in that direction. As soon as he did, he picked up a second whinny from Nyx himself. He didn't want to move too quickly with the wind pushing him in that direction, but just a minute later, he spotted Nyx, and right below her, he saw Laura curled up in the snow.

He quickly dismounted and trotted to her inert form, then knelt beside her.

"Laura! Laura!"

There was no response, but he had to act quickly. He first stepped over and tied Nyx to Mars and then scooped Laura into his arms, stepped up on Mars, then began riding back south. He held Laura tightly as he continued to fight the wind and snow. He had one big advantage. He had just ridden the route and Mars was going home. They were moving as fast as Luke thought it was safe and he estimated they could reach the house in another forty minutes.

Twenty minutes later, he quickly checked his compass. He was still heading due south. If he went too far to the east, he'd run into his own fencing, so he shifted slightly to the west. Laura hadn't moved since he picked her up and he was already worried sick.

Ten minutes later, he knew where he was, picked up the outline of the house five minutes later, and headed around to the back door so he wouldn't have to fight the wind. He didn't worry about the horses for now, but just stepped down with his precious cargo and walked carefully up the steps, opened the back door and walked inside, then kicked the door closed with his heel and walked Laura quickly to the new bedroom. It was still warm from the heat stoves and fireplace.

He laid her down on the four-poster and began taking off her heavy outerwear. Once she was down to her shirt and pants, he pulled off her boots and slid her under the blankets. He felt her chest and wasn't sure that he felt a heartbeat. Luke fought panic and ran back out to the kitchen. He went outside and quickly moved both horses to the stables, stripped them both quickly, and tossed some more wood in the heat stove before jogging out of the stables and back into the house. As he ran to the big bedroom, he began stripping off his outerwear. Jacket, gloves, scarf, and hat all littered the hallway as he reached the bedroom, then he yanked off his boots and crawled into bed under the blankets with Laura.

"Laura, we can't keep meeting like this," he whispered as he hugged her tight.

She was deathly cold as he contoured his body to match hers to transfer as much heat as he could to her.

Twenty minutes later, she still hadn't moved, but Luke could feel her heart beating. He relaxed somewhat and continued to hold her close. With no lamps lit, the only source of light was from the fireplace, and despite everything, Luke drifted into sleep, still clutching the unmoving Laura.

Laura was still in a mental fog. She remembered lying down in the snow but now she was warm again. She was less confused than she had been that horrible day in the barn a year earlier, but she still had no idea where she was. *Was she in her room in her house on the Star H? Where was her mother or Hal?*

She rationalized that they were with Martha, her sister. She had a baby sister and smiled at the thought before realizing that she wasn't alone under the blankets. There was an arm draped across her chest, and she should have been startled, but she knew that it was Luke. She could feel the heat of his body making her warm. He had found her again, somehow, answering all of her prayers.

"Luke?" she whispered without a response.

Laura saw the light from the fire but had another worry, so she slipped out from under Luke's arm and found the chamber pot, then had to wrestle with the union suit. It was a close race, but she made it. She discarded the garment in case she needed another sudden trip and just put her shirt and pants back on before sliding back under the blankets.

When she did, she came face to face with a wide-awake Luke.

"Laura," Luke said normally, "you had me worried."

She ignored him momentarily as she snuggled in close and pulled his arm back around her.

"I'm sorry, Luke. I just wanted to see you. I didn't think it was that bad."

"It was still a silly thing to do, Laura."

"I just wanted to thank you for my birthday gift. It was so beautiful."

"Laura, you are never going to make the ride to the Circle S again without me. That is final. No arguments."

Laura was unpleasantly surprised and asked, "Why would you say that, Luke? It's as if you don't want me to show up anymore."

"No, Laura. I don't want you to make that ride anymore. It's a totally different thing."

"But it's not bad most of the time. Today was different."

"I'm not taking that risk with you anymore, Laura. You won't make that ride alone anymore."

"And that's final?"

"Yes, Laura. No more solo rides. From now on, when you need to go visit your mother, I'll go with you."

Laura was going to protest again when the context of what Luke had just said was interpreted by her still mildly foggy mind.

"You want me to stay here?"

"I don't want you to ever leave me again, Laura. Forget about waiting until spring. I want to marry you tomorrow."

"Do you mean it, Luke? You really want to get married tomorrow?"

"I don't ever want you to have to make that ride again without me by your side. I never want to be away from you, Laura."

“I never want to leave, Luke. Luke, could you help me roll around?”

Luke helped to turn Laura until she was facing him and pulled her in close.

“Is that better?”

“Much. I can see you now and I can feel your heart. It feels good to have you so close, Luke.”

She paused and asked, “Luke, where is Nyx?”

“She’s in her stall appreciating the warmth of the heat stove.”

“Is she all right?”

“She’s fine.”

“How did you know to come looking for me? How did you find me? I was lost.”

“I was in the stables and looking at Nyx’s stall. As I was leaving, I just had a vision of you fighting against the snow. I knew it was my imagination and totally illogical, but I couldn’t take the risk of you being out there, so I left. As to how I found you, you can thank Nyx. I would have missed you by a few hundred yards, but Nyx must have smelled Mars and whinnied. Mars turned to the east and I let him go. When Nyx whinnied again, I heard her and found you.”

“I owe my little filly so much.”

“What made it impressive when I found you was that she was still standing over you. She didn’t go wandering as most horses would have, and because she stayed, I was able to find you much faster.”

"She's my friend, Luke."

"Now, I'm going to go and fix you some hot coffee and food. You stay under those blankets and keep warm," he said before he clambered over Laura and stepped out into the chilly room, "I'm going to get the heat stoves and fireplace refueled and going strong. With the cook stove, the house will be like a hothouse in a little while."

Luke was pulling on his boots when Laura said, "Luke, you need to empty the chamber pot."

"I know. You woke me up when you got out of bed."

"Did you see me when I was taking off that union suit?"

"Not as well as I would have liked, but enough."

"I suppose I should be embarrassed, but I'm not."

"From what I saw, Laura, you should be proud and not the least bit embarrassed. Now you just stay curled up under there and I'll be back in a while."

She closed her eyes and said, "Thank you for saving me again, Luke."

As he left the bedroom he said, "It was completely selfish on my part, Laura."

After Luke left the room, Laura began to wonder why Luke, after seeing her at least somewhat naked, hadn't even kissed her when she returned. *They were going to get married tomorrow, so why didn't he want to make love to her now?*

Luke started the cook stove fire and then went out onto the back porch and emptied the chamber pot before taking care of his own natural necessities.

He returned to the kitchen and cleaned the chamber pot before setting it aside. Next, he fired up the original heat stove and then added wood to the new heat stove and fireplace. Before he began to cook, the house was already warming nicely.

He had coffee made and was cooking a stew similar to the one he had made for Laura that first day, but using smoked beef rather than canned, and adding some different spices. He poured two cups of coffee and walked back to the new bedroom, letting the stew simmer.

Luke entered the room, set the cups down, and lit a lamp before sitting on the bed and waiting for Laura to sit. He handed her the hot coffee and took his own in his hands.

Laura had both hands wrapped around the cup as she sipped her coffee.

"Luke, where are you going to sleep tonight?"

"With you, unless you'd prefer to sleep alone."

"No, I never want to sleep alone again, Luke. I was just wondering."

"Why were you wondering, Laura?"

"Well, you saw me with little or no clothes on, and then when I returned and was close to you again, you didn't even kiss me. Luke, don't you want me?"

Luke set aside his cup of coffee.

"Laura, you have no idea how much I want you. I want to make love to you so badly it aches not to."

"Then, why didn't you?"

"Because, my love, you almost froze to death a few hours ago. I wanted you to be strong and fully recovered. I don't want to take what little energy you have now. It's just that I love you too much, Laura."

Laura looked over the rim of her cup at Luke, understanding just how much he really did care for her. It was far beyond what many passed off easily as love. She understood because she felt it as well. She would do anything to make Luke happy.

She smiled softly and simply replied, "I love you, Luke."

Simple words, so often spoken, but seldom with the full meaning of the phrase behind them.

Luke smiled and simply touched her face with his fingers.

"If the weather gives us the chance, we leave early tomorrow to get back to the Star H in the morning to calm your mother's concerns. Then we ride into Colorado City and complete the loop with a return ride to your new home."

Laura nodded, still smiling. The idea of being Mrs. Luke Scott so suddenly dawned on her at last. It would be tomorrow, the day after her seventeenth birthday. At least it would be easy to remember their anniversary.

Ann had been frantic with worry when she first discovered Laura missing, and Hal had offered to go and find Laura, but Ann said there was no point in risking his life as well. But after she'd been gone for several hours, instead of getting more upset, she found herself becoming almost serene.

"She made the ride hundreds of times, Hal. She's probably safe with Luke right now."

"Maybe he'll finally come to his senses and marry the girl sooner rather than waitin' till spring."

"That would be nice. Hal, it's been just a year since Luke first brought Laura home. When Les was killed and my Laura taken, I thought my world was over. I had nothing and thought I would die alone. It was a terrible, horrible feeling. Then Luke brought my daughter home and took us to meet you.

"Now, I have a wonderful husband, and my girls are both happy and I even have a new daughter to love. There has been so much happiness to come from that hopeless situation. All of it brought about by that terrible storm. Now, Laura is caught in another blizzard and I should be sick with worry, Hal, but I'm not. I just know that Luke has her all wrapped up and warm. Isn't that strange?"

"No, my love, it isn't strange at all. It's called faith."

Laura was dressed warmly as she sat at the kitchen table with Luke having dinner.

"I'm feeling really good now, Luke," she said as she smiled.

"I'll be the judge of that, Miss Harper."

"Tomorrow, you won't be able to call me that anymore."

"No, but I'll come up with something. Maybe I'll start calling you 'Miss Blizzard' or something."

"I wasn't the one who got lost in the first one, Mister Blizzard."

"No, but I didn't almost freeze my butt off twice, Miss Frozen Butt."

"It's not frozen now. Did you want to check?" she said as she smiled and wiggled her eyebrows.

"Maybe. You've got to finish off your stew first."

"Yes, Mama."

"And no cookies until you do, young lady!" he admonished with a ticking index finger.

Laura laughed. It was going to be a fun marriage.

Forty minutes later, they were back in bed and Luke found that she was warm everywhere. Laura found that Luke had not the slightest inhibition of making love to her once he was sure she was all right. And once that concern vanished, any other restrictions vanished as Luke made love to Laura with more passion than she thought possible. She found herself freed from any societal boundaries and allowed herself to feel the pleasure of just being loved. Luke discovered just how extraordinary Laura was again, as she became a full partner in their unbridled enthusiasm. As each level progressed, they branched into new ways to pleasure each other. Laura was in ecstasy, something she never thought possible after those horrible weeks more than a year ago. With a warming blanket of love covering them both, they reached the ultimate of physical and emotional peaks.

An hour later, as they lay entwined under the blankets, each was content and secure in the knowledge that theirs would be a complete union of two souls for eternity. They were meant to be together. It may have been a wailing wind that drove Luke to that barn, but both were convinced that it was an unseen hand that had steered him to find Laura…twice.

The next morning dawned as if the storm had never happened. The flat spots were almost devoid of snow, with giant drifts along the windbreaks. The coating of ice was still there, but as Luke and Laura set off on horseback, there was no wind and the sun was already blasting the glossy, ice-covered ground.

They reached the Star H before nine o'clock and noticed two saddled horses already tied behind the house as they arrived. They stepped down, leaving their horses saddled for the ride into Colorado City later, then walked hand-in-hand up the porch steps.

As they approached the house, the door swung wide and Ann trotted out and hugged Laura.

"I was worried about you, Laura. Why did you leave in the middle of a storm?"

They all walked inside as Laura explained that the weather wasn't that bad when she left.

Ten minutes later, the mood inside the house changed dramatically with the announcement that Luke and Laura were going to go to Colorado City to be married.

Beth and Larry congratulated them both and offered to watch Martha, so Hal and Ann could join them and the offer was readily accepted.

It was an oddly dressed group for a wedding that stood in Judge Stevens' chambers. Luke had remembered to bring the bridal set that matched the sapphire ring he had given Laura at Christmas.

The marriage ceremony was short and devoid of all the trappings normally associated with weddings, but it didn't matter a bit to either Luke or Laura. They knew it was right and that was all that mattered. After they had exchanged vows, rings, and their first kiss as husband and wife, they completed all the necessary paperwork and left the courthouse. All four went to the hotel restaurant for a post-wedding luncheon and then Luke and Laura bid farewell to Hal and Ann to return home.

After they had consummated the marriage for the third time later that day, Luke and Laura lay together bathed in sweat despite the frigid temperatures outside.

"Luke," Laura began, "do you think I can have a baby?"

Luke was surprised at her question but shouldn't have been.

"Of course, you can have a baby. Probably five or six. Why do you ask?"

"It's been kind of nagging at me. Ever since that day when I could tell you that I wasn't pregnant after all and was so happy about it but now, I wonder if I'm barren."

"Laura," Luke replied softly, "remember the man who explained to you that you might not be pregnant after all?"

"Yes, I remember him quite well," she answered as she smiled and slid closer.

"That same man is now telling you that you are going to have babies. Not just one baby, Laura. You will have a lot of babies."

"How do you know?"

"Because, Laura, we're meant to have children. I feel it. I don't know how long I can be with you to enjoy them all. I'd be happy with twenty years. But they'll complete us, Laura. You'll be able to sit your grandbabies on your knee and tell them how their grandpapa found you frozen in a barn and knew from that moment you were the most precious person in the world."

EPILOGUE

Laura was overjoyed when she told Luke six weeks later that she was pregnant already and Luke immediately began preparing one of the bedrooms for their new arrival.

The spring also brought the arrival of nine new foals into the herd and Ira Pearson came down from his farm and admired the newborns and helped to educate Luke about raising horses. They became fast friends and visited each other often.

Laura thought Nyx needed to join the harem, so she could foal the next year and Luke agreed.

Beth gave birth on June 11th, to a little boy that she and Larry named James. He would be their only child.

On October 18th, Laura went into labor and six hours later, little Rachel Scott was born.

On Laura's eighteenth birthday, Luke left her gift, a soft, fleece-lined robe in a box outside their door. She pretended to be surprised to find it there in the morning, beginning a lifelong tradition.

She also came into possession of the large award by Judge Stevens in the Sheriff Crenshaw case. It was a substantial $15,760.67, which they just added to their account.

Laura found herself pregnant six months later and had little Max on March 28, 1874.

That summer, Hal died of a massive stroke, devastating Ann. Luke had a new house built for her on the Circle S, preferring to leave the small house as a library. Ann sold the Star H and moved into the new house with little Martha.

He continued to add to the library, and by the time Laura had their third, another little boy they named Sam, the library was the largest in the county. Luke had an unusual honor system for anyone borrowing a book. There were six easy chairs in the main room now and some just stayed and read there. Most would borrow a book without any form of recordkeeping. Luke would lose books now and then, but not a significant amount.

Ann recovered from her loss by being close to Martha and her new grandchildren. Having all the young life around her soothed her aching heart and Luke and Laura were happy to have her close, and not just because she helped with their growing family.

The horses continued to multiply, and Luke had to hire a hand to help. He was Larry Talbot's younger brother, Frank. Frank loved horses and was in heaven working with so many handsome animals. Nyx had foaled twice and her second was a very handsome black colt that looked very much like his father, Zeus, but after the second foal, Laura removed Nyx from the harem.

Laura continued to have a baby a year until she and Luke had seven children, four girls and three boys, creating a lively house. Ann was a godsend, relieving Laura of much of the day-to-day upkeep of the household, but Luke hired a maid/nanny anyway to take the pressure off both women. Young Mary Williams was very good at her job and was pretty besides. Naturally, she attracted the welcome attention of Frank Talbot, requiring yet another small house to be constructed on the ranch which was quickly becoming a compound.

Ann Rawlings passed away after fighting a losing battle with cancer in September of 1881. Martha was legally adopted by Beth and Larry as Beth had wanted a daughter badly but failed to conceive after James. As much as Laura and Luke would have loved to keep Martha with them, they knew how much it would mean to Beth to have a little girl to love, so they let the adoption go forward.

The tradition of leaving birthday gifts for Laura continued until her seventy-third birthday. Despite his belief all those years ago that he would never get to spend enough time with his beloved Laura, Luke Scott celebrated their fifty-sixth anniversary with her the day after delivering her birthday gift.

The birthday/anniversary was celebrated by their seven children, their thirty-one grandchildren, their ninety-six great-grandchildren, and sixteen great-great-grandchildren.

Luke Scott finally left his Laura when he died of a brain hemorrhage on April 9th, 1928. He was out riding in the east pasture when he suddenly fell from his horse, a great-grandson of Zeus.

His funeral was attended by the entire family and dozens of friends. For two more years, Laura continued to tell her great-great-grandchildren how their great-great-grandfather had saved her from two horrible blizzards and had faced all the bad men and saved her again. The children, just as their parents and grandparents had done, listened with awe at the tale.

When she died on January 28th, 1930, it was with a smile on her face. There was a raging blizzard howling outside and she knew that her beloved Luke would find her.

BOOK LIST

1	Rock Creek	12/26/2016
2	North of Denton	01/02/2017
3	Fort Selden	01/07/2017
4	Scotts Bluff	01/14/2017
5	South of Denver	01/22/2017
6	Miles City	01/28/2017
7	Hopewell	02/04/2017
8	Nueva Luz	02/12/2017
9	The Witch of Dakota	02/19/2017
10	Baker City	03/13/2017
11	The Gun Smith	03/21/2017
12	Gus	03/24/2017
13	Wilmore	04/06/2017
14	Mister Thor	04/20/2017
15	Nora	04/26/2017
16	Max	05/09/2017
17	Hunting Pearl	05/14/2017
18	Bessie	05/25/2017
19	The Last Four	05/29/2017
20	Zack	06/12/2017
21	Finding Bucky	06/21/2017
22	The Debt	06/30/2017
23	The Scalawags	07/11/2017
24	The Stampede	08/23/2019
25	The Wake of the Bertrand	07/31/2017
26	Cole	08/09/2017
27	Luke	09/05/2017
28	The Eclipse	09/21/2017
29	A.J. Smith	10/03/2017
30	Slow John	11/05/2017
31	The Second Star	11/15/2017
32	Tate	12/03/2017
33	Virgil's Herd	12/14/2017
34	Marsh's Valley	01/01/2018

35	Alex Paine	01/18/2018
36	Ben Gray	02/05/2018
37	War Adams	03/05/2018
38	Mac's Cabin	03/21/2018
39	Will Scott	04/13/2018
40	Sheriff Joe	04/22/2018
41	Chance	05/17/2018
42	Doc Holt	06/17/2018
43	Ted Shepard	07/16/2018
44	Haven	07/30/2018
45	Sam's County	08/19/2018
46	Matt Dunne	09/07/2018
47	Conn Jackson	10/06/2018
48	Gabe Owens	10/27/2018
49	Abandoned	11/18/2018
50	Retribution	12/21/2018
51	Inevitable	02/04/2019
52	Scandal in Topeka	03/18/2019
53	Return to Hardeman County	04/10/2019
54	Deception	06/02.2019
55	The Silver Widows	06/27/2019
56	Hitch	08/22/2018
57	Dylan's Journey	10/10/2019
58	Bryn's War	11/05/2019
59	Huw's Legacy	11/30/2019
60	Lynn's Search	12/24/2019
61	Bethan's Choice	02/12/2020
62	Rhody Jones	03/11/2020
63	Alwen's Dream	06/14/2020
64	The Nothing Man	06/30/2020
65	Cy Page	07/19/2020
66	Tabby Hayes	09/04/2020
67	Dylan's Memories	09/20/2020
68	Letter for Gene	09/09/2020
69	Grip Taylor	10/10/2020
70	Garrett's Duty	11/09/2020

71	East of the Cascades	12/02/2020
72	The Iron Wolfe	12/23/2020
73	Wade Rivers	01/09/2021
74	Ghost Train	01/27/2021
75	The Inheritance	02/26/2021
76	Cap Tyler	03/26/2021
77	The Photographer	04/10/2021
78	Jake	05/06/2021
79	Riding Shotgun	06/03/2021
80	The Saloon Lawyer	07/04/2021

wtn

Made in the USA
Las Vegas, NV
13 July 2023

74621466R00229